"Westin knows how to write romance!"
—New York Times **bestselling author Suzanne Enoch**

Praise for *Lady Katherne's Wild Ride*

"Westin recreates the bawdy Restoration era to perfection with colorful historical detail and each rapier-sharp piece of dialogue. A delightful action-packed read à la *Shakespeare in Love*." —*Romantic Times*

"Jeane Westin once again transports her readers back in time to a bawdy, dangerous, and yet thrilling age. . . . And if there's one thing Westin does best, it's draw her readers inside this fantastical place and this time in history. . . . A ride that's well worth taking." —*Romance Readers at Heart*

"A big wow of a book! The characters are fabulous, and I truly adored them all." —*Fresh Fiction*

"A terrific Restoration romance starring a likeable woman in peril and her champion, who not only risks his life to keep her safe, but mentors her that you only have one time at living so make the most of it." —*The Best Reviews*

"This beautifully written book is impeccably put together, and the language is gorgeous. . . . This book is for the intelligent romance reader (is there any other kind?), so sit back and enjoy a well-crafted historical romance with all the little touches that make you feel as if you are right there with the central characters."
—*Historical Romance Writer Newsletter*

"Jeane Westin's new book has two of the most loveable characters in fiction to date. . . . Katherne and Jeremy just jump off the page as you read their adoring story. . . . Please run to your bookstore and pick up a copy. . . . You won't be disappointed!" —*Book Cover Reviews*

continued . . .

Praise for *Lady Anne's Dangerous Man*

"A seductive pleasure—indulge yourself! Stories like this don't come along often. Jeane Westin weaves sharply observed historical detail into the tale of a seductive battle between a rascal and a bluntly spoken young lady: It's a true pleasure to read!"
—*New York Times* bestselling author Eloisa James

"Jeane Westin brings Restoration England to life in a sweeping tale of passion and adventure."
—Lauren Royal, author of *Tempting Juliana*

"A spirited lady, a dashing highwayman, and a rich cast of characters make for a delightful swashbuckling romance."
—*New York Times* bestselling author Jo Beverley

"An old-fashioned swashbuckling romance with smart, sexy overtones."—Suzanne Enoch, author of *An Invitation to Sin*

"In her dazzling debut, the author deftly combines a cast of colorfully original characters with a richly detailed historical setting to create a vivid and satisfying tale of adventure, intrigue, and passion."   —*Booklist*

"The era, the people, and the story are brilliantly brought to life by a shining new star on the romance horizon."
—*Romantic Times* (Top Pick)

Other titles in Jeane Westin's
Restoration series
from Signet Eclipse

Lady Anne's Dangerous Man
Lady Katherne's Wild Ride

LADY MERRY'S
DASHING CHAMPION

Jeane Westin

A SIGNET ECLIPSE BOOK

SIGNET ECLIPSE
Published by New American Library, a division of
Penguin Group (USA) Inc., 375 Hudson Street,
New York, New York 10014, USA
Penguin Group (Canada), 90 Eglinton Avenue East, Suite 700, Toronto,
Ontario M4P 2Y3, Canada (a division of Pearson Penguin Canada Inc.)
Penguin Books Ltd., 80 Strand, London WC2R 0RL, England
Penguin Ireland, 25 St. Stephen's Green, Dublin 2,
Ireland (a division of Penguin Books Ltd.)
Penguin Group (Australia), 250 Camberwell Road, Camberwell, Victoria 3124,
Australia (a division of Pearson Australia Group Pty. Ltd.)
Penguin Books India Pvt. Ltd., 11 Community Centre, Panchsheel Park,
New Delhi - 110 017, India
Penguin Group (NZ), 67 Apollo Drive, Rosedale, North Shore 0745,
Auckland, New Zealand (a division of Pearson New Zealand Ltd.)
Penguin Books (South Africa) (Pty.) Ltd., 24 Sturdee Avenue,
Rosebank, Johannesburg 2196, South Africa

Penguin Books Ltd., Registered Offices:
80 Strand, London WC2R 0RL, England

First published by Signet Eclipse, an imprint of New American Library,
a division of Penguin Group (USA) Inc.

First Printing, August 2007
10 9 8 7 6 5 4 3 2 1

For my sister, Reno

Chapter One

A Serving Maid Is
Mistaken for a Countess

Meriel St. Thomas raced up the sweeping oak stairs of Cheatham House in answer to Lady Judith's urgent call, clutching up her rough woolen gown to speed her way. A lady's maid soon learned that swift response was necessary to her work, if she wished to stay above the scullery. And who would not wish it? Yet Meriel could not keep from slowing, her hand caressing the richly carved and highly polished banister and finials, smiling all the while.

She was beguiled by the fine furniture and rich tapestries of her master's house, though she knew it would not do to admire them too openly, pretending to a station that could never be hers. Or so the other servants constantly reminded her. Meriel's smile grew wider, for such pretense was the true and deepest part of her. But she was no idle dreamer. She knew her place as any servant would, but always wondered who she was meant to be. No strange thing in an orphan.

Hey, well, I could be a princess bewitched by an evil demon. When looking for an answer, don't overlook a possibility.

Stopping on the second-floor landing, Meriel laughed aloud. She had always had a sharp inner voice, a saucy tongue that spoke as it liked and often said what a servant could not.

"Meriel! Meriel! Where are you, girl? Come up to me and at once!"

The shrilly pitiful calls echoed along the hall toward Meriel, her name cried with increasing urgency. Lady Judith was in good carrying voice today, despite her head aching sorely with her near-constant megrims.

"There you are!" Lady Judith said, one hand squeezing her head, the other dangling over the bedside as Meriel opened the door. "Girl, how can you desert me when I am in much pain?"

"I'm sorry, m'lady. I was delayed by other duties."

"There is no excuse for poor service when I am ailing," Lady Judith said, her petulant voice spiraling higher, full of her need for attention. "I need my physic. And I need your healing rub. My head pounds this morn. You know you are the only one who can halt my aching. . . ." She trailed off, unable to think of more requests for the moment.

Meriel gave her the laudanum she wanted, which was reduced by two parts wine and sugar, lest her ladyship fall into a daylong stupor. Gently turning her to her side, Meriel began to knead her well-fleshed neck and shoulders, making soothing noises as to a babe. Once Lady Judith began to snore, Meriel straightened the bed linen, removed a plate of ginger cakes from under the coverlet, swept away the crumbs and gently closed the bed curtains. Sunlight was sure to provoke more anguish in her ladyship. Bending to her work, Meriel cleared the floor of hairbrushes, combs and pillows, which Lady Judith threw about when her cries were not answered with the speed due to quality folk in an advanced state of noisy misery.

Finished with her task, Meriel stood alone in the middle of the room and closed her eyes, inhaling a goodly breath. Up the stairs. Down the stairs. Fetch this. Fetch that. Please God that this was not the sum of all her days. There had to be more of life for Meriel St. Thomas, although even that name was borrowed, since she'd been abandoned as a new babe on the steps of Canterbury Cathedral where Thomas Becket, the old saint, was entombed. She knew in her heart . . . had ever felt . . . that she must be destined for more than a serving maid's life. But what? And when would it begin?

The hours she'd spent in the schoolroom while young Edward and his older sister, Elizabeth, were being tutored, and in Sir Edward's library of books, maps and ship's plans, had opened the world beyond Canterbury to her and closed the world below stairs. The other servants had grown to spitefully resent her learning and the master's preferment. Their constant criticism and lying attempts to force her from favor had driven her from them and deeper into her books.

Meriel heard the crunch of carriage wheels and fairly danced to the windows overlooking the drive next to the River Stour as it flowed near to the town. At last! Sir Edward was returned from London. Perhaps he would take her sailing in his shallop again, allowing her to helm the little ship as it raced before the wind, the freshening breeze blowing away every care.

She breathed deeply, feeling safer now. He had rescued her once from the workhouse near ten years gone, and he would keep his jealous servants in check. Or she would. 'Od's life, but she would.

Since Meriel was sure that the house servants were

gathered at the entrance to greet their returning master, she climbed out the window, tying her shoes about her neck, and walked sure-footed, balancing along the ridge with her arms wide in a delicate roof dance to the lattice that reached down beside the library windows. She was yet slender enough to descend through the vines as she had since a child, when this had been her preferred way of visiting an always welcoming Sir Edward without the other servants knowing.

Stepping through the window, which reached the floor, and into the library, she brushed her long dark curls from her eyes and removed stray ivy leaves from her hair. Grinning at her own foolishness, she curtsied to the marble head in the form of a Greek god sitting on its plinth. The silent, handsome face of Lord Giles, the Earl of Warborough, had been commissioned by the king to honor England's bravest hero after the Battle of the Four Days against the Dutch fleet in the last year. He was a friend of Sir Edward and the idol to whom she had told all her private womanly secrets. And Lord Giles had always listened, never scoffed or scolded.

Today with a soft laugh, she bent to kiss the curving, cold stone lips with as much enthusiasm as a woman hoping for some return. "There, my love, that should keep you satisfied until next we are alone." Although it had been all in fun, the shock of meeting his cold lips and finding they added to her own body's heat halted her amusement. Could she be taking this impossible playact too far even for a jest?

Meriel was still searching for amusement in her own foolery when Sir Edward threw open the paneled oaken doors and entered the room, tossing his great traveling cloak to the porter. "Welcome home, sir," she said with a curtsy, truly delighted to see him.

"Meriel, you are too much a woman grown to be climbing about the roof like a young boy," Sir Edward said, but his kindly voice had as much good humor as censure.

"Aye, aye, Sir Admiral," Meriel said, giving a sailor's two-fingered salute to her forehead. It had been this pert address that had first drawn Sir Edward's attention to the dirty-faced young girl while he was performing his charitable duty to the parish orphanage. After he had taken her into his service, she had continued to address him impudently in private as a sign of the real affection she soon held for him.

Returning her smile—for what man of any age does not delight in a mischievous woman?—Sir Edward flopped into his great chair and held his legs aloft for his manservant to remove his boots.

"Sit, girl, and tell me the news, though I doubt if all of yours will match the least of mine."

"Then I would hear yours the sooner, sir." Meriel poured a glass of Portuguese Madeira, his favorite wine, served him, then perched on the edge of a stool nearby.

"Leave us," Sir Edward said without a glance at his sullen porter. He might have been surprised to see the sudden flare of jealousy. Or he might not. Sir Edward had commanded men at sea, and knew that favorites were resented or even thrown overboard, as Meriel had no doubt was the fate the porter hoped for her.

When the door had closed, rather more sharply than need be, Meriel gave an account that Lady Judith was sleeping from a draught to cure her megrim.

Sir Edward sighed, but quickly brightened since he was ever an optimistic man. "Soon I will have the royal physicians to physic her. They will surely have a cure."

Meriel felt in sudden need of physic herself. "Sir Edward, are you leaving Canterbury? Will you take the little ones? Will you . . ." She took a deep breath.

"Hold, m'girl. There is excellent good news. I have been given an important post at the Admiralty, overseeing the design of new warships to send against the infernal Dutch. They continue to challenge our sea power in the Americas and our East India trade. Though we are in peace negotiations, the Admiralty believes they are coming against us again. Whitehall is abuzz with the sound of young bucks sharpening their swords." He stopped, teasingly pretending to inspect his fingernails while she stopped breathing altogether. "This is a post so important, m'girl, that I'm to have quarters in the palace so that I may consult with His Majesty and the Duke of York upon their least desire. You may not know, but our king is greatly interested in all sciences, especially those that concern the architecture of the fleet."

"But, sir—"

"Quiet, now, and listen well. I will be taking my family." He stopped to loosen his neck cloth for another excruciating moment. "And, by the by, you will be coming with us." He grinned at her.

"Me? To the palace of Whitehall? To see London? To see the king?" She was already on her feet, twirling about, her cap flying off, her curling black hair tumbling about her shoulders. When she reached the plinth, she threw her arms about the handsome marble head and asked, "And will I see the Earl of Warborough?" Oh, what would she do if he was before her, or even brushed against her in a palace passageway? She put up her hands to cover her cheeks and hide the high color rushing to them.

"Eh, what's this? Calm yourself, girl. The earl serves the king as Gentleman of the Bedchamber so you may well see him from a distance. But you go to London because the children will have need of you, as will my lady." He smiled slyly. "And perhaps we can find a husband worthy of you, a lord's majordomo, or even a tradesman. Surely your beauty will urge men to apply to me for your hand."

No! She would not marry a servant, no matter how high, or a tradesman. True, it was said of women in this modern day that they had two ways to spend their lives: through the back door as a servant or through the front door as a wife. But she would spend hers in some other way. She knew not how she knew it or what it would be, but she knew. "Sir Edward, I am determined in my mind to remain a maiden. For now."

"I will not force a marriage on you, Meriel, but I must warn you about the perils of the court and London for a young . . . and I do freely admit it . . . a most beautiful young woman."

"Perils?"

"Aye. Kidnappers, pick-a-pockets, innocent country maids bought for whores as they enter the city gates, every evil temptation known to godless man on offer in the byways, not to mention in the coffee and chocolate houses. And theaters are even worse, m'dear, where the low and most licentious of this age bargain in the pit for the orange girls and—"

"But, sir, the king is said to be a most willing patron of—"

"Yes, yes, but what is suitable for a sovereign is not for a young and innocent maid."

Meriel bowed her head, unable to argue against such accepted logic, though Sir Edward did not know that she had left her chastity at the orphan's workhouse. It was no fault to a young girl when rapine was forced by a hulking, foul-smelling, grunting stable hand behind the byre. Nonetheless, she was determined to see for herself if all Sir Edward said was true. This was the age of proving by experiment, was it not? Galileo and Bacon had written so. Sir Edward taught her this, as well. So, how would she truly know if a thing such as the theater was licentious unless she observed such for herself? She decided, though, not to remind him of his own words. Men did not seem to admire a good memory in women.

"Ah, I see that sharp mind of yours at work. By the Lord of Blessed Name, I hope I have not ill suited you for the natural world. But I cannot blame myself. Who would not take delight in your intelligence? Why, you can cipher as well as any of my lieutenants, helm my shallop as well as any seaman, write a very fair hand and read where many an Oxford lad would be confounded." He sighed. "Yet you are a weak and helpless woman, and must be protected from that mind carrying you too far. Too far, Meriel!"

She nodded dutifully and hid her laughter, since he could read her face so well.

He frowned, cleared his throat and lowered his voice to emphasize the important instruction contained in his next words. "Although the king is head of the church in England, his court is an ungodly place, Meriel, though it is said the queen is pious, perhaps to excess, as she is also barren." He cleared his throat again. "I would be better in mine own mind if you were married within the year."

Meriel ran to him and knelt for his blessing. "Oh, sir, I am most grateful for all that you have taught me, and I will use it well, on my oath. I do not mean to get above myself, but I will know the man I can love when I see him."

"Very well," Sir Edward said, laying a hand on Meriel's bowed head in blessing as any kind master would do. "You are fortunate if you find a man to love and marry, since you have no property to dictate who you will marry and who you will not. Ah, yes, young Meriel, you may be very fortunate indeed."

Meriel looked up at him, because his usual jovial tone had fallen into sadness. She wondered if he had been forced to join property with property instead of finding true love. Her heart ached at the thought. He was more than a master to her. He had taken her into his home, helped her rise from low scullery maid to schoolroom nurse for his children and indispensable personal maid to his wife. When he had early discovered that she was quick to learn, he had taught her and delighted in her ability, passing from master to teacher, and finally at some time during the decade she had lived at Cheatham House, to the only father she'd ever known.

Two weeks later, as a very cold April turned to the flowering of mid-May in the year of our Lord 1667 and the seventh of the restored reign of Charles II, the Cheatham family and servants approached crowded London Bridge from the Kent road, their carriage followed by two wagons heaped with household goods.

Meriel was busy holding back the children, who wanted to hang out of the windows. Sir Edward fanned Lady Judith, who was in a faint from the city odors and perhaps the sight of traitors' heads mounted on pikes. But they drove quickly through the crowded bridge scarce twelve feet wide with all shops and houses perched atop.

Late-spring showers had not washed away the odious refuse of all kinds that lay in the narrow streets of Cheapside, but mixed it with the ashes of old London. The city had suffered a great fire in the last September, the greatest ever known, destroying more than thirteen thousand homes, churches and shops, a number Meriel could hardly conceive.

The king and Parliament had decreed that the new city rise in stone and brick so that fire would never destroy so much again. And so it was. From amidst the rubble, Meriel could hear the sounds of the stone masons' chisels and the rasp of the saw pits. She was astonished to see that some houses were nearly rebuilt, standing two and three stories proud in the tumbled wilderness of charred ruins.

As the dizzying scenes of London's death and rebirth passed before her, she sensed that her own life was changing forever, but she could not imagine what that would mean.

"The palace!" shouted young Edward, pointing.

Meriel squeezed past the boy to get her first glimpse of Whitehall, her new home, after all. *Mine and the king's,* she thought, and with a nervous inner laugh at the rush of warmth carried on this thought . . . *Lord Giles's.*

She had expected battlements, a curtain-walled castle, but what she saw was a forest of chimneys, a huge and rambling white timber and red brick building, or rather a series of buildings connected by stairs and steps, courtyards and gates running in every direction, like a giant puzzle not well put together. A long garden walk beside the Thames was full of strolling lords and ladies in lavish plumed costumes.

"The Royal Horseguards Parade," murmured Sir Edward, answering her unspoken question.

A line of servants in scarlet-coated livery carried their goods behind them as they were shown through endless rooms and down numberless marbled, mirrored halls to their apartment. Although Lady Judith was disappointed in its size, Meriel thought the three large rooms, an anteroom and two bedrooms (one for the master and mistress and one for the children and her own sleeping pallet), were wonderful, especially since they overlooked the river full of boats of every description. She stopped arranging Lady Judith's clothes and her many physic bottles to stare as the royal barge, banners flying, docked at the palace water stairs.

Her ladyship complained from her own tapestry chair. "Don't dawdle, Meriel, when I am sick unto death."

"Aye, Meriel," Sir Edward said, concern crowding his voyage-weathered face, "the rough roads have quite undone your mistress. Go for a royal physician and bring him quickly. Ask any guard where to find their offices."

Meriel rushed to this new duty and an opportunity to see more of the palace, which Sir Edward had said contained more than two thousand rooms, a tiny number of which she had glimpsed, wide-eyed, during their swift passage from the parade ground. But she had no more turned a corner, then another, and she was hopelessly lost.

"Please, sir . . ." But her appeal was not heeded. Everyone was rushing somewhere, with candelabra, platters of steaming meats, bowls of towering fruits, pitchers of drink.

She hurried on and rounded another corner, colliding with a stern-faced older man, of narrow hooded eyes and pressed lips. He bowed low. "My dear Countess of Warborough, what a delight." His voice held no delight, but Meriel quickly looked behind her to see whom he bespoke.

"Quite amusing, Lady Felice," the man said, although he didn't smile. "You are dressed as a servant for masquerade. Or an assignation, since I do not see Lord Giles at your side. Let me guess which it is, since you are unmasked."

A shock at the familiar name surged through her. Was her secret affection for this lord writ plain on her face for anyone to see? She stepped back. "Sir, you have mistaken me for another. I am on a duty for—"

The man twisted his lips into what he obviously thought was a smile. "My lady, you have wit, but even you do not have the skill to deceive William Chiffinch, the king's spymaster. It is a truth you would do well to remember. . . . During your ramblings in the city . . . and beyond."

She tried to squeeze past him, but he took her arm, squinting in her face. "Leave hold, sir, or I will tell my master, Sir Edward Cheatham, that I have been accosted on my first night in the palace. As he did warn me."

Chiffinch laughed heartily now. "Excellent imitation of an innocent country wench. I would believe it most readily if it were not for—" He held her wrist hard and lifted the hair behind her left ear, then stepped back so suddenly, Meriel was pulled forward. "Where is the scar? Who are you?" he demanded.

"Well, sir, for a spymaster, you do have trouble hearing plainspoken words. I speak in no foreign tongue, sir. You mistake me for another. My name is Meriel St. Thomas and I am in service to Sir Edward Cheatham, who is here at His Majesty's request, and he will certainly hear of this."

William Chiffinch looked hard at her, and Meriel had a sinking feeling that her face and form were being memorized. "Have you seen all, sir?" she said, her anger at such treatment completely escaping a servant's natural caution when confronted by the rude behavior of her betters. *Hey, well, there are limits to even a servant maid's forbearance!*

"My apology, Meriel St. Thomas," he said, and left her shaken and greatly bewildered, even frightened, most especially when she heard him laughing heartily. The laughter echoed from hall to hall as she hurried uneasily to her duty.

Giles Mathew Harringdon, the Earl of Warborough, stood by the heavy tapestry curtains held up by golden eagles atop the king's bed and positioned double steps for the royal feet. "Your Majesty," he said in the low, measured tone of a Gentleman of the Bedchamber, "the sun is rising over the river, and I recall we are to have some swordplay." He heard a delightful girlish laugh, which told him the king had been at play of a different kind. No one slept alone in Whitehall Palace, as indeed he did not, although not with his wife, and not through desire. He satisfied his manly need only. His wife had long ago turned his heart to ice, though his cod seemed not to know it and to rise hot and demanding with great frequency. He frowned, not much liking the bitterness that ate away at his natural light heart.

Two little spaniel dogs jumped from behind the curtains, and long manly legs followed until Charles II stood naked on the floor. "My lord Giles, we seem to have misplaced our breeches," he said, amused as he was quite often in the morning. Further feminine laughter erupted behind him.

Giles bowed, expressionless, and went to a chair near the vast fireplace to retrieve the embroidered suit and fine small clothes laid out sometime during the night. "Your breeches, sir," he said, acting as valet, which was one of his duties.

A timid knock sounded on the door leading to the king's privy closet, barely audible over the sound of his many closet clocks striking the hour.

"Enter," the king called, and a barber with steaming bowl and gleaming razors on a towel-covered tray hurried in while the king sat to receive his morning shave. "My lord earl," the king said, waving a hand toward a food-laden table, "unless you have eaten, it would please us to see you break your fast. Try the figs from Her Majesty's own tree."

From the other side of the royal bed, a naked young woman with exquisite curving buttocks exited. Carrying her gown and slippers, she tiptoed to a side door. "A merry farewell, m'dear," the king called cheerfully through his sandlewood-scented lather. "You take with you your sovereign's gratitude."

Giles knew that the king's gratitude also consisted of

good payment doled out by His Majesty's keeper of the privy closet and chief pimp, William Chiffinch.

Giles poured a glass for himself and one for the king, then took some bread, dipped it in his wine and parted the draperies on the windows overlooking the Thames. A low fog hung above the water.

He forced himself to a calm he didn't feel and his mind fled to Harringdon Hall, his ancient home in Norfolk. On a morning such as this, the bright May sun would soon be swallowing the dew on the buds in his rose garden. His espaliered apple and cherry trees would be in full blossom against the warm south brick wall of his small private garden. He should be there, his wife beside him, children tumbling in the long grass while a nurse tried in vain to manage their youthful spirits. His wife's hand would steal into his and they would look long at each other, knowing that they were blessed.

But this was an old scene played out long ago. The loving husband and happy wife had been his mother and father, the children his sister, long dead of the smallpox, and his young brother, torn to pieces by a Dutch cannonade.

Giles steadied himself by widening his stance, as if he stood aboard a ship.

All that was left of that happy time was Giles Harringdon, a peer of the realm, with title, manor, wealth and all of everything except the family he yearned for. His wife, Felice, continued to betray him in every way a man could be betrayed. At first she had hurt his heart, but no longer. He had numbed himself to real love with every eager lady, of which there was a great supply in this most bawdy palace in Europe.

For three years, Felice had seemed a willing partner in every drunken, ribald, lascivious charade of the court of

Charles II. A court ruled by Barbara Castlemaine, the king's fascinating and sexually insatiable chief mistress. A court where husbands and wives were laughed at if they objected to cuckholdry; where satiric poems were written about them by Lord Rochester and pinned to their doors at night; where ribald plays about them were performed at the Theater Royal for the commoners in the upper galleries to enjoy. Giles had withdrawn into naval service, or into his gardens in Norfolk, and when at court, he seemed uncaring, taking a mistress to show his indifference to all who might think otherwise, a mistress whose beautiful face he could not remember the moment he left her bed.

Giles drew in a deep breath and caught the musky scent of the king's recent dalliance. Although his sovereign had no legitimate children by the queen, he had many bastard children, whom he loved extravagantly. Giles expelled air from his lungs in a whoosh. Damn all! He wanted to be like the king, to take love for a night or a month, make bastards and then happily move on. But he was not such a man. Nothing could recompense him for not being able to pass on something of himself to an heir who would go on after him into the centuries to come. When there was no love, no children, what did honors mean? Even the blue sash of the Garter at his waist only held up his breeches.

Damn and twice damn Felice! Giles clenched his fists, forgetting that he held the stem of a Venetian crystal wine glass. It broke and sprayed his coat with fine Portuguese Madeira.

The king came to him as Giles shook off his coat. "M'lord, you need exercise. You're like one of our pendulum clocks wound very much too tight."

Giles smiled and bowed his head, appreciating the friendly gesture. Perhaps he would be able to broach the subject of leaving Whitehall for an extended stay at Harring-don Hall, for the peace of his gardens—although the last time he'd asked, the king had said no. The reason had been flattering: "Giles, you are our one gentleman who does not want to get closer to us for some higher office. Therefore we want you ever closer."

Giles had stopped asking the king for a squadron of ships to take against the Hollanders, since it was His Majesty's duty to protect him, the only heir to an ancient earldom.

This morning Charles II put his arm about Giles's shoulder, and as comrades they walked into the Presence Chamber, down the Stone Gallery and through the king's privy garden, past the scent garden to the covered tennis court, meeting only sleepy servants at this early hour.

Attendants had prepared blunted practice rapiers and a sword master stood near to count the points as they were scored.

Giles shed his wine-stained coat and in his loose shirt open to the waist took a few practice parries, lunges and di-agonal swipes from left to right, high to low, just to hear the familiar hiss of a blade and to loosen his taut leg and shoulder muscles. The king was right; he was wound too tight. He assumed the *en garde* position in salute.

The king returned the salute. "Do you know why we like to practice at the sword with you, m'lord of Warborough?"

"I would hope Your Majesty enjoys the exercise."

"Aye, that is part of it, but we most like it that you do not allow us to win easily."

Giles lowered his rapier across his heart. "That would be disrespectful, sir."

"Just so," the king said, and made a diagonal swipe from high to low with a step forward.

"Point to His Majesty," called the sword master quickly.

But Giles had seen the move coming and evaded to his left, stepping back. Shouting, "Ha!" to add momentum to his lunge, and staying low, he thrust to center, while the king's blade passed harmlessly over his shoulder.

The king shouted, "Point to you, m'lord earl," but he recovered and briskly extended his sword arm to meet Giles's onslaught.

Giles saw that the king was overextended and performed a perfect glissade, sliding his sword along the king's blade, immobilizing the hilt.

The king fell back and saluted. "Ah, Giles, you are masterful at the *pris-de-fer*. No man attacks the blade as well as you."

"Majesty, you are too generous," Giles answered, *en garde*.

"No, we are not, as you will see," said the king, attacking with renewed energy.

They fought round and round the tennis court, which rang with the sound of sword on sword until time was called.

Giles dipped his perspiring face in a bowl of cool water held by a servant, rising to swing his dripping dark curls about his shoulders to shed excess water.

The king pointed to Giles, laughing. "M'lord, you look just like one of our lions at the Tower, and perhaps as hungry."

Hearty applause and trilling feminine laughter came from several court ladies on seats opposite, all furiously waving fans about bosoms spilling out of their gowns, though the day was not yet warm. Both the king and Giles, who was taller even than the tall king, bowed formally, Giles making an elegant leg in the ladies' direction. He was answered with a shrill, "Oh, la, m'lord," from a young lady who covered her face with a feathered fan.

"It would seem," said Charles II, "that the ladies do also think you a hungry lion and have it in mind to feed you."

"The applause was for you, sir."

"Partially, we must agree, but we do see a bed rival in you," the king said, laughing.

Giles laughed, as well, which brought another flurry of whispers and sighs from the ladies, who quickly formed two lines at the door, through which Giles and the king marched. When Giles reached the door, he turned back toward them and very slowly winked an invitation.

The king grinned as they strolled away. "Is it your intent, m'lord, to drive all of these ladies to your bed?"

"Well, sir," Giles said, pulling a serious face, "I try always to give them what they want."

The king rolled his eyes toward heaven. "M'lord Giles, we urge you to have a care, for we have discovered that there is no end to their wanting."

The king and the Earl of Warborough had passed the sundial in the privy garden, their feet crunching on the graveled path, before Giles realized that for an hour by the dial he had not once thought of Felice and had even felt a brief happiness without that burden.

Chapter Two

A Maid Looks Down
upon a Royal Ball

Meriel returned to Lady Judith with a royal physician, one Josiah Wyndham by name, a funny little man with a soaring periwig, who took many small steps at a run but knew his way about the endless palace. They found her ladyship in a near-hysteric state.

The doctor checked her for the fever of ague, murmuring that there were three degrees. "Quotidian, tertian and quartan," he pronounced as to himself.

"You are most learned," Lady Judith whispered, while he bent to listen at her chest, and lifted her eyelids, which had been clamped against the light.

"My lady," he began, and got her attention with his deep, rumbling voice, "you have no ague, but severe megrims. I like not that you are over-pale and lack strength."

"That is exactly what I have been telling Sir Edward, my husband, but he has no more time for my pain." Her voice was petulant. "He is gone already to his work for the Admiralty, and this worthless girl, Meriel, dawdles about the palace."

The doctor glanced at Meriel and smiled. "Nay, my lady, she is excessively dutiful for one so young and fair, hurrying me almost off my legs."

"Well, perhaps. But I do need a stronger physic, good physician, as you can see." Her arm flopped limply over the bedside.

"My lady," he said most gravely, lifting the green glass bottle at her bedside and sniffing it, "you are the victim of a grievous distemper, true, but made worse *by this very physic.* I have observed such results many times in my practice in London and during my student days at the University of Padua, Bologna, et cetera."

Her ladyship's eyes opened a little wider for a better look at the small doctor who, nonetheless, spoke with the impressive authority of a large acquaintance with knowledge.

"Sir, the best physicians of Canterbury have tended me and prescribed—"

"Indeed, I have no doubt of it, my lady. It is a common cure for humors of the fragile female organs and to still the pains brought by the monthly flux. . . . Or pain of any kind. But I think this physic is vastly overpraised except for very brief use against pain"—he sucked in his cheeks—"*in extremis.*"

Her ladyship sputtered to a seated position in her bed, impressed yet alarmed. "But, good doctor, I have had this physic for more than two years and I must have it, or I will surely die."

"My lady, may I be forthright? Indeed, it is that very character that brought me to the king's attention, along with my specialty for women's complaints, of which there are . . . er, many such in the palace. My lady Castlemaine, the king's high friend, is great with child at this moment."

He raised a perspective glass and looked through it at her

face. "What I see before me, madame, is a woman of squandered beauty in great pain, and no doubt no longer esteemed by Sir Edward to the loving degree. . . ." He raised his brows.

She raised hers in mutual understanding, nodding eagerly at such an agreeable diagnosis. "Exactly so, sir!"

Meriel could see why the little doctor was an expert on female distempers, for his patient was vastly improved by a single moment of true male understanding. She determined to learn the secret of his insinuating manner, for he was an obvious master.

"My lady, you must follow my prescribed cure, or I cannot promise release from pain and restoration to health and youth," he said, his voice rumbling lower so that Lady Judith bent forward to better hear him.

"Yes! Anything," she said, entreating with feeble fingers.

Meriel, too, leaned closer to hear, for the doctor was obviously thinking deep thoughts, perhaps in Latin. And she divined his secret physic: understanding followed by absolute demands. But was that all?

The doctor continued. "If you are faithful, dear Lady Judith, I promise a complete cure and your girlish bloom returned."

Lady Judith extended a reinvigorated but still supplicating hand.

The physician grasped her hand and held her gaze. "You are to take nothing to stomach but watered wine, mutton broth and honey-dipped bread for three days, while I cast your horoscope. I do not doubt, my lady, that yours is dominated by Venus and the Moon in conflict. Since Mercury is also now in retrograde, I will leave with your maid my Oil of Privet to take away the megrims, and my famous red

Counteracting pills, which she will give you to purge your body of the harmful effects of your physic and stars."

Meriel curtsied to acknowledge her part and to hide a pleased smile. She thought the little man could probably talk those same stars from the sky.

"But, good doctor, are you not going to bleed me? Where are your leeches?"

"Bleeding is a sovereign cure. . . . As is a purge, but your stars are not propitious for such. Listen carefully now." Dr. Wyndham put two fingers to his temple, signing a deep thought. "On the fourth day, you will rise and dress yourself in your finest gown and walk each morning in St. James Park when many in the palace walk with His Majesty. You have great need of fresh air, sun and charming company."

"But . . . but—" her ladyship sputtered. "It is said the king walks so fast that many must run to stay in his company."

"Exactly so. His Majesty is of a vigorous constitution and very fond of exercise. I would advise, therefore, that for some days you stay back with the slower courtiers until you begin to show roses in your cheeks."

Her ladyship's face had already grown rosy from his close attention, but not so much that she forgot her desire. "My old physic, sir? Indeed, I need it most urgently."

The little doctor bowed low, nearly disappearing under the high bedstead. "My lady, you will need it no longer in a very short time." His voice brooked no challenge to his authority. "I will instruct your maid here, who looks to be a well-minded girl, though such a pretty person will not escape the notice of the lads in the palace." He sighed. "Ah, yes, well—but I will show her what your doses are to be. For now, I want your mirror to be brought."

He nodded to Meriel, who retrieved her ladyship's ivory-handled mirror. *Ah,* she thought, *the final piece of the cure . . . vanity.*

"From this time forward, your looking glass must not leave your side. I have here"—he pulled a black lacquered box from the large carrying case he had over his shoulder— "Wyndham's Infallible Miracle Salve, used exclusively by Lady Anne Gilbert, formerly of Her Majesty's bedchamber, and Lady Katherne, one of the brightest comic stars of the Theater Royal and a great favorite in the court. My salve will quicken that beauty which lies hidden beneath the laudanum and hurry Sir Edward to your side." He bent closer to whisper. "And if Sir Edward has lost a vital part of his nature, then"—he dropped his whisper even lower, although Meriel, stifling laughter, could not understand why, since it carried to all corners of the room—"its use will quicken that noble part, as well."

Standing very upright, he bowed, smiling at his quite revived patient. He closed his case, and firmly taking Meriel's arm, walked her to the adjoining sitting room. "Now, young maid, where have we met afore?"

"Never before today, sir." Was she again being mistaken for a countess?

He frowned in concentration. "Your face is very familiar and I do not forget faces, especially a beauty such as you."

She curtsied because it was a compliment and not an invitation. She knew the difference.

"Well me, I will think of it," he said, puzzled, but came back to business. "Now," he announced, taking a paper packet from his case, "these are my red emetic pills to give her ladyship after each dose of laudanum, which you are to make weaker by the day. The lure of the laudanum—"

"Sir," Meriel said, refusing the packet, "these will give her ladyship vomitus."

"Aye, girl, but will save her life. I have treated those who have an overfondness for poppy syrup with my little red pills. They soon blame the poppy for their retching stomachs." His face was stern. "Otherwise they waste away and die. And keep her mirror close to her and my salve upon her face, and you will assist nature in the discharge of her duty. Your lady is suffering from a pernicious disease of long marriages called *Inattention.*"

"And the stars, sir," Meriel asked slyly, "won't you wait for their answers?"

He grinned, taking her meaning, and giving her another close look. "My pills are faster than the planets, I vow."

And with a shift of his bag on his shoulder and another quick study of her face, Dr. Wyndham left Meriel to wonder whether the man was a mountebank or a true physician. She inclined more to the latter since it was obvious that he believed in experiment and observation. A modern doctor, indeed, though a strange one. Yet for the rest of the day, she smiled whenever she thought of him.

That night Sir Edward found his wife somewhat improved and praising a court physician to the heavens. Sir Edward was so pleased that he allowed Meriel to take young Edward and Elizabeth to walk about the palace.

"Remember to give way and to bow and curtsy if the king or other high lord should pass," he instructed his children, and then they were off.

The richly paneled halls, with all sconces alit, were filled with people: lords, ladies, mere gentlemen and common servants, hurrying in one direction toward the sound of music.

Meriel stopped a boy wearing the king's scarlet livery. "Where is the revel?"

"In His Majesty's Presence Chamber beyond the Stone

Gallery, girl, but such as you cannot attend, though you be a pretty miss."

Meriel shrugged. *Hey, well, life is unfair, but at least it is life in a palace. Someday . . .*

The lad grinned, giving her cheek a pinch just before hurrying away. "Go up the stairs at the end of this side hall to the gallery opposite the musicians and you can watch the quality until the majordomo sees you and gives you his boot."

"Yes, please, please, Meriel," begged young Elizabeth. Edward tried to hide his eagerness under a lordly pose, which he could not quite, as yet, maintain.

"If you promise to be quiet and obedient." But Meriel was off and leading them by the hand down the side hall and up the stairs to the gallery, the sounds of strings, hautboy and bassoon and many feet tapping a pattern upon marble floors coming closer and closer.

Meriel crept, bent near double, the children holding to her gown, along the wooden gallery and came to a wide place that afforded a view while hiding them well. She looked down through the thickly carved railing on a mass of lords and ladies moving in the stately pattern of a French sarabande, the colors and rich cloth of their gowns and doublets, many inlaid with jewels, glowing in the light of a dozen glittering candelabra. Immense gilded mirrors at each end of the Presence Chamber magnified the swirling color and light until Meriel had to squeeze her eyes tight for a moment against the dizzying splendor below.

She put a finger to her lips to shush the children, and realized that it had been herself who had said, "Ahh!" Best she keep her finger where it was since she could not trust her own mouth.

Meriel's gaze was drawn to the throne dais, where the

king sat laughing with a chestnut-haired young woman standing before him whose lithe body seemed to be dancing, though she did not move a step. Meriel realized at once that this must be Nell Gwyn, the king's favorite actress, notorious for her high wit and japes about London, the delicious gossip having carried her fame as far as Canterbury. It was said the king was besotted with her entertainment, while not neglecting the queen or his other mistresses and . . . some nights it was rumored . . . seeking further sport at Madame Ross's establishment with the Duke of Buckingham and the Earl of Rochester. No wonder commoners called the king "Old Rowley" after his amorous stallion. Meriel flushed hot at her thoughts and the images they evoked, which were ones that no decent maid should entertain, although she suspected many did because they came unbidden and refused to leave. *Hey, well, everything to excess is the motto of this golden age.*

Her attention was next drawn to a couple dancing near to the throne, the lady, wearing a dazzling gown of lilac velvet trimmed with large pearls, just turning into Meriel's view.

She sat suddenly and very hard down upon the wooden gallery floor, in as much amazement as she had ever felt. Was she looking in a mirror? It was her face she saw, her black hair, her olive complexion, and though she could not see the eyes, she knew, somehow, that they matched her own gray color.

Meriel removed her finger from her lips, for she no longer feared that she would make a revealing sound. She was incapable of words, but her mind was swiftly dealing with the amazing resemblance. This must truly be the Countess of Warborough, wife to the Earl, Meriel's hero. Felice, the spymaster had called her. Meriel was no longer surprised by his mistake. It was perfectly natural, and no doubt would happen many times until Sir Edward was forced to send her away or dismiss her. Back to Cheatham House or into the London streets. On her oath, she knew that a countess and a common maid could not share the same face in the same place.

Meriel gathered herself to leave. She must speak with Sir Edward at once, before some high personage came to him with a complaint. Quickly, she looked one last time through the gallery railings to assure herself that she had not suffered some sudden malady of the eyes, seen what was not there. The countess and her partner had exchanged places. . . . From the gold braid on his doublet, glittering medals, the blue sash of the Garter order . . . he must be the Earl of Warborough! Meriel knew that she was looking upon the form of Lord Giles Matthew Harringdon, her beloved hero.

She could not see his face, in shadow from his wide hat, although one side was turned up. They had danced away from the nearest chandelier, but she did not need to see, since she knew that face from tracing her fingers across his marble features countless times. But now his form caused a quick intake of breath that made her dizzy enough to grasp the railing. Though she knew she should take the children and leave rather than be discovered and draw all eyes, she could not move from staring at her idol made flesh.

He was a man of more powerful manly stature than she had ever seen, taller even than the king, and with greater shoulders and a more elegant turn of leg, although few would probably say as much aloud. And who had not heard of Lord Giles's courage during the Battle of the Four Days against the Dutch? He had been splattered by the blood of his slain younger brother and yet had stayed on the deck of his burning warship, spars and sails raining down upon him, fighting against a dozen Dutch sabers, astride the boy's body. Every Englishwoman had sighed with pride to think of such a courageous lord, who was said to be the most handsome man in all the court, a court swarming with handsome men.

Meriel's cheeks blazed as a sweet and fiery elixir coursed through her, heating her blood with a need she had never acknowledged before and could not now name. Still, she recognized what that need meant. It was what kitchen maids whispered about and then hid behind nervous laughter as one of the footmen passed by. Even the kitchen spit boy came in for his share of glances and sighs from the younger maids.

Against her will, which she realized at that moment was not as strong as she had thought, Meriel looked again. His lordship held himself rigid and apart from his wife, as if her body's touch would turn him to ice. Could it be that Lord Giles disliked Lady Felice? His own wife! Meriel fought a wild desire to laugh, admitting the crazed thought. What did it matter to her? That it did . . . there was no denying . . . frightened her because it made no sense. And she had a sensible mind. Or so she had always prided herself. She needed more courage and she needed it now.

Grasping the children, she crept along the gallery to the stairs where they had entered, casting glances behind her as if Beelzebub himself were flying after her with all the imps of hell.

She must get to Sir Edward before she was exposed to Lady Felice or to the earl. And how would his lordship react to another face he so obviously disliked? Or worse, she could be taken to the king. Though this was a modern age and she did not have to worry that she would be burned for a witch, still she would have better treatment from her master than from offended quality. *Hey, well, how dare a low-*

*born maid have such high, mocking features? A natural
death begins to look good.*

A further thought propelled her toward the door leading
to the stairs. Was she bewitched? How else could she account for her close likeness to Lady Felice? Although she
had rejected witchcraft as lacking reproducible proofs, as
had many scholars of this modern age, there seemed to be no
explanation but wizardry. Unless . . . Meriel almost laughed
in her flight. An abandoned noble babe on cathedral steps
was a thing of fairy tales, like a princess spinning hay into
gold in a castle tower, or fairies dancing in the night woods.

Shushing Elizabeth and young Edward, who did not want
to leave the king's ball, though their eyelids were drooping,
she hurried them down the stairs.

William Chiffinch stood at the bottom.

He bowed to her, very low and mocking, his hand upon
his heart, as if she were truly the aristocratic Lady Felice,
throwing his shadow high up on the polished wood walls
until it seemed to hang over her with dark menace.

"Sir," she acknowledged with a hasty curtsy, and did not
breathe again until she turned the corner and was out of his
sight.

Chapter Three

Kidnapped!

Sir Edward was up and away in haste at first light to break his fast with the Duke of York and thence to the Admiralty, promising Meriel his full attention when he returned for his supper.

"But, sir—"

"Have a care with Lady Cheatham," he said, frowning and rapidly bundling ship's plans under his arm. "She does seem to have a new ailment, and this of her belly."

Meriel bobbed a curtsy, but could say nothing about the cause of his lady's new complaint. The little doctor had guessed right, and Lady Judith did blame the laudanum and had earlier refused it. Yet Meriel's greater concern was to give Sir Edward quick knowledge of her own desperate problem. . . . That the king's spymaster had mistaken her for Lord Giles's wife! . . . And that the news of her remarkable resemblance might reach court officials at any moment. Or worse, reach Lord Giles. *Hey, well, as I think it, I have to admit that I desire that he know I exist.*

Tom-a-Bedlam! She must be crazed. His lordship would demand to see her, and when she faced him, she would suffer his scorn and—what?—anger, a demand that she be shipped immediately to the Sugar Isles and Jamaica plantations? White slaves brought a high price, and lasted a year if they were lucky.

"But, sir—" Meriel protested, yet Sir Edward hurried away to the duke's apartments, seeming not to hear.

The children were now with palace tutors, so she busied herself with airing her lady's gowns, while glancing often out the windows to watch the boats on the Thames, their lanterns yet alight against the morning fog drifting atop the river. She wondered if Sir Edward would ever take her sailing again, perhaps all the way down the Thames to the sea.

Although determined not to go about the palace, such proved impossible. Lady Judith insisted the little doctor attend her, since she could no longer take her physic and was feeling such flutterings of her heart as to put her in fear for her life. Meriel tried kneading her ladyship's shoulders and neck, but nothing would quiet her mistress except that the royal medico, who so completely understood her problem, should come to her. And at once.

So, pulling down her cap, clutching her shawl about her and lowering her head as any humble maid would, Meriel walked quickly along the halls. Up and down the stairs and across a connecting courtyard, morning sun shining through breaks in the mist, she made swift passage to the offices of the royal physicians.

"Doctor Wyndham is not yet from home, girl," an attendant told her.

"Please tell the good doctor that Lady Cheatham requires his physic most urgently." She retraced her steps, again as quickly as possible.

Perhaps too quickly.

"Surely a healthy young maiden is not in want of such

vigorous exercise. Indeed, I think you could o'erwalk His Majesty."

The king's spymaster sat on a bench beside the sandy path where he had not been just two minutes earlier.

Breaking her stride, she dipped a curtsy, then before she could hurry on, the sun disappeared. Her shawl had been pulled over her head and two hard hands held her in their tight grip.

"Quiet, now," said Chiffinch close to her ear, "and I vow you will not be hurt. Indeed, you may be grateful to me, girl. In time."

Meriel drew what breath she could against the cruel hands that clasped her, and shrieked, "Help!"

That was all she remembered until she awoke with a throbbing head to the rocking of a boat and the slapping of oars against water.

"She be stirring, sir. Do I give her another crack?"

Meriel heard the spymaster answer as from a distance, through a buzzing in her ears.

"Nay, leave be as long as she is silent. Pull in at the Traitor's Gate. It is less used."

Meriel's eyes opened wide against the dark cloth. Silent was all she could be with a cloth around her mouth. Then the full import of the words she'd heard caused her to struggle against the rope that bound her upper body and hands. Traitor's Gate? They were taking her to the Tower. Why? What had she done that she would be taken to a prison for high lords of the realm, a prison that many did not leave with their heads still atop their necks?

A hand rested on her shoulder, squeezing slightly, in what felt like an attempt to reassure her but had no such effect. Close to her ear Chiffinch's harsh voice whispered: "Silence, girl, or you will rue it, soon and forever."

Meriel shuddered and ceased her struggle, though her mind was screaming questions. Not that she had much hope of answers.

The boat bumped hard and the oars were shipped. She heard water lapping against what must be the water stairs and sensed by the violent rocking of the boat someone stepping over her to the landing.

"You know the work you must do by nightfall," Chiffinch said, and Meriel heard what sounded like the footfalls of two other men. "Take her gown from her."

Meriel kicked out with her feet and hit something, but was firmly held and stripped to her undershift. *Oh, Lord of Blessed Name, they are going to rape me and throw my body in the river!*

"Sweet lugs on this 'un, Master," said the coarse voice attached to two groping hands.

"I have other plans for the wench, Jack. Have a care you don't end in the river your own self," Chiffinch said, in his threatening tone. "Now cease your struggle, m'girl, and walk. Have you never been taught to obey your betters?"

"You whoreson pissabed!" She spat the worst oath that she'd ever heard into the cloth gagging her. Though the sounds made no sense, even silent defiance gave her new courage.

Meriel heard the boat push away while a firm hand thrust her ahead and she stumbled up the slimy stairs, scraping her shins. She could see nothing, but she could hear everything. A rusty gate rasping open, the cawing of the ravens that had lived in the Tower grounds forever—it was said they would stay as long as there was an England—and that distant roar of animals was probably from the hungry lions and tigers in cages at the king's menagerie. She had heard that the king's elephant swam in the Thames on a long lead, a grand sight she'd longed to view. All these things that she had heard in traveler's tales and hoped to see for herself, she was now walking amongst, unable to see. And glad of it. She shivered, for the thought of ravenous lions did not hold the excitement for her that it once had. Catching her toe on a cobble, she nearly fell.

"Hear me well, girl," Chiffinch's voice said near her ear. "If you vow to be silent, I will remove the bag from your head and the bindings. I wager I can trust your vow. If I cannot, you're a dead woman."

Meriel took a deep breath and nodded. She would promise the devil his dinner to be able to see where she was being taken, and perhaps a means of escape.

Her eyes were uncovered, and Chiffinch pulled out the gag. Her mouth was too dry to spit at him, though she was able to loose one word: "Villain!" Before she delved further into her store of vile words learned from the many seamen who'd visited her master the admiral, she struggled to pull away her arm, which he held all the tighter, though his sober face broke into a grin. The bastard enjoyed the struggle.

Meriel had never been so furious. Chiffinch must be high in the king's favor, if he thought he could kidnap any woman he fancied. And him twice or better her years. She rounded on him, though chilled in her shift. "You foul goat! Do you think that you can abduct me from Sir Edward and use me as you will? Are you so poor for women that you must drag unwilling maids to the Tower!" Her voice gathered sarcasm with every breath. "Or are you up to some magic, pretending that I'm the real countess to give your failing cock new life!"

Chiffinch was no longer smiling. "You are here on His Majesty's business, so say more of insult to the king's chief servant at your peril." He pushed her faster up the hill toward the green, which had been watered with the blood of traitors who had defied a king's will.

With great effort, Meriel kept her tongue in her head, determined to retain both until she could get away, for she would get away from this evil condition, if only to death. Although she preferred something more pleasant and less permanent.

They bent to enter at a low doorway and she was led past barred cells, some holding men in chains, who looked up hopefully and then sank back into their stinking straw. She heard groans and imagined, swallowing hard, that she smelled the acrid odor of blood over the other all-too-human odors. She was pushed round a corner and up narrow tower steps, circling past a series of landings with doors. She fought down waves of terror when again she heard the moans of men and a woman's cry. Or was it her too-vivid imagination? All her life she had heard stories of the bloody Tower; none of them she wanted to recall in detail at this moment or even the next.

Dizzy from climbing, Meriel put out a hand and touched the scream-soaked stones, ancient and cold, then quickly withdrew her fingers, wiping them against her shift.

Finally, Chiffinch opened a door at the very top and pushed her over the lintel.

Meriel was amazed that there was a cheerily glowing fireplace and food steaming upon a trestle table before it. An older woman of a good thirty years was rising from a pallet against the wall to curtsy to her. *To her?*

Meriel faced the spymaster. "If you don't intend to use me for your private pleasures, what do you intend? You must tell my master where I am, for he will look—"

"You have a confident air for one born so low," Chiffinch said, his eyelids drooping but nonetheless seeing everything.

"I begin to think me that I have not been mistaken in my plan."

Before Meriel could scream, *What plan!* the heavy oaken door slammed shut. She quickly tried it, even as the huge lock clicked.

Furious, she stomped to the window to jump, or to yell rape, but she saw that she was very much too high for the one and too without any rescuers for the other. "'Od's wrath!" she yelled, whirling on the other woman, who curtsied again. "Who are you, and what—"

"My pardon, your ladyship, won't you please sit and break your fast. I have here some warm ale, cakes and a haunch of good English beef."

The woman's eyes were lowered as Meriel's mouth dropped open in amazement. "Why do you call me that?"

"Call you what, your ladyship?"

"Your ladyship!"

"Is that not the correct address for the Countess of Warborough?"

Chapter Four

A School for a Countess

The sun was setting through the stone mullioned window when two Tower yeoman guards came for her. She had paced miles back and forth in the room, but had also eaten well, sensibly deciding that she could not escape if weakened by starvation. And the odor of fresh bread, still warm, was irresistible, as it had always been. Orphans learn early that food is never to be rejected for reasons of temper. Or any reason.

The maid, who said her name was Agnes, although Meriel could pry little else from the sly wench, had helped her into a dress that Meriel recognized immediately. It was heavy lilac velvet trimmed in large gray pearls, and as she put it on, Meriel could smell the lavender scent of its former owner. It was indeed the same gown worn by Lady Felice the night before as she danced the sarabande with her husband, Lord Giles Harringdon.

An image of the tall earl, moving stiffly with his partner in a body that seemed made for grace and lithe movement, came at once to her mind. Or perhaps had never left it as the features she'd adored for so long were never far from her thoughts. *Hey, well, I always try to be honest with myself, or what is the purpose of a mind?*

But how came the dress to be here in the Tower and not on Felice? And why should Agnes playact that Meriel was the Countess Felice?

Meriel sneezed violently, and Agnes rushed to provide a handkerchief. "The lavender," Meriel said, her eyes tearing. "Such flower scents do make it happen."

"Then I wonder that your ladyship loves this scent above all others," Agnes said in perfect seriousness. Too perfect.

Meriel nodded. So Agnes was part of the game, whatever it was. Well, Meriel would play it out, until she could escape back to . . . where? In the palace she would be mistaken for Lady Felice again and again. In the city, she had no money.

She sneezed mightily and walked quickly to the window, leaning between the bars for fresh air, but she had not long to breathe it. The door lock clicked and two Tower guards with wicked-looking double-bladed pikes appeared, one standing aside for her to proceed him.

"I will wait here for your ladyship," Agnes said with a low curtsy.

"Very well," Meriel said, her head high, since she knew right well what angle highborn ladies held their chins.

"Where are you taking me?" she asked the guard, wondering why she was so richly dressed if she were to be placed in a dungeon, raped, racked or even executed. *Are these the sporting games of idle lords and spymasters? And perhaps especially for this spymaster, who might enjoy dressing me as a noblewoman who is unattainable to him?* There was no gag in her mouth now, and she would call Chiffinch what she had not been able to call him aloud before. She practiced the oaths silently as she descended, rolling them about on her tongue with some little satisfaction.

They wound down the stone steps and along an echoing hall, out across the green sward, Sirius the Dog Star already faintly visible in the evening sky. They entered the side door of a chapel. Meriel lifted her head and squared her shoulders as she stepped into the candlelit, rich tapestry-hung room. If they wanted to play at her being a countess, then she would be a . . .

She dropped to her knees, half from fright, half from duty.

There was no mistaking the straight, dark figure standing before her. Though his suit was unadorned, it was of a very rich tabby cloth with crested buttons of polished silver; his great hat sat firmly on his long black curling wig. Even had she not seen him on his throne in his glittering Presence Chamber, she would know him from the face on the coins she took to market each week.

King Charles II advanced a step and held out his beringed hand, a slight smile spreading his lips and lifting his mustache. Meriel didn't know whether she was supposed to kiss the hand or take it, so she used her energy to keep herself from shrinking away. The king bent and lifted her by her elbow.

"Don't be afraid of us," he said in a pleasant, light voice. "Yes, Chiffinch, the likeness is quite remarkable. Speak, girl, let us hear you."

Meriel stifled a sneeze, trying to remember the elegant tone she had practiced often enough since a girl. "Your Majesty, I dare only say that my heart o'erflows to greet your most sacred person at last."

The king laughed, and she could see that he found her answer most enjoyable. "Well spoken, lass." The king turned to Chiffinch. "Her voice is far more resonant and pitched lower than Lady Felice's, but since that lady brays like an ass e'en when not using hers"—the king smiled broadly at his shocking turn of phrase—"it is vastly more pleasing to our ears."

Chiffinch bowed, smiling widely. *A king never smiles alone,* Meriel thought, storing the knowledge, as she did all things newly observed.

The king stepped away, speaking to the spymaster, who followed. "The earl is no fool and neither are the Dutch. It will take more, we think, than a face and courage, which you do assure us this lass has in abundance. Where is her carriage? Her manner? Her knowledge of our court? Even for you, William, this may be too great a task to accomplish in so short a time."

Chiffinch bowed, his hand on his heart. "In one week, Your Majesty, this girl will be Lady Felice, only better for our purposes. She has a brain and is very quick, I vow, which is more than I can say for the countess, who was caught spying for the Dutch because her arrogance made her stupidly careless."

"Where do you keep her now?"

"Secure in the Bowyer Tower, Your Majesty."

"Secure, indeed, William, since those ancient walls have held many traitors. But we have yet to hear how you exposed her."

"Lady Felice was observed entering a glover's shop of known Dutch sympathies. My agents later followed her and stopped her carriage on the Norfolk road late last night. She had coded messages on her person. The admiralty will soon decipher them, although the code is a strange one." He bowed again.

"Then we place our realm in your hands and in the hands

of our beautiful new countess, William." The king smiled again; indeed the smile indicated a long-practiced secret amusement at all schemers.

Ah, Meriel thought, storing away another bit of knowledge, *he is not ruled by others as so many in the palace and the commons think.*

The king stepped near to Meriel, and looked hard at her from his great height. "Are you willing to do your king and England a great service to the risk of your very life, m'lady?"

Hey, well, what can I do but nod with some enthusiasm? How could she find other words in the chaos that was her brain, pleasing voice instead of a braying ass, or no?

Then true words came to her. "Your Majesty, I can hardly do less than m'lord Giles and show him the honor all England owes its heroes."

The king didn't hide his pleasure at her answer. "Ah, excellently spoken again!" The king looked to Chiffinch, who bowed. "Continue with our new Lady Felice and give us news of her progress and your plans as they unfold."

The yeoman guards marched Meriel out, but not before she heard one final command from the king. "And William, see what you can discover about this young maiden's parentage. We think this remarkable likeness and delicacy of feature are only possible with a noble family connection, perhaps Lady Felice's own. Wasn't there some scandal . . ."

Crossing the Tower green, Meriel lost the rest of the king's words, nor did she hear the lions' roar or the elephant's trumpet. She allowed her gown to brush the wet grass, while her fingers explored her face. For a moment, her mind raced with a question. She was certainly in a tower, so why couldn't she be a princess? Then she laughed aloud, to the amazement of the yeoman guards tramping beside her.

*   *   *

Meriel's training began the next day with a formal dinner laid before her, including ivory-handled silver forks from Italy, now all the mode.

"Your ladyship," Agnes prompted twice when Meriel forgot, "meat is no longer speared with the knife at Whitehall, but forked into the mouth in small pieces."

Later, through a secret spy hole, Meriel observed Chiffinch closely as he endlessly questioned the real Lady Felice about her Dutch contacts, under threat of the headsman's ax if she did not cooperate. Meriel thought that the lady probably lied as often as she told the truth. And Felice most certainly lied when she tried to implicate Lord Giles in her spying schemes. It was obvious to anyone of any discernment that Felice was determined to destroy her husband, if not with her many lovers then with her false charges. It was said, and she happily repeated, that she led the Duke of Buckingham and the Earl of Rochester around by their cods, and had even bedded James, Duke of York, His Majesty's brother and head of the fleet.

Meriel was amazed as the intricate tale of spying unfolded at the spymaster's masterful questioning, a mix of promises and threats. Felice had access not only to the Duke's person, but also to his plans to resupply the fleet and to the number and location of English vessels and garrisons guarding the Thames. She even had information about the number of cannonballs stored in the river forts, especially Sheerness, which was the first line of the Thames defenses. It seemed James had left naval plans on a table near his bed. When Felice had swived him to exhaustion and deep sleep, she had learned all the Dutch needed and put it into cipher.

Everything Meriel heard at the spy hole caused her to question what Chiffinch had in store for her. He didn't trust her with more information than for her immediate needs, preferring to tell her only what she must do next.

That night she confronted Agnes. "I must know what I face, or how can I be prepared? Chiffinch trusts no one, probably not even you."

Agnes looked about their tower room, frightened. "Nay, I can tell you nothing."

"Who would hear?"

Meriel watched as Agnes went to the oaken door and ran her fingers over every inch of it. "What are you doing?"

"I checked this the first day, m'lady, but a hole could have been bored since. Whitehall itself is full of spy holes, especially into a lady's bedchamber." She returned to the table where Meriel sat. "I know little more than you do, m'lady."

"I know almost nothing."

"Why should I risk my employment, m'lady? And what does it matter, since you will be sacrificed, whether you succeed or fail. Chiffinch cares nothing for his people, only the game. Even if you win through, he will not risk that you would reveal your part and thereby reduce his glory. He's after a knighthood."

Meriel leaned forward and clutched Agnes's hand. "Confide in me, because we are together in this venture. Don't you see that if I do not survive, you will not be allowed to live to tell of failure, either? If I do win, I will see you bettered. . . . Somehow, I swear it."

Agnes looked alarmed at that, but the truth of Meriel's words at last softened her face. "What do you want to know?"

"What lies before me? Chiffinch will not tell me the whole of it."

"I think because he does not know himself more than a few steps ahead. Lady Felice was caught with plans for the defense of the Thames, or rather how unprepared we are. Chiffinch had been on the watch for someone who was close to the Duke of York to appear at the shop of a known Hollander spy. Her ladyship's noble arrogance and greed caused her to fall into his trap. But Chiffinch cannot risk the Dutch knowing her ladyship has been exposed. I overheard him say he means to use you as a lure to bring out more at Whitehall in the pay of the enemy. That is all I know. Mayhap you will learn more as Chiffinch questions the countess."

"But why chance sending me to the palace where Lord Giles could expose me?"

Agnes sighed. "Because no one would believe that Lady Felice would stay from court in the country for longer than a week. Not even for her health, as has been put about. Mayhap 'tis one of Chiffinch's tests. If Lord Giles does not discover your identity, then the Dutch might not. The Dutch fleet commander has seen Felice but once while with her husband on a diplomatic mission several years ago. That is probably when they recruited her."

Meriel's patriotic anger flared. "The woman has betrayed everything!" Then abruptly she sat down, shaking. "You mean he intends to send me to the Dutch fleet as Lady Felice." Agnes didn't answer. Meriel fairly shrieked at her, "Doesn't he?"

Agnes shrugged. "Expect anything."

After each session at the spy hole, Meriel was sent away to repeat an imitation of Lady Felice's haughty speech and practice her carriage and manner of walking, first with Agnes and then each evening with Chiffinch to that hard taskmaster's rare satisfaction. Now all this learning took on a life-or-death meaning and Meriel's mind was wonderfully concentrated on her lessons.

A simple thing though it was, Meriel found it was most difficult to learn that a countess never looked down because nothing was expected to be in her path.

Yet all was easier than the formal court curtsy. The hasty dip of a servant maid would not do for a highborn lady. Bending one knee, stepping back on the other leg, sweeping the three-foot train of heavy velvets and silks attached to her court dress to the rear while sinking to the floor, all with eyelids languid, took two full days of almost endless, exhausting practice.

On her third night of training, she was awakened by Agnes, who helped her dress. "What? Not more curtsy practice. Please, Agnes, I beg of you, allow me to sleep."

Agnes looked away. "I promise your ladyship. Not more curtsy practice this night. Be brave."

Meriel stumbled sleepily after her. "Brave? What could be worse?"

They came to a lower room with a burning brazier, and the funny little doctor, Wyndham by name, standing beside Chiffinch. The spymaster pointed to a stool near the brazier, and Meriel sat down.

"You have done well, Meriel St. Thomas. But to be Lady Felice in truth, both to Lord Giles and to the Dutch, you—"

To protect Agnes, Meriel had to pretend shock. "What do you mean be Lady Felice to the Dutch, sir? I know I'm to pretend to be the countess at Whitehall so that the enemy will not know they have lost their spy. I am even prepared to pass false information, but—" Quickly, Meriel stood, backing away from the brazier, for she had focused on a metal rod with a flattened end, glowing red hot in the sea coals. "No," she said, having no doubt as to the spymaster's plan.

"I must protest, sir," the doctor said, horror writ on his

features. "The wound could fester and suppurate, beyond my powers to cure."

Chiffinch ignored him. "It is your choice, girl. You submit to becoming Lady Felice in all ways without question, or I am pleased to offer you a quick boat trip to the Clink prison, where you will be bound and thrown into the Thames some foggy night. I cannot risk that you might trade what you know to the Dutch for some revenge or benefit."

Meriel shivered, feeling the water close over her head.

Chiffinch smiled, which did not restore her confidence. "Submit to scarring, m'girl, and be successful in this wifely masquerade for only a month and—"

"A month! Blessed lord, how could I not be found out in such a time?"

"Mayhap two weeks," Chiffinch said impatiently. "Our captains report that the Dutch are on the move in the Channel. As soon as their fleet sails south, you will be substituted for their spy, Lady Felice."

"How substituted? And then what?"

"You will be told what you need to know as you need to know it. If you succeed in convincing the Dutch that you are Lady Felice, they will give you a fortune and sanctuary in Holland. If you do not succeed—" He made a cutting motion across his throat.

"Holland! Nay, I will not leave my country, not for any fortune."

For a moment, Meriel thought he would hit her or order one of the yeoman guards to put a pike through her chest. Still, she stood straight and as resolute as her quavering insides would allow.

Chiffinch spoke through clenched teeth. "If you are successful and make your way back to England from Holland, or perhaps convince the Dutch there is more service you can render from London—" He stopped, squinting at her.

She realized that he would promise her anything without any thought of keeping his word. Actually, the promise was less than she expected.

"—You will have a pension at one hundred pounds per annum and receive a small house and garden off the Strand. You have but one charge: never to tell your tale during your lifetime if you wish to end it in your bed."

Meriel flung his offer back at him, marveling at courage that did not seem her own. "One hundred pounds for a hot branding like any common pick-a-pocket, for being a false wife to an English hero, who has done no wrong, and lastly, for making a fool of a fleet of Dutch admirals, who are not fools. You demand much of a countrywoman and hold your spies cheap, sir."

The spymaster ground out the words: "Perhaps we could arrange marriage to an ailing country squire of good estate." He lost the last of his sorely tried patience. "Now choose, girl! I have not all night to argue with a serving wench!"

"No serving wench, sir, but the Countess of Warborough." She resumed her seat, and lifted her hair. It was obvious which course was easily the most desirable, and truth to tell, had ever any English maid been pensioned so well for playing the wife of a handsome hero? The memory of Lord Giles keeping his posture erect and perfect in the king's Presence Chamber caused her to forget fear of danger and of the burning pain for the moment. She would do nothing for Chiffinch, but for the Earl of Warborough . . . A plan began to take form in her mind. Lord Giles would never know, but *she* would know that he had been spared discovering his wife a traitor, and the following public humiliation. She would do this for him. Meriel St. Thomas, an orphan girl, would save the honor of an earl.

The little doctor turned his face away as the yeoman guard lifted the iron, saying, "You must be very still."

"No, not you," Meriel said to the guard, knowing that this was one time she could give the orders. "You do it, spymaster. A man should be first to do the deeds he commands of others." She looked in his eyes, and saw surprise and something more: admiration. *Hey, well, a very little admiration, but there.*

Meriel swore to herself that she would not scream, not shake in her skin and not cringe away. If she was to be worthy of the hero of the Battle of the Four Days, she must bear this as he would.

She felt the heat of the poker flattened into the shape of Lady Felice's scar before she heard the sizzling of her own flesh and more . . . the smell of it, like an animal on a kitchen spit. The pain was instant, flashing through her entire body, and she did not think she could keep her oath a moment longer, when the poker was removed, taking her skin away with it. She looked up into Chiffinch's face, her own eyes swimming, but no tears falling.

"I have indeed not been mistaken in you, my lady," he said, bowing. He replaced the poker in the brazier and left the room without another word.

The little doctor hurried forward, a salve on his fingers. "England is fortunate in her women, my lady."

He was a royal physician, but Meriel believed she had a friend in him. One she might need again.

Five days later, Lady Felice, Countess of Warborough, returned to Whitehall from Harringdon Manor near Great Yarmouth on the Norfolk coast. Meriel's training had taken one day longer than the promised week to reach a perfect degree of court curtsy. *Hey, well, a real countess would practice a lifetime!*

Her ladyship's majordomo met the coach. He informed her that Lord Giles was inspecting the river forts and escorted her and a line of servants carrying many cases to her apartments, where her ladyship dismissed all with a wave of her delicate bejeweled hand, claiming utter fatigue from her long journey over racketing coach roads from Norfolk.

Meriel collapsed into a large tapestry-covered chair, one of a handsome pair placed before a cheery fireplace. She was grateful for the heat, the old palace being chilled most nights and mornings even in May. Meriel knew that she had passed the first test. A servant who saw her daily had accepted her without question. Now she must gather her thoughts before she had to use them for the ultimate test, her first meeting with Lord Giles.

Alone, Meriel had time to examine what had brought her to this moment. She would take Lady Felice's place to save her own life. . . . Yes . . . for a way out of servitude, no matter how gentle . . . yes . . . but for far more. For the hero of her dreams. For the Earl of Warborough. For Giles. She tried to halt her fantasies about a man she had seen but once from a distance, yet they fed her starved heart as they had for more than a year.

Taking a very deep breath, the new Lady Felice touched her soft linen handkerchief to the still aching, weeping scar, but sat straighter in the chair, folding her now softer hands on her emerald green silk gown. They were shaking slightly, so she smoothed the wrinkles, which certainly indicated hard travel, smiling at the delicacy of material that was nonetheless appropriate for this difficult job. She heard maids in the next room shaking out her clothes and putting them away. She could smell the lavender and raised a finger under her nose to stifle a sneeze. Would she have to face the ultimate test of a wife on this first night? For king and England, after all. She smiled because she could not deceive her own heart.

A delicious shiver traveled through her and she stoked the fire higher. She had only to call for a servant to perform that duty, but she wanted to be alone in this place, surrounded by a room that had often held Giles Harringdon, a place that had more luxuries than the whole of Cheatham House. The marble floors were covered with turkey carpets that were meant to hang on a wall; a japanned cabinet on a gilded stand with enough scrollwork to cover an entire bed was in place against one wall. A pendulum clock and a giant marble vase with dancing gilt goddesses stood in one corner. She doubted any of it had more purpose than just to be beautiful.

Pulling a chess table nearer, she delighted to see finely carved and polished mahogany pieces. But the delight faded when Meriel remembered that her good Sir Edward would not be able to play at endless games with her, since he thought her to be dead. Chiffinch had thought of everything. He'd ordered a girl's corpse with battered features dressed in Meriel's own plain stuff gown thrown into the Thames at low tide, to be fished out by men paid a bounty for such work. It was reported that Sir Edward accepted the death of his maid, saying the girl had wandered into London alleys against his express warning.

Meriel poured a small glass of brandywine from a decanter near her and drank it down, knitting together her frayed nerves. Leaning her head against the chair back, she closed her eyes, going over in her mind how she would greet the Earl. . . . Er, her husband, when he returned. Coldly, she had been taught. Lady Felice had said in plain speech that she and Lord Giles rarely had use for their marriage bed, at least with each other.

She would have time to prepare herself for their first meeting, to practice concealing her secret love for him. And it would take practice, though she'd learned early and often to conceal her true feelings. Yet none of them had been of love.

Dozing, she found herself dreaming quite a different idea. *Hey, well, a young woman can be forgiven such dreams, can't she?*

Upon a knock, the door opened, and the majordomo stepped inside. "The Earl of Warborough, your ladyship."

Giles Matthew Harringdon strode through the door, so tall he bent his head to the side, then stood erect, a heroic statue become full living flesh. He stopped and bowed stiffly.

Meriel was too astonished by his unexpected appearance to move, though she did manage to exclaim, "But I thought you engaged at the river forts."

Giles dismissed the servant and shrugged. "Then I cannot be here."

There was so much sarcasm in the words that Meriel was jolted from her reverie. She gathered her trembling legs under her, stood and curtsied, calling down blessings on Agnes for the long, difficult hours of practice she had supervised.

The earl moved with long strides toward her across a richly hued carpet, his sensitive mouth clamped in a hard line, his face without expression. "Are you going to swoon at sight of me, m'lady?"

"Is that what I'm supposed to do?" Meriel answered with

a little sarcasm of her own to stop herself from reeling toward him.

"I doubt you ever do what you're supposed to do."

Her dreams of their first meeting collapsed, since she was doing exactly what she was supposed to do, very much against her own desires. Why had she ever thought it could be gentle?

"My apologies, Lady Felice, for this probably inconvenient visit." His mouth tightened with irony as he glanced toward the adjoining bedroom. "I hope I have not interrupted your plans for the evening hours."

Meriel had never heard so much proud bitterness come from such a full and sensuous mouth, and although she understood the anger that burrowed deep within this man, she saw it surface for a moment, and knew that his wife's faithlessness pained him still. She also understood that he would never in this life admit to it. "No, Giles, I have no plans other than to greet you. I pray you, be at ease," she said, motioning to a near chair. Despite the flash of unfair anger she had felt, his name sat sweetly on her tongue, as if she had been born with it in her mouth. And perhaps she had.

After the Battle of the Four Days, the king's sculptor had captured the features of Giles Harringdon so exactly that it was as if Meriel were returned by magic to Sir Edward's library, and her beloved hero had sprung to full life before her. She took a firm grip on her heart and her face lest she show how overwhelming this moment was.

The earl felt his face soften before he could stop it. "Giles?" he repeated after her in a voice that intensified the pain he felt whenever he confronted all that he had lost. "You haven't called me that for years, Felice." He feared a yearning behind his words, and steeled himself to bring back a stern glare to bear on her. He had learned well to guard against any softness with this wife. Learned early and many times too often. "Felice, if you are playacting for gain, you waste your time and mine. I will state my business and leave."

His wife continued her unusual silence. What was her game now? Giles heard himself making conversation. "The country air did you good, I see. You look younger . . . er, rested—"

He veered away from the path that would lead him close to her, walking about the room, as if inspecting his possessions. He needed a moment to gain full control. Felice's face was somehow different. Something in her expression was softer, her gray eyes like early morning clouds. He had even glimpsed hurt at his words. Bitterness washed through him. A fresh lover, no doubt, had helped her regain the face and feeling of her innocent youth.

The bitterness of that thought allowed Giles to laugh, though he forced his mouth to do it and stepped deliberately toward her. "Indeed, Felice, you look quite another woman."

Chapter Five

The Earl and Countess of Warborough at Play

Meriel reached behind her to grasp the chair arm and sat abruptly, while Lord Giles settled into the chair opposite. Had he seen through her disguise so quickly? Was there something of the orphan serving maid about her, something like Beelzebub's brand that no training could ever erase? Oh! He was staring at her.

For a moment, Meriel felt like a butterfly pinned under glass in Sir Edward's collection. She had to move or be frozen with fright. Pouring another glass of brandywine for herself and one for Giles, she offered it to him. He bowed slightly and took it, then turned his face from her to stare into the fire.

Meriel took a deep breath, holding tight to the stemmed glass. Although she could see the brandy sloshing from side to side, she hoped Lord Giles would not notice and question her nervousness.

In profile, the earl's visage was taking her breath and leaving her empty: a magnificent strong brow and chin, straight proud nose and lips fuller than she'd realized. The sculptor hadn't quite gotten his lips right. She liked the real ones better. Quite a bit better. He had a strong beard that already marked his jawline with stubble, and it not yet supper by the clock.

But the dark line of beard only accented his strong features and her despair at how she was betraying him as much as Felice with this pretense. As he stared into the fire, the silence seemed to howl about the room. Or was it a roaring in her head now that she was looking at a face that she had known, a face she had talked to, caressed, and a mouth she had kissed? As she watched him, he swiftly surpassed even the perfection of her marble god, but then such warm, manly flesh would. She reminded herself to breathe slowly lest she swoon, as he'd thought, like some empty-headed wench with her first love. And yet, he *was* her first.

She took another deep breath to stop the slight dizziness that seemed to seep through to her bones.

Was Lady Felice insane to turn away from such a man, or brainless as Chiffinch thought? Probably both, Meriel decided at that moment.

Though tall and lithe, the earl was well muscled—the body of a man who practiced at the sword every day, who rode to horse with the king and played at tennis with him. Then, it was said, they doused their heads with water or leapt into the Thames to cool themselves.

Meriel, feeling overwarm herself, thought a leap into the river a good thing.

The earl was grace itself, sitting there, his long legs crossed, his black knit hosen stretching tight around his calves without a wrinkle, his lengthy, strong fingers entwining the glass. She tried not to stare, but the cordovan leather–booted foot slightly swinging in front of her captivated her gaze.

"And do you find me so changed, as well, Felice, or have you forgotten your lawful husband's features?"

Meriel swallowed hard. "Your pardon, Giles. Was I staring? I vow I'm but weary from travel."

"Ah," he said, looking away again because he had forgotten how, when Felice was in a pleasant mood, her body and face relaxed, her beauty made his stomach knot and his cock ache. He had remembered how strikingly beautiful she was, although he had tried to erase that memory along with many others. Hell's fire, she had even grown in beauty in these last days. Her dark hair was glossier than a young blackbird's feathers. Or did everything taking on new life shine like that? He could not understand why he thought so. Had it happened when he had not been looking? And her dark-lashed gray eyes were larger and even lighter than morning clouds, more like smoke against a clear sky. They would haunt him again later as he tried to sleep this night, finding no comfort in the warm body of his mistress next to him, though he would surely try. And was Felice's firelit face more alive, or were the flames playing tricks on a mind that he had ever had in his stern control? Now it was he who stared, for how could a man not gaze on that which gave off so much radiance?

"All is well at Harringdon Hall," she said, struggling for wifely conversation.

He nodded without speaking.

She struggled on. "Wallace has trimmed the yew hedge surrounding the parterre behind the main hall most perfectly, and spring has arrived early." She prayed that she'd remembered the correct name of the chief gardener and the plan of the old manor she'd studied for hours. What could be worse? The man facing her was known to design his own gardens and dig in the soil like a farmer while she had avoided flowers her life long.

"And the centifolia roses I planted when their roots were bare?" He looked at her with mounting curiosity.

"Ah, the roses," Meriel said, smoothing her gown, playing for time. Were these the large roses Sir Edward had brought from Holland before the war, the ones with one hundred petals? She did not recall that they had bloomed yet in Canterbury and most certainly would not have bloomed next to the sea in Norfolk. "Well budded, I believe I heard Wallace say, but you know I pay little attention," she responded, praying that she had not been too clever by half, and saying amen to no more talk of roses.

"I am surprised you remember that much, Felice, since you take no interest in my gardens."

Meriel decided at the moment that she must be bolder or give herself away. "I seem to surprise you much this evening, m'lord." She tried to make her words hold a suggestion of much more than she said, as Lady Felice could do only too well.

The earl straightened and put both feet on the floor. "Not so, Felice, for I doubt you could ever truly surprise me. A wife who aborts my son and heir with the help of a whorehouse midwife could ne'er surprise me again."

Giles stood abruptly, gripped with tension. He was surprised that these words defining Felice's betrayal spoken aloud still had the power to twist his insides like a powerful colic. And yet, some new gentleness in Felice's face, something that felt like an effort to reach for him had touched him. He had almost made a fool of himself with this woman whom he could never again love, nor as yet divorce. "I will not take more of your precious time, my lady. I came merely to ask that you join me on His Majesty's walk in St. James Park on the morrow morning. He has particularly requested your presence, and so I am obliged to relay it."

Meriel clamped her lips together before she could say, *Hey, well, I wager His Majesty has.*

Then the full import of all that Giles had said hit her body like a foul blow, and she struggled mightily to keep the shock from invading her face. 'Od's grace! The countess had not revealed such infamy under questioning. What more had she hidden? Meriel could scarce imagine worse than aborting one's own son, though something told her there probably was worse, since Lady Felice had mentioned several lovers by name. Had she named them all?

Meriel felt rooted to her chair. "Please, Giles . . . stay the while." Somehow she could not allow him to leave believing such a terrible thing of her, a thing not only against man's law, but God's law, though she knew this sudden desire for Giles's esteem was wildly dangerous in a spy who only pretended to be his wife and in a short time would be gone, never again to see him.

He bowed, stiffly formal. "My apologies, your ladyship. I have a late . . . appointment." As soon as the insinuating words were spoken, he regretted them. Although Felice flaunted her lovers, it was not his way to allude to his mistress with his wife, though she was little wife to him. And was that disappointment on her face? He could not believe what he saw. Felice was a consummate betrayer and liar. Yet . . . ?

"I'll remain for a moment, since you wish it," he said, sitting again before he could stop himself, bringing his sword to the front and leaning on its basket-weave hilt. "To what do I owe this desire for my company? Is it a debt to your booter or seamstress you want paid, or you wish to argue for more of a pension than what I grant you. . . ."

Meriel scrambled about in her head for a reason to keep him by her. She had not done with memorizing his features, comparing them to the hero she'd adored, hearing that hero speak with the deepest of commanding voices.

He made a move as if to rise.

She glanced desperately about the room and then at the chess set, gleaming in the firelight. "Giles, we could play a game," she said, motioning to the pieces laid out upon the board.

"You continue to surprise me, Felice. I thought you despised chess in favor of cards. . . . Basset, if I do remember the debts I've paid to my lady Castlemaine, that notorious cheater." Giles heard his wife laugh, and it was sweeter than he remembered. But it had been some time since he had heard that laugh, and perhaps time had made it more musical. He determined to close his ears and eyes and notice no more, else every little thing he would take with him and play hell to be rid of.

"You fear a match, my lord earl," Meriel said, need making her bold. She arranged the pieces, moving her queen to challenge him.

Giles stared at the board. "The queen's gambit, I see. So Buckingham has been teaching you."

"Nay, my lord. I had a far better teacher than the duke. But beware, or I will capture your king."

"Will you, now!" He laughed before he could stop himself.

Meriel watched his long, lithe fingers with trimmed, clean nails as they danced about the board. They moved the pawns and rooks deliberately and with artless grace, although he must have seen she stared. Meriel forced her gaze away. These were the hands she was supposed to know by sight and by touch, two hands that had made love to her. Despite the fire, she shivered.

They played with concentration for some time, and although he took her king at last, he bowed to her with his hand over his heart, his eyes seeming to see inside her. "I commend your teacher, my lady."

She smiled slightly, her mouth hesitant, wondering who this man was behind the high-court manners. Would he demand his marital rights this very night, taking her with all abandon? Perhaps where she sat? On the floor? Oh, surely in the bed.

Meriel held tight to the chair arms. She shivered again, preparing herself to be wife to him. *Hey, well, duty is duty!*

Meriel took a very deep breath, but let it go quickly when she realized that her bosom had risen to a degree that she doubted Lady Felice could accomplish. She had noticed in the Tower that the countess was not endowed to the same degree as a humble orphan girl. Women do notice such things. And unless she was mistaken, the earl had noticed, as well, and was staring.

The majordomo knocked and entered, bowing. "Your lordship, I have an urgent message from"—he bowed again and said to the floor—"reminding you of an appointment."

Giles nodded, pushing away regret he did not want to explore. "Your pardon, Felice, I must leave you."

She said nothing, fearing she'd revealed too much already, but she guessed he went to another woman. She could do nothing to stop him.

He bent to kiss her hand, which she gave up to him as if it were the most natural of things. The lips that touched her skin were firm as she'd expected. And hot as she had hoped.

Still she had not anticipated the swelling warmth that enveloped her. She jerked her hand away to save herself from the very un–Lady Felice behavior of leaping upon him and winding her legs about his torso.

The earl stepped back and the firelight lit one side of his handsome face, leaving the other side in shadow. His voice was low and rough. "I don't know what game you play, Felice, and I have no desire to discover it. If you think to charm me, spare yourself the effort. You cannot put new wine into an old bottle." Then he was gone in an instant, and the majordomo bowed to her and closed the door softly.

Immediately upon the door closing, Meriel thought of a perfect riposte. *That may be true of new wine, sir, but I am a new woman. Hey, well, why do just the right words always seem to come too late?*

The next minutes Meriel passed in cursing Lady Felice, then Chiffinch and, with a hasty look around and in a softer voice, the king. God would have been next on her list if she had not quickly quaffed another glass of brandywine. She did not need blaspheming to add to her list of crimes: being born a bastard, educating herself above her station and, finally, agreeing to this monstrous spying madness.

She had been forced to betray her master, Sir Edward, and now she was betraying the earl. His lordship. Giles. Her husband. All because her face resembled that of a traitor countess. How she wished she had been born with a wart as big as a goose egg on the tip of her chin!

"My lady?"

One of the maids was standing at her elbow.

"Does my lady wish to remove her traveling clothes? I have her favorite *robe de chambre,* if my lady expects . . ."

"Inform the majordomo to admit no one. I will to bed at once." Meriel stood, a bit dizzy from too much brandy, and drew on the imperious visage of Lady Felice. She found it fit her well when she had need.

Two maids washed her hands, arms and feet in rosewater, while she berated them for using water not near warmed enough. *Hey, well, that's what a countess would do!*

Another servant brushed her hair until she shivered with delight. Meriel could not help but enjoy receiving attentions she had once only given. Although service to king and country and escaping prison and death should be compensation enough for spying and impersonation, a few luxuries made it somewhat more worth living every minute on the precipice of discovery.

After dressing in the heavy silken robe, she was given a bowl of mulled spiced Spanish wine and some figs from the queen's own tree rubbed with a sugar loaf. Her head whirled with questions about the morrow, but she doubted she would stay wakeful long. . . . Wine laced with dread cured wakefulness faster than Lady Judith's laudanum.

"Leave me, please," she ordered, relishing the imperious words, as she snuggled into the plump goose-down mattress and pillows so thick that her head was forced almost upright.

She had pushed all thoughts of Lord Giles from her mind, or rather she continued to push at them. There lay her worst fears. He would be the one most likely to give her away as an imposter. Or would he? Would there be anything that she could say or do that would make such a man forgive a masquerade so unforgivable?

Meriel, exhaustion creeping inside her very bones, was dozing when a secret door in the paneled wall slid open, almost but not quite soundlessly, and Chiffinch stepped into her room.

She clutched the covers to her and tried out Felice's smirk. "How dare you invade my private rooms?"

He laughed. "Excellent. You are good enough to play a countess at the Theater Royal."

"I am good enough, sir, to play a countess before the earl, my husband and the entire court."

Chiffinch laughed. "Dam'me, but your spirit will make you a good spy yet. Did his lordship accept you without question?"

"I think he believes me Felice, though he thought I looked rested."

Chiffinch laughed again, or what he thought was a laugh. Humor ill befitted the man. She allowed the thought to rule her face.

"Stay your anger, m'lady." He used that address without sarcasm for the first time. "When you are well into your work, you will learn that every man can be fooled by a woman. If not, then you would be no use to me, no use at all."

She fought the pillows to sit straighter. "I would not fool Lord Giles beyond what is necessary. I have honor of my own," she said, almost biting at the words. "You think ill of me—at your peril, sir—for taking the only door out of the Tower open to me . . . when I did not belong there. You may find I have honor enough for this work or any other. Perhaps an orphan serving maid can have honor enough to save what a noble countess would betray."

"Perhaps," Chiffinch said, serious now. "Howsoever, I will rest easy when I am certain the earl accepts you as Felice. . . . When I see him in your bed, madame."

"He hates his wife."

"Perhaps, but the king believes that a man is more easily fooled if his head is next to a beautiful woman's on her pillow. His Majesty is very wise in these matters." He bowed, touched a carving on the wall and disappeared through the sliding door.

Meriel heard his voice from inside the secret passage. "Get the earl into your bed, madame. Prove that he accepts you, or sleep out your last nights in prison."

"You poxy pimp," she yelled after him, throwing a pillow. "I want Agnes here. I cannot bear to have no one about who knows me."

Where the pillow had lain on her bed, Meriel saw an enormous silk sachet of lavender and dissolved into helpless sneezes. She must call the good doctor for a cure, or her nose would give her away before her mouth did.

The Earl of Warborough reached his apartments swiftly after leaving his wife. He called for strong beer and a goodly haunch of venison for a late supper, waving away the other six dishes he was provided by the palace kitchens, as was due his rank. He sat long before his fire, legs stretched in front of him, scarce eating what was on his silver plate, toying with his knife, unable to answer all the questions swirling in his head. Something had changed. Felice was changed. There was now a softer face, something even mischievous. A thing more alive than he had seen for so long that he had almost forgotten she had once been innocent and endearing.

It had taken three years and all his strength to forget that younger Felice. He would not endure such misery again. Would not!

An hour, then two passed, and he did not move or notice that his majordomo was yawning, until the servant opened the door to a soft knock. There was a whispered conversation that Giles did not need to have repeated.

"Tell her that I cannot come tonight," he said, his voice a little rasping from ill use.

As the two servants exchanged looks of surprise, Giles stood, moving rapidly toward the door, his stride containing a slight roll from his years at sea. "Leave me and follow my orders!"

The servants backed away, bowing.

Giles snatched up his rapier and jousted furiously with his shadow and then with every piece of standing furniture in his rooms until, exhausted, he fell fully clothed into bed, his body demanding sleep.

Chapter Six

A King's Exercise

At full light the morning after her first meeting with Giles, Meriel sat in front of her mirror while her black curls were dressed in the latest *hurluberlu* scatterbrain fashion, with two lovelocks, one draping on either shoulder. She could scarcely recognize herself for the serving maid she had been. But she did in some amazement recognize that the aristocratic woman of mode staring back at her was more the woman she had always wanted to be. Yet at what cost to the real Meriel? And to Lord Giles?

Giles was never far from her thoughts, having strode into her dreams last night carrying breeches, shirt and boots, as if he belonged naked in her bed. He'd stormed the ramparts of her sleep and plundered her body like a pirate taking a ship without its firing an answering shot. Bent on taming her, and though she should have resisted such an assault, he had easily overcome her puny efforts to pretend maidenly struggle. To an alarming degree, she had surrendered, giving him all that he demanded . . . and that was everything. A degree alarming, that is, for an unmarried maid. Or rather an unbedded wife. Or, indeed, an imposter wife, she reminded herself, having lewd dreams of a man on whom she had no claim and who, nonetheless, climbed aboard her in full and quite magnificent arousal.

'Od's bods and damn the devil! Her mind was awhirl in its attempt to describe what she had seen and felt and still felt all these hours later, her body at this moment flushing with heat and a wet prickling that was far more than memory. She was forced to admit that she wanted this dream to come again, to crawl back into her bed and repeat the thrill of Giles the pirate's body hard against hers and his . . .

"My lady, please! Take some ease. Ye be all flibberty this morn."

"You take a great liberty, m'girl," Meriel replied sharply, thinking her squirming about too easily understood.

"Begging yer pardon, Lady Felice, but yer scar be scabbed and weeping," said the maid curiously, lifting a lovelock.

Quickly, Meriel pulled the long curl back into its place on her shoulder, repeating her rehearsed answer. "A careless country maid pricked it with a sharp comb. Have a care if you don't wish to receive dismissal from my service."

Another servant quickly held out a jewel chest. Meriel chose simple pearls so lustrous they looked like milk in moonlight. Fortunately, she had remembered that Lady Felice was known to wear jewels only at night, and then all of them.

Three ladies' maids circled about her as she was dressed, but she did not speak except to complain. And it worked. If there was one thing on which she needed no tutoring, it was a personal maid's duties and a mistress's imperious behavior.

She rejected, in a petulant tone so near to Lady Felice's that she could not help but silently congratulate herself, the wood-stave corset laid upon her bed. "If I am to walk for His Majesty's exercise, I must be able to breathe." She stamped her foot under the dressing table for emphasis.

The maids jumped to tie her petticoat ribbons about her waist and her silk hosen to her drawer ties. Next came all the fastenings on her gown.

"My lady," whispered the forward maid in all amazement, "your bosom is high and full without the corset. Be you with child?"

It was an impertinent question, but Meriel did not dare to chastise her further. She was too busy suppressing sneezes. Besides, there was no way of knowing which maids, if not all, were also in the pay of the Dutch. Chiffinch had warned her that spies were everywhere in the court, and those not with the Dutch were paid by the French ambassador. Or the Spanish. "I have been using Wyndham's Infallible Miracle Salve prepared for me by that royal physician." She smiled at each of them and pointed to the black lacquer box on her mirrored table. "You may make reasonable use of it as well."

They curtsied, murmuring thanks, and from their longing looks at the salve, Meriel knew they would strip to their skin as soon as the door to her apartment closed behind her.

"By the by, I would see that good doctor."

"Now?" questioned a maid.

"Immediately!"

Dr. Wyndham was ushered in as soon as Meriel was completely gowned and her shoulders and bosom powdered.

He bowed low and waited for her to speak.

Meriel dismissed her women, and took the little physician's hands. "Doctor, I need your help most desperately, or I will be discovered."

"Anything to assist you . . . m'lady. My skills are at your command, but first allow me to examine your burn." He did so and nodded. "Healing slowly, but that is the way of such wounds. Continue with my Infallible Salve. Now, how may I serve anew?"

Meriel explained her problem with lavender and indeed, many flowers, especially in the springtime, the doctor nodding sagely as she spoke.

He opened his kit and after searching its contents withdrew a small stoppered bottle, which he gave into her hands. "Distillation of onion flowers, m'lady, a sovereign cure much used at the University of Padua. To make it yourself in future, allow the flowers of onions to sit in a bowl of water in the sun for several hours, then mix with half brandy and take four drops beneath your tongue once each hour when in gardens or fields and—*et voilà!* as we said at the University of Paris—your sneezes vanish."

"Doctor, I am mightily obliged. You are a genius."

"Perhaps I am," Wyndham said with a grin.

Meriel answered with her own amusement. "Surely, there is nothing you do not know."

"There may be something . . . possibly," the doctor answered, looking up at her, his eyes very merry.

Without hesitation, she placed four drops of the tincture under her tongue and stored the bottle in her concealed pocket.

"And my mint lozenges to sweeten the breath," the doctor said, handing a paper packet to her.

"Good doctor, you think of everything."

"Indeed, a genius must," Wyndham agreed, and they both laughed.

She waited for the doctor to open her bedchamber door, marveling how easily she had transformed from servant to highborn lady, who expected to do nothing but take in air for herself. No doubt it would be much more difficult to reverse the roles, though she was determined, somehow, never to return to her former servant state, even to so kind a master as Sir Cheatham.

Meriel found Giles standing before the fire in the anteroom, as if he'd never left. He wore a wonderful black velvet suit with silver embroidery and silver hose, with the longer coat that was the new mode. She curtsied, and he bowed handsomely. She searched her mind for a proper greeting, since she could hardly remark that he'd spent the night in her dreams.

Hey, well, spent *is quite the proper word, since in my dream Giles was no milksop!*

"Are you ill, Felice?" Giles asked after he watched the doctor bow to him and be ushered out. What other explanation was there, since his wife's face flushed when she saw him, as if in a fever or embarrassed, which was all the more puzzling since Felice never suffered from shame.

Meriel shook her head, took a deep breath, and said the wrong thing. "Good morrow, my lord, I see by your own high color that you have already been at tennis with His Majesty."

Giles stiffened, damning his high color, which he knew was from honest early exercise. Was Felice hinting that he had been at some libertine act, as she no doubt had? He need feel no shame for sleeping with a mistress when his wife had whored with most of the peers of the realm. Yet there it was, deny it as he would. . . . The warmth of shame was upon his face, and he had only *thought* of visiting his mistress last night. Cock's life! He would stop this new nonsense about Felice if he had to exercise his cod day and night.

Meriel drew back in alarm at the sudden fierce look that flared on his face. "I beg pardon, my lord, if I have said aught to offend. Your angry face does give my fault away."

He shrugged and tossed his scarlet-lined cape over one shoulder to offer his arm, which she took, albeit hesitantly. "Felice, you don't need to make polite conversation. We are well beyond that."

Stung by this changeling man so different than the one in her dream, Meriel could not stop her reply though she had no idea at all if this would have been Felice's. "Evidently well beyond polite conversation, my lord, since our talk together is neither polite, nor even conversation."

A look of anguish passed so swiftly across the visage he turned away from her that she could not be sure she had seen it, but it did make her contrite. "A face can be a burden, Giles." She had good reason to know this since her face, so like Felice's, had brought her all these troubles.

He began to walk toward the door that the majordomo had opened in anticipation, Meriel upon his arm. "A face will be what you make of it, Felice. Since you've used your beauty to become a court whore, you know this as few women are given to know it."

"Ah, Giles, it seems we come to an agreement at last, and face to face." She laughed because that is what Felice would do, though Meriel hated doing so.

He heard a hesitation, but he thought her laugh as pretty as the first birdsong of spring. "Yes, it seems we have come to agreement." He was close to amusement and wondered how he could laugh at the jest of a faithless wife, though he wondered even more if there was a hidden meaning. Felice had always been easier to read than she had been these last two days, exposing her unfaithfulness to the point of callous folly. It had been her uncaring that had sundered them so everlastingly. A woman with a small heart makes a man with a generous one bitter. And a bitter man does not trust love.

Ever. But now came this changed Felice, who was not so easy to read. Not easy at all.

They emerged upon the Royal Horseguards Parade into one of those perfect English late-May mornings: woolly white clouds floated in the pale blue sky above Whitehall, the trees waved tender green leaves in a gentle breeze, and on all the carefully raked paths men and women in morning costume strolled arm in arm. As Meriel watched, almost breathless and trying to contain her interest in what she was supposed to have seen countless times, a company of marvelously scarlet-coated soldiers marched out from the direction of Westminster.

She almost stopped to watch their white-hosed legs swing in unison along the parade, until she saw Lady Judith walking with other ladies. Meriel was relieved to see a Lady Judith with careful posture and right good roses in her cheeks. The ladies curtsied low as Meriel and Giles passed. She buried her face in Giles's shoulder and gripped his arm, though she doubted a knight's wife would examine a countess too rudely on a public path.

"You must be ill!" Giles exclaimed, puzzled by her clinging to him. He had forgotten the sweet sensation of Felice's head on his shoulder, where once . . . He stopped that thought before it took him where he had refused to go for these years past.

"Nay, a moment's dizziness is all. I have not yet broken my fast. Hurry, Giles. His Majesty's party is entering into St. James Park."

Giles hesitated, sniffing the air. "Mmm, I can smell the onions growing in the king's physic garden from here."

Meriel held her breath until she coughed daintily and slipped one of the doctor's mint lozenges into her mouth. They moved on quickly to join the crowd of lords and ladies trailing the king and a dozen of his floppy-eared dogs chasing about, nipping at heels. She tried not to smile when no one kicked out at the spaniels. Not even when they tore at hosen and scratched new boots. The dogs were the king's favorites and allowed great liberties, even whelping in the royal bed.

Giles saw her effort at a straight face, and smiled for her. "These walks are for the spaniels' exercise, I vow. I doubt His Majesty cares as much for the health of these courtiers."

"Yes, he does love his little dogs so. Perhaps because they ask for little and give much."

Giles lost his stride, and Meriel looked up into his face, knowing she had noticed something Felice would never have observed or understood. She shrugged and said in a tone of complete indifference, "Oh, la, at least that is what Buckingham says. Very witty, don't you think?"

"Very," Giles responded, grimly resuming his pace. What game was Felice playing now? What purpose to constantly confound him? She had taken as her own all the freedom a lady in this modern age and libertine court could want. True, he had matched her cuckold for cuckold. Though in truth he took only a man's release in it, no one would ever know he had anything but delight in other women. Especially not Felice.

They were walking fast because the king had long legs and he stretched them mightily on the paths in St. James Park. Most of the other walkers were falling behind so that the king and his dogs were ahead with Meriel and Giles staying hard by.

"Come up to us, Lord Giles and Lady Felice," the king called over his shoulder. "We are all amazed, my lady, for you have never kept our pace before."

"Your Majesty should decree that all your ladies wear no corsets, if you would have them keep your pace."

The king laughed. "Perhaps we should, Lady Felice. We will think on it most diligently."

Meriel curtsied and took the arm His Majesty offered. Giles dropped a pace or two behind, a hidden scowl marking a deep vertical line between his eyes.

She sensed that the king was enjoying her bold masquerade. Well, she wished him joy of it, for there was little enough for her. At any moment she could be exposed, and she never forgot that she was in constant danger. *Hey, well, if I am to hang or drown, a jest or two along the way will make it easier.*

Charles Stuart pointed to several trees and groves as they walked, noting that his father had planted them. Meriel bowed her head and closed her eyes in quick prayer at the mention of the late Charles the First, who had been beheaded on a Banqueting House balcony by Cromwell and his regicides. The king saw her homage and his face softened for a moment, though he must know that his father, once reviled as a tyrant by the commons, was now revered as a saint.

Meriel thought she would not wish to pay such a price for popularity. Behind her back, she thrust her thumb between her first two fingers to form a cross and ward off evil if the devil was watching. *Hey, well, he usually is.*

"My lord earl," the king said over his shoulder as they approached a pond teeming with ducks and swans. "The food for our cobs and signets has unfortunately been delayed with one of the cooks." He turned and pointed to a man in plainclothes near half a furlong behind. "We would be obliged if you would fetch it to us."

Giles bowed. "A great pleasure, Your Majesty." With a

sharp glance at Meriel, part distrust, part anger, he spun
about and walked swiftly away.

"He suspects?" The king pursed his lips in thought,
searching her face.

"Nay, how could he, Your Majesty? But he senses that I
am not the same Felice."

Charles nodded. "We can see that, as well. There is a
lively spirit about you. Lady Felice was always weary from
too little sleep. For good reason, we fancy." He laughed,
covering his mouth with a beringed soft kid glove. "Go to
Chiffinch when you return to Whitehall, and without delay."

"I did not expect that you would be my messenger, sir."

"Who better, m'lady?"

Now Meriel covered her mouth. "Would anyone suspect
the king of spying for the king?"

Charles laughed aloud, and the swans honked and
flapped their wings before settling back into the water, too
fat from the king's attentions to fly. "Chiffinch chose well,
we say again. We will reward him. And, of course, you will
better yourself if you succeed . . . if you have not already."

She took his sensual meaning since he glanced in the direction Giles had gone, but refused to satisfy his curiosity,
since all she had to report was a dream. "What of Lady Felice, Your Majesty? Must she die?" Meriel stared into his
eyes, knowing it was impertinent to question an anointed
sovereign. Yet she did not fear him, for she recognized a
sweet melancholy that he kept well hidden, but not from her.
She saw this sadness with no condescension. Even a countess would not dare remark it; most certainly not a nameless
maid.

"*We* have not condemned her. She condemned herself
when she first sold England to the Dutch."

Meriel knew the subject of Lady Felice's death was for-

ever closed to her, but she also knew that it would continue
to haunt her mind. Her heart ached to think that she had been
the instrument of a woman's death, traitor or no, perhaps a
woman of her own blood, though she hardly knew how that
could be. She determined to ask the king if he had learned
of her parentage, but she had no chance.

"Ah, Lord Giles comes. He will think that we are seeking
to bed his wife."

"And are you, sir? Lady Felice did not mention you as
one of her . . . her sporting friends, but . . ."

"Nay, we did not, finding that lady too much the bawd
e'en for our appetites, although we might have, at some future time, upon a whim. Our manly need does betimes o'er-
whelm our good taste."

Meriel sensed that the king spoke the self-mocking truth
and, though sad of a fault, was also forgiving of it, as if the
knowledge cleansed the act.

His Majesty greeted Giles, who bowed and handed over
a large cloth bag of food scraps from the royal kitchens. "We
thank you, Lady Felice, for a most delightful conversation."

Dismissed, and with a bow and a curtsy as the rest of the
king's party arrived, Giles and Meriel backed away and then
began their return to the palace.

Giles set his face toward Whitehall and did not speak. His
mind was all awhirl. What now? Had Felice set her cap so
high as the king? And had Charles turned to Felice for his
comfort, with his chief mistress, Barbara Castlemaine,
heavy with a babe, her fifth by Giles's reckoning? He had no
desire to be made cuckold again, even by the king he served
and would die for, and he would not stay at the palace to witness this further disgrace, pretending not to see as Castlemaine's husband did. The man, though created an earl, was

an object of pity and laughter. Damned if he would ever submit himself to either!

"I will ask the king's leave to go to Harringdon Hall two days hence, for how long I cannot say."

Meriel was startled because the words came as if bitten from a rotten haunch of meat and spit out upon the path. Giles was furious. Felice still had the power to make him unhappy. No, not Felice the countess. It was Meriel, the serving maid, who had reached inside that unyielding body and squeezed his heart. And God forgive her, she was gladdened to know it.

As keeper of the privy closet and of the king's jewels and unofficial purveyor of women for His Majesty, Chiffinch's office was near the top of the outside stairs that led to the king's private closet and bedroom. Meriel climbed the dark stairs, lit by one lantern, and Chiffinch answered her knock. She found him pissing in his fireplace. Born low or high, a fireplace was every man's pisspot. What was it with a man and fire that he had to try to quench it?

"Sit down, my lady," Chiffinch said, pointing to a large leather chair. Thankfully, he pointed with his finger.

Averting her eyes as he arranged his breeches, she sat. It was not that she was so dainty as to go all to vapors at the sight of a prick; there was simply no more she wanted to know of this man. His face was the one she'd see forever when recalling the unspeakable pain of the fiery poker sizzling on her skin.

From a bowl, Meriel picked a fig still fresh from the queen's tree. Surely, it was not required of her to starve for England!

Chiffinch moved the bowl beyond her reach, which explained his bulging paunch. "Galling news from the north," he said, sitting very much too near her, before his writing table.

She moved a few inches away. "Your pleasure is not part of our bargain, spymaster," she said, licking fig juice from her fingers.

"Have a care. I am a high servant of the king."

"You bring him women for his pleasure up these back stairs, and it is said you take your own pleasure before they leave."

"The palace is full of gossip, my lady. What I do is not your concern. You have but one man to bring to your bed if you wish to keep him from suspicion. Pretend to be reformed, to have found a renewed love for your husband. A man aroused is not a man who questions or notices change. Then as soon as we are ready for our next move, you can make a quarrel. Get to your enticement, m'lady, or find yourself swimming with the river rats or jigging at the end of a rope."

She clutched the chair arms, holding herself straight, though not doubting him. "I cannot. Giles has said he leaves for Norfolk in two days, if the king permits."

"Then I will ask His Majesty to deny him leave, or busy him with our capital ships at Chatham until the Dutch fleet is on its way south. Then you must go to Harringdon Hall. . . . Alone."

"Why must I go alone?"

"Surely you cannot have the earl in residence when you go to sea to meet the Dutch fleet. He might attempt to stop you."

"Do you really mean to send me to the enemy?"

Chiffinch puffed up his cheeks, wrinkled like a grandfather's although he had no kindly eyes. "You are a vain, prating woman to think you should know more than I need to tell you." Lifting his wig and scratching his newly shaved head, he took a deep breath: "Aye, perhaps you do need to know, since you must play a more sincere part than any actress at the Theater Royal. If you will stop your questions of me, I will tell you a little more."

"You will tell me all, sir, if you want no mishaps. I will not suffer discovery and death by the Dutch because you fear to trust me. You have no other choice, as I do not. We are in the same bed, sir, to put it into words a whoremonger would understand."

Chiffinch raised his eyebrows very high, his face reddening. "Where does a serving maid learn to challenge her betters with such words?"

Meriel grimaced. "Why, from her betters, sir. Now tell me all I will need, or you can throw me to the river rats and be damned to your plans. I'll not die by Dutch hands for your need to keep secrets for your own glory." She held her breath, fearing she had gone too far.

But Chiffinch answered her demand in part, although he continued to refuse to tell her until the last minute how she would reach the Dutch fleet.

In the last two weeks, he explained, his hand tracing down a map of the Channel, a Dutch fleet of twenty ships had come against England's ships off the coast of Scotland, and captured valuable coal ships bound for London. Then just days later, they poured above four hundred shot into the Firth of Forth, doing little damage but showing their might and creating alarms.

"My spies in Scotland and in Holland tell me the Dutch are not finished, but will increase their fleet to as many as one hundred sail and move south," Chiffinch said, "laying-to off the Norfolk coast to gather information."

"But why do they risk their fleet when we are in peace

negotiations at Breda? My maids are all abuzz with talk of it," Meriel asked, puzzled.

"The Hollander, Cornelis de Witt, might take such a risk to improve the Dutch bargaining position, indeed, *must* take the risk, for they want Suriname in South America and the return of their New Amsterdam colony in the Americas. And I suspect that he is planning some notable thing upon London to force us to give way to all the Dutch demands, else why would he want so much knowledge of our river defenses? We must assure him that we can repel any force with great loss to him."

"Can we?"

"You now know more than you need to know. I cannot risk that you would expose my plan under torture."

Meriel's stomach turned queasy as she stared at Chiffinch, who was growing more obviously uncomfortable at the questioning of a lowborn woman. "And I am the counterrisk you take? Cheap at that, and little loss to you if I fail."

Chiffinch shrugged. "Unfortunately for England, your highborn face provides us with our only chance. Now, enough of this prying chatter. We know that Lady Felice planned to meet de Witt in the Channel. He expects to see his spy in person and to receive cipher messages from her hand. We have the ones she prepared and have broken the cipher. We must substitute false messages telling the Dutch of overwhelming force ready to repel them in the Thames."

Meriel was near breathless. "And the messenger will be—"

"Lady Felice, of course . . . our Lady Felice."

"What if there is much the countess has not revealed?"

"That is a problem. She has bargained for her life with the names of other agents, though she will not gain her freedom thereby."

"Nay, that is my problem—if they learn of her imprisonment and warn the Dutch."

"We hold a close watch and will take them all when you have finished this business," Chiffinch said. With another shrug, he added, "Or are finished by it." Although the words were harsh, his face told her he was reluctantly forming a respect for her ability. *Hey, well, not fast enough!*

She stood and paced to the fire, since it had sprung to life again, holding out her hands, colder than they should be for May.

She was still standing there moments later when the door opened and she looked up to see Sir Edward Cheatham, wearing the uniform of an admiral. She cried out, unable to stop herself. She knew that she would never in this world be able to deceive Sir Edward.

As it was, she did not need to try.

"Meriel, my child," Sir Edward said, approaching with his arms spread wide. "I do most humbly beg your forgiveness," he whispered in her ear as he held her to his breast. "There was nothing I could do to save you from this."

Chapter Seven

A Day at Court Takes
an Amorous Turn

Sir Edward gently led a shaky Meriel to a chair. Motioning Chiffinch away with the back of his hand, her old master sat near to her. He spoke in a low voice. "Nothing! Nothing I could say or do, Meriel. Your resemblance to Lady Felice was not to be denied or wasted and, believe me, I did not know. I had never met the countess." He blinked moist eyes. "And the good Lord forgive me twice. All unknowing, I had fit you for this task since the day I took you into my service. I gave you speech and manners, and knowledge of cipher and the sea. But your courage and beauty tied the knot, and these were not given by me but were ever your own."

Not quite speechless, Meriel began, "But, Sir Edward—"

He shook his head. "I will never forgive myself for the wound you had to bear, my brave girl. The little doctor did assure me that he has started your healing."

She laughed, her shock wearing away. "Was ever a spy so well-known?"

"Only to those who need to know. Meriel, hear me out

before you rightly tell me that I have proved a poor master and false friend to you."

She held her tongue, for her old teacher was in obvious deep distress.

"England is in grave peril. From the moment I came to the Admiralty, I have had terrible news. The seamen of the fleet, now unpaid for months or paid only in worthless tickets, are close to mutiny. The Lord Treasurer is recently dead, and Parliament withholds monies from the king, fearing he will spend all on his mistresses and pleasures."

Chiffinch coughed. "Beware, sir, I am the king's most loyal servant."

Sir Edward raised his head. "As am I, but I am repeating what is commonly said on the streets, sir, in fear that rebellion is coming." He spoke brusquely, then continued in a kinder tone for Meriel. "The city is in shambles from the Great Fire. The Dutch, thinking us weak, grow bolder by the day. If they disgrace us in any way, the commons could rise up and the king lose his throne as in Cromwell's time. Anarchy would rule in the country once again." He gave up her hands that he had grasped, placing them gently in her lap, one over the other. He sat back, staring at her. His gaze pleaded for understanding and forgiveness.

"The children? Lady Judith?" Meriel asked.

"The children miss you, but are children and easily distracted. My lady misses you greatly, finding two maids not sufficient to the service you performed."

Meriel smiled at that. She was happy to have finished with such servitude, though serving the king seemed little better and far more dangerous. A thrown pillow or hairbrush was more quickly ducked than a cannonball or noose. But she said none of this because Sir Edward was sad enough, and she did not forget that she owed him affection and understanding for his many years of care.

Chiffinch growled, prowling the room. "Sir Edward, you give far too much knowledge to this lass. If you tell her more, she will think herself Jeanne d'Arc and bargain for half the gold in the treasury."

Meriel gathered her wits. "Little enough as Sir Edward tells it," she said, laughing at the idea of leading a cavalry charge in armor on a white horse, although she would avoid becoming a saint at the stake. *Hey, well, what is left but to laugh?*

Her life was fast turning to low farce that would play well in any tavern if luck held, or she could find herself dead, either by Chiffinch or the Dutch. "I'll ask for no more gold, Master Chiffinch," Meriel said, her chin up.

Chiffinch looked relieved but still wary.

"However, I will ask for one addition to our bargain now that you so blithely risk my life."

Chiffinch puffed his lips and glared at Sir Edward. "Did I not tell you?"

Meriel answered for herself. "Not gold coin, Master Chiffinch, but something worth as much to a brave man. His reputation. My bargain is that Lord Giles suffer no public calumny for his wife's treachery no matter what happens to me. He is never to know Lady Felice is a traitor. No public execution at the Tower. No bloody details in the *London Gazette* to thrill the commoner in the street. No head on a pike at London Bridge."

Meriel took the deep breath she needed to continue, and stood to face the spymaster. "You fished a dead servant girl, one Meriel St. Thomas, from the Thames. When I am done with my work, whether successful or no, and if Lady Felice is yet to die, you must find her body identified by her dress and jewels in the same watery tomb. I leave it to you to re-call how to accomplish the deed."

Chiffinch looked nonplussed. "You dare to dictate new terms. For a lord you do not know. A lord who hates his faithless wife, and would hate a lowborn wench such as you even more. If he discovered the ruse, he might murder you with his own hands, and suffer no punishment for it."

Meriel curtsied expertly, unable to be turned from her purpose. "Aye, that same lord, sir, who deserves better than he has received from his country's spymaster."

The spymaster blustered about the room, rolled some pa-pers, tied them with ribbon and left, slamming the door and cutting the word "Agreed!" in two parts.

Sir Edward broke the silence. "You cannot trust him."

"I know."

"You are so much changed, Meriel."

"I will not see Lord Giles suffer more than he already has."

"You have formed a quick affection?" Sir Edward asked, worry writ plain in the question.

"Nay, sir," she said, sitting again before him, "I would but do him a . . . a justice, since he has no fault in him." She knew this reason was not the total truth, but she was just be-ginning to know how far from full truth it was.

She smiled at Sir Edward because he was as trapped as she. "I am still the Meriel that you took to your service in the scullery and later raised to the upper floor and taught well." She smiled and winked impudently. "But as a countess, I may say exactly what I think to a spymaster, to an admiral and even, perhaps, to a king."

"Just so, your ladyship," Sir Edward said, bowing where he sat, "but that is not so much changed from before. I was speaking of a certain look. The way you hold yourself as if born to your station. I say nothing of the glow in your eyes that I've not seen afore."

Meriel looked away. Was her affection for Lord Giles so apparent? Would others see this glow and her masquerade be over? All Whitehall knew that Lady Felice betrayed Lord Giles at every turning. If Meriel could not match the countess's indifference, it would surely expose her to . . .

"Attend me, for we have little time and must not be seen leaving this office together," Sir Edward said, unrolling dispatches. "This is the cipher used by the Dutch fleet with their London agents. Very simple, yet very clever. It is especially good for our purposes because you will not have to duplicate Lady Felice's unique handwriting with the new wooden pen that holds its own ink."

Meriel picked up a sheaf of papers. "But this looks like music, the same that Lady Judith used at her virginal."

"Aye, but the notes descending the staff represent letters in the alphabet, not all in strict order to add a complication. Only *K* and *Q* are omitted because they can be substituted with *C*. You must learn to read this cipher quickly and to write it, since Lady Felice will have had much experience."

Meriel bent over the manuscript and noticed that the vowels were placed on the lines and the letters *w, x, y, z* were extended below the staff. She could learn this cipher. All the hours spent with maritime codes and turning music pages for Lady Judith had not been wasted. Indeed, Meriel thought in some amazement, it seemed that everything she had learned in her life had been to school her for this moment. Was God's will at work here? Amusement rose inside her, so much that it reached her mouth.

"What amuses you, Meriel?" a puzzled Sir Edward asked.

"Perhaps the greatest jest of all, sir. I have to believe that God knows what he is doing."

*   *   *

Meriel returned to her apartments to find that Agnes had arrived to act as the Countess of Warborough's personal maid.

The maid dipped a curtsy. "It does please me to serve you again, your ladyship."

Meriel nodded. "Due consideration to my rank, m'girl." *Hey, well, now Chiffinch has a spy in my apartments and will not need to creep behind walls and disturb my sleep!*

Although her other maids showed sour mouths to Meriel, she ignored them and ordered a bowl of sweet Portuguese wine for dipping bread. An invitation to dine with the king at the Banqueting House lay on her chess table, the sealing wax still warm. She had scarce time to change into a very pretty white taffeta gown with a pearl stomacher, its hem looped high to reveal a scarlet petticoat and a generous glimpse of ankle.

"Ah, my lady," Agnes said, tying her scarlet sleeve ribbons, "white does set off your black hair and high color most well indeed."

Meriel frowned, not satisfied, as ladies never were. "My hair does not shine as it should."

Two other maids rubbed it again vigorously with silk cloths and arranged the curls with thick sugar water. They would not move out of their coif in a North Sea gale.

Followed by Agnes carrying her train, Meriel left Whitehall by the Holbein Gate and walked down King Street to the Banqueting House, marveling at the beautiful building designed by Inigo Jones. In Sir Edward's library, she had studied this architect's book of draft plans for several of his noble structures, never dreaming that she would one day dine with a king in the most famous of all his public buildings.

Meriel waved Agnes away. "You may return to Whitehall," she said, and then in a whisper, "My eyes are happy to see you, Agnes."

Agnes smiled. "I will do your bidding in all things, m'lady."

"After Chiffinch's," Meriel whispered, an eyebrow cocked.

"But yours with greater pleasure."

Meriel watched Agnes retrace her steps, wondering if this was a friend or only a very clever spy for companion. 'Od's grace! It mattered not. Meriel felt less alone than she had for near a fortnight.

A young courtier escorted her into the hall to a seat near to the king and his dark, childlike Portuguese queen, Catherine of Braganza, seated amidst her pious ladies. Meriel curtsied very formally.

The king smiled a greeting, his mustache newly trimmed since she had left him with his swans and ducks. The Duke of Buckingham was serving the king and knelt, as was custom, to hold up a large platter for His Majesty's inspection.

"Ah, Lady Felice," the king said, "it is some time since you have dined with us. We thought we were all forgot during your absence." His Majesty made an elaborate pretense of introducing Meriel to the company, mostly of his mistresses and ministers. Everyone took it to be an amusing game, and the king's way of chastising a woman who had made herself too absent. There were a few astonished faces, since the king had never paid her any more attention than courtly manners dictated.

Meriel played her part, pretending new delight at each introduction, and blessed the king for the clever way he had given her knowledge of all present.

Barbara, Countess of Castlemaine, sat to the king's left, her hands caressing her belly as if to remind the king that she gave him sons while his queen did not.

The queen stared into her plate, her ladies-in-waiting seeming to murmur continuous prayers.

Yet for all Castlemaine's advanced pregnancy, she was very beautiful and very sensual. Her smoldering gaze rarely left the king's face. Until it was turned on Meriel.

"My lady Felice," Castlemaine said in a sharpened tone that could slice through the mutton bone on her silver plate, "I've never seen you look so well. It is little wonder that His Majesty is newly taken with you."

"Babs?" the king said, but the warning tone was lazy and he looked on with interest to see what might come next from these entertaining women.

Commoners crowded the gallery under Peter Paul Rubens's spectacularly painted ceiling cherubs to watch their monarch dine. The hum of their conversation did not drown Meriel's reply, which she meant to reach to the end of the table where Giles sat, watching her with dark, secret eyes she longed to read.

"My lady Castlemaine, is it not the duty of all His Majesty's subjects to serve him"—Meriel paused for emphasis—"in any way that furthers the king's many interests? Indeed, every lady in England might take lessons in that duty from you, madame."

There were a few indrawn breaths and some titters, though Castlemaine's fury and influence stifled any real laughter at her expense.

Meriel thought she saw the queen suck at her cheeks.

Castlemaine's gaze measured Meriel, who held her breath. "You think to fish in my pond, Lady Felice?"

Meriel's stomach misbehaved so that she was forced to press on it under the vast table. "Never, your ladyship. My own stream is too excellently well stocked." Meriel turned and deliberately smiled at Giles. All heads turned with her to Giles, then back to Meriel and on to Babs, as if they watched a very erratic tennis match.

Before Castlemaine could proceed as she would have rather than be bested by this upstart rival, the king signaled his musicians, who began to play energetically.

Meriel wanted to steal a glance at Giles, but she could not. She wasn't supposed to care what he thought of her antics, or how he was used by two women fighting for dominance. She turned her attention to a dinner of dandelion sallet, roast beef, mutton, goose, chicken, rabbit, steak pie, four breads, Gascon wine and endless sweet tarts. She could scarce swallow, partly due to her corset and partly due to her stomach, which was in her throat. But she ate something of everything rather than appear chastened.

Lady Felice and Castlemaine had been enemies before today, so the nature of Meriel's ripostes had been anticipated. Babs rejected any woman she could not rule, and Lady Felice had been one who had not sought her favor, being too busy with the men at court. An omission Babs would not forgive, since they were often rivals for the same lord, although Babs sometimes exhibited even lower taste than that of Felice. One Jacob the tightrope walker had captured her interest, since he could bend his body into especially exciting poses, wearing only tight breeches, and that on a rope over Babs's bed.

The meal lasted for two endless hours, although Castlemaine left early, pleading her belly.

At her leaving, the little Portuguese queen finally lifted her head and smiled at the king. Meriel's heart went to the twice-burdened woman. Not only was she barren, but in love with her lusty husband. Strange though it was, Meriel felt a kinship, bearing as she did the double burden of being both lowborn and an imposter in love with the man she deceived.

Everyone sat until the king stood, then all stood.

Meriel waited quietly when Giles approached, standing tall

and strong and handsome enough to steal any woman's breath. He bowed slightly. "My lady," he said, his eyes piercing her to her core. "I will escort you to your apartments, lest there be further talk of my countess strolling alone upon the streets."

"I can think of nothing that would give me greater pleasure," she said, answering his mockery with her own. Yet she had never meant any answer more sincerely.

It took them thirty minutes by the clock to walk the short distance, since everyone must be greeted; bows, curtsies and pleasantries exchanged.

When they reached her apartment, Giles strode swiftly to the adjoining bedroom door and closed it, ordering her twittering maids to remain inside and allow their mistress privacy.

Hesitating, Meriel remained by the entrance.

"My lady, you astound me!" Giles said, his voice a husky growl, moving quickly to the fireplace to pour a stemmed glass brimful of brandywine. He sat abruptly in a chair, sloshing strong drink on his embroidered coat, flinging one leg over the chair arm. He looked exhausted, breathing deeply, as if he had been at recent hard exercise, though she knew he had not.

"I do not take your meaning, m'lord," she said quietly, seating herself across from him, as if his bad manners had gone unnoticed.

"I think you do, Felice. There is every sign of conspiracy about you, although I do not understand it. The king has ordered me this day to remain at court. Why would he not want me gone if he is to cuckold me?" He poured another glass of brandywine.

"You are in drink, sir."

"Not as drunk as I wish to be, or soon will be," he growled. "Felice, this is not the first such conversation we have had, although I did think me never to have another. You are engaged in some plot, no doubt, with Buckhingham or Rochester. I promise you, my lady wife, I will go again to the House of Lords and petition for divorce on grounds that you are barren and I need an heir to protect my title. You will be banned from court."

"This court where notoriety is exalted?" Meriel fought to stay in Felice's careless character, when as Meriel she wanted to deny these other lovers, to tell Giles the truth that if she were his wife there would be no other man for her. Ever. But she had knowledge that the Dutch planned mischief against England, and she felt Chiffinch's noose tighten about her neck and forced herself to respond in disguise again. "Giles, petition all you want, but the Lords will deny it. I am still young enough to produce an heir."

"Then you will, wife. Dam'me, but you will!" Giles stood so violently, the chair crashed down behind him. He pulled Meriel from her seat, hurting her arms. Crushed against his chest, she could only plead, "Giles, it is not what you think."

His eyes narrow, his full lips pulled back from his teeth, he was a man driven too far. A man to fear. And yet she did not fear him, nor yet pity him. He was too brave to pity. She knew him for an honorable man living in dishonorable times, keeping his head and courage high. That he still wanted his wife, Meriel was sure, and some of that surety reached her eyes and softened them. Not even cold Felice could resist this man's hungry gaze.

Giles almost stopped himself before he captured her mouth. But he was not in control, and there was some look on her face that angered him more because he couldn't understand it. At first he hurt her. He meant to hurt her. He knew he had because she cried out against his cruelly pressing lips.

And he hoped she'd fight him so that he could master her, take her on the floor as a common slattern. But she did not fight him. The harder he pressed, and the more he bent her backward as if she were a slender branch he meant to snap, the more she went limp in his arms. And she wasn't wearing that damned lavender scent, which he'd always hated.

Cock's life! He felt a surge of heat from deep within and a longing he had not allowed himself for many long nights. Gradually, his punishing arms slackened and his mouth softened without any intent on his part. He heard a groan rising deep in his throat, as if dredged up from his heart. Her full lips fit into his, and he tasted her on his tongue. He felt himself going a little mad.

Meriel seemed to exist without breathing, Giles's kiss giving her all she needed for life. She had eaten a sweet at the Banqueting House, though nothing to compare with the sweetness of his kiss. Yet there was one thing Chiffinch hadn't thought to teach her: how to kiss the Earl of Warborough. What if she was kissing as Meriel and not as Felice?

Giles loosed his hold and pulled her upright. She thought she had made a kissing mistake and was exposed for the imposter she was. Still, she could not allow him to cease his kissing. She was well past wanting him to stop when she slid her arms about his broad back, her fingers tracing the hard muscle under his coat, wishing that coat was warm, moist skin.

Meriel had been kissed before, always hastily and without her permission. But Giles was her husband and needed no permission. His body was close against her full length, and she could very well feel what was hard other than the muscle of his back. This hardness made her breathless, dizzy, or something did. The kiss. His long, lean body. The smell of him, all leather and wine, shaving lather and sandalwood oil on his long hair as it brushed her cheek. Would he take her now? For a fleeting second Meriel knew the ravishment she had endured as a child would now save her from being exposed for an imposter. The Countess of Warborough could hardly be a virgin.

Had the moment come to face her ultimate test? Would she now bed Giles for king and England? Or for herself?

She felt her breasts press against his fine linen shirt, his neck cloth caressing her throat, his hands sliding down to cup her buttocks and draw her closer into him. Now she was not throbbing with a duty to any but her own need, a need that had flared into a flame that put the coal in the fireplace to shame.

He swept her into his arms and moved rapidly toward her bedchamber, kicking in the doors. "Out at once!" he yelled at the maids, who ran tittering from the room.

Giles threw her into her feather-down bed, where she almost disappeared, though several feathers went whirling into the air to settle on the floor.

Before she could do aught but open her mouth, not to scream as he must think but to welcome him, he had thrown aside his coat, dropped his breeches and was atop her, his cock pressing against her, while his hands tore at her gown and shift.

"Giles, *please,*" she cried, almost sobbing, feeling him at the entrance to where her fire burned hottest.

He sat atop her, his cod touching her hot nether lips, suspended between the demands of his body and his conscience. She was his wife. By right he could take her in the street if he so desired. Why not? She had mocked her vows to gently love. So could he.

But he could not. Damn! He could not.

Giles broke away from her, his chest heaving, his eyes wild, and stumbled from her bedchamber.

Frantic, Meriel slid from the bed and raced after him, throwing her arms about him, caring no more how Felice would act, shaken, only needing him and at once.

Giles took her arms and pushed her firmly into the chair he'd pulled her from only minutes earlier. He turned his face away so that he presented his strong jaw and high cheekbone, his skin brown from the sun. She saw the thick, dark lashes lying on his cheek as his eyes closed, scarce keeping his chest from heaving and his hands from shaking by his side. She matched his effort with a shiver that ran from her bruised lips down to her woman's place. And burrowed inside where Giles had not entered.

"Your pardon, Felice," he said in a voice that sounded as if it were strained through rough wool. "Of late you have reminded me of a long-gone love. I will not mistake you for her again, for she is dead to me."

Meriel knew she was in great danger of revealing the truth and was scarce able to return to her Lady Felice tone. "Giles, I think it is you who are ill. Perhaps you should have Dr. Josiah Wyndham, my royal physician, purge you or give you an excellent spring tonic."

"Ah," he said, bowing, almost laughing, thankful for the full return of his senses. "The little doctor can do what the House of Lords cannot."

He walked toward the door, his linen shirt half out of his breeches, his hand on his rapier, turning back to face her so suddenly that he tangled his boots in the turkey carpet. "The king's coronation anniversary ball is tonight. We are naturally expected, and we will appear." He kicked the carpet aside.

She stood, sinking into a very low curtsy to mask the

still-glowing desire on her face and a brighter glow hidden elsewhere. If any behavior would make him suspicious, it would be what she would forever have trouble hiding from him. . . . Her utter adulation.

What she couldn't hide from herself was her growing sense that this fraud on Giles Matthew Harringdon would land her in a far worse place than the Tower of London. A place a good deal hotter even than the poker she had suffered.

Chapter Eight

In Which a Spy Is Spied On

Giles opened wide the door to his apartments, having sent his servants in all directions on meaningless errands so that he could conduct this shameful business alone.

Agnes curtsied, her head bowed. "You sent for me, my lord," she said, holding a folded note containing only his seal in it, since few servants could read.

"Aye. Enter." He took the note, walked stiffly to his chair by the fire and threw the paper into the flames, watching his seal quickly melt back into dripping wax. Back erect, he motioned Agnes to approach.

"How may I be of service to your lordship?" she asked dutifully, hands folded at her waist.

"You are new in my wife's service."

"Just so, my lord earl."

He cleared his throat since his words near choked him. "Thus you owe her no loyalty."

"I owe her the loyalty of a good maid to a mistress, my lord," Agnes replied, eyes downcast, all demure.

"Yes, yes." An expected answer. "But you have no especial liking for her as yet."

"My lord, she is a demanding mistress, but she has a sweet nature at times."

Giles frowned with surprise. Perhaps this maid would not be so easily brought to his side. Yet often gold sovereigns bought more loyalty than the sweetest nature. And the woman's praise was most probably the lie of a wary servant anxious in her new position.

He picked up a bag of coins from a nearby table and rattled them near her face so that she could sniff the scent of gold. "Here are five sovereigns if you tell me who my wife entertains. And one more each time you report the times and the names of those who come and go from her apartments." He was paying an outrageous price, and he knew it was to salve his conscience. Swallowing hard, he thought to end this business, not liking to play the spymaster. Dam'all, but Felice had given him no choice if he was to plead his case for divorce or annulment. "And I want to know where she goes and whom she sees—and beds—especially if my lords Buckingham or Rochester." He took a deep breath. "Or the king. Do you understand these requirements?"

The maid smiled.

Giles stepped closer to her, on the edge of fury, grinding the words between his teeth. "Have I amused you, Agnes?"

"No, my lord, nothing of the kind. I take my commission seriously. Most seriously. I but smile to think of the new gown I may buy."

He dropped the bag of coins, and they clinked into her hand. "Then go to your duties for Lady Felice, but keep your duty to me in the vanguard." He spoke softly, unable to really threaten the woman. It would be even more dishonorable than what he was now bringing upon himself.

Agnes curtsied and let herself out quietly. She went hastily to Chiffinch's office and found him at his desk.

"A complication," Chiffinch muttered after hearing her tale. "Will he interfere with our plans for her, or do we merely see a jealous husband seeking to rid himself of a faithless wife once and for all time?" He stood and paced to the door and back. "The Lady Felice has been ever open in her dalliances. Why make this move now?"

"I think this new Lady Felice does bother him greatly, sir, and he knows not why." Agnes waited for a reply, while Chiffinch mused silently.

Finally, Chiffinch said, "I fancy it makes no difference to our plans. We will learn what we need either way. Keep your eyes open when you are with him, as you do with the counterfeit."

Agnes clasped the bag of coins to her bosom. "I may keep these, sir?"

Chiffinch shrugged. "You will better serve me since better paid, though not from my pocket."

Agnes curtsied, but didn't leave.

"Yes?" Chiffinch said, and the maid smiled.

"Sir, I am now a double agent of which I have never heard."

"Eh?"

"A double agent for the same side."

Chiffinch squinted. "That jest is worthy of your current mistress. Beware you do not grow too like her, or you'll share her fate. You would not want it, I assure you. You don't think that I can allow her to live, mayhap to blackmail me with all she knows. She has already asked for more than our bargain."

He watched Agnes leave with a hasty look back over her shoulder. He had always known fear to be the last and best coin, and thus it was proved again.

A thought struck him and he pounded the desk before he rushed to the door and called Agnes back.

Worried, she reassured him, "'Pon my word, I will do my duty to you, sir."

"Yes, yes. But I think we can stir this pot and rid us of one earl." He squinted at Agnes, pleased with himself. "Report to Lord Giles that you saw the Lady Felice enter this office. He will think it proved that his countess is sleeping with the king, and withdraw from this renewed fascination with her. I will ask the king to send him to inspect the river forts or some such. I don't want his interference with my plans."

Giles arrived that night at Felice's apartments as the clocks in Whitehall chimed nine. Mischance had made him late: a missing silver button on his embroidered waistcoat.

Agnes opened the door, whispering one word, "Chiffinch," by way of report.

The name stopped him. The king's royal procurer. He clenched his fists. So it was true that the king desired Felice, and his wife, ever practical, bargained her price. Cock's life! Not again! Not if he had to kidnap her and lock her in Harringdon Hall for the rest of her days or until she produced a son. It passed his mind that she was behaving just as he had known she would, but this time not giving him a way to sue in the House of Lords for annulment. An earl did not sue a king. Felice must be secretly laughing at him despite that untamed behavior in her bed this very day. Briefly, he remembered her curving lips, swollen from his kisses, and how she had opened her passion to him as he neared its door. What a fool he had been, thinking . . . what? He couldn't remember and didn't want to remember, then wondered that such knowledge did not anger him to more rage as it always had, or sent him rushing to a woman, any woman. This time he shook off the question, determined to stop Felice.

Giles saw her waiting by the fire, her lovely face in quiet repose, showing no hint of the treachery she planned. Felice, who had ever been openly wanton and uncaring, had grown cunning. Why?

He saw she was gowned in a shimmering green satin with matching satin slippers, silver laced and ribboned, a coronet of large gray pearls to match her eyes across her shining black curls, a large ruby pendant at her throat. The ruby he had given her the first night of their marriage. He pulled back from that memory as he moved toward her. Closer, she looked like a spring morning, her dewy face turned up to him. With what? Delight, apprehension? Both?

Meriel had never seen Lord Giles look so magnificent, not that first night when he had danced with Lady Felice, not earlier this day—was it just hours ago?—when he had kissed her so hurtfully, with a desperate hunger . . . and . . . and nearly committed his husbandly duty upon her. His kisses yet heated her mouth, kisses that she had repeated in memory all the day until she was half-crazed with remembrance of the rich sense of them.

Crazed enough to wish for work to do. *Hey, well, at least as a maid, I was busy every minute.*

All the hours since dining with the king, she studied and practiced writing the Dutch music code when alone. The Dutch would expect her to read and write it, especially if they had messages for her to deliver back to their agents. And she had no book to pass more time. Felice read only the *London Gazette.* Gossip was the air she breathed, not learning for its own sake. The idleness of a countess would drive Meriel to Bedlam! Yet when she left this idle world, she'd be leaving Giles behind. The thought was unbearable now that she had felt what she had never known with a man.

Giles bowed. "My lady," he said quite formally, attempting to look bored.

She curtsied. So that was the way it was to be. Nobles could pounce on a woman in her bed of an afternoon and forget it by evening. "My lord Giles," Meriel replied. "I hope I find you rested . . . from your labors."

"Quite," Giles said, refusing to allow any guilt for his behavior to reach his face, and alarmed that he would feel any at all. He must gain back his control and soon.

"I can readily see that you are rested . . . as well as late."

Giles laughed, a little too loudly. "Felice, we have never accounted for our time as do other husbands and wives. It surprises me that you would suddenly want or need such knowledge."

Meriel could not bear to argue with Giles. Perhaps she played Felice a little too well. She went to meet him, putting her beringed hand on his bent arm, and following brief formalities with servants, they walked out the door and down long corridors, not speaking again, toward the sound of a grand trumpet voluntary—the king and queen's ceremonial entrance music, with every man bowing and every woman sunk to the floor, their legs probably shaking under them. It was a sight that few commoners had witnessed. And she'd missed it.

Still, Meriel faced the king's ball with misgivings, though she couldn't confide them to Giles. She knew country dances. Common dances. She had watched the sarabande and knew the steps, but executing the intricate dance would surely give away her inexperience. And dancing all the court dances was a thing that Lady Felice would know expertly. Chiffinch had forgotten to supply her a dancing master.

The high doors were opened wide to the king's glittering Presence Chamber, chandeliers alit and jeweled tiaras sending sparks as heads turned, all double reflected in the huge gilt framed mirrors at either end. Meriel took a deep breath, or as deep as her corset would allow, and stepped forward. Giles did not move, and she was pulled back by the strength in his unmoving body.

"Felice." His voice was thick with her name, and Meriel was frightened by the overwhelming anger she heard.

She did the only thing she could do. She became Lady Felice. "Giles, don't be so wearisome. The ill-tempered husband is fit only for the Theater Royal, and then is the butt of all humor."

Meriel scarcely dared look up at him as he towered beside her. Still, her eyes went to his face on their own order, as if she had no real command of them.

The line of his jaw straightened and she saw his heart pulse in his throat. "I know what you scheme," he said, and the words cut through her like winter wind through a cheap knit shawl.

She couldn't stop the sharp intake of her breath. Satan's breeches! What did he know? Had she been betrayed? Who could— She had no time to think more before the door porter announced in a loud voice: "The Earl and Countess of Warborough!"

As they stepped into the Presence Chamber, to lights, music and a buzz of voices, Giles bent to her ear and said words that chilled her more. "Believe me a fool at your hazard, wife."

Before she could offer any answer, which she certainly didn't have ready on her tongue, a very handsome man approached, took her hand and kissed it with a smack of his lips, as if eating a sweet. Meriel sensed Giles go rigid. "My lord Buckingham," she said, recognizing him from the miniatures she had studied in the Tower. He was already showing a small second chin that would grow with time, but as yet he was quite good to look upon, and from his smirk, knew it well.

She showed him the half-lazy sensual smile of Lady Felice, the smile that seemed to say *I know what you want and I've got it.*

Hey, well, I cannot help but feel some small chagrin: I have never been so all the rage, and now I don't want it. Meriel had always amused herself with her own unspoken wit. But now she was far too unhappy even for silent amusement.

"My lady Felice, Lord Giles," Buckingham said, bowing extravagantly. "My lord earl, I look forward to jousting with your great wit this very hour."

Giles inclined his head.

Meriel tried hard not to look aghast. Wit? Giles a great wit? She'd seen none of it.

Buckingham inclined his head, not taking his gaze from her. "My lord earl, you will surely grant me this first dance with your wife, since she returns more beautiful than when she left us," Buckingham said, not needing permission to strip her naked with his eyes.

"No, your grace, I will not grant your wish," Giles said, matching Buckingham's easy tone. "I have a sudden need for this particular partner tonight. For the entire night."

Buckingham's hand reached for a rapier that wasn't there, since he was dressed for dancing. Indeed his arm was so beribboned that he would have made a poor parry and an exceedingly awkward long thrust.

Giles grinned. "You are indeed a fortunate man, Buck," he said, not having to explain his meaning.

"And so I have always thought myself, Giles, though I have bested a husband or two who came against me. Still, would I challenge one of the best swords in England without extreme cause, since I but needs wait for another night?" He smiled, but the smile was more a twist of his lips than an expression of genuine mirth. "Yet what occasions this heartfelt desire to dance with a wife . . . a desire to amuse the assemblage, indeed all London, when the word gets out . . . which it will?" Buckingham waved a heavily perfumed handkerchief under his nose as if encountering a noxious odor.

Giles smiled without care at the harmless insult. "A sudden whim, Buck, that I would exercise fully. I fancy a man needs no better reason to dance with his wife, not even in this court."

Buckingham was not taking Giles's refusal well. Meriel could see red creeping up his neck to his cheeks. A high noble of the realm, cousin to Barbara Castlemaine, a member of the king's merry gang of favorites, he was not often refused any expressed request.

The duke bowed abruptly and walked away.

"I have made an enemy in your name, Felice," Giles said, bowing to a promenading man, who bowed to him.

Meriel curtsied, beginning to weary of it. "There was no reason to do so."

"It depends on what you mean by reason," Giles said, continuing to bow to all who greeted him.

Was he toying with her? She made another curtsy to a handsome couple. There seemed to be no one without some claim to beauty in this court. "Reason means many things, as I'm sure you know, my lord husband. Do you refer to logic or to justification?"

Giles continued to bow, but she saw a startled change of

expression. "Where comes this new and more learned Felice? Or have you been sitting at the knee of that great philosopher, John Wilmot, the Earl of Rochester?"

Meriel decided to fall back on Felice's indifference, since she had gone very much too far in this debate. All the while, she was trying with great difficulty to keep her mouth from dropping open in utter amazement, since she had never been so close to so many richly dressed aristocrats, each adorned with a king's ransom in jewels. She couldn't help but think that the whole navy could be paid and outfitted if the wealth were stripped from these bodies, although she thought better than to say so or even allow the thought to reach her face.

The door porter tapped his standard upon the floor and called the country dance: cuckolds-all-a-row. The dancers applauded with delight as Meriel sighed with relief. Giles led her to the center of the floor, where dancers were forming into fours. This was a dance she knew well. The Earl of Rochester, as handsome as his portrait, and his petite partner, the comic red-haired actress Nell Gwyn, made their foursome.

The sprightly music began and they took hands and all moved forward, then back. Next they weaved round, first with the right hand and then with the left. For a moment Meriel forgot that she was dancing in Whitehall, masquerading as a countess. She might have been back on the Canterbury green with a maypole ribbon in her hand. The temptation to throw back her head and laugh was stifled when Rochester bent to her ear on her turn round him, whispering, "Midnight, same place."

Her heart began to pound in time to the music. What same place? What would Rochester do if Lady Felice did not appear?

Now the foursome became eight and they locked arms,

marching down the chamber at a quick step. At the other end, the men changed places, and it was hands all around again, weaving in and out, almost skipping. It was a sight to make the maid Meriel laugh to herself to see elaborately dressed and coiffed courtiers larking about like country lads and lasses. As she took Buckingham's hand, he bent into her ear and licked it. *Midnight,* he mouthed into her face, as she twisted away.

Fear gripped her. All was beyond her control. She knew not what these nobles planned. The solution came to her when she noticed the long silver ribbons on one of her slippers were undone. Wait till she got her hands on that clumsy maid: She'd reward her handsomely for this way out of her dilemma!

As the eight became four again, Meriel flung into a turn and crumpled to the floor. She held her ankle and moaned, perhaps too loudly, for she noticed that Nell Gwyn had a little smile on her vivacious face. *Hey, well, she is a real actress.*

Those dancers nearest stopped and stood looking down on Meriel as if she showed plague signs. A very good thing she wasn't mortally wounded.

Giles rushed in and knelt beside her, his mouth tender as she had never seen it. "Felice, what is it?"

"My ankle," she said, grimacing with what she hoped was the right amount of pain to convince him.

He scooped her easily from the floor and started for the Presence Chamber door, Meriel against his chest, his warm breath moving in her hair. Her heart beat faster for finding herself in his arms again. The music and dancing stopped as the king stood.

"My lord earl." It was the king's voice, and it was a command. "Take my lady Felice into the ladies' tiring room behind the Court Theater stage, so that she may rest and perhaps rejoin us later. I will send for a physician."

His Majesty motioned to the door porter, who pounded his staff and called, "Make way. Make way."

Giles had no choice but to obey. He followed the porter, his wife light in his arms, groaning softly. Every groan tore at his heart. He felt responsible for her pain, although he berated himself for the feeling. What was this new hold Felice had on him when he believed himself rid of every fond emotion? Obviously, he had not been thorough. But he would be more painstaking in the future, struggling to push down any further nonsense about a different Felice. Hadn't she proved by her visit to Chiffinch to be the same high whore?

He placed her carefully on a cushioned settee and checked her ankle. It was not swelling as yet. "Where is the damned physician?" he yelled at the porter.

"He has been summoned, your lordship."

A little doctor in a black medical robe much too long for him hurried through the door. He reached scarce to Giles's chest but carried an air of high consequence.

The doctor bowed low. "Josiah Wyndham, royal physician, your lordship, and as you know, I have treated Lady Felice before."

Giles frowned. "For what ill, doctor?"

"My deepest pardon, my lord earl, but the first thing I learned in my studies at the University of Padua, and later at Bologna and—"

Meriel interrupted his familiar speech. "Giles, I consulted the doctor when my scar was opened by a clumsy maid with a sharp comb and needed healing," she said, reaching up to touch behind her ear.

"Now 'tis a turned ankle, doctor, in addition to an open wound," Giles said. "All the more reason I insist that my lady must be abed in her apartments until I can remove her to the country."

Dr. Wyndham nodded, tapping his cheek in deep thought. "Rest is a cardinal remedy, Lord Warborough, but may I examine the ankle to determine if any bones are broken? A lady's ankle is a fragile thing."

Giles nodded, but watched, frowning.

Without looking upon the lady's naked flesh, the doctor felt along the ankle through the gown, a look of concentration on his face.

Meriel tried to stare a warning, but he didn't need it.

"My lord, I prescribe a cure-all salve, which I have with me, and a tight binding. Then your most excellent suggestion should follow: three days abed." He busily applied the salve and wrapped Meriel's ankle in strips of clean linen.

Giles nodded and drew a coin from his waistcoat, which he gave to the doctor.

Bowing, the doctor said, "I will call for a litter from my office for her ladyship."

Giles raised a hand to stop him. "Stay by her, and I will tell the porter to do so." He rushed from the room to give the necessary orders.

The earl was no more out the door than another opened, Rochester and Buckingham crowding in.

"My lords—" the little doctor began, but spoke no further when faced with a cocked pistol and lordly disdain.

At that, Meriel jumped to her feet, a mistake she quickly regretted, knowing she would be allowed few mistakes if she wished to live past two and twenty. She stepped easily on the foot bound with linen, oozing the doctor's miracle salve. Aye, indeed miraculous, since she was cured on the instant.

A mischievous lord pulling on either arm, she was suddenly racing through the marble halls of the palace to an exit.

There, Rochester and Buckingham laughing in high glee, they were joined by Nell Gwyn, who helped all to cloak and mask themselves. Grooms held two horses.

Scarcely containing himself, Rochester smirked. "Felice, what have you done to Giles? Is he trying to seduce his own wife?"

Buck roared. "He needn't try so hard, eh, John?"

Rochester laughed and made a drunken rhyme. "Our noble fine countess has got a good trick; she cuckolds her husband for the sake of his prick!"

Buck doubled over with laughter. "She cuckolds her husband, for the—" He stopped, nearly choking on wine-fueled merriment.

"Felice," Rochester added, pleased with his success, "that was another merry trick you played on your lord. I knew you'd divine some way to escape his sudden interest."

Meriel winked and laughed as Felice most certainly would. But inside she was thinking, *'Od's life! What is the lady Felice facing now?*

Chapter Nine

A Midnight Caper

Grasping Meriel around her waist, the Duke of Buckingham plucked her from her feet and placed her sidesaddle in front of him. "Now, my pretty passion," Buck said, "we have planned a wondrous midnight caper to welcome you home. You will adore it after those dull days in the Norfolk countryside. Dam'all! And those unwanted attentions . . . despite John's verse, I do not believe them wanted . . . they are so very far out of the mode. M'dear, did he think to make himself the jest of all Whitehall, demanding you dance with him?" His lordship licked her ear again, and a waft of wine enveloped her nose.

'Od's life! Did this duke have some particular liking for ladies' ears, as some men did for a dish of ram's testicles, thinking to increase their manly prowess? She turned her head, but that only exposed her other ear to a licking.

Buckingham whipped the horse and they were off at a canter.

"Buck!" yelled Rochester, reining alongside with Nell astride behind him, her skirts pulled between her legs and the ends tucked into her waist ties, her face alight with mischief. "Let us see what sport we find on the Ring Road in Hyde Park."

They were off at twice the speed, pounding along cobbled streets, empty but for the watch with his lantern calling the hour. They clattered into the park, Meriel's skirts flowing against the horse's flanks. She thought to be dead of a stabbing corset stave before Chiffinch worked any revenge. Instead of finding Giles come to her bed this night—she shivered at that thought—she was racing about London without an idea how she would escape two amorous and drunken lords intent upon tomfoolery. And probably more. But her thoughts went to Giles and what he would think when he returned to the tiring room to find her gone. And what he would do.

Giles arrived with a litter and its bearers scarce minutes after Meriel disappeared. "Where is she?" he asked, his voice harsh. He knew immediately that he'd been a fool to trust Felice. He also knew that he wouldn't repeat that mistake in this lifetime.

The little doctor perched on the settee with his head in his hands. "My lord earl, I am most grievously—"

"Where did she go?" Giles said in a voice that would have brought a general to attention.

"I know not where, your lordship. My lords Buckingham and Rochester spirited her away, but a few minutes gone. They had a pistol—"

"Her ankle?" Giles said, his face demanding the truth.

"Better, your lordship," the doctor said, standing, and in his towering peruke nearly reaching Giles's chin.

Giles was away before the little doctor, obviously distressed, could tell a longer tale of his miraculous salve, and was quickly out the side door and to the palace entrance.

Two grooms in their lord's livery were playing dice against the wall. Giles collared both on their knees. "Where did your masters go?" His command was not to be denied.

The groom in Buckingham's livery sulked. "The duke does not consult me as to his comings and goings."

Giles tightened his grip, and the groom's face reddened. "If you do not wish to end in the Clink as party to wife kidnapping, speak all you know and speak it quickly."

The Earl of Rochester's groom spoke for him. "I heard my lord say"—he coughed, trying to get his breath past his tightening neck cloth—"they would make a great jape on the Ring." Then he hesitated.

The groom's face bulged as Giles tightened his hold. "Tell all!"

The two grooms looked at each other, and the duke's groom added, "And then to Spring Gardens, my lord. I beg you do not inform—"

Giles dropped them and they sprawled on the ground, scrambled immediately to their feet and, leaving their ivory dice behind, fled.

Giles was already racing for the royal stables, yelling for a stable boy to saddle his horse well before he entered the stalls. While his horse was readied, he called for pen and ink, wrote a short note, giving the boy a penny to deliver it to his majordomo. "Run like the wind, boy," he said, flinging himself into the saddle. Within minutes, he was pounding toward Hyde Park.

Not this time would he forgive her. Felice was finished at court if he had to hold her prisoner at Harringdon Hall until she delivered a son. She would give him an heir and then he would not care what she did, where she went or whom she loved, but he would see her banned from court. He had that power. He berated himself for believing her injured for an instant. What had made him not see so transparent a trick? What had induced him to believe that she had changed, or was changing? Even the knowledge that she treated with the king's procurer had not completely dampened his wonder at the new Felice he'd seen or, rather, sensed. And it was a lie. She was a lie!

"Never again, Felice. Never again!" He yelled the words into the streets, slamming them against houses and into the trees that lined the Ring as he passed through the great entrance into Hyde Park. And then there was only the sound of hooves, pounding the packed road that by day held the carriages of London's nobility and by night served as London's dark, airy starlit brothel with every known vice for sale in its shadowy glades.

From behind some trees at a turning well inside the park, Meriel asked, "Buck, what do you plan?" She used Felice's indifferent voice, drowning Nell's excited laughter.

"While you were moldering in that ancient country manor of yours, we were planning a wonderful new game, Felice."

"Aye," Rochester said, "and, my love, you will adore it."

Meriel did not like the sound of these lords. One called her *his passion* and another *his love*. She feared that both were only too true, for the real Felice was an equal to Castlemaine in her need for male service. Yet as a spy, Meriel was in too deep to back away from this trouble without giving herself away.

"Do tell me, what is this game called?" Meriel asked, allowing Felice's aristocratic voice some excitement. Concentrating on being Felice kept Meriel from succumbing to the unclean odor coming from the duke. And to her own fear. At least for the moment. The arm about her waist was not loosening, thus she doubted if her protests would raise more than reminiscences of other such games and thence questions she might not be able to answer. Best these lords stay well occupied with present sport.

"I name this game rogues-all-round," Nell Gwyn answered for them. "It seems you high courtiers do tire of your station and love to act like common road rogues, though you are the poorest rogues ever I beheld. Now for a real highwayman, you'd want Gentleman Johnny. Once on Bagshot Heath he stopped my carriage and took my jewels, but when he learned my name, he returned them for a kiss, and rode away laughing. I called him back and gave him ten guineas and another kiss." She threw back her head and laughed softly.

"Say you so, Nell?" Buck answered, taking up the challenge. "I don't trust a thief who trades money for a kiss when he could take both." He adjusted his mask and then Meriel's.

"The devil, Buck," Nell whispered urgently. "I'll have nothing to do with robbery of some poor slut angling for her penny bread behind a bush. Or even a pretty-arsed Molly Boy. Though I would not mind lifting the fat purse of a bishop, taken from the poor box."

Rochester laughed softly. "Our Nellie has a sweet sensibility, Buck. Best we humor her."

A slow-moving carriage came around the turn.

Buckingham leaned into Meriel's ear, as she relaxed to think that Nell had put a halt to this madness. "What say you, Felice, shall we show these pale ninnies real roguery?"

Before Meriel could think of how to back away from this trouble, the duke had spurred into the road with pistol drawn. "Stand and deliver, my good man!" he yelled, then chuckled. "'Tis easy. I know their rogue language."

The carriage halted, the horses shying.

"Place your hands where I can see them, my man," Buck ordered the driver.

Meriel looked into the carriage, dimly lit by a side lantern. A naked slattern was scrambling away from a man whose breeches were about his ankles, though his manhood still stood proud.

"Fie on you, sir," the Duke of Buckingham said, laughing. "You owe me your purse for saving you from this poxy wench, else you'd be in the mercury baths within the week."

The man thus saved sputtered indignantly. "Villian! While I'm in the baths, you'll be dancing from Tyburn's tree. Let me go free, and I'll say no more as I do discern by your speech and dress that you are a gentleman with a lady. And that lady wears a coronet upon her head that outweighs my purse by many guineas. Rob her head, sir, and leave me to my pleasures."

"I thank you for your advice," Buck said, though now there was no humor in his tone. "But it is *your* head that is a target for my pistol. Toss over your purse. Carefully and *now*!"

The word was so loud, Meriel was near deafened, and it caused her to jerk in his arms.

"Keep your nerve, Felice," his lordship whispered. "We'll laugh together later, as well as share other delights."

Rochester with Nell, their hoods low over their heads, spurred onto the road.

Faced with this double threat, the man in the carriage threw his purse, and Buck, leaning from his saddle, deftly caught it.

"Begone," Buck called to the driver as the girl jumped naked from the moving carriage. Her dress came flying

after, her customer wanting no reminder of this evening's
thwarted pleasure.

"Let the whore go, Buck," Nell said, in a low but commanding voice. "There is no sport in taking her hard-earned
shillings."

"Aye, humor Madame Gwyn," Meriel whispered. And
then thinking what Felice would say, added, "It would be
more amusing to mix the honorable with roguery." She
laughed and was happy to hear Buck and Rochester join in.

"Begone, whore," Buck called, as the terrified girl struggled into her only garment, a worn and grimy gown. Opening the purse he'd stolen, he threw her a shilling. "Catch a
new customer, girl, or better buy some oranges and take
them to the Theater Royal, where you can catch a king on a
good night."

Meriel looked quickly at Nell, because this was a studied
insult, since Nell had been an orange girl before becoming
London's most famous comic actress and then going on to
bed the king. The Duke of Buckingham might never forgive
this spoiled bit of japery.

"Nay, girl," Nell said, throwing her a gold guinea from
her own purse. "The king is fairly caught," she said in a
proud, carrying voice that easily reached to the upper gallery
most nights. "Go home to the honest cottagers you left.
There is no fortune for you here, nothing but early death."

The girl scuttled away into the darkness, the guinea between her teeth.

Meriel knew that she would forever wonder if the girl
took Nell's advice. But on that instant she liked Nell Gwyn
exceeding well. Whatever else she was, she was kind of
heart and had a rough honesty.

"A pretty couplet. Most sweet and warming," Buck said,

but there was anger in his tone. "You seek the approval of the lowest commoner and deny mine."

Nell threw back her pretty head, red-gold streaked hair loosened by the ride streaming behind her. "Buck, I do remember recently when the commons ruled England, and if they do so again, it won't be my head on the block."

Buck's body went rigid against Meriel. "You speak treason."

"Fie, my lord. His Majesty has no more loyal whore. I merely speak history."

Before Cromwell's civil war could be fought again, the sound of a swift-approaching horse sent them spurring back behind the trees.

Somehow Meriel was not surprised to see that the lone rider was Giles, making swift passage, rustling the leaves about her in the warm May night. She saw his white face as a blur in the dark and shivered, imagining his fury and at the same time longing for him to rescue her. Yet she did not call out. These lords, who seemed to recognize no limits to their pleasure, could run him through or shoot him dead. Who was there to know? Indeed, that might be their ultimate game, to push against all decent limits until they crumbled.

Buck whispered in her ear, "Your husband will make himself the court jester yet, chasing after a wife in the dark." He chuckled.

To Meriel, the laughter sounded forced. "La, Buck, if Giles is going to continue so tiresome, perhaps we should return to Whitehall."

Lord Rochester took a long drink from a bottle in his saddlebag. "George Villiers, if we let husbands dictate our sport, we will be mightily inconvenienced." He offered the bottle to Buck, who matched him draught for draught.

With a laugh, Buck clasped Meriel tighter. "John Wilmot,

Giles is such a fool. We'll lose him easily. He makes for Spring Gardens, at the Fort Millbank river crossing. We'll take the closer Westminster stairs and get to the gardens first." The idea delighted him so that she could feel him shaking with laughter. "What a tale to tell the court! While the Earl of Warborough beat the gooseberry bushes looking for his lost wife, I had her on her back almost within his sight."

His laughter beat upon Meriel's ears as she leaned into the pommel, hoping to put some few inches between the duke's body and hers. There was no doubt now as to his intent.

All four set off in seeming high good humor in another direction, soon coming to the Thames. Leaving the horses with an idle boy at Westminster, they hired watermen to row them to the Kensington side. It was low tide and the river had shrunk to one-third its size. Thus, the boatmen had to carry all through the mud to the stairs, where Meriel nearly slipped on green slime, but came at last to the Spring Gardens entrance. Lanterns and flares were everywhere, making her midnight surroundings into the dusk of eventide, not light but not dark.

Nell complained immediately of hunger and thirst, and after Meriel suffered an interminable kiss from the Duke of Buckingham, who made liberal use of his tongue in any opening he found, the two nobles were off in the direction of string music to find food and drink.

Nell walked about rubbing her arse. "I don't find our companions at all amusing tonight, my lady. They are too drunk, and Rock is intent upon some coarse mischief."

Meriel did not think that Felice and Nell had been friends. Felice was too haughty, though not above using her acquaintance with Nell to gain admittance to the men's tiring room at the Theater Royal. Still, Meriel doubted anyone used Nell without her knowing it, or for longer than she wished. Or without comic retaliation. She was as full of intelligence as she was of fun.

Meriel rubbed her own arse. "Why don't we play a trick on two lords who so overreach themselves?"

"A trick for a trick," Nell said, smiling. "You have more of wit than I knew. I think we should surely do it."

Giles realized that he'd lost the two lords and Felice somewhere in the park. When he reached the fort, he stabled his horse with instructions to return it to the royal mews, crossed to Spring Gardens and walked swiftly into one of the gravel paths, which divided the formal squares of plantings and fountains. Ordinarily, Giles loved walking in these gardens of a May springtime morn, when all blazed with jonquils, gillyflowers and borders of berry and rosebushes. But this was the middle of the night, and its darker walks and arbors were used for other purposes also known to nature.

He strode purposefully with one hand clenched into a fist, the other on his rapier hilt, vowing silently to find Felice wherever she was. And if he had to fight Buck for her and break the king's no-dueling law, he'd do that, too. Better the Tower for killing a duke than any further disgrace to his ancient name or to his manhood. He refused to include a thrust to his heart, or the memory of skin like silk, or the rhythmic rising of her bosom as she talked, so that he could not attend her words. He clenched his fist so tight that pain stopped him and he stood very still.

He wanted her again as a man wants a woman for the first time.

Strollers passed him by. He was unaware of their questioning stares, while he struggled against a truth he despised. He was falling in love with his wife again, or with this changed creature that was Felice. The scent of her, where he had held her close in the dance, was on him and might never leave him. He groaned and hoped no one heard.

Hand in hand, Meriel and Nell raced down one of the dark paths, their long court gowns draped over their other arms, past some fully occupied arbors until they found an empty one. Meriel collapsed onto the bench, and Nell, laughing, sat down beside her.

"They will spend half the night looking for us," Nell whispered, a chuckle in her voice. "That should cool their cods!"

Meriel leaned back. She was exhausted, not so much from the long day of walking, scheming, dancing, and the long bouncing ride through Hyde Park, but an exhaustion of pretense. It was so much more difficult to be someone she wasn't, all the day and night long, than she had ever imagined, especially with Lord Giles. She ached as his name swept through her, but her corset would not allow her to breathe in and out too deeply.

Nell leaned back, as well, thrusting her legs in front of her, though she was so petite they swung clear of the ground. "Something has changed you, my lady Felice."

Meriel was immediately on her guard. "How changed?"

"That is what I am trying to discover. You joined me in freeing the whore though you pretended it as part of the jape. I knew it and I think Buck knew it, as well. He will not like it that you—"

"Are changed, as you say. Hey, well, then he will have to live with his dislike!" She knew this last was what Felice would say, but it was also pure Meriel, and comforting. She wondered if she could trust Nell with the truth, then she wondered if the king had already confided the secret and Nell played her own game. 'Od's life! Spying was like a Tudor maze, and she was trapped in the middle without an idea how to reach open ground.

Meriel's wondering was soon over.

"His Majesty asked me to pass this message to you during the dancing, but I had no opportunity."

"Yes, Nell," Meriel said, one of her questions answered.

"You are to go to Chiffinch this night without fail, as it is time for you to act. . . . Something about word finally come down from the north. I know not what the message means, and I don't want to know. If I am asked, I can deny all knowledge, though I am an excellent liar, learning that part early in the alleys off Drury Lane."

"My thanks, Nell. I didn't know—"

"If I had the king's confidence? He knows I would never betray him. And he tells no more than needs be."

"Then I must get away from this place as soon as I know where our lords are, so that I can go in the opposite direction," Meriel answered. "They are both so taken with their idea of cuckholding Lord Giles under his very nose that they would never give me leave."

"Aye," Nell said, "Rochester will make a poem about tonight and hang it on your door. Tomorrow all will know. He says he is bent on outrunning impotence, yet I think, in some strange way, he seeks it."

"It makes him cruel."

"Aye, he may seek that, too, and I don't doubt he knows it."

Meriel and Nell waited some minutes before they heard their names being called, as Buckingham and Rochester searched the gardens for them. Then they heard cursing and heavy boots racing down the gravel path, coming closer.

Meriel opened her mouth to bid Nell a good night before slipping away.

From behind, a hard hand clamped across her lips before she could speak. An arm surrounded her upper body in a crushing hold. Terrified, she began to claw at the hand on her mouth.

Giles bent to her ear and said, "Quiet, Felice. This is the end of your career as chief court whore. My pardon, Nell, but we must take our leave."

"I see that, my lord, although I challenge your lady's position, when all know that I am chief whore at Whitehall."

"Madame, I would give you the better title of friend, if you delay your companions."

"Gladly, sir. They deserve a trick and will have it. Two drunken lords will not exceed my gifts as an actress."

Meriel had ceased struggling once she heard Giles's voice. If he would only allow her to speak, she would tell him that she must return to the palace, though she couldn't tell him why. Yet would she say how relieved she was to see him and be saved from Buck's tongue. And probably the rest of him.

She felt no softening in Giles. He thought her a lying, cheating wife, and she could not blame him. With his strong arms tight about her, she could summon no strength to fight him. Nor will.

He didn't remove his hand but lifted her bodily and, carrying her under one arm like a sack of oats to a barn, walked swiftly toward the rear of the Spring Gardens, scarcely keeping his anger under control.

Straining to catch her breath, but having it bumped out of her at every step, Meriel said, "Gi-iles . . . put . . . me . . . do-wn. I am no lamb, sir, to be truss-ed and tied—"

Giles didn't flinch, keeping his ears closed to her pleas.

He couldn't trust her, not for one moment, though his hands burned where they touched her.

"Sir, what do you with that lady?"

Giles glared at the gentleman who stood in his path and questioned him. "I take my wife away from this place, sir. She has not my permission to be here."

The man bowed and stepped aside. "My pardon, sir. A husband may do as it pleases him."

"Did you hear that, Felice?" Giles questioned, his voice harsh again as they neared the exit. "Prepare to hear that daily until you give me what you owe me."

Chapter Ten

Catch as Ketch Can

Giles carried her from Spring Gardens through the rear gate to a small grove of elm saplings, where he put her none too gently on her feet. "You will remain silent, or you will force me to silence you."

Dizzied from being carried near upside down so unceremoniously, Meriel spoke in a thin voice: "I could scarce talk if allowed." She felt the distinct need to point that out to him.

She had no doubt that Giles would use almost any means to silence her. His rank and manhood demanded he master her. The wonder was that he had not already done mayhem upon Felice for her debauchery. That he hadn't was all the more to his credit. He deserved the best a woman could give, which made her own deception of him a great wrong. "What will you do with me?" Her voice trembled.

His hand hovered before her mouth, then dropped to his side, and he set his face away from hers. "You need not be frightened, if you do not call out to your fellow pranksters."

"As you well know, they are part of the king's merry gang. They are not *my* pranksters."

His lips twisted with bitter sarcasm, his famed wit entirely missing. "Have I here a victim of a vile kidnapping?" But he turned his face away from her to save his determination from the innocence she managed to so artfully display on that beautiful face and in those tender, trembling lips.

Meriel did not try to answer him or quiet his anger. She could not tell him that calling to those raucous lords was the last thing she would do even if Nell were not leading them away at this moment. She could not tell Lord Giles anything at all. 'Od's grace! Though she never gave in to self-pity, at that moment she felt sorely tempted.

Because she could not look on his hero's profile without feeling great confusion (she refused to call it lust), she was the first to see the lanterns of a small ship moving toward the shore. She recognized it for the kind of shallow draft coastal ketch she'd seen many times come up the Stour River to the markets at Canterbury.

"Ah, they received my message and here she is," Giles said, great relief in his voice. "Bid London farewell, Felice. You're going home."

Meriel almost repeated his last word, but swallowed it as she always did, so that it lay as a familiar lump against her heart. The word obviously held a deep meaning for Giles, as it did for her, though she had never had a home beyond a straw pallet in the work house or a maid's rope bed in an attic. Yet had she lived all her life within the hearing of that word, and cherished it all the more because she longed to know its truest meaning.

The Thames was now at flood, fog rolling in and tide ebbing. The ketch came in close enough for a gangway to reach the water steps. Giles handed off Meriel to a sailor . . . with a determined shove . . . and jumped aboard himself, helping to pull in the gangway. "Take Lady Felice to my cabin below," he ordered, "and bar the door."

"Aye, my lord," the man said, touching two fingers to his forehead in salute.

"Giles, I must return to Whitehall, for . . . clothing . . . and, er, my maid Agnes." He turned his face from her, but not before she caught his look of utter scorn.

"If I promise to tell you the truth," she said, desperately searching her mind for some truth that she could tell, "could I plead my case?"

"There is no truth in you."

She couldn't argue that.

The sailor knuckled his forehead, amused at the goings-on of his betters. "This way, yer ladyship, and be watchful on the low overhead."

Meriel glanced back to see Giles already in command. He stood on the rail, holding to the standing rigging of the mainsail, leaning far out to guide the helmsman tacking lee-ward. The wind had picked up and the ketch caught the current. Giles dipped his knees, riding his ship like a great racehorse. For an instant she felt resentful, because love and joy were writ across his face and she had not put them there.

Meriel scrambled down the wide ladder and stepped across the high threshold into Giles's small cabin, the door closing behind her. She heard a bar fall into place. Quickly crossing the small lantern-lit cabin to the stern windows, she saw that the ketch had now come about and they were head-ing down the Thames toward the English Channel.

She mounted the bench seat to push against the middle stern window and it opened, allowing the smell of the river carrying away all London's waste to assail her. She had ever been too tender in her nose. Still, she would wait until they came to the river's turning near to Whitehall Palace, then she would hold her nose and jump. Since Chiffinch had sent a message by Nell that the Dutch fleet was moving south and he was ready to act, she would be expected. There would be ciphers to prepare and instructions to memorize. . . . One all important: How was she to get to the enemy fleet?

And what would Chiffinch do if she did not return tonight? He would never dare harm Giles. Or would he? Thanks be, she could swim. Like all the orphans at the work-house, she had escaped to the Stour River for swimming on hot summer evenings.

Minutes later, Meriel unlaced her gown and let it drop on the cabin deck, happily followed by her corset. She kneaded her stomach, erasing the welts left by staves, and smiling at the thought of arriving at Whitehall wet through her cling-ing scarlet silk petticoat, she thrust a leg through the stern window. She'd think later of what lie to tell about her attire. Now she must away, and quickly. Then she saw the dinghy bobbing below in the dark waters.

The sailor who'd brought her to the cabin grinned up at her, mostly toothless, but still able to spew a warning. "I would not do it, my lady. 'Tis colder than a whore's cunny, the river is, and my lord has promised me a guinea if I catch ye. I be swimming ter hell for a guinea."

"I'll give you *two* guineas to row me ashore."

"Ye must think me daft, my lady. As well ye know, all us Barnes's been Harringdon men fer all time. Lord Giles be sendin' a midwife for me woman when her belly was big and her all bleeding and screaming. He be the kindest, bravest lord in all England, and begging your ladyship's par-don, pull yer pretty leg back in afore I whack it with me oar."

In no doubt as to his sincerity, Meriel obeyed rather too hastily, falling backward into the cabin, sprawling on the deck, her shift over her head, her drawer ties ripped asunder.

It took her a moment to catch her breath, and then she began to giggle, a giggle that turned into a full laugh. It was so ridiculous to be kidnapped and lying near naked on a boat making way past the Tower for the second time in a fort-night. There was naught else to do but laugh. *Hey, well, nothing I try seems to be working. At least my humor still does.*

Directly above, Giles leaned against the richly carved taffrail and heard all. He was not surprised that Felice had tried to escape. He'd expected it. What surprised him was the helpless laughter that followed. It was the kind of infect-ing glee that made others laugh though they knew not the jest. He found himself smiling before he could stop it, though he tried to close his ears. He could not allow his heart to rule his head, a head that knew all Felice's former tricks and now this new pretense at change. He moved quickly amidships to better stifle the sound of her, resting his fore-head hard against the mainmast as they made passage be-tween the pillars, the mainmast just clearing Tower Bridge, toward the open sea.

Nell raced up the king's private stairs as the sun rose, and burst into his closet to find him, always an early riser, exam-ining one of his many pendulum clocks with Chiffinch. Breathless, she collapsed into a chair. Only two people in England—the king's spymaster and chief procurer, William Chiffinch, and the king's younger brother, James, Duke of York—had the right to enter Charles II's closet without in-vitation. And not even these high persons were allowed to sit if the king stood.

The young actress fanned herself with a rather bedrag-gled feather fan, one feather floating away, where it was im-mediately pounced on by the king's spaniels.

At once, the king came to Nell. "Are you not well, Nellie?" He looked over her small body, obviously not displeased and seeing far more than infirmity.

Chiffinch approached, cautious as always. "Madame Gwyn," he said, bowing.

"I have news for Your Majesty and for you, Spymaster. Lady Felice, your new agent against the Hollanders, has been abducted and spirited away by her amorous husband, I know not where." She repeated the adventures of the night, omitting the highway robbery.

Chiffinch struggled to keep his face respectful. "Your Majesty, I had not realized that Madame Gwyn had your confidence in secret matters of state."

But the king heard no censure because he expected none. Indeed, the king almost smiled. "My lord Giles is a more jealous husband than we thought. If we know our man, he has taken her to Norfolk." The king clapped his hands. "What a story we will tell when we may!"

Chiffinch was not amused. "Sir, I beg your most humble pardon, but this is a story we may never—"

"Yes, yes," the king admitted, hearing the censure this time.

"Your Majesty," intoned Chiffinch, "this is a most grievous turn. I have urgent dispatches for that lady to cipher, and instructions we intercepted from the Dutch for a rendezvous, and now that we have taken up the last of their agents, there is no way to delay them other than our Felice."

The king nodded. "Yes, yes," he said again, now obviously impatient with instruction. "We see the problem clearly, but we have full confidence that you will discover that particular lady, no doubt at her husband's estate, and settle the matter to our benefit. You may go to your duties, William."

The king now looked upon Nell with more than interest. "My dear, it is against protocol to sit in our presence."

Nell's small pouting mouth spread with a smile, since she was quite recovered. "But, great sir, is it against protocol to lie down in your presence?" She stretched her slender body, a goodly amount of pretty leg showing.

The king's eyes half closed, and he held out his hand to her.

Chiffinch hastily bowed and left by the rear stairs, closing the door rather sharply so that he could be heard departing.

By that afternoon, he had questioned Nell, gaining the full tale, which she exchanged for knowing that Meriel was a false Lady Felice, though Nell had half guessed something of the like. "Have I a rival for the Theater Royal?" she asked, laughing.

"I must swear you to secrecy," Chiffinch responded severely, having no humor.

Nell was sworn to secrecy, which she exchanged for Chiffinch's silence about the Hyde Park adventure.

While decrying to the silent walls of his office that he had ever begun this scheme, Chiffinch had also determined on a course to follow without allowing more gossiping courtiers knowledge of the plot. The king could not resist pillow talk, which meant that a dozen ladies might know before long, and every day brought the Dutch fleet closer. Their last communication with their Hollander spies in London had convinced him that they planned an attack on the capital. And soon! The English fleet was anchored in the Medway, and must be prepared to sail, lest they become a sitting target. But where and with what monies and crews? Best if his counterfeit Felice could warn them off, since she had not succeeded in ferreting out Dutch spies in the court.

It was the last gamble he could take, and if he won the wager there was surely a knighthood in it . . . mayhap a peerage.

Chiffinch sent for Dr. Wyndham, who was attending Admiral Cheatham's lady. It was an hour by his clock before the doctor was announced.

"You are ailing, sir?" the little doctor said, his peruke askew from his hurry, opening a tapestry bag of pills, powders, elixirs, leeches and all such nostrums.

"Nay, Doctor. I have need of your other services."

Dr. Wyndham sniffed. "I have no other service than to physic, sir."

"You serve as royal physician at the king's pleasure, and therefore, at mine. I have need of your knowledge of a certain lady."

"I carry no tales of my patients, sir." Wyndham stood very tall, though still quite short, and Chiffinch saw the man had dignity, which was to say, self-regard. A bad thing in the spy trade, when spymasters must rule men by money or fear. Chiffinch clamped his teeth. He'd get rid of such unwanted dignity. Wyndham turned for the door. Quickly stepping behind the little doctor, Chiffinch pulled his coat over his head and kicked his arse.

Stumbling against the wall, the doctor whirled upon the spymaster. "Sir, I call you out. I am a graduate of the Universities of Padua, Bologna and—"

"You will be a graduate of the Tower lion pens if you do not shut your gob," Chiffinch said in a low, menacing voice that had chilled many a man of higher station. "You twice gave physic to our counterfeit Lady Felice and thus are part of our secret plans against the Dutch, whether or not you wish it." He let his words have their effect. "I speak for His Majesty in this matter."

"Lady Felice," Wyndham said, straightening a peruke that was hanging off one ear. "Yes, I would help that lady in any way a true gentleman could. You have sorely used her beauty, sir, and will reap God's—"

Chiffinch put up a warning hand, wearying of teaching such a numbskull proper respect. It might take more time than he could spare. He gathered documents together from his writing table, wrapped two bundles in silk and then oiled vellum and attached two red wax seals. "You are to take these to Harringdon Hall in Norfolk at once. The smaller is for the earl, explaining that His Majesty has sent you, his personal physician, to tend his wife's health. . . . Her injured ankle and burn, if you will. That will ensure you are not denied. The other packet is to be delivered into Lady Felice's hands by her maid, without the knowledge of her husband. On your life, sir, promise to accomplish this."

Wyndham remained full angered. "I am no member of your secret service, Master Chiffinch. How do I accomplish such a feat?"

"That is for you to determine. Surely a graduate of universities beyond number will be clever enough . . ."

Dr. Wyndham listened no further, but interrupted bluntly, "What mode of transport?"

"A carriage and four will be waiting below the king's outer stairs within the hour. Lady Felice's maid, Agnes, accompanies you as my accomplished agent. You will be under her orders."

Wyndham braced himself for another assault, but raised his chin and spoke boldly. "I leave not before two hours' time, sir. My wife, Kate, is with child again and I must take my leave of her and provide for her belly sickness, which comes every morn like the sun."

He asked for no leave, waited for no assent, but left the office immediately, slamming the door with great vigor.

Chiffinch poked at his sea coal fire before removing his cock from his breeches and pissing in the flames. He chuckled softly. The little man had courage and might yet be a good choice for a doctor. He could use some physic himself. Of late, he'd had a hurtful swelling in a big toe that he did not like. And the king swore an oath by the doctor's salve, which added vigor to the male part that would not always obey a spymaster's desire.

Meriel awoke on the cushioned bench under the stern window, rocked by the ship's motion, her hand brushing spray falling against her cheek through the open window. For a moment or two, she rubbed her eyes, not remembering where she was, until full memory rushed in on her. She swung her legs to the floor, half expecting Giles to be waiting there intent on . . . *Hey, well, he is no eunuch.*

But the room was empty, except for bread, ale and beef laid upon the small table. Had Giles placed all there, and looked down on her sleeping? Had he touched her, made her breasts swell, her stomach ache? Was her dream real?

Hungrily, she tore at a piece of bread with her teeth, gulping ale from the green glass bottle. Pale light from the stern windows lit the cabin, the lantern candle having long guttered out. Her gown and corset lay in a tangled heap on the floor where she had dropped them. She turned back to the windows and saw nothing but water and fog not yet burned away by the feeble morning sun.

Looking below, she could see plainly the dinghy was gone. At least Giles did not think her mad enough to swim the English Channel.

There was a high-backed chair at the table, a chest and

piles of rope to complete the sparse furnishings. A small, cloudy mirror was nailed to the wall. She could imagine him before it, tying his hair behind his head like a sailor.

Chewing her bread and beef, she rummaged inside the chest, removing canvas breeches and a rough linen shirt, rather too open at the throat. She tied the breeches on with a short length of rope, rolled up the legs and stepped into her satin slippers, smiling to herself. After having four maids to attend her, she could still dress herself. If she ever became Meriel St. Thomas again, she would not have forgotten such necessary skills.

The mirror showed her to some disadvantage, the pearl coronet tangled tightly in her hair. She removed it along with some long strands of black hair still attached, placed it carefully on the table and began to beat upon the door. When pounding brought no response, she began to yell and hector the guard outside until Giles opened the door.

Although she had wanted him to come to the cabin, now that he was before her, she bit her lip like a shy maid. The light, reflected through the window from the sea, danced across his face, playing along his proud jawline and nose. His shirt was open to a place where a trail of dark hair began to make its way down to . . . She had to hold fast to a sharp intake of breath else she'd give her feelings away, though she would hardly know how to describe them.

"Felice, you are free to come up on deck," he said, observing with some astonishment her new clothing.

Meriel knuckled her head like a common seaman, as the best way to hide her unease. "Aye, Captain, my lord earl, and if, as I warrant, you have a yardarm ready for my hanging, or a plank ready for my walking, I'll gladly oblige."

Giles bowed to hide his grin. "I have no such plans for you." He had not expected this Felice: playing the part of charming hoyden, her face bright, her dark hair a curling confusion, her color high, prettier than he had ever seen it. If she had any thought as to how ravishing she was all unkempt, a rope accenting her slender waist and even more her full bosom, which he could clearly observe, her mouth all yielding, she would appear this way always. His nails bit into his palms and he turned abruptly and climbed to the deck, leaving her to make her own way before he was undone and behaved foolishly once again.

Sorry for my attire, your worship, Meriel mouthed at his . . . well, at his arse, since it was practically in her face all the way up the ladder, and in her memory for quite a time after. Though he had abandoned his coat and medals, he was still wearing his tight breeches for dancing. They exposed every line of muscle and tendon as he brought his weight to bear upon first one leg, then the other, then . . .

Once on the small deck, she saw the sky was changing to gray to match her mood. Clinging to the rail in the choppy seas, she went hand over hand toward the short bowsprit with its jib full.

It was a stubby little ship, but a sweet body as Admiral Cheatham had said as they pored over the ship's plans together.

She stood in the stern, breathed in the sharp odor of the sea, lifting her eyes to watch the crying seagulls circling overhead. She felt the ketch meet the waves under her feet, spread her legs to keep her balance and turned her face to the blowing spray. She felt cleaner at that moment than she had since becoming Lady Felice, and somehow safer. . . . Then thought herself mad. Safer with this man who hated her as Felice and would loathe her as a commoner pretending to be his wife?

Still, he could not control the regard in his eyes or mask

his kindness. Nor could she ignore the good man beneath the hard, protective shell. She did not want to know that. It made it so much harder for her to use him, though she had no choice.

She felt the warmth of his presence close behind her. *Hey, well, more than warmth, since his body is pressed hard against mine, assuring me that this lord is blessed with as much manliness as any man could expect. . . . Or woman desire.*

She tried to move farther into the stern, but his body followed hers with increased pressure, his arms going around her, his hands resting on the railing. She was trapped in a warm, fleshly prison cell, and any wish to escape fled immediately.

"If you crush my breath, Giles, there will be little left of me. . . . Whatever your plans for tonight."

He moved back, but just enough to allow her to inhale, which she did, fairly swallowing the salty sea air. Needing more, she raised her face and breathed deeply, realizing too late that her head now rested on his shoulder. She did not move away.

"You know well what my plans are."

Meriel had never been the coquette, though she felt herself about to become one. "I've heard what pirates do to captured women."

Her head resting against him softened the answer he might have given. "Perhaps my plans are sweeter, though nonetheless inescapable."

"But, sir, I can't believe a peer of England, especially one with such a worthy little ship . . ."

Though he could not see her face, Giles felt her joy in his ketch as a kind of shiver. "I thought you hated my ship, Felice." There was even more puzzlement in his voice than when he'd released her from the cabin below. "You always refused to sail with me, preferring the wilder shores of Whitehall Palace."

"Giles," she said in Felice's voice, "you seem unable to allow me any change at all, but would keep me forever a nineteen-year-old bride."

"Untrue. Indeed, I demand change in you." He felt her body stiffen against him.

Then she spoke in Meriel's humor: "Do you give no quarter, then, upon your pirate ship?"

"Nay, I will give you none, wife. What I will give you is a son and heir to my title. You'll walk that plank tonight."

Chapter Eleven

~

Home to Harringdon Hall

Meriel gripped the bow rail long after the warmth of Giles's body left her. And without a *by your leave,* too! She waited, hoping he'd return. He did not. And she scarce suppressed a desire to blame him aloud for the chill she now felt through her sailor's canvas breeches.

Instead she began to pace the deck, head high, gaining two good sea legs, while trying not to show more suspicious delight at the sea and the wonderful little ship. She knew that Felice must have exhibited loathing for both. It would not have been in her character to enjoy what was windy and wet.

As a girl, Meriel had been out on the Stour River with Sir Edward in single-masted fishing shallops, but this ketch was a good forty feet in length with a topsail mainmast and a short mizzen, lateen rigged. Still, for all the sea knowledge gained from her master and his library, she had never felt deepwater swells lifting the deck beneath her feet, driving the ship forward like a live thing. Meriel's body tingled with fresh life, finding her balance as if born to it.

Through narrowed eyes, she watched Giles while pretending to be bored. He was more relaxed that she had yet seen him, more as she had imagined from his noble statue that he might look on a ship deck. And she saw his full smile for the first time, blazing against his dark face, as he gazed up through the halyards at the sails, snapping and billowing in a gusting language he obviously heard and understood. At that moment, the wind changed direction and the square-rigged mainsail emptied. Giles climbed hand over hand up the shrouds to the mainsail, balancing along the yard on the footropes. He grasped the sheet rope to adjust the sail, so that it would catch the next change of wind. His muscles tensed and he finished just in time for the sail to fill.

Meriel saw Giles look down to where she stood near the pin rail. She gave a sailor's two-fingered salute. He answered, raising an arm in triumph, holding on with one hand, laughing aloud, master of wind and water. And master of her heart, if she could allow him to know it.

Minutes later, they sailed through a gray fog bank, through the swells around a sandy headland and into the sun, which lit the ship and all in it. Or was it Giles's smile as he climbed down to the deck, his joy obvious at being in this time and place, a joy that she had never once glimpsed at Whitehall?

Lord Giles immediately went forward and climbed out on the short bowsprit, his long legs wrapped around the spar, making love to the ketch and hauling on the headsail like any shilling-a-week seaman. He lost his hold, slipped and swung under the spar. His name caught in her terror-tightened throat.

Giles righted himself, grinning broadly. Relieved, she saw that this lord could acknowledge his own mistakes. She liked that in anyone, but more so in a man because so many men thought they were served only by blame. Yet Giles had no such need. Meriel was more convinced than ever that

Felice was the greatest fool in the realm for turning away from such a lord, whose real charms would long outlast Buckingham's or Rochester's foolish ones.

Meriel sat on a coil of rope, languidly leaning against the mainmast, and tried to keep her eyes from him, maintaining a frown on her face. *Hey, well, I am supposed to be abducted against my will, aren't I?* Perhaps she should worry about her mission to the Hollander's fleet, and she would worry soon. But not yet. Her gaze on this man wouldn't allow it.

Giles's black hair damp and curling with spray, his shirt clinging to his wide shoulders and well-muscled arms were in sharp outline against the blue water. She swallowed hard because she could scarce believe what she saw, though she doubted she would ever forget. Giles was a picture painted on her mind for all time. Whatever happened, she would be able to conjure the colors of sea and sky, the sound of waves and wind and the picture of a happy man, legs spread wide, riding the swells like he meant to tame them. Indeed, she would not be able to erase this picture no matter if she tried.

And why should she? Tonight he had sworn to bed her. And although it had sounded a threat because he thought her an unloving, wicked wife, the words had not frightened her.

Being bedded by a Garter knight, who looked to be her Adonis come to life, hardly compared to what she'd already experienced. And it wasn't as if she were totally unaware of what happened when a man mounted a woman. Men were men. They did what they did for their own satisfaction. Yet she could not help but think that the Earl of Warborough might be very much better at it than most. Suppressed laughter settled in her belly. She was being wishful, when she never had been afore.

Giles called for sail to be shortened, and as the wind fell away on a larboard tack, they steered the ketch into Great

Yarmouth harbor to a dockyard just past the mouth of the North River. He went over the side into the longboat that towed the ketch into its berth, pulling an oar and singing loudly with the men. Leaping to the dock, he called for a hawser to tie up to the ring bolts, and saw Felice overlooking the rail.

"Rig a steady ladder for my lady, Tom."

Tom pulled his forelock. "My lord, it 'pears yer lady be not needing one."

Giles managed to hide his astonishment, but only just. Felice was scrambling hand over hand down the rope ladder in her seaman's breeches as if born to it. What was this? He refused to believe his eyes. Felice was not above such a trick to put him in ease of mind so as to work some secret will on him. He was no eager bridegroom to be duped by a beautiful face and curving form, not to mention very pretty legs. He had himself well in hand, though he was feeling heated. He'd not deny that he wanted this wife, but only to get an heir. No more.

Giles looked quickly away from Felice's ripe body as she clambered into the boat. When his eyes returned much against his will, she was pulling the end of an oar with Tom Barnes, singing with the men. What was Felice's game, with this constant effort to amaze him? She had always been far too indolent to work so hard for his approval. Why now? He must watch her closely. And take hard hold of his thoughts, remembering that he had but one use for the woman. She must deliver an heir to him. That was her only function. Then she could descend to the hottest level of Hades. His heart would not be involved, as hers would not.

Having been sent for as the ketch rounded the sand spit into the harbor, a small coach-and-two with a coat of arms painted in gilt on its door soon arrived on the dock from

Harringdon Hall. The arms were quartered with a lion ram-
pant. Meriel knew little of heraldry, but everyone knew the
lion quartering was a sign of royal ancestry. 'Od's grace!
She didn't want two kings in her tragic life.

Giles handed Meriel inside the carriage, but not before
she saw the name on the bow of the ketch. Or rather *No
Name,* for that was writ there plain. It was lettered over another name, still faint in outline: *Felice.* Meriel's belly tightened. Giles detested his wife so much that he had scraped
her name from his beloved ship. She no longer felt at all sure
that she could survive the plank Giles prepared for her this
night.

But she scarce had time to worry or to watch the lovely
Norfolk countryside unfold outside the carriage window.
Giles was ignoring her as best he could with his knees near
touching hers, once meeting sharply over a rut in the road.

"Pardon, my lady."

"None needed, your lordship."

Good manners briefly observed, they traveled on. Meriel
was occupied with a worry about how she would be greeted
by Harringdon Hall servants. Even Chiffinch couldn't force
a hundred servants to agree their lady had recently spent a
week there. Although magic was akin to witchery, she kept
her fingers crossed to hex a forward maid or manservant
from speaking of her long absence in front of Giles. Her
only excuse for lying to him was to admit another lover's
assignation. And she was loath to hurt him anew.

"You will want to change your clothes after astounding
the porter and housekeeper," Giles said, noting her sailor's
garb.

Meriel answered as Felice. "I am not overconcerned with
the thoughts of servants."

"They are part of our family, and their fathers before. You will have a care for their good opinion."

"As you command, husband."

"Yes, as I command. Do not mistake me for one of your court fools, Felice. You have not earned my trust by this docile turn. I'll post guards everywhere."

She nodded, lifting one shoulder to show her uncaring. Yet she was rapidly losing her taste for pretending to be a woman the equal of the Borgias or the Medicis, if not all of Louis the French king's scheming courtesans combined.

They said nothing further to each other as the carriage turned through a gate and into a wide road, several furlongs in length, that led to Harringdon Hall, its towers barely visible through a forest of ancient oaks, light slanting through mossy branches, a few lone seagulls swooping inland across the barely undulating landscape. The coach came around the trees and out into a long green deer park with sheep-cropped meadows, still sporting uneaten white daisies and yellow chamomile.

Though her heart swelled at the beauty of the place, Meriel kept her mouth firmly under lock. She had studied an ink drawing and memorized a plan of rooms, yet she had been unprepared for the stone majesty of the old house.

Like Giles himself, it was tall, strongly built and handsome in the extreme. Many gabled buildings, old and new, with mullioned windows from the old queen's time and of later Palladian design, gray slate roofs, tall chimneys, a church spire, all connected as if planned from the ancient beginning of the three-story central hall. It was a rare thing when adding to perfection did not undo original beauty.

The majordomo stood waiting in the wide carriage turn-around near the front entrance. Meriel took a deep breath as he opened the door and lowered the step, bowing as Giles leapt to the ground.

"Welcome home, Lord Giles, Lady Felice."

Meriel relaxed. She had hoped, indeed expected, that it wasn't a servant's province to comment upon his mistress's comings and goings. Still, she was relieved. For the moment.

Giles held out a hand, remembering that his household was watching. "My lady, welcome to our home," he said.

Meriel clasped the strong hand and stepped down upon the earth. Here she would be mistress until she was discovered or escaped to her spy's duty. Meriel instantly loved the old estate as if she had known it always as a yearning in her heart.

Though she had felt guilt early and often for the cruel deception of an honorable man, all the intrigue was almost worth the price she'd paid for the first moment she stepped into the Earl of Warborough's vast central hall, its brightly lit sconces flaring into the far corners. No drawing or plan had done it justice. She was unaware that she had stopped in the center of the soaring hall and turned around to take in all the rich carvings, crisscrossing rafters, wide-planked floors and paneled walls.

Giles was puzzled, stopping very suddenly close behind her. "Nothing is changed, Felice. You look as if you have forgotten Harringdon Hall."

Meriel stiffened. Was he suspicious? Had she given herself away in some word or act? Or was he merely trying to elicit some delight from a jaded wife, who had starved him for companionship? Not for the first time, she almost wished herself back in the orphanage where all had been simple: steal enough food to stay alive and not be caught at it. She pressed a palm against her forehead.

"Does your head ache?" Giles asked, showing a husbandly concern. "I will have the cook send up a decoction of feverfew, or would you prefer it be chamomile?"

"I would prefer it be a hot bath, since I have been pummeled on land and at sea now these many hours." She walked away lest she respond to his kindness in a way that would compromise all. She knew her rooms were at the head of the gallery stairs.

"You shall have both," Giles said, mastering his anger at her rebuff. "Then we will sup together this evening as is expected of the Earl of Warborough and his lady. You will do as I command, Felice."

Meriel climbed the elaborately carved stairs to her rooms, without turning back to Giles to say . . . what?

In her room, she found two maids removing gowns from a chest full of lavender in silk sachets. She enveloped herself in Lady Felice's manner. "Take those gowns and air them," she commanded, huffing about the room. "I no longer use lavender. And bring my bath. Stoke the fire before I take a chill. Mind you, hot water in plenty. With no dried rose petals for scent, or you'll feel my wrath."

Meriel laughed aloud at herself as the maids fled in two directions to do her bidding. Being a demanding mistress was not a matter of birth after all. It was a matter of opportunity.

Yet she urgently needed to be alone, to avoid pretense for a quiet minute, not to be Felice, not to be Meriel. To be nothing.

Exhausted, she threw herself upon the huge bed, her eyes heavy with—oh, she didn't know what—perhaps preparing for her husband's promised bedding. Yes, indeed, unable to think of any other thing. "Am I truly undone?" she whispered into the coverlet, letting her yearning woman's body speak through the whisper that escaped and lived on unanswered in the room all during the long, steaming bath.

They supped in the intimate library, hung with tapestries, off the great hall. Giles had chosen this room and dismissed the servants after the food was laid out so that Felice would sit closer to him than at the great table. He wanted to observe her, to satisfy himself that what was different was superficial, indeed artificial.

Perhaps some new and redder cochineal to make her lips fuller and more sensuous. A softer powder, perhaps of finely ground pearls, to add a luminous quality to her skin. A henna dye that inserted lights in her dark and tumbling curls. Some trickery of art learned from her theater friends that caused golden flecks in those enormous dark-lashed gray eyes, which were surely larger than ever.

While busying himself with poker and fire, adjusting his chair and everything he could think of, he managed to observe her, and although he could not choose one thing over many changes, he could see that there was no artifice to his wife's enhanced beauty. There was nothing to conclude but that his own eyes deceived or he had simply forgotten how beautiful she was.

As was fitting and custom for a wife of any station, Felice took the most tender slices of meats and placed them on Giles's plate with several seeded knot biscuits from a mounded basket.

Nodding his thanks, he heated a rich mutton broth in the fireplace for her. It had arrived too cool from the kitchens, but he was loath to recall the servers, since he had dismissed them for the night. He wanted no interruptions to his desire, no matter when it arose.

He leaned against the high leather back of his chair and,

though pretending to drink his broth, he observed her every move. He had never known Felice to have such appetite. Although he could tell that she was trying very hard to observe courtly etiquette, she was obviously ravenous. He poured a sack posset into her bowl, which she downed immediately.

Meriel saw Giles smiling and realized she was not nibbling daintily as Felice would have done, nor in any semblance of her lessons at the Tower. "The sea air," she explained, knowing that she had eaten like an orphan afraid of losing her portion to a stronger child, and feeling the rich warmth of the posset's eggs, wine and sweetened cream slowly seeping into her limbs, already too much weakened from the bath.

Giles laughed and his good humor reached into his dark eyes. "Would you like a pear tart? Or two?"

Meriel would have liked nothing more, although she knew she must observe her easily abandoned court manners. She sighed and declined the sweet with a wave of her hand. "I must watch my flesh."

"I see nothing wrong with it," Giles said, trying not to grin anew. "Neither too much, nor not enough . . . except—" He was staring at her breasts.

"Although what? I'm not wearing a corset, thus—"

"Don't twist my meaning. I merely noticed that your bosom is greater than I—"

Meriel knew that this was one feature in which she differed significantly from Felice. She thought fast. "I've been taking the Turkish sweats." Since he seemed unbelieving, she added, "And Wyndham's Infallible Miracle Salve, which the good doctor does claim to add flesh where it is lacking—"

Giles laughed aloud. "And take away where overmuch. Felice, you were ever ready for magic and quackery."

She managed to look uncaring at his raillery. She was

sated and sleepy, drugged with food and wine posset and the warmth of the crackling oak fire. And the man before her, his fine, long, tightly hosed legs stretched to the fire, a help to her imagination, though it needed little help with such manly reality in front of her.

Giles saw her in quite another way than he had seen his wife of late. Her rising color told him she was like a woman ready for lovemaking, eager as a bride, virginal as the tender young girl he thought he'd married. And lost. Maybe that was the difference. Felice's face and body had hardened to his eyes, losing all soft curves of emerging womanhood. Now they were back. Everywhere! Could she have come to regret her actions in denying him a son? Could he forgive her numerous betrayals? He doubted he ever could, but he would know after tonight.

Giles felt his reckless cod ripen. Damn! And damn again! Too soon. He stood quickly to walk it out, circling the library, taking a book from the shelf and returning it unopened. Then another, which he did open. "Ah, my favorite," he said. "Remember, Felice?"

Meriel bit her tongue, not wanting to hurt him, but having to in Felice's brittle, yet languid tone. "My memory is so poor for books, Giles. Surely, you know that."

"Cervantes," Giles said, not allowing disappointment to show. "Miguel de Cervantes."

He began to walk about the room, reading aloud to her as he once had on their wedding night: "*'Tis said of love that it sometimes goes, sometimes flies, runs with one, walks gravely with another; turns a third into ice and sets a fourth in a flame—*"

Meriel was alert now, turning to watch him as he passed behind her, lest she be taken by surprise and he pounce on her. At last he moved beyond firelight into candlelight.

"—*Love wounds one, another it kills; like lightning it be-gins and ends in the same moment; it makes that fort yield at night which it besieged in the morning; for there is no force able to resist it.*"

As the sound of his voice throbbed through her, tears rose in Meriel's eyes, and for a moment, she thought that if she failed to fool the Dutch, one night with this man would be worth a hanging.

Giles was like one of the Tower lions, pacing softly in his cage, muscles rippling under tawny skin, ready to leap out and devour her if she let down her guard. She stood, un-nerved by his prowling. "My lord, shall we walk about for our stomachs' sake?" Yes, she was delaying the promised bedding. Would she know what he wanted or would he just take it? She prayed for the latter and wondered if the God of blessed name answered such bold prayers from a woman forced to sin, if not against heaven, against this wonderful and worthy man.

Giles lit a lantern, which he held before them. "As you say, let us walk about. The servants will want to greet you."

They strolled through many connected rooms, each one splendid with turkey carpets, polished paneling, and soaring fireplaces a man could stand in upright. Meriel nodded to servants she couldn't call by name. To her relief, the ones who passed merely bowed and moved on with all speed. She doubted that they had much love for Lady Felice. For a mo-ment she allowed herself a dreamy vision: Meriel, mistress of Harringdon Hall, a kind lady beloved by all the servants, who wondered aloud that she was so much changed. She bowed her head, ashamed of her earlier behavior with her maids. She had played her role too well when there was no need, and she would not repeat such a performance.

They entered into a long gallery with a barrel-vaulted

ceiling, hung with many portraits, moonlight wavering upon the tiled floor from a bank of diamond-paned windows. Giles stopped in front of a painting of a very young man, a beardless, boyish version of himself, with a fleet of ships over his shoulder and a spyglass in one hand propped on his knee.

Meriel knew it must be the younger brother Giles had lost in the Battle of the Four Days. "He was so young and so full of promise," she whispered, needing to let him know she understood such loss, but not wishing to disturb what might be a prayer. Her own heart near broke from the pain so obvious on Giles's handsome features.

"Six thousand lost their lives in that battle. It was all bloody confusion."

"Do you blame the king?"

"Blame my anointed sovereign? I would not so break my oath of loyalty." Giles turned away and walked on, holding the lantern before him. He stopped and held it up before the portrait of a woman in the court clothes of Charles I's time. A young girl-child, no more than two, in the same elaborate dress stood beside the woman's knee, holding a bright-plumed bird.

"I had it reframed," Giles said, his voice expecting some response.

"Yes, it's lovely," Meriel acknowledged, her eyes staring at the picture, not daring to say more.

"I know you were very young when your mother killed her— er, died, but I have never understood why you hated her. . . ." He allowed his voice to trail away.

So this was a portrait of Felice's mother. But why did Giles hesitate about her death? Had he almost said she killed herself? Why? What had happened?

Giles raised the lantern so that she could see the portrait better.

Meriel stared into the woman's face, the eyes, a half-parted mouth. The resemblance to what she saw in her own mirror was obvious, or probably what she would see in a few years to come. Was she looking into the face of someone she should have known? Someone of her blood? No, it was all too fantastical. Ladies of position and wealth did not leave their children on cathedral porches. It might happen in a play about a lost princess waiting for her prince to rescue her, but not in life. She shook her head to rid herself of such thoughts, and real tears started, amazing her. She was not prepared for their coming.

Giles saw and his heart was stricken. He had never seen this tenderness in Felice. He wrapped his arms about her, and she was smothered against him. "Felice," he whispered, and sought her lips, tasting the salt of her tears. Her lips trembled against his, and he almost lost himself completely.

Meriel could not stop kissing him, realizing that she had longed for this moment since those first hard, angry kisses at Whitehall. She wanted those lips in warm, urgent flesh as she had first tasted them in hard marble. Her heart pounded faster, forcing heat to rush to her limbs and face from the furnace of her womanhood. Surely, he would feel it and stop. She clung tighter to hold him, to feel his lips taking hers as she had thought they could from her first sight of them, clung tighter to draw him deep into her and cool this demanding flame.

Giles lifted his mouth first, breathed deeply and stepped away abruptly. He rebelled against believing what he saw and more against what he felt. Desire had been a trap for man since Adam. Pulling away, he silently vowed to plant his seed until he got his heir. Then he would let her go. But, he had to admit, he would release her with a great deal more regret than he had ever imagined.

Meriel knew she had done something very wrong. How did Felice kiss him? Perhaps not as insistently, or with such bold demands. She had no idea, and she could not think rationally with her insides a melting torrent of guilt and yearning. She tried a jest to cover her vexation. "'Tis true the church has banned kissing on the Lord's Day?"

Giles nodded, his eyes everywhere but on her face, his voice barely controlled along with his desire to smile at the jibe. "The belief is that kissing leads to other carnal acts."

"I certainly hope so." *Hey, well, that might not be what Lady Felice would say, but it is true, and I need truth.*

Giles laughed aloud, and the sound reverberated down the long picture gallery. He laughed as he had on the ketch, but this time with her, because suddenly Meriel could not stop laughing, too, as if a terrible tension were released.

She walked on before he did, fearing she would say or do the wrong thing, if she had not already done so. She could sense Giles studying her as he would a new book that held a secret, trying to understand what she could not explain.

They came out of the long portrait gallery and stood in front of her apartments.

Meriel halted by her door, scarce breathing, though she could not stop her mouth. "Does the plank end here, my lord?"

Giles rested his hands on her shoulders, his long fingers curling into her back. "I swore I'd never bed you again, Felice."

"Yet here we are." She touched his sleeve. Meriel caught at her breath, excitement racing through her, and out of her mouth came exactly the question she needed to know the answer to. "What changed your mind, Giles?"

"I never changed my mind," he said huskily. "I'm not thinking with my head."

And indeed she noticed by the lantern light on his tight fawn breeches that another part of him was urging him to act, and, she suspected, most uncomfortably, too.

She threw open her bedchamber door.

Chapter Twelve

A Wife in Truth

Giles held his body away from Felice's, watching to see what she would do now that they had entered her bedchamber. For some reason that he did not know, he couldn't fall on her like a ravening beast. Though he knew she would despise him for treating her with tenderness—indeed, he would despise himself—he could not remember her wide smoke-gray eyes and bring himself to ravish her with no regard for her comfort and need. He had never been such a lover and would not be one now.

Moreover, Felice had responded to him in the picture gallery. Like a virgin, full of wonder.

He damned himself for a fool. It must be a clever act for her own purposes. Could the Felice he knew have so changed that she could return love truly, or was she playing some hideous game to amuse herself and her fellow libertines when she returned to court? Why should he believe her now? Why had this new and aching love risen in him from dead fire? He had tried in every way to halt such crazed feelings since she had returned to the palace so changed. He was near consumed by anger at his own stupid impulses. Yet that same mixture of anger and desire drove him on. He must finish this business, get Felice with child and be done with the woman.

Her back to Giles, so he could not read her face, Meriel came to a quick decision. She would not be Felice this night. She had no doubt that Chiffinch would have her followed to remind her of her mission to the Dutch. . . . The man had a single purpose to stop the Hollanders and she was his only means to that end. . . . So this night might be her only chance to lie in Giles's arms. A night to remember for all her life, or at the moment of her death. Whichever came first. And why shouldn't she have it?

She purposely shut out all moral doubts that she was taking what was not hers. And she was not thinking of furthering the king's cause or of England; only of her need to be loved by this man, praying that he would never learn the truth.

Not for her sake. For his.

When he looked upon Felice's dead body, he would believe that she died truly loving him. Meriel convinced herself that he would live out his days the better for that.

Giles moved in closer to her back, touching all of her, fitting his contours against hers, and again she felt the warmth of his body as she had in the bow of the ketch. "Help me from this gown, my lord husband," she said in a small, choked voice she scarcely recognized as her own. They were words she had never uttered before, indeed had no right to say, but they sounded wonderful in her ears.

She felt his hands on her shoulders, his fingers untying her ribbons, his moist, hot lips on the back of her neck where it curved into her shoulder.

"Felice," he whispered, and she felt his breath like summer wind beating against her skin.

She twisted around in his arms to look up into his adored

face. *Meriel! Meriel!* She wanted to scream her name at him. She wanted him to know the true name of the woman he would love this night.

Finally, she wanted as much truth between them as she could tell. "Giles, I love you," she breathed, burying her head in the hollow of his neck. "Only you. Always you."

Felice spoke of love. What did she think she was doing? He stopped her lies with his mouth, or tried to, but the lie continued in the pressure of her soft, yielding lips on his, the hesitant tongue she thrust out to mock his. Lies, all lies! He didn't need them or want them. But her hands were at his neck cloth, pushing at his coat buttons, as he pulled at her waist ties. Perhaps he could not have all, her honesty and her desire.

She wanted him. He could see it, feel it, despite his constant denials as if to remind himself of the rage that was being pushed aside in his need for her. He shrugged out of his coat and untied the sash at his waist, one hand disrobing himself, the other tearing at her clothes.

He hated the words as they came from his mouth, but he could not help himself. "It's been so long," he said, "so very long."

Meriel, in all honesty, could only nod in agreement. Never was indeed a very long time.

In between his words and her thoughts, she was not idle. Her two hands joined his until four hands were flying about in haste, sometimes entangling, with laughter inevitable. Their lips touched and parted, touched and parted, bringing a moan from deep within her, some place that had held it for all her life, waiting for this man to rouse it. She had never felt such stinging urgency. If Giles did not fill her, and soon, she would die, consumed by rolling waves of heat near to melting her body. And that throbbing, beating against her swollen woman's place like a storm surge against a ship's hull, threatening to wreck her on some far rocky shoal. This is what it was to hunger for a beloved man. And it was beyond anything she had imagined or heard whispered.

At last in her shift, and Giles in his drawers and hosen, Meriel felt her feet leave the floor as he carried her cradled against the broad, hard planes of his bared chest, from candle sconce to candle sconce around the paneled room, blowing out each light in its turn.

They were left in a room lit by pale moonlight and the glowing coals of a dying fire, sending flickering beams over the down coverlet on the huge bed, its curtains gaping open to receive them.

His lips descended on hers again, and he laid her gently on the bed. As he straightened, he tried to slow himself before he spilled his manhood into his drawers like a lad with his first maid. "My lady, shall I call a servant to help you with your *robe de chambre*?"

"Do you need help?" Meriel asked, unable to resist being herself.

Giles smiled, his eyes crinkling in the corners. "What think you, hoyden?"

He bent over her and held her gaze with his for so long that Meriel thought his dark eyes must certainly see through her disguise when she wanted them only to consume her.

"Do you yet ache from my kidnap?" he asked, his voice low and thick, as he sat on the bed, pulled off his hosen and dropped them, adding to the trail of clothes about the room.

"I . . . I ache, yes, but not—"

Giles turned her over as if she weighed not half a stone. Then he slipped her shift from her shoulders and began to knead the soft flesh of her back and buttocks, her skin dewy with need, or he was much mistaken. Why was he delaying? Why not just take her, spill out his seed and leave? Getting a son was what he was about this night. No words need be said, no promises made, nothing to remember or regret. And yet he wanted to linger over her body, trace her shoulders with his forefinger, place his hands on her sides where he could feel the first swelling of her breasts. *Rot me!* He was teasing himself as if this were his first true love.

Meriel felt the warmth of his palms, the pressure of his lithe fingers, each one making their separate way down her spine. She shivered. She knew how to resist a man. How to scratch and kick. But she did not know what Giles wanted from her unless she could see his face.

She rolled onto her back and pulled him down beside her, acting the wanton. She was sure this was the right way. A man could not expect a woman to be a lumpen thing, a mere receptacle. Then why was surprise writ plain upon his face? Without doubt, loving a man was like the science of experimenting. She would have to do it many ways, then replicate those ways that worked. *Hey, well, repeat them more than once!*

Giles thought she played the practiced wanton well, but her wide eyes, drowning in firelit innocence, did not show him an experienced courtesan. "You didn't like my fingers kneading your back? They say the Moors do it with scented oil in their harems. But you would know that."

Meriel was not angered by that insinuation. He had a right to believe Felice a slattern. Still, she could not accept his thinking it of her.

"I adore how *you* do it, Giles. I have never known such strong, warm hands that were yet gentle. I feel safe in them." She wanted to add, *I hope that's what love is,* but she didn't dare.

"Felice," he whispered.

Meriel could not bear that name. Not tonight. So she went back to a childhood memory and pulled up a name the youngest orphans had given her when they couldn't say her real name. "My lord, call me Merry tonight, since happiness is my mood."

He jerked away from her touch. "Do you think me such a fool that I would honor Buck and Rochester and the rest of the merry gang in my own house and bed? Earlier, I had a hope—"

"Shush, Giles. That is not my intent," she said, the words shaking with as much truth as she could tell him. "It is a name for a new beginning." She had some sense that she had gone too far, and held on to any other words.

"You're shaking. Are you cold?"

"No. Frightened."

Now the anger and uncertainty lurking beneath Giles's surface exploded. "I frighten *you*!" he shouted. "I have never so much as—"

Meriel clasped him to her. "No. No. Hear me, my lord. It is not you who frightens me." Although he did a little in this mood. All his arm muscles were taut. Even the dark, curling hair on his chest seemed to be angrily erect. She could see him taking gulps of air.

"Then who?"

"Me, Giles. I am the frightened one . . . at how much I need you. Want you more than—"

The words were too real to ignore. Not even Felice could be that skilled at lying and was very much too lazy to bother. He stood and quickly unloosed the ties of his drawers.

Meriel's mind whirled at what she saw, and she heard the trapped-animal sound again deep within her throat. Giles was magnificent. The king had made a grievous mistake commissioning a statue only of his hero's head. His body was fit for the finest Carrara marble. His wide shoulders tapering to a narrow waist atop long, lithe legs . . . and those curving tight buttocks . . . could have been copied from Michelangelo's David. And in between, prominent—indeed, most prominent—rose the insistent manhood that reminded her of an illustration on a wicked ancient papyrus Sir Edward had brought from his Mediterranean voyages.

Which she had not been allowed to view.

But had.

Giles slid into the bed, parting her legs, and she quickly gave up all thought of ancient art. He bent to her breasts, kissing them, holding them like cherished heirlooms, relishing, licking greedily, taking the perfect white orbs into his mouth until he could consume no more. He dragged his mouth up to her neck, thinking it the most stunningly beautiful neck he had ever seen.

And she tasted a bit like the sea with a freshening southerly breeze blowing from on shore. Clean, salty and with the scent of mint—and wild onions?—rising to fill his nostrils.

Lifting his mouth, he stared down at her, pausing to breathe, and saw what he would never forget. The moon now high in the windows, beams spread thin by thick glass to give her curving body a soft, wavering glow, adding moonlight to her black hair spread upon the scarlet silken pillow. She was the most beautiful creature he had ever known, a Lorelei singing a song to lure him upon the rocks. No mortal man could resist what he was seeing and tasting. At that moment he forgave himself for wanting all of her.

Meriel raised her head to reach his mouth. "Kiss me hard, Giles," she said, her voice husky and a little demanding. "Don't stop kissing me, not even if I ask you to stop. And I won't." She wanted all of him this way once, just once, and then she would face the whole poxy Dutch navy single-handed.

There was amazement mixed with her need for him. He was between her legs. She was begging. "Please, Giles, I want you. I need to have—" She stopped, not wanting to sound like a common back-alley whore. What did wives say to husbands? She couldn't think if she'd ever heard; she could only feel, and what she was feeling was Giles with his cod moving back and forth, torturing her woman's place. He was kissing her everywhere, eyes, lips, throat, the nipples on her breasts that were so erect they ached. She surged against him, beseeching without words. In truth, he would send her all crazed to Bedlam if he did not take her. Now! This minute.

But Giles was at that instant exerting stern control over his own pounding heart. This was not what he had planned. His plan had not included this roaring need to give himself completely as he took her, to show her his searing desire, thus becoming her slave. But his cock ruled tonight and it was an uncompromising master.

Still, that was not the sum of these feelings. Strangely, Felice was a more loving wife beneath him tonight than she had ever been. He was too heated, too full and hard to think of all the ways in which he now found her to be witty and brave and even more lovely . . .

Have a care! Giles told himself firmly. But he could not rule his emotions. She was arching against him, grasping his cod with her hand, demanding him and, God of blessed name, he could no longer think at all.

"Giles! Please, please!" It was a demand, a scream of need to surprise Meriel's own ears. She had thought herself a woman before tonight and been wrong. Giles awakened a fire that had its spark from her very soul.

She raised her hips higher and felt Giles lift her legs to wrap around his buttocks, an image of their tightly muscled contours on the ship's ladder leaping to her mind and remaining there.

She pulled him into her as he pushed, both, for once, in perfect agreement.

Meriel would not have thought it possible that anything could increase her desire, but as he entered, driving deeper, then deeper still, a molten heat rampaged through her limbs.

She heard her own voice, but could not understand the words she cried. They were foreign to her ears and, she feared, most embarrassing. Was she begging for more? Challenging him?

Giles's had held himself back for so long, he feared to hurt her with a cod as strong as Spanish steel. And she was crying something that he couldn't understand, except that he was urged on by the sound. He took her with fierce thrusts and they dropped into a wet trough between stormy waves, then rose up to ride the crest and down the other side, over and over, meeting each wild swell with equal rhythm.

When the storm broke over them, it was violent, like lightning flashing, thunder crashing down from the top of the world, and they held each other for a long moment, floating together, until at last they lay exhausted on their silken beach.

"Oh, Giles, my only lord—" She had finally come to a place of lassitude, unable to lift a limb, but remembering Cervantes's words, which she whispered: "Love—truly there is no force able to resist it."

Giles had fought his hunger for this woman who had betrayed him. Now, finally the hunger had won. "We begin anew this night, Merry," he whispered.

He paused, his lips brushing her shoulder. "Merry," he repeated, as if it had always been the name in his heart.

Chapter Thirteen

~~~~~~~~

An Idyll Interrupted

The following morning, Meriel awoke but did not open her eyes, wanting to hold on to the dream that she knew had been no dream this time. She stretched her arms and legs and found them amazingly light, as if they were floating. Stretching farther to reach Giles, she realized that he had gone. In the depression left by his head on their scarlet pillow lay a perfect white rosebud with dew still sparkling on its tight petals, all pricking thorns stripped away.

Her heart quickened at the thought that he had come back from his garden to silently bring her this gift and stare down at her while she slept. She pressed a hand to her throat, caught her breath and sneezed.

Roses and onions and mint; such was her life. She reached for her pocket hidden under the pillow and tipped four drops of the doctor's tincture under her tongue, quickly followed by a lozenge.

Still she could not put the rose from her, since it had last been touched by Giles. Perhaps he'd left a kiss on it.

Since she dare not smell it, she shook the dew onto her fingers and sucked them, and discovered her lips were swollen. And her breasts were tender to her touch. More, there was an aching emptiness below her belly. She smiled. Wasn't this the logical outcome for a woman who had been thoroughly loved by a man, a lover born to pleasure a woman, an artist with his hands and mouth; indeed, a man who was in no doubt about what to do with his manly part in the bedchamber?

She pulled aside the heavy tapestry bed curtains to find the sun streaming in.

A dozing maid sprang from a chair. "M'lady, how may I serve ye?"

"With sunshine and roses." Meriel smiled, wriggling lazily, reaching for her undershift, which peeked from under the coverlet where it had been wantonly discarded and forgotten. "Have you ever seen such a glorious morning?" she asked the astonished maid.

The young servant blinked and then stared as if she couldn't believe her eyes.

Was a naked mistress so uncommon a sight in this room? Meriel hoped that this was so with all her heart, wanting to believe just for the moment that last night had been the first night of love for Giles as it had been for her. She told herself she was being an idiot. Then she told herself again without really believing it.

The maid approached tentatively.

"Warm water for washing would be won-der-ful," Meriel said, drawing out the word, toying with it, rolling the sound of it on her tongue. The maid ran from the room as if she'd seen the devil's mark. Obviously, a happy and satisfied mistress was an eerie apparition in Harringdon Hall.

Meriel, slipping into her shift for modesty's sake, ran to the leaded glass window and opened it. All windows were closed at night to keep out the noxious vapors formed in the dark, but in the fresh morning air what could be the harm? And she needed to breathe in as much of Harringdon Hall as she could hold.

Giles, in rolled-up shirtsleeves, was below on a greensward enclosed in high, perfectly cropped yew hedges, engaged with another man in practicing with a flashing rapier around the edges of a rectangular pond. It was a handsome space, ordered and closely tended, yet with spring wildflowers allowed to grow in abandon amongst its grasses. All framed the master who had made it.

Meriel bit her lower lip to remind herself that this was the same untamed man who had pressed his body . . . indeed, every part . . . upon her most urgently just a few hours earlier.

She watched Giles bound forward, aggressively slashing his rapier as with a broadsword, then pivot and step back, parrying with great style. She had to applaud. He looked up, and his opponent, seeing opportunity, sent the earl's weapon flying from his hand and into the pond. Giles bowed, slapped the fellow's back and roared with laughter.

She waved, smiling down at Giles, her two men in one: the artistic earl who had planned such a simple but elegant garden, and the fierce lover who had conquered her. She had first desired him as a distant hero; now she adored him as a man, especially when he laughed. Had he laughed so with Felice? No, impossible.

"Merry, break your fast quickly and join me for a morning walk. There is a place I want to show to you," he called, holding his arms wide as if to embrace all of her and Harringdon Hall together. Then he jumped into the pond to retrieve his rapier, emerging with his wet shirt and breeches clinging to him. To his utter advantage.

"My lord, you will take a chill."

He grinned up at her and squinted against the morning sun, brushing away the dark, wet hair clinging to his cheek. "After last night, my lady, I doubt I shall ever feel cold again."

She blushed and moved back inside, but not before she heard him shout for her to hurry her toilette. Which she did with no further urging.

In the great hall at the head of a double line of servants holding various items, Giles waited in dry shirt and black breeches with highly polished, red Spanish boots turned down at the knee. He watched her descend the wide stairs with eyes that devoured every curve of her. She was dressed as a country maid in a gown of fine gauzy lawn, much embroidered and beribboned, a shepherdess in want of a crook to complete the picture. And exposing finer ankles than he remembered. Her black hair was free and tumbling about her shoulders, held back by a scarlet ribbon, as if she had never heard of formal court styles. He thought she could charm the cows away from the tender spring grass, the bees away from their flowers and the ewes away from their lambs. He bent to kiss her hand, then turned it over and kissed her palm most thoroughly. "Utterly charming, my lady," he whispered. "You grow younger and more beautiful by the hour."

When he began to slide his lips up to her wrist, she teased: "I thought we were to walk. Have you changed your mind?"

"My mind is not for changing, my lady, although I beg you not to tempt me lest I fail in that faint resolve." He took a deep breath and gathered himself, since he always felt somewhat off balance with his wife, especially of late. "But walk we will, Merry, and dine in the woods. The French call it a *pique-nique,* but I'll take good English fare under fine English oaks to any French bower." He swept his hand down the rows of servants, holding heaped cloth-covered hampers, a table, two chairs, and linen. Two men brought a virginal and its stand.

'Od's grace, did Felice play and sing? Meriel knew she could fake neither no better than fine court dances. *Hey, well, will I now have to sprain my hand and tongue both together?*

Meriel stood on tiptoe to reach his ear. "Oh, my dearest lord, nothing so formal, if it please you. Could we not just send a food basket ahead and stroll together and alone? I would look into the parterre and at your rose garden."

He looked at her, astounded and delighted. "If you wish it, my shepherdess." This was, in truth, a strange new Felice, who had always expected that comfort follow her if she agreed to walk at all.

Meriel took the arm Giles offered, holding on tight lest the dream slip away, as all dreams must with waking and as this dream surely would before another day had gone. All too soon, she knew, the joyous pleasure of being loved would be a memory. Yet it was worth the risks she would soon take. Thus she determined to treasure every moment.

They walked through the great gothic arched entrance into the sparkling sun, saw a manservant off with the basket of food and wine, and turned down the carefully raked carriageway to the gardens. Along the sides of the road, workmen were lifting spent bulbs to repot and divide for the next year. Giles and Meriel strolled hand in hand round the hall to the main garden, past roses beginning to open full behind their carefully trimmed privet hedges. The beds were laid out in the most cunning geometric patterns with intersecting paths all leading to a center fountain. It was charming, a window into Giles's gentle soul. They continued on the wide central path to the far edge where two seedling trees stood ready to plant near a road.

"No," Giles said to his aproned gardener, Wallace, reaching for the man's shovel. "I'll do this planting, chief."

"Aye, sir."

Giles kissed Meriel's cheek, brushing his lips softly across her skin, then began to dig in the rich soil. "These are horse chestnuts, Merry," he said, soon reaching a proper depth. "They will grow and flower, arching high over this road and giving us shade long before we are old. I will plant a new one for each of our children on the day they are born until our family marches in an avenue down beside the hall."

Meriel's face convulsed and tears flowed down her cheeks. This lie was becoming hourly more unbearable. She struggled not to tell him the truth; she could not spoil his dream. Soon enough it would lie dead.

Giles tamped the dirt around the saplings before he looked up to see her tears. Wiping his hands on the grass, he came to her, taking her in his arms. "Sweet Merry, dry your eyes, for you are now the woman that I always knew you could be, and that is an occasion for joy, not tears." He pulled his shirt from his breeches, and smiling, gently wiped her face. "Come now, there is something I've never shown you."

They moved on toward the meadows. She threw back her head, closed her eyes and drew in a deep breath past a tremulous smile.

Once more, Giles looked on her in amazement, wondering why a kind God had given him at last the woman he had always wanted. Felice had hated his country estate and all his lands about, second only to her hatred of the sea. He had known her to be changed last night in the abandoned yet shy way she gave herself to him, but he had not expected so complete a turn in her character. This new Felice, this Merry as she now named herself . . . and what a true name it was! . . . loved this country air she breathed, full of animal and plant scents. If he had tutored a wizard to conjure a perfect wife, Merry would be the result. He could have no further doubt that the Lord of blessed name had intervened, for this woman was surely heaven-sent.

"Come," he said, taking her hand in his, "let us walk through the fields to the woods. At my prayers this morn, I ordered a perfect day for you. A hot sun and a cool westerly sea breeze."

"You have great powers of communication beyond the common man," she said, smiling again.

"Ah, you well remember." His low tone held a throb of meaning.

Meriel blushed and clasped his hand tighter, pulling on it. They had reached the great fields of wildflowers she had seen from the carriage. She must hope the little doctor's onion elixir was up to this country air, though she must pass this way quickly before she began sneezing, which would surely be very unlike Felice. Even the onion drops could not protect against so many blooms. "And do your powers extend to foot races, my lord, or is the man not as fast as the boy?"

"Faster!" he said, laughing.

She ran away toward the oak woods, her eyes red from a sneeze, or several, denied.

He chased her, marveling at this playful spirit. Perhaps it had been part of her all the time. How could he have missed such jollity? Could he have been too demanding, too eager to mold her? Had he missed the real woman these last years? Though she dodged in and out of the tall grasses, he caught her easily and, laughing aloud, they walked on with their arms around each other's waists.

He loved the sense of her hips moving under his arm. He took great warmth from her body, warmth he still needed. He would never be without it again.

Meriel felt strength from his closeness. She would need strength to let him go when that time came, and a prickling on her neck told her that her time here was short. Chiffinch's plans would not be stopped by her kidnapping in Spring Gardens.

They crossed the carriage track and reached the woods and walked under its green-scented canopy, stepping onto a carpet of bluebells. She turned her face to his. "Why are you sad?" he asked.

"I've never been so happy," she said, sniffling.

He turned her to him and touched her cheek. "Here is a tear."

"My eyes are unused to—"

He put the moist finger to his tongue. "Tastes like a tear." He wrapped her in his arms, cupping his hand around the back of her head and pushing it gently into his shoulder. "Whence comes such tears? Sadness, and on this day of all days at our new beginning?"

Oh, how those words stabbed her because she knew that a sure ending was part of this beginning. "These are not tears of sadness, Giles, but of joy and love."

The past still kept him from instant belief in miracles. "Are there loving tears?"

"There are for a woman." Meriel could not tell him that she had adored him as her marble hero in a library far and away in Canterbury, an ideal of manhood that she had never hoped to actually hold in her arms. So she spoke all the honesty she could. "Giles, I love you because you are brave.

And because you can forgive. And because you are a man who makes gardens."

"Is that the truth?"

"The only truth that matters."

He gently closed her eyes and kissed them, both in turn, holding her as near as she held him.

"I can scarce believe that you are here with me like this." He shook his head as if to clear away any remaining doubt. He did not want to deny what he was feeling any longer. Suspicion was dropping away from him, taking anger and ill memory, everything but what he saw and knew at this moment.

Meriel bit her lip hard to keep from crying out all that he did not know. She would pay with a lifetime of emptiness for these few enchanted moments, but she was determined to leave Giles with a happy memory of his wife. She convinced herself that the masquerade must continue for as long as possible. Everything in life was a choice. At that instant, she could imagine no other.

They walked on through the slanting light, crunching under their feet the acorns missed by the manor's pigs, coming at last to a small shaded glade surrounded by a canopy of giant oaks, some with limbs as thick as trees. Meriel thought these must be the grandmother oaks of this forest, the oldest from which all the others had been born.

Giles dismissed the servant waiting beside the laden basket. "Merry, have you an appetite?" he asked, his dark eyes crinkling at the corners.

A comic twist of his mouth described the appetite of which he spoke. Laughing, she ran away so that he would give chase again. She wanted to be caught, to be carried by the weight of his body to the ground, to be loved here on the ancient earth of the Warboroughs. Mistress of all for a brief moment.

Giles chased her to the biggest oak of all and began to climb it, pulling himself up, then taunting her with a grin. "I challenge you, Merry."

"A countess doesn't climb trees," she said, fearing to become so much herself that she would be unmasked.

"I saw you climb from the ketch as no countess would." He balanced along the branch and back, showing his prowess. "I used to climb in this tree all the day, hiding from my tutors and the whipping that most often followed. It is one of my fondest memories."

"The whipping?"

"Definitely not. My Latin tutor could lay on with a will. It was a day alone in the forest that I could not resist, a day without conjugations and sums. I had always rather be on the land than in the schoolroom."

At that moment, Meriel loved him so completely it near took her breath. Giles was a peer of the realm, a Garter knight, but at heart he was a farmer, a sailor, a man at home everywhere but at Whitehall. There was no guile in him. He was showing her who he was. And she loved all that she saw.

Looking up at him standing tall on the huge limb, shaded by leaves, he seemed an ancient green man come to life. Before Meriel could stop her mouth, she blurted, "As a child, I swam in the river for just such escape to make my own private place."

Puzzled, he peered down at her. "You never said you swam the Stour. I thought you would have hated it."

The Stour? Her river had been Felice's? The thought tumbled about in her head while she tried to find the sense in it. What she found was a warning to watch her tongue.

Any unguarded word could create questions she could not answer and expose her deception. She couldn't risk it.

He stooped to give her a hand. "I grow lonely. Come up to me."

Without a thought, she reached high and grasped his strong fingers and he pulled her easily up to a perch beside him. The tree enclosed them, and higher up she heard the four-note love call of a hopeful woods dove.

"Look, Merry!"

She followed his pointing finger to a huge forked branch higher up, where young hands had built a platform.

"I haven't climbed up there for years."

"Take me up, Giles. I want to see where you went as a boy."

"I never thought you would want to see it."

Faintly in the distance, she heard horses on the estate road and knew that her time with Giles was short now, for if not this carriage, then surely the next would bring Chiffinch's orders. Meriel clung to Giles until he climbed to the next limb. "Quickly now, help me," she said, looking up and seeing Giles's happy face above her. She would make that smile last as long as she could.

Pulling her skirt between her legs and tucking it into her waist ties, she exposed her legs, but she was beyond modesty with this man. Quite beyond. She held tight to his hand as they climbed higher, the rough bark catching at her ribbons and untying them.

"Don't look down," he said.

"I have never been fearful." She was proud of that truth. She'd been born with nothing, not even a name. There wasn't much to lose after commencing life as an orphan. At least there hadn't been until Giles.

He grasped a rope hanging from the platform, but it came

away rotted by time. "Wait here," he said. He inched up the trunk, tested each branch for strength, then reached back for her. They clambered finally onto the rough planks lodged in a fork between two large branches. Giles brushed away old acorns and dried leaves.

Meriel could well see the proud boy building his woodland hideaway with railings like those on the prow of his ketch, a little ship sailing among a sea of leaves. Large square-head nails still held it sturdy.

"Are you dizzied?" he asked.

"Probably. Don't let go of me."

"Never and a day," Giles said, pulling her closer as he leaned his back against the huge trunk.

He lowered his voice so that the sound stayed between them. "I want you here, Merry. I want to give you our son here where I dreamed as boy and youth of the woman I would love."

"But you are neither now, my lord, but quite obviously full grown." She tried harder to shut out the sound of approaching horses and the rattle of a carriage now clearly heading toward Harringdon Hall. *Please God, just a little more time.* The begging words echoed through her.

He kissed her. It was a starved kiss and she felt all the years of his hunger at once. When she pulled back from him, she saw he was smiling.

"How could you kiss me like that and smile at once?"

"Merry, how could I not?" His hand found hers and put it on his manhood.

She held her breath. "I need no further proof that you are indeed full grown."

"You shall have it, nonetheless."

Chapter Fourteen

Leaving Love

As Giles pushed into Merry, the force of his desire so soon after their long night of love ripped through him like a sudden storm at sea and came to rest in his full and swollen cock. The memory of loving Merry only hours before was not enough for him. He needed to touch her, to taste her; he needed to hold her in his hands, to pull her so close that they became one person, one flame, one primitive emotion.

He saw her throw back her head, her mouth open and her hands grip the railing lest she fall overboard. "Merry, my love—"

He felt Merry's tightened hold on his manhood, felt her pushing her legs against his back, wordlessly urging him on. He needed nothing further.

Meriel's thighs ached with tension. She wanted more of him and got it, rocking backward until he thrust into her deepest woman's well and completely filled the emptiness that she knew she would need only him to fill forever.

They cried out in ecstasy together, and the sound of almost unbearable aching throbbed through the old oak forest, sending birds flying from their perches and leaves quivering on their fragile stems. For a full minute the forest was still, then gradually birds returned and began to chatter and a breeze rustled the leaves, making it a forest again.

In the late afternoon, the earl's majordomo greeted his laughing master and mistress as they strolled arm in arm to the entrance of Harringdon Hall, Giles carrying a now empty food basket. "My lord, a Dr. Wyndham awaits below in the hall. He says he is sent by His Majesty, and indeed a carriage bearing the royal arms brought him." The servant handed his master a letter with the red royal seal and bowed again to Meriel. "Your ladyship, your maid Agnes accompanied the doctor from Whitehall. I sent her to your rooms."

Giles nodded and Meriel felt his arm muscles tense under her hand. He looked a question at her, and she shrugged. Although she had suspicions, she truly did not know why the doctor had been sent. No one could fathom Chiffinch's tactics, but he used everyone for his purposes. A royal physician would not be exempt if he wished to keep his position. What she did know was that her time with Giles was now very short, and she moved closer and clung to his arm.

The little doctor was seated by a wood fire in the ancient stone hall that seemed to hold the chill of winter even in June.

Giles had loosed Meriel's arm, and she could sense the suspicion that had returned almost as if it had been biding its time.

"My Lord of Warborough," the doctor said, rising and sweeping his hat before him, bowing so low that he almost lost his wig.

"We meet again, Doctor, I hope in better times," Giles said, though his voice held no such hope.

"Alas, your lordship, I'm afraid better times elude all true Englishmen. After plague and devastating fire, the people cry out for order. Yet we must now contend with the Dutch navy."

Giles drew himself up even taller than his normal height. "Has the king ordered me into naval service at last?"

"That is not why I am come, sir."

Giles's voice was rigidly polite, but along with the pulsing vein in his neck, his tone took on a noticeably harder edge. "Then I must ask why you are come, since I have no need of a palace doctor."

Wyndham cleared his throat and took a deep breath. "His Majesty is greatly concerned for her ladyship's health and wishes a royal physician"—he bowed again to indicate himself—"to attend her. I am charged, sir, with—"

Giles stepped closer to the doctor, lowering his voice so that servants, always curious, would have no further gossip to carry to their quarters. "Her ladyship, Dr. Wyndham, is in excellent health, as you can plainly see. And mark you, for the king's ears only, we are in hopes of a babe by the coming spring."

Indeed, Meriel knew that the doctor could witness her health and possibly much more. Her gown was near undone from its ribbons catching on the climbing tree; grass and wine stains . . . and perhaps the mark of lovemaking . . . had soiled the skirt during their wild *pique-nique,* where she had acted the wanton shepherdess to Giles's highway rogue. That a babe had been conceived had not been far from her thoughts, either, though she could not visualize a future beyond the next few days, indeed the next hours. She could not imagine what she would do if she lived on and had Giles's babe. All her future was emptiness, either from quick death by the Dutch or a slower death without Giles.

The doctor cleared his throat several times and blinked rapidly. "Ah, yes, my lord, I do see great health in her ladyship, and I pray that God grants you the child you long for."

His face reddened and took on further confusion so that Meriel could not help but have sympathy for him, though he stumbled on. "Er, yet, sir, I am charged by the king's appointment as royal physician to examine her ladyship's healing of both her ankle and the scar opened, as you may know, by a careless maid, since . . . er, His Majesty knows my skill in treatments of both bones and burns."

The doctor reached into his roll of instruments and salves, withdrawing a small clay pot, cradling it against his chest as if it were precious, though he did not leave off his flow of words. "I have mixed my famous miracle salve, a certain cure for burns and swelling joints." He paused, clearing his throat once more with much puffing up of lips. "Mixed even more infallibly, I must say, for her ladyship's specific use, since it was discovered that she left it behind in her haste to . . . er, accompany your lordship to your Norfolk estates." The doctor was by this time completely breathless, but showing a more contented face now that a difficult royal message had been well and truly delivered.

The earl had watched him closely for any sign of dissembling. But the doctor was by nature so fidgety Giles could not tell, making him an admirable choice for king's messenger.

"That was most kind of His Majesty, but as you see you may carry to him the good news that her ladyship is fully recovered. . . . And happy." He looked to Meriel for confirmation, and she gave it with a brilliant smile.

The doctor bowed to her, his hand spread upon his heart.

"As my lord says, good doctor, I am the happiest of women. As to fully recovered, I must beg your good offices. I have great need of your pot of salve. I have sorely missed it, and my face and burn have suffered its absence."

He held the small pot out to her. "Your ladyship's beauty shows no ill signs. Indeed, the country air has brought back all the roses of early youth. London air is no aid to the complexion."

"Yes, yes," Giles said somewhat impatiently. "You are welcome to rest here the night before your return."

"And may I examine my patient, my lord earl, so that I may give a true and medically considered opinion to the king?"

"Only in my presence, as is fitting, and after we sup. We will welcome your company at table, Doctor."

"Your lordship is most kind." Dr. Wyndham bowed his acceptance.

Giles ordered a porter to prepare a room for the doctor, and firmly escorted Meriel up the great hall's stairs to her rooms. "I have only one question," he said when they were alone on the stairs.

Meriel smiled up at him a little sadly, sensing the happiness of the last hours slipping away faster. "I suspect, my lord, that you have many more than one question. But I will answer the one you want to ask first."

"Are you witch that you know it?"

She smiled again, this time at his anger, since she knew it was born of deep confusion. "Because it would be my question. And no, I did not expect the doctor. Now I will answer your other questions. I am not eager to join the troupe of king's mistresses. Every word of love I have spoken to you in our bed and in our tree is whole, blessed truth, or the devil may have me for his plaything."

Giles scowled, his mouth tightening to stop any unmanly softening. "Do not tempt the devil, my lady." He took a deep breath and expelled it before he asked what he feared to know. "Then why did you visit Chiffinch on that last day in Whitehall if not to put a price on yourself and secure the king's favor?" As he said the words, his face reddened.

Meriel loosed his arm and grasped the banister. "You had me spied upon? Is all the world after me?"

"You ask me this after you disappeared with Rochester and Buck to Spring Gardens? And after I found you and the king in St. James Park with your heads together? What else am I to think?"

"That perhaps I was kidnapped by those courtiers and that I had the king's confidence in St. James Park."

He stared at her in disbelief, and she knew that Felice had won. There was no way she could finally and for all time overcome such a rough history and win back his full trust. Meriel could feel the wall between them, the one that had tumbled into fragments over these past hours of loving, being rebuilt stone by stone as they spoke.

"Try to find it in your heart to forgive me once more, Giles. Just once more," she whispered and ran up the stairs to her rooms. There was nothing further to say without exposing her sham and Felice's perfidy. Better to leave Giles with the memory of what little she had been able to give him. For a moment she felt virtuous for her tender sacrifice, the greatest any woman could make, though she doubted that the feeling would last for as long as she would need it.

She flung open the door to her room and quickly shut it again, leaning back against its solid wood, gathering some strength from it. When she opened her eyes, Agnes was standing apart from the other maids. She curtsied a low court curtsy, putting Meriel in memory of their long lessons in the Tower, which seemed years past, but was only little more than a fortnight.

"I am happy to see you, Agnes."

"I thank, your ladyship. With me are various gowns, pomanders and certain *necessaries* left behind at Whitehall."

Meriel heard the emphasis and waved away the other

maids. "I will rest now and call you when I dress for supper. Agnes may stay by to bring me gossip from Whitehall."

The door closed somewhat louder than necessary on what appeared to be jealous servants, who did not like the intrusion of a fancy court maid into their provincial domain. Meriel drew Agnes close: "Chiffinch?" It was an entire question.

"Aye, your ladyship," Agnes whispered in return. "I am come with orders and documents for you to cipher, and then to deliver to the Dutch."

Meriel heard and understood, but could not resist an accusation. "And you are here to ensure that I do your master's bidding."

Agnes bobbed a shorter curtsy. "As well as make certain of the doctor's loyalties, although he proved a perfect excuse to follow you when you were . . . abducted by your . . . husband."

"You have many talents, Agnes, dissembling being the chiefest."

"I thank your ladyship. If I may say so, you are gifted in your own right far above my poor talents."

"You may say so," Meriel said, tempted to smile. Somewhat more wearily she added, "So the time is come?"

"Yes, we intercepted a message for Felice that said the Dutch fleet under Cornelis de Witt will pass offshore some time tomorrow on its way to the Thames, and a possible attack on our capital warships anchored in the Pool of London. You must away tonight." She thrust her hand into a slit in her skirt and drew out a pocket of parchments tied around her waist. "You will meet their fleet with the proper dispatches to draw them away. If they think we are prepared for them as these messages reveal, then they may turn back north or return to Holland." Agnes handed the parchments to Meriel. "You will recipher messages from their agents—

Chiffinch wrote what to say—telling the Hollanders that the chain across the Thames has been strengthened, many fire ships readied and soldiers and cannon line the banks all the way to London."

"Is this true?"

Agnes frowned. "I trust to God it is by now, your ladyship. Sir Edward Cheatham, Samuel Pepys and others in the Admiralty are working furiously, but there is little money and the sailors are still in revolt from want of pay, even proclaiming they will not fight."

"Giles could lead them!" Meriel bit her lip for giving away so much. Agnes would know her feelings for Giles now, if she hadn't guessed.

"I do not doubt it, my lady." The words were soft and it was a comfort to Meriel that Agnes—that someone in the world—knew her true heart.

Meriel closed her eyes the better to take all Agnes's words into her memory and retain them, slowly repeating them in a low voice. One question remained. "What if I am unable to fool the Dutch?"

"If Lady Felice's own husband accepted you, there is no reason for the Dutch not to be completely taken in. Try to get them to give you ciphered instructions to return to their London agents, and the means to get you there . . . not knowing that we have gathered them all up to the Tower. To their loss of comfort as with all traitors," Agnes added, grim faced.

Meriel shivered, remembering the bloody Tower, the night screams, the pungent scent of fear. She thrust the memory from her. "What if the Hollanders do not believe these dispatches or are so close to battle they do not want to stop?"

"Then, Countess, you will have to make good use of any other talents you may have."

"Even Daniel had help in the lion's den."

Agnes smiled, though it quickly waned. "The Lord of blessed name will be your only help, too, if you are discovered. Guard your life with your tongue. Do not mistake the Dutch for complete fools. They are strong, good seamen and have a score to settle with us for burning two ships at the port of Vlies and pillaging the town of Terschelling on the Dutch coast. Yet tomorrow you will be the first subject of King Charles in this battle."

Meriel rolled her eyes. "Hey, well, remind me to appreciate my opportunities."

Agnes curtsied, a formal court curtsy again, ignoring Meriel's irony. "I salute you, my lady, and hold you in great esteem."

Meriel's lungs craved air. She walked to the window and opened it, looking down in the gathering dusk on the orderly garden below, seeing Giles as he had climbed from the pool into the morning sunlight, wet clothes outlining the muscles of his body. She stopped herself before she thought longer on that body as it had been in the oak tree, though she had to dig her fingernails into her palm to halt the memory.

She tried not to long for this life and the man . . . in his garden, sensible, sweet scented, with interludes of wild loving. That way led to melancholy and eventual madness, not to the courage she would need and need in abundance.

Then she set to work on the messages Chiffinch had intercepted from the Hollander's London agents. She rewrote them into the Dutch musical cipher with all the military detail Chiffinch had given her for the supposedly superior English defenses.

Meriel descended for supper at eight of the giant pendulum clock that stood just inside the open library doors. She was gowned as a countess, perhaps for the last time, in bright blue satin looped to reveal a pearl-colored petticoat with matching hose and shoes.

Giles and the doctor, both wearing fine satin suits all the mode, waited by the fire with wine in crested crystal glasses. The two men bowed in response to her deep curtsy.

The library's paneling gleamed from beeswax. The linen on the table was crisply white, and the silver shined as if no hand had ever touched it. It was a room of no disorder, a room for which Giles had overseen the preparation, she was certain. His way of controlling the part of his world that yielded to control. She understood why he had needed to make the effort.

"My lord husband, good doctor, please be seated. I thank you for your greeting." She bowed her head so that Giles could not see the suspicious glint of tears in her eyes.

A servant held her chair, and she was seated. Wine was poured. A rich oniony broth was served.

Giles motioned to her bowl. "Since you have a new delight in this vegetable."

The doctor covered his mouth to erase a smile.

"I thank you, Giles. I hope you don't mind."

"'Tis my great favorite, as well," Giles said, taking an enthusiastic spoonful.

After this exchange, they fell to silent eating while the doctor desperately made conversation about the healing nature of onions, to fill the emptiness the host and hostess did not seem inclined to satisfy, and commenting further, in as many ways as mud and ruts could be described, on the roads that had delayed his trip from London.

The second course was of light meats, including boned pheasant laid out in a symmetrical pattern so that all could choose as they liked. The third course was of fruits and sweets with cottager farm cheeses circling a large platter.

"Merry, are you not hungry?" Giles asked Meriel, who had eaten little.

Hey, well, the lump in my throat is too large to admit solid food!

Meriel noted that he had not called her Merry since their return from the oak forest, and she could not stop the pleasure she felt at hearing that name on his lips again. "I did dine fully during our *pique-nique,* if you recall."

"You did not seem to indulge in *eating* overmuch."

She thought the real subject of their talk ill disguised from the doctor. She dared risk those dangerous waters, needing to signal Giles that her memory was as good as his. "Indulgence is a matter of appetite, my lord, and my appetite was most fully satisfied this day." There, that should give him full knowledge of what she had taken away from their forest romp!

"Aye, but you did have much of . . . *exercise,* which should have renewed your hunger." Giles's voice was laden with other meaning, and it would have delighted her any other night but this one.

The doctor was following this exchange with interest, his gaze going back and forth between them. He made a feeble attempt to join in what seemed raillery. "My lord, would that there were magic drops that husbands could give wives to get at their real meaning," he said, looking to Giles. "Or the same for a wife," he floundered, looking to Meriel.

She knew that she could not continue this conversation that had no other place to end but in her bed or a furious argument, either of which would take too much time with Agnes waiting. "Much of exercise," she said, looking at Giles and assuming her Felice voice. "No more than that to which I am accustomed."

Giles's voice grew predictably harsh. "I doubt it not."

Because Meriel was drowning in shame and sorrow, she answered his anger with anger. "Strange, m'lord, since you seem to doubt so much of late."

His eyes flicked toward her, and their dark depths reflected her own emptiness. Meriel wished she could recall the words she had said in necessity and a little anger because she had needed to put a distance between them. But it was too late. She knew she had already squandered the best of this last hour with Giles.

The doctor stood before his host rose, a breach of etiquette that went unnoticed. "Perhaps your lordship will allow me to examine her ladyship now before I retire."

Giles waved a hand in agreement, his face set with no expression.

The doctor gave her ankle a cursory glance, but examined her scar more closely. "It is healing well. Use the salve morning and night, your ladyship, to double its value."

"I thank you, Doctor. I will do as you advise now that you have been kind enough to bring me a new supply."

Dr. Wyndham bowed to Giles. "I will be leaving very early on the morn, my lord, so I thank you now for your generous hospitality. I will remark it to His Majesty."

"I say farewell and Godspeed on your journey," Giles said, in a pleasant host voice, though his gaze was still on Meriel.

"And, Doctor," Meriel added, "please take my maid Agnes with you, as I have sufficient servants at Harringdon Hall for all my needs. I doubt I will soon return to the court."

The doctor bowed his acknowledgment, and a servant opened the door for him.

"Did you speak true?" Giles asked her, and she saw hope again in his face.

"Who knows, my lord. I am a woman of changing appetite and a need for variety." Her voice was now pure

Countess Felice. "And with your permission, I will take my leave. You may remember that you have exhausted me."

Since her words pulled him in all directions, for some relief Giles lifted his fork and stabbed the linen with its three tines.

Frightened, Meriel stood and backed toward the door, which was opened for her by a porter who showed nothing on his face.

"I have given you no leave as yet, m'lady," Giles said, and waved the porter out of the library.

The door closed softly behind him, but Meriel knew servants and expected his ear was pressed close to the keyhole. "Why are you demanding my presence," she asked, swallowing hard, "since it is obviously so unpleasant? Let me go and you will surely be more at ease." She put a hand to her forehead in good imitation of fatigue.

"Then go as you wish. I have no need for company that is ever changeable." He turned his back and faced the fire. A log fell, spraying sparks against his hose. He did not move.

Meriel knew she should say nothing further to Giles, but she had no will to stop herself. "Always remember the oak tree, my lord."

Giles whirled about, hiding his puzzlement, as the door closed behind her. He longed to call her back, to demand an explanation of such a curious good-night. How could he ever forget this day? And what had this quarrel been about?

Chapter Fifteen

A Midnight Flight from Harringdon Hall

Slowly climbing the wide staircase from the hall to the gallery, Meriel shut away all thought of the angry and haunted look on Giles's face as she had left him in the library. She had to. That memory would be too heavy a burden to carry forward when her own feet seemed unable to lift up to the next step.

She faltered more than once, half turning to go back. The need to tell him the truth almost choked her. But fear stopped her. Fear for what the knowledge of Felice's fate would do to him. Fear for England. And fear of Giles's hatred for her pretense, which she could never bear.

She reached her rooms to find Agnes holding a heavy traveling cloak. "Wait until deep dark," the maid whispered, "and then the little doctor will take you to Great Yarmouth harbor to meet with a chandler on the waterfront. The chandler was caught smuggling by Chiffinch's men, so he will do as he is told to escape the hangman. He will take you out to the fleet as it passes on the morrow. Your boat must be standing offshore when the Dutch arrive."

Meriel questioned what she'd heard. "Dr. Wyndham will deliver me to the town?"

"Aye, we cannot ask a man from the earl's household. They would be loyal to their master, and the earl—"

"Would be informed and follow me on the instant. Or perhaps not."

Agnes smiled. "You jest. He is besotted with you . . . as if he had you for the first time."

"That was cruel as only unwanted honesty can be cruel," Meriel said, and her voice trembled.

Agnes nodded. "Aye, forgive me. A spy learns she must take her amusement where she may . . . as you will learn, if you have not already."

"I have had little of amusement in latter days." And as so much in her life lately, this was as true as it was untrue for Meriel.

Agnes insisted: "But you do see why we cannot involve the earl's men."

Meriel nodded her agreement, not trusting her voice. Never would she put Giles's life at risk for the spymaster, the king or— She nearly added heaven to her list, but decided that would be impolitic at this particular time of her life as a king's spy, when about to be at almost sure risk of her life. If a Dutch matchlock or noose from a yardarm sent her to death, she would not arrive at the gates of heaven with blasphemy on her tongue. She would have enough to answer for with lying, adultery— She pinched herself hard to intercept such thoughts. She would not fail. *Could not fail!*

Agnes and Meriel waited together, without speaking more, until a moonlit midnight was faintly visible through the diamond-paned window. Meriel tied the pocket, containing all her reciphered messages from the Dutch spies in London, beneath her gown and fastened the ties of her cloak about her throat.

Agnes attempted to hand her a small pistola. "You may have good use for this."

Meriel thrust it from her. "It would be madness. More like I would shoot myself!"

Agnes shrugged and handed her a small sheathed knife, untying it from around her leg.

Meriel could not help a nervous laugh. "You are as armed as a grenadier, Agnes."

"Take it," Agnes insisted, and watched with approval as Meriel tied it about her thigh under her gown. Then they shook hands in the new style of farewell.

Meriel clung to Agnes's hand. "Do you wish that you were accompanying me?"

"No, Meriel St. Thomas," Agnes said, all but shuddering. "I am clever, but not brave."

"Ah. I think there is a compliment in that somehow." Meriel pulled her cloak tighter. "Agnes, you know what you must tell Lord Giles when he discovers me gone."

Agnes nodded, expelling a deep breath. "I will tell him that the king did send for you and you obeyed as a loyal subject to save the earl from His Majesty's displeasure. What can even a peer do against his monarch?"

"He would defy His Majesty for me if he knew." Meriel was certain of that answer though the words quavered on her tongue, but she could delay her departure no longer.

"He will never know the truth, m'lady," Agnes said. "An unfortunate carriage accident on the dangerous roads of this shire will take the Countess of Warborough's life, leaving her battered body for the Earl to inter in the family crypt."

Meriel clenched her fists. "Chiffinch thinks of everything."

"Aye, he is always one plot ahead. Don't doubt it."

Silently, Meriel slipped out the door and down a back-stairs to the box parterre exit. There was no guard barring her way. Giles trusted her. The thought stabbed under her breast for he would soon know his trust misused. Until he got the terrible news of her death, he would think her at best a liar and eager whore to His Majesty. Better that, Meriel thought bitterly, than to know the worse truth. A man did not forgive a woman who had played him for a fool.

She had gone no more than a few steps when the worried white face of Dr. Wyndham appeared on the raked gravel path. He brought a finger to touch his lips for silence and motioned for her to follow him across the lawn away from the pole lanterns edging the garden. She breathed in the heavy green odor of newly scythed grass and knew that whenever in future years, that scent would come to her it would bring her back to this night at Harringdon Hall, the moon hanging high in the sky. And to the sound of her own feet running away from Giles and the happiest hours of her life, against which she would measure all future pleasures. And find them wanting.

The doctor took her arm and guided her some distance before they reached his coach and they were off, slowly at first, and then faster back down the rutted road to the harbor at Great Yarmouth.

Meriel wrapped herself in her cloak and turned her face from the doctor, looking out the window into the night and seeing nothing. She could not converse. She was too busy blocking all the emotions that threatened to overwhelm her as they pulled away from the place that had been so briefly her true home. She had belonged there for days as she had never belonged for years in Sir Cheatham's home and cer-tainly not in the charity orphanage at Canterbury.

She gripped tight to the upholstered seat. If she allowed

tears to begin, there would be no end to them and no way she would fully be the Countess Felice for yet another few days. And she must deceive the Hollanders and live on to hold Chiffinch to his word that Giles never know Felice had not gone reluctantly to the king, having regained her love for her husband. *He must believe that!*

The coach clattered from the dirt road onto the cobbles of the town and on through streets that were dark but for an occasional watchman, crying the hour and weather, holding a lantern high on its pole. At last they reached the wharf and stopped in front of a shop that showed no light.

"Lovely lady," the doctor said in a rumbling, sad voice that refused his effort to soften it. "Pray, let me tell you of my complete admir—"

"No, Doctor, there is no need. You have done your whole duty under duress, I don't doubt, and I thank you for your particular kindness. Now return with a restful conscience to your family and to Whitehall."

He took her hand and put a small glass vial into her palm, closing her fingers about it. "If you are found out, and put to the torture . . . this will help."

"Surely the Dutch are civilized people—"

"In war there is no time to be civilized."

Meriel shook her head with finality. "I cannot meet my God as a suicide."

"No, no. You misunderstand. This is not a poison, though I studied poisons and their antidotes during my student days at the University of Padua, Bologna and . . . ah, yes, but 'tis a strong poppy juice." He lowered his voice as best he could. "It makes pain bearable, e'en the pain of death. Indeed, e'en the pain of parting from a great love, sweet lady."

She nodded, grateful for his thought of her, then could not resist a way to jolly him. "But, good doctor, if I take this physic, will I not then need your red Counteracting pills, and I do not fancy—"

"Pray, dear lady, do not jest more or you will break my heart with your courage."

She bent across to kiss his cheek. "Doctor, I must jest, for it is all in life that ever saved me." She stepped from the coach without another word, but in the dark, she slipped the vial into the pocket that held the doctor's other physics. It made a comforting weight.

The chandlery door opened and she was pulled inside as the coach moved on slowly down the quayside. Two shadowy figures confronted her, dressed, as far as she could see from a guttering candle, in rough sailor's canvas breeches and shirts.

"We be clearing the harbor just afore first light," said one. He led her to an upturned keg beside a barrel table. "There be small ale, my lady. No wine."

"Ale with my thanks. The nights are cool by the sea."

The man grunted. "Be hot enough when the Hollanders get on to ye."

Ha! A chandler who thought to bandy words with a countess, e'en a counterfeit countess. Cromwell's Roundheads and their republican teachings had much to answer for. She grinned into the dark of the shop. *Hey, well, I am beginning to think like an aristocrat.*

Meriel drank off most of the ale and put her head on her arms and dozed, though she was aware someone turned the hour glass thrice.

"I almost regret this is what we must do to save our necks from the king's spymaster," one of the men said to the other.

"Aye, she be a calm 'un," answered a gruff voice.

Meriel smiled. If they could only hear her heart pounding like all the drums of a regiment of foot. She slept no more after that, but watched as the men gathered coils of rope and lashed several small kegs together.

"'Tis time, lady."

"You don't know my name?"

"Knowing nothing is safest, though we see ye're quality."

Meriel finished the last of the ale and followed them outside to a small fishing shallop with a half deck, oars for rowing and two sails fore and aft. She walked down a short plank, and the men threw off the mooring ropes. They rowed away from shore and then set the sails and tacked with the wind around the breakwater toward the open sea.

"Best get ye belowdecks," a sailor told her, as the wind rose and the little flat-bottomed shallop bounced through the waves, spraying the rowers.

She felt as if she were in Charon's boat, crossing the river Styx to dark hell. Though she shook her head to deny the thought, still it lingered.

By full sunup they were in the Channel, with nets out to lee and stern, hauling in fish. Meriel watched the fish flop to their gasping death under the rowers' benches, and thought she might not so enjoy breaking her fast with a plaice or cod next time, which reminded her that she was not hungry, though she should be.

It was near to noon and clouds had overcast the sun when they came up a swell and saw many sails massed in the distance.

"There be the damned Dutchies, now," said the chandler, who had never mentioned his name and did not now.

Giles sat long in the library after his wife retired. He sent his porters to their beds and stared at the door, half expecting it to open once more and Merry to appear in the flickering light of the dying fire. He imagined her rushing to him, throwing her arms about him, begging his indulgence of a brief womanly distemper. She sat on his lap, and he bent near to reach her lips and felt the full fire of them envelope his, the tip of her tongue came out, all shy yet heated, to amuse his.

He groaned, needing to send the sound of it into the far corners of the room, needing to fill the room with his desire. He stood and strode to his books, his comfort, looking at the familiar titles, books that he had loved to absorb and to smell the supple leather and to feel the rich paper crinkle under his hands . . . and now not even Cervantes could delight him.

Giles wanted everything to be as it had been for that too-short time in her bed and in his oak tree. . . . His no more, but theirs because they had shared their love in it.

The pendulum clock struck one, then two, and he knew that there would be no sleep for him this night. He rose and walked into the night chill of his sunken garden and saw the moon reflected in his pond. Or was it a light from her window?

His heart beat faster to see the light. She could not sleep as he could not. He smiled. She wanted him to storm her room, lay siege to her heart and halt her vexing behavior like a young spark come courting.

Along the yew hedge, a gardener had left a long orchard ladder. He rejected the idea at first, but on second thought, and uncaring what anyone looking on might think, he carried the ladder to the wall under Merry's window and climbed up. It was off the latch and he pulled it open and swung his legs over the sill and into the room.

A startled and fully clothed maid rose from the bed.

"Who are you?" he said, his eyes searching the far corners for Merry.

"Agnes, my lord, her ladyship's maid."

"You are the maid from the court," he said, and advanced

on the bed, his voice almost guttural. "Where is she? Tell me if you value your life!"

The chandler hauled in the sails of the shallop and hailed the Dutch flagship *De Zeven Provinciën.* "Passenger for ye."

Meriel stood on the half deck of the little fishing boat, trying to keep her footing as sailors peered over the side of the huge warship. There were so many gun ports, she could not count them all. Her legs felt like water, ebbing away under her, and the ale she'd drunk had long ago lost its ability to warm her. She took hold of the mast and remembered why she was here. Giles had not been all the motive with which she had begun this adventure in the Tower. . . . She had needed to save herself. . . . But he was now the whole reason why she must finish this job without discovery.

An officer, judging by his gold braid and lace, leaned over the top rail and lifted his broad-brimmed hat in salute to her. A ladder was lowered. The chandler held the bottom of it as the shallop bumped against the Dutch ship.

"Here's luck to yer, m'lady," he said, touching his forehead. "Whatever ye be doing, God's blessings on ye."

Meriel nodded, not trusting her voice. Taking a deep breath and sending a quick prayer aloft, she began to climb the ladder, moving up and down in the Channel swells. She almost smiled, for it was what Sir Edward would call a lubber's ladder, as easy to climb as a hall staircase. The rail swung open and she stepped across onto a deck almost white from holystoning.

Sailors watched her with obvious suspicion as they pretended to go about their duties. She remembered that females aboard ships were supposed to bring bad luck. She allowed herself one second to wonder whether she would bring it or suffer it.

The young officer bowed, and she shook out her skirts and rearranged her cloak, checking to see that the ciphers were still securely tied about her waist. She glanced at the stern and saw the Dutch flag, a red lion on a gold field. She was truly in enemy territory.

"*Goedemorgen,* Countess," the young officer said, smiling widely. "*Mijnheer* de Witt waits eager for you in his cabin."

She nodded, since no other acknowledgment was required, and the officer, smiling betimes, led her to the companionway aft, carefully helping her down the stairs. He knocked on a well-crafted oaken door with a brass handle, opened the door and announced, "The Countess of Warborough."

Meriel stepped across the high lintel, and for a moment she was back in the cabin on Giles's ketch, the sun slanting through beveled pane windows, casting diamond shadows on the deck at her feet.

De Witt came forward immediately and kissed her hand. "*Met plezier,* Lady Felice. I have never seen you in such health and beauty."

He was a man of about forty years, bewigged and with a thin mustache and goatee very much after the Spanish fashion.

"A flattering greeting," Meriel said in her haughty Felice tone. "And now to complete my business with you."

"*Ja,* and why not, when you bring me dispatches from our agents in London? Good news is my hope."

He bowed again, smiling to an extent that Meriel thought excessive, but that might be the Dutch way. "Yes, I have here dispatches from three of your agents in London. I doubt you will be pleased, Admiral."

"I am not an admiral," he said, "but, as you should know, a representative of the States-General."

Meriel had made her first mistake. Why hadn't Chiffinch

or Agnes warned her? "A courtesy title, sir, since you head a great fleet."

De Witt bowed, smiling still, and Meriel continued. "I fear you will not be pleased to hear that King Charles and his Admiralty are rapidly strengthening all the Thames defenses."

"*Nee!* I am sorry to hear it. We had earlier news that the king thought our fleet just a feint while peace talks were concluding, and did not intend to meet us with force. This is most disturbing. May I see these unhappy dispatches?"

Meriel, not showing the relief she felt that her explanation had been accepted, indicated that the dispatches were beneath her skirts, and he bowed again, turning his back gallantly to face the row of windows aft. She lifted her skirts and untied the pocket, placing the dispatches on de Witt's map table, which she could see contained a detailed map of the Thames estuary. She took as long as she could, trying to memorize the red arrows on the map that must indicate attack plans. Meriel couldn't help but notice the plate of rich Dutch butter and new-baked bread. She thought she would be able to sniff out warm bread even at her last moments, then quickly retreated from that thought.

"I cannot tell you, dear Countess, how much I have longed for your arrival," de Witt said, turning.

There was a strange shiver in his voice, almost as if he were laughing uproariously under that curled wig and intelligent face.

He opened the packet and removed the dispatches, looking up at her occasionally and nodding. "Good work, my lady. I have never seen better."

Meriel nodded as if praise was her expectation. "Of course. Now, if you will show me to my quarters, I will await transfer to the first ship leaving for Holland. . . . With all promised treasure . . . unless you have dispatches to send back to London." She couldn't mention what that treasure would be, since it had not been discovered as she left the Tower. She added, "According to our bargain."

De Witt bowed, most courteously. "It is indeed my bargain with the great Countess of Warborough, and I do not forget."

The cabin door behind Meriel opened and she turned abruptly, the skin on the back of her neck giving her a sharp warning too late to heed.

Felice, Countess of Warborough, stood in the threshold, light from the companionway making a halo around her head, but it was a devil's voice that issued from her mouth. "This serving wench is the poor counterfeit I told you Chiffinch bragged about before I escaped from the Bowyer Tower. Throw her overboard!"

De Witt shook his head, looking on Meriel with pity. "Ah, my dear Countess Felice, we Hollanders are a gentle nation of traders and tulip growers. First, we must take her to our country and duly try this imposter for an enemy spy. Although it would be a shame to put a rope around that pretty neck, and if you will pardon me for saying it, Countess: Whoever she is, she has the loveliest neck on this ship."

Chapter Sixteen

In Which a Plot Unravels

Lord Giles waited in the shadows outside the garden wall where the carriageway turned past Harringdon Hall and connected to the Great Yarmouth road. As Dr. Wyndham's carriage stopped, one long-fingered hand loosened its firm grip on Agnes's throat. "Call him to you," Giles said in a low, rasping voice.

Giles meant her to fear him more than she feared failing whomever she served. Her answer confirmed his success.

"Doctor," she choked. "Over here, quickly."

The doctor's desperate whisper answered, "Agnes, we must away before we are discovered!"

Giles stepped into the lantern light. "Your confederate is my prisoner, physician. And if you attempt to leave before you fully answer my demands, I'll have the sheriff on you both for kidnapping my countess . . . providing you escape my mercies."

Reluctantly, Dr. Wyndham lowered himself from the carriage and gave a little jump to the ground. He bowed. "I am truly at your service, my lord, for I am ready to quit this ugly business, even to losing my post at court."

"Keep your court position, sir, but tell me what I demand. Now follow me, and no trickery. I have guards about the grounds and you could not leave . . . not alive. Those are my orders, so doubt me at your peril."

If nothing else had, the methodical, uninflected cadence of Lord Giles's anguished words convinced the little doctor to obey.

Giles turned his back in scorn on the slow-moving pair and walked into the great hall. A sleepy spit boy on his way to light the roasting fires stopped and stared in droopy-eyed alarm until Giles waved him away toward the summer kitchens.

Agnes settled into a chair by the fireplace, from all appearances in a near faint.

Giles roared at Dr. Wyndham. "Now speak, Doctor. Where did you take my wife?"

"To a chandler's shop in Great Yarmouth on the quayside, as I was instructed."

Agnes cried out. "Doctor, beware of saying more!"

"No, mistress, this mission is unworthy of a great country and a great king." Dr. Wyndham straightened his shoulders and his jaw, his face full of resolve.

Giles kept all puzzlement from his face. He would learn more from them if they thought he knew more than he did. He stepped toward the doctor, his large shadow high on the wall, overwhelming the smaller one. "Tell me what I ask, but answer me true on your life. You took her to await a ship back to Whitehall and the king."

Agnes interrupted: "A carriage, Doctor . . . a carriage."

The doctor shook his head vigorously. "Your lordship, on my honor, I know naught of any plan for either ship or carriage. I am a simple physician, graduate of the University of

Padua and of Bologna, renowned for healing in the capitals of Europe—"

Giles took a menacing step nearer, blinded by his anger and the clouds of deception that rose from these two, obscuring his deep need to understand . . . whether or not Merry had gone willingly. "Then, as with most doctors of physic, sir, you are a master at confirming what your patients don't know."

Dr. Wyndham drew himself up to a height he rarely obtained. "My lord, you may do as you will with me for this sorry business, but I will not agree to listen quietly to the scorn of my noble profession."

If Giles had any humor left, he would have smiled with admiration at such valor from so unlikely a source. Instead, he rounded on Agnes. "Is this the tale of it? The chandler made passage for her ladyship to London one way or the other. Why not by the doctor's coach? I cannot believe the king would send her into the Channel with the Hollanders lurking offshore."

Agnes was speechless, her mouth gaping, her face ashen in an obvious near faint, or at least a worthy imitation, which Giles thought as likely. A woman who spied had little to protect her when caught out but the appeal of her feminine weakness.

Giles paced the full length of the hall, his shadow looming over all. He could make no sense of this. He had known the king from the day of his coronation and had been a gentleman of his bedchamber on daily intimate terms with his monarch. Yes, Charles Stuart was a man led by his cod, and with an exceeding need for women beyond even a growing lad's, but he would never take a woman against her will. There was less need for this king to corrupt a countess for his bed than there was need for more water in the ocean. Did

that mean that Merry had gone willingly? That all they had
shared these last days had been playact? That all he had felt
true in his deepest soul had been false? That he could never
again trust his own heart? He tried to make himself believe
it, for it was the only seeming answer. But each time Merry's
face rose in his mind, her lips begging for his kiss, he could
not.

He stopped abruptly before his two captives. "There has
to be more to this that I am not told. Tell me now, or I will
surely hold you both for the next assizes on the charge of
kidnap. It will not go easy for you, I promise that on my
honor." He disliked threatening a servant maid and the doctor, whom he admired against his own desire to despise him.
But he had no choice.

The doctor looked at Agnes and shook his head sadly. "I
can no longer do such work, e'en for His Majesty, and most
certainly not for William Chiffinch. Since I know little, you
must tell his lordship everything. At once!"

Agnes's hand trembled against her breast and, eyes
avoiding Giles's face, she said, "My lord, she is under orders
from the king's spymaster, as am I. She has gone of her own
will to deliver ciphers to the Dutch to warn them off an attack with false tales of huge new defenses of the city and
many fire ships in the Pool of London. The doctor played no
part except as forced messenger."

Giles straightened, shock writ on his face and in the
stonelike stiffness of his body. "A spy? Against the Dutch?
The king and his spymaster have sent my wife into the
enemy's hands, knowing the enmity they hold for me from
the Battle of the Four Days!" His voice was rising beyond
his efforts to control, while his heart sang a song he had
never thought to hear: *She is no whore, but an English sub-*
ject working for her country. All this time, she appeared to

play me false, but was true and brave as no woman ever be-
fore. . . . My valiant lady playing a dangerous game.

"My lord," the doctor began, "your wife is not—"

A swift kick from Agnes had him bent double, clutching his shin. "Say more, Doctor, and lose your head!"

Giles roared. "I command you to say it!"

Dr. Wyndham mumbled, "I beg your pardon most humbly, your lordship, but what is left to be told must come from . . . your wife." He gulped air into his lungs and concluded, "You must realize that all is now too late."

Agnes looked up as the gray light of dawn began to fill the high windows in the hall. "Aye, my lord. Felice is taken to the Dutch warship *De Zeven Provenciën* at first light. I will pray for her. It is all that I can do."

Giles's voice returned from some dark depth. "How was she to escape?"

"Our information is"—Agnes took a shallow breath—"that she would be taken to Holland by a packet sent for that purpose with ample treasure for her services . . . if they believed her ciphers."

"There is more you are not telling me. I cannot take the time to wring it from you, but I promise you will both suffer if any harm comes to her." Giles thrust a pistola in each boot, drew on a cloak, and called for his majordomo, who appeared as if he never slept. "Have my horse saddled and brought round. Pack my saddlebags with a plain black suit and sturdy boots and send to Tom Barnes at once and tell him to ready the ketch, dismount the bow culverin and take it below out of sight. I will be with him at the dock within the hour."

Giles grasped his rapier and baldric from the great table, buckling it under his cloak. "I leave you to pray, Doctor, and you to hope, Agnes. But I will go for her and bring her home if I have to fight both Cornelis de Witt and Admiral de Ruyter."

Agnes shrank into herself. "You cannot hope to win against all their guns."

"Obvious. I must outsmart them, and you've given me the way."

The doctor looked up from his clasped hands. "Are we free to return to London, your lordship? I have a wife with a babe in her belly, and patients who are ill served by others' physic."

Already the tail of Giles's cloak was disappearing out the high stone entrance of Harringdon Hall.

Two sailors helped shove Meriel from de Witt's spacious cabin into an adjoining room scarcely the size of a large horse stall.

Felice ordered her captive's body wrapped in a hammock until she could not move. De Witt confirmed her wish to his men in the Hollander's tongue.

Felice stood over her, triumphant. "Whoever you are, you are not even a good counterfeit. Sir, do you not think her features are much coarser than mine?"

Meriel, staring defiantly between the rope loops, assumed Felice had a heart, but saw no sign of it. Felice had lost the fresh beauty she claimed, but Meriel kept these observations to herself. Though young, perhaps twenty and five, Felice's face had begun to reflect the hard use to which she had put her body and her soul.

De Witt made the politic answer. "*Ja,* nor on close observation does this spy have your experienced manner, Countess."

"Or the burn mark, which I have carried since a childhood accident." Felice reached between the hammock's coils and lifted Meriel's hair, taking a step back, amazement and more anger on her face. "This cannot be!"

De Witt bent forward and lifted Meriel's hair. "William Chiffinch is a most formidable spymaster, *nee*?" He looked on Meriel with some pity in his broad face. "We Dutch have need of such a one. Indeed, only France with its Cardinals Richelieu and Mazarin is more clever than England with its Chiffinch. And perhaps not as ruthless."

Meriel had been countess for long enough to dislike being talked over as if she were a brainless servant. "Well, get on with it," she said, liking the defiance of the words, although being trussed reduced their intended bold effect. "Throw me overboard or hang me, but don't waste my remaining time when I would be about making my soul's peace."

Felice kicked her. "You make no demands here, you low-born bawd."

"Oh, la, how different from a highborn bawd? If you must talk so much tittle-tattle, then tell me, Felice, how you escaped the Tower." Meriel pretended the kick had not hurt, though her hip would probably bear a mark tomorrow. If she had a tomorrow. "I may have need of such knowledge if Chiffinch gets his hands on me ever again." It pleased Meriel to deliberately omit any title or servile speech.

She put on an impish grin and a broad wink for de Witt, who was frankly admiring her through the hempen ropes tightly crisscrossing her bosom. "The Tower would surely be my lot, if you let me go." Meriel pretended anguish. "What a dilemma for a representative of the Dutch States-General, sir. Hanging a woman from your yardarm would surely alter your country's gentle reputation for coffee trading and tulip growing for some time to come." *Hey, well, I will gain more admiration with defiance, though I doubt much more leniency!*

"*Ja,* I am tempted to return you to your spymaster with my compliments. Unless—" He let the word hang in the air. "You might be persuaded to work for us in truth. We will not have my lady Felice in London, and we could use a bold one like you, who, I don't doubt, has intrigued Chiffinch and half the court. . . . Perhaps Lord Giles himself." His face suggested more than his words. "*Ja,* quite tempted."

Although he didn't sound as tempted as Meriel would have liked, she laughed gaily. It proved an unsuccessful attempt and sounded more a gargle. "Are you offering a bargain, sir?" At least if she kept de Witt engaged, even challenged, they would not be putting a rope around her neck in the next few minutes.

Felice was furious, almost spitting the words at her. "You make no haggle here, bawd, as in the whore that spawned you!"

"And what whore would that be?" Meriel spit back.

"I will be the questioner, spy. Tell us your story and take care, for we know much already."

Meriel ignored her, looking to de Witt and keeping her voice vivacious to engage the regard for her that was all too apparent. "Then, sir, if you do not command here as it appears, make an end to me. I might enjoy a little hanging, since that would tend to lengthen the graceful neck you earlier admired, and stop this traitor's prattle in my ears." Meriel had always observed that what was first requested was usually last granted. She hoped this request would be no exception.

De Witt grinned. "Mistress, you make me happy we do not fight Englisher women."

Meriel laughed. "Do you not, Cornelis?"

This angered Felice more. "Cornelis? Do you allow her to cozen you? Take her below with the rats. That will loosen her tongue, or I will do it for her."

He bowed to Felice, but without a flourish. "*Ja,* I believe you would, but you forget yourself, my dear countess. I command here."

Felice held her next words, though Meriel thought her only temporarily halted.

De Witt stepped to his main cabin door and spoke to an officer in words that Meriel could not understand. She did understand the two sailors who appeared and carried her trussed up on deck like an ewe for market and thence down into the hold.

Thus far, she thought, as the seamen climbed back up to the deck, leaving her in the dark, Felice and her Hollanders were trying to frighten her in hopes of discovering more of her business. And from the way her heart thudded under her breast, they might be close to success. Was she a coward? Would she tell all when faced with the noose?

Her mind raced to find some plausible story. She had not exactly admitted to being Chiffinch's spy. They had assumed so and she had jollied them. But she could think of no other explanation for her presence on this Dutch warship that did not involve witchery or angels. Nor could she think of any escape. Except for de Witt, who might prove to be an unexpected friend, for it was certain he neither respected nor admired the Countess Felice.

Giles galloped toward Great Yarmouth in the glow of first light without his usual appreciation of morning sun flowing over pastures and fields already showing good spring crop growth. Everywhere in his mind, he saw his wife as she was now: the sweet curve of her body under his hands, the hard and bitter shell of the court beauty replaced by a soft and yielding girl, who must always have been there and who seemed touched by new love.

As he was.

He would not lose her again to Whitehall as once he thought he had. Now he understood her behavior of last night and those last words: *Remember our oak tree!*

With his heart pounding in time to his horse's hooves, he clattered onto the streets of the harbor town and straight into a fruit seller's stall, scattering Spanish oranges everywhere. Giles reined in, his horse dancing in a circle. He untied his purse and tossed it to the vendor, leaving him openmouthed and richer by a month's receipts.

Tom Barnes waited quayside, the bow ropes half untied in his hands. "The crew be here, my lord, though I had to pull them from their warm beds."

"Gather on the foredeck, Tom."

With a quick touch of two fingers to his head, Tom wrapped the bow ropes securely and ran aboard, returning with four men, all deepwater sailors by their weathered faces and rolling gait.

Giles stepped to the deck and stood amongst his men. "My lady is now aboard a ship in the Dutch fleet, which is sailing south and up to some mischief against England. This ketch is of Dutch design. I mean to go out flying their flag as a packet sent to take her to Holland. A gold sovereign for any Englishman who helps me."

One man studied his bare toes. "That be temptation aplenty for a poor man, my lord, but the Hollanders have seventy-gun warships. They could blow us to smithereens, if ye don't fool them."

"I speak their language. I'll make them believe me."

"And what if they don't, my lord?"

"Any man wishing to go ashore is free to leave my service," Giles said in a tone that said he was finished with talk. "The rest of you cast off and make all sail."

The sailor who had no taste for Dutch cannonballs jumped to the dock. The rest cast off and hauled on the mainsail, which caught the wind and propelled them into the Channel.

Giles took the helm, setting an easterly course, shouting for all sails to be raised, and steered the ketch with the wind until it seemed to skim the waves like a seagull looking for a fish to break its fast.

He tried to keep a lighter touch on the helm as he changed into his solemn Dutch captain's clothing, but he found himself gripping the wheel, as if he could urge on the little ship faster with the sheer strength in his arms. He shouted continuous orders, raising and lowering sail to take advantage of every shift of wind.

Tom brought him ale, which he drank down quickly to warm his stomach, and bread, which he ate wet with spray, not tasting either. Nothing mattered, not comfort, not safety, not even his ketch, which he had built with his own hands and loved above all ships. Only this new Felice, this Merry, as he thought of her now, held his regard. She had become his world.

Meriel awoke in the dark hold, smelling rotted salt meat and worse. She tried to move but was still wrapped in the hempen hammock. It proved a tighter binding even than those she'd worn as a child at the charity house when punished in the miniature stocks thought fitting for orphans: those who swam in the Stour, disobeyed the master, stole bread or failed to beg enough pennies with their fake crutches.

Her stomach growled at the very thought of bread. She'd gladly sit in the stocks again for a piece of that warm bread and thick Dutch butter resting on de Witt's map table. For a moment she was grateful for the hunger that kept her mind from Giles, and what he was doing and thinking.

She felt the knife along her thigh, but could not reach it.

A rat's claws skittered on the wood deck, a scrambling rat brushing against her foot. She kicked out as best she could in her rope cocoon. Shuddering, she turned her mind to anything but what was happening to her. And what Felice might be planning.

The little doctor and Agnes must be well on the south road to London by this time. And Giles? She smiled ruefully. *Hey, well, so I can't keep my mind from him.* Had he gone after the doctor's coach, thinking to find her? Or was he so angry that the old Felice had come again that he had finally ceased to care?

Against her will, she dozed and woke several times. With the overhead hatch closed she had no idea what time had passed, whether it was yet day or dusk. She was still wondering when she heard many feet running on the deck over her head, back and forth, and the sound of faintly shouted orders.

Meriel looked up as if she could see through the planking, and waited to hear the loud boom of a great gun. She had not long to wait. A cannon boomed and the ship rocked to starboard, then she heard nothing. After the silence came worse. She didn't need to know the language to understand shouts of triumph.

Was an English warship taken so easily?

Though she tried to force her mind to focus on all the reasons why it could not be so, there was one answer that resisted all her effort to reject.

Giles!

Chapter Seventeen

No Greater Deceit Confess'd

Sabers drawn, Dutch sailors swarmed down the starboard side of *De Zeven Provenciën* and boarded the ketch.

"Steady on, men," Tom Barnes said to the three English crew. "Give the Hollanders no cause ter kill yer. Lord Giles be needing us."

One English sailor held Giles's bleeding head as he lay on the deck, barely conscious, a handkerchief tied about his blood-matted hair.

Cornelis de Witt called down to the English seaman, "Bring Lord Giles up—carefully now. We'll take your ketch in tow. We may have use of it later."

A sling was ordered, but by the time it was lowered, Giles had staggered to his feet and stood braced against the shattered railing. "Tom, make all fast," he said, holding his voice steady for his men. He pushed away all help and slowly climbed the ladder to the enemy deck, gripping each step and blinking hard to force his eyes to see the next rung clearly. He scarcely felt the prodding pistol of the Dutch officer behind him.

On deck, de Witt bowed to him as the English crew was marched to the forward hold with muskets at their backs.

Giles returned de Witt's courtesy, and unbuckling his baldric surrendered his sword, saying in perfect Hollander formal words he had never thought in this life to say: *"Ik ben uw gevangene."* He had always planned to die before losing his sword or telling a triumphant enemy *I am your prisoner.* But Merry had changed his wish to die gloriously in battle to living gloriously for her, though he thought her much crazed to take on spying, no matter how well intended. And without consulting him. True, they had been estranged much of the time. Finally, his head ached too much from the wood splinter that had grazed him to assign blame. Damned foul luck! How was he to know that de Witt would be on deck and he'd recognize the Dutch captain come out to take the Countess of Warborough to Holland. Would knowing have stopped him? No, but he wouldn't have risked his men's lives. If it was ransom the Hollanders wanted, he'd pay it.

De Witt motioned for Giles to follow him below, and Giles did so, holding himself rigidly upright, refusing to take hold of his head though it pounded like all the demons in the bottom of a brandy barrel. "My wife, sir, the Countess Felice . . . is she well? What have you done with her?"

"All in good time, my lord of Warborough," de Witt answered formally enough, though with an attitude of high good humor that would have brought a challenge had Giles been in any position to deliver one.

They descended to a bright cabin obviously occupied by Cornelis de Witt, a Dutch plenipotentiary and brother of the leader of the governing States-General of Holland. Giles recognized him from his earlier diplomatic missions before the war and had been known in turn. So this was indeed a real attack on England and not a feint to gain advantage at the bargaining table. Giles accepted subterfuge as part of war, since he knew that English ships were attacking Hollanders at sea, peace talks or no. But his mind swarmed with other questions, real questions. Why was he not taken to Merry immediately? De Witt was a gentleman not given to mean-spirited games.

"Be seated, your lordship," he said, motioning for his men to search Giles.

They removed his boots and took his pistolas, while de Witt smiled amiably.

De Witt dismissed his men. "It grieves me, my lord, to see you injured, though it was exactly the foolish bravery I might expect of you. And you might have fooled any other captain. . . . Ah, m'lord, please accept my deepest apologies for foiling such a courageous act. You have great spirit, *nee,* though I could not have imagined so bold a move." De Witt bowed again, real admiration on his face accompanying a puzzled frown. Briskly tapping his map table, he added, "I have sent for my surgeon and will try to give you what comfort a warship can supply to an enemy during your stay with us, which will not be long if our business goes as I and Admiral de Ruyter plan it." He grinned widely, his round face flushed with patriotic pride.

Since de Witt chose to speak English, perhaps not to be overheard by his crew, Giles answered him in like manner. "I need no comfort, sir, beyond knowledge of my wife's safety. How long are we to be your guests?"

"An uninvited guest on your part, my lord," de Witt corrected. "And do please sit. Head wounds can be grievous hurtful."

Giles decided it would be churlish to refuse, and his head was spinning with the effort to remain standing, though he could see that towering over the shorter, thicker Hollander gave him some small advantage.

The surgeon bustled in, cleaned the wound and pronounced it not serious, a glancing blow from a piece of the rail smashed by the single cannonball. He bled Giles, produced a foul-tasting blood tonic for which he rattled off a list of ingredients, which included the full-moon-picked leaves of a rare scarlet tulip. Then he applied a stinging poultice bandage and left, ordering the patient to rest and stay clear of too much exposure to fresh air. This last was said with a smirk.

De Witt offered food, which Giles refused, hoping not to regret it later, and a tankard of strong beer, which he accepted with thanks. "My wife, sir," Giles insisted in a tone not to be longer denied. "I fear she has been misguided by those who would take advantage of her . . . innocence."

Taking a seat behind his map table, de Witt nodded, though with one eyebrow raised. "I believe you think it, my lord of Warborough," he answered, now clearly amused. "I could not possibly agree. The Lady Felice did come to us of her own will in want of funds you would not supply a needy wife, according to her tale." He shrugged as one husband to another. "Yet has she been long a loyal courier to the States-General, e'en while you warred against us in the Battle of the Four Days." Though there was some triumph in the words, a gentleman's regret was there also.

Giles pretended ignorance, but it was difficult to keep the shock from his face. Had not his wife taken up spying but recently, and not years past when he had restricted her allowance? "I do not believe it, sir," Giles said. "Bring me to her, for I would hear it from her own lips." Was de Witt playing an enemy's game to discover what a husband knew of this business, or could add to save the life of a wife he loved enough at risk to his own? Had Merry made a triumph of her work for Chiffinch? Or been exposed? Questions rose one after another like surf pounding against Dover's cliffs, and nothing was answered, each question making his hard-sought sureties murkier, bringing him to ask the most difficult question: Was the change from Felice to Merry that he had gloried in to be the last and most cruel betrayal?

De Witt lowered his voice. "My dear Lord Giles, I regret that we meet again in such circumstances, for I know you to be an honorable man who wears his love for his wife on his face and is a patriot of renown in both our countries. Yet must I ask you for information, as is my duty when an Englisher nobleman is captured pretending to be a countryman. By the law of the sea, I could have you hung for a spy."

Giles held his aching head even higher. "Do your duty, sir. As I will do mine and refuse you information."

Undeterred, the Hollander tapped a feathered quill against a map, showing the mouth of the Thames and its islands. "You are of the court and in the confidence of your king, close to secrets of the Admiralty. If you tell me what we need to know of the strengthening of these defenses during the month past while your lady was . . . er, sojourning in the Tower"—he ignored Giles's leap to his feet—"and, my lord, the defenses from the fort of Sheerness to Upnor Castle." He raised his quill. "And thence on upriver to Chatham. I especially want to know how the chain across the river at Gillingham is now situated and at what depth, and beyond to your city of London—"

Giles, his head spinning from all de Witt had said and the sudden lunge to his feet, nevertheless was incredulous at that last statement. "You intend to strike at a city laid waste once by plague and again by fire! That is dishonorable, sir, and I would not have thought it. And you are mistook about the Tower. My wife was with me except for a week at Harringdon Hall." He tried to remember. Was not it on her return that he began to notice such a great change?

De Witt tightened his jaw. "Seat yourself, my lord. War is not honorable or dishonorable, as is spying, but merely nec-

essary, all men being but men and most easily bought."
Amused as well as triumphant, he smirked a bit. "Or in this
case, women."

"You insult me, sir, to think me capable of being traitor
to all I e'er fought to defend. Or that my countess is such.
What I *will* tell you is that you lead your fleet into certain
disaster against superior forces."

It was obvious to Giles that de Witt's generous smile
meant that he had better information. Merry? His heart felt
squeezed between what he had heard and what he desperately wished to believe.

De Witt continued, "Then many Englishmen will die that
you could have saved."

"No true subject of His Majesty, King Charles, would
want his life spared to the ruin of his country's fleet or
chiefest city, sir."

A side door opened and Felice, the Countess of Warborough, stepped into the light of the cabin windows. "Oh, la,
my lord husband," she said, highly amused in her turn.
"Here is one subject of the king who will have her life
spared and a goodly treasure into the bargain. You are yet
impossibly noble, attempting rescue of Chiffinch's slut. She
must have given you a very good ride indeed."

This was Felice, but the old Felice, her face hard again as
if her new sweet vulnerability had peeled away. Giles took a
hesitant step toward her, nearly losing his balance except for
grabbing the map table that stood in his way. "Merry?"

"Halt!" Two men answered de Witt's shout. One of them
using his pistola butt hit the back of Giles's head as he
reached for Felice.

"The wound has affected his mind, Cornelis," Felice said,
rounding the table to stare down with curiosity at her husband's

crumpled body. "He thinks me the other when the difference is more than plain."

"Indeed, my dear countess, I believe he does think you the counterfeit, the woman he risked his life for, which answers some questions and raises other quite interesting ones."

Meriel had ceased to strain her ears, unable to decipher any of the faint sounds coming from the deck above. She was aware that the ship, which was hove to after the cannon fire, had turned her bow once again to meet the Channel waves, running before the wind.

The hammock ropes had loosened from her tugging just enough for her to sense the lump in the purse tied round her waist, which had slipped almost to her knees. Wyndham's Infallible Miracle Salve! She felt the small waxen packet she had happily thought to bring with her. *Hey, well, a young miss already in the prime of youth must always care for her face upon the sea, if she wishes to remain . . . prime!*

Meriel inched up her gown and between two fingers was able to open the packet on one end, squeezing the dewy, slippery salve against the ropes until she was able to slide up the knife in its sheath on her thigh. She said a prayer of thanks for the little doctor's nostrum, then busied herself severing rope loops along her leg as far as she could reach until the hatch opened and light came streaming in, almost blinding her.

She rolled to her side to hide the opening in her rope prison, wondering if Felice or de Witt or both would descend into the hold to taunt her. Several seamen carried a heavy bundle to the bottom, shouting words she did not know but could readily guess were aimed against such work. They dropped their load none too gently before retreating back up through the hatch, slamming it shut.

The bundle groaned and cursed. "Cock's life!"

Frantically, Meriel began to roll in the dark toward the hatchway, crushing the little vial of laudanum the doctor had given her to help her withstand torture.

Giles gasped out a challenge in Hollander. When she didn't answer, he shouted in English, "Who shares this rat's den with me?"

Meriel could have touched him if her hands had been free. But would she have dared without knowing what he knew and what he thought about it? Had he changed from the lover he had been at Harringdon Hall to an avenger?

"Speak your name!" Giles ordered.

"Merry," she whispered.

"But—"

The one word was followed by silence, though she could almost hear him organizing what he did know and guessing at what he did not. "For Christ's sweet sake, Giles, please . . ."

Finally, after agonizing in the black darkness and even blacker silence, he spoke in a tone of inquiry, as if sorting the words into recognizable heaps. "I left my countess in de Witt's cabin, claiming you a counterfeit. You are Merry? Your voice is as I remember it . . . in a recent night. And that was not the voice I heard in de Witt's cabin." There was a short, thick pause before he spoke words she had hoped never to hear: "Damn you for a liar. Who are you?"

There was nothing left but truth before death, either from the Dutch or from Chiffinch . . . or perhaps from an enraged Giles himself. Any magistrate would grant an earl that he had just cause. Her breath trembling, she said, "I am Meriel St. Thomas . . . the Merry of the last days at court, the Merry of your bed and of the oak tree." Then, her heart pounding in her throat, she was completely breathless, done, destroyed.

His voice rasped out a denial. "But your face . . . we do not live in an age of miracles."

Her breath hardly came to her in time. "You are most wrong, Giles. In any age, the love we shared is a miracle."

"You dare speak of a lie as love! My meaning is of your perfect match to Felice, as a twin babe from the same womb, and yet there were differences from the first. I saw them, and didn't believe them."

"You believed them. You wanted to believe them. I know you did."

He hated her at that moment because he knew she was right. He'd been a willing dupe, but he would not admit it. "You know nothing, girl, but how to turn love to lies! In that even Felice is not your peer."

Giles's words had been wrung from some deep, wounded place in his soul. Meriel knew his heart and mind had snapped shut against her. It was in his tone, in his words, in the air, suffocating her. And yet she had to hope for his understanding, or what use was her next breath?

She could hear him moving, perhaps sitting, his breathing labored. "Are you hurt?" she asked.

"What I am is not your concern. Speak the truth or speak not at all."

"Yes, my lord, I will speak the burden that I have carried these several weeks, and rid myself of it, no matter what the cost." Being practical, she added: "But I could speak more clearly if I were not choked in rope."

"My hands and feet are tied."

"I have a knife and have it free of its sheath. They ne'er thought to search a woman."

"I will not make such a mistake now that I know any gown can hold a Judas."

Ordinarily, Meriel would have disputed how men thought

women incapable of cleverness, but she could not answer this accusation. "When you hear my story, you may see I had no choice."

"There is always choice." He grunted with some great effort. "Can you reach my bindings?"

"Move to the sound of my voice, as I have almost freed one arm." She felt a little hope return as he inched closer, and wondered briefly if he remembered all that had passed between them as she did, or if those gentle hands would reach for her throat. Somehow, the possibility did not concern her, since if Giles was lost to her, she would end her life as it had started. Alone.

It took some interminable time, but she sawed through the ropes on his hands, and he, taking the knife, freed his legs.

For a minute Giles hesitated, holding the knife in the faint light from the hatch rim, and staring into its dull glint.

"You would get no blame from me if you plunged the knife into my heart." Her voice caught on the last word. "You would have my blessing, for I have done you a great wrong . . . though the fault was not mine."

"Whose fault then, Mistress Merry, although that is not your true name?"

"It is my truest name, and I followed Chiffinch's orders and the king's to save my life and for England. It is not just men who can fight for their country." She paused, breathing deeply, so many words trying to crowd into her mouth, she hardly knew what to say first. "Believe me, I always thought to do more good than harm in my pretense to be your countess. . . . And I had always—" She stopped as she felt the knife begin to cut through the hammock ropes and they fell away from her body one by one.

"Always?"

"Esteemed you above other men."

He laughed a bitter laugh she had heard before when she had first met him at court in what seemed a far-gone time. "Then, Mistress Spy, I pity the man you do not esteem."

When she was free, he moved away from her, keeping the knife. She saw no blame in that. He wanted no tale of hers, and none she told would he believe. She knew that she had lost him. No man under God's heaven could forgive what she had done. A man can be cheated of his money, of his property, even of his honor, but not of his given love. That is an unforgivable and bitter acid that eats at all manly pride, for it is the rejection of his essence. This was a truth any woman grown knew without a need to be told.

In the dark, she heard him breathing, steadier with each breath, and she began to speak quietly. Whether he wanted to hear or no, she would speak. If she were to die in this hell of a Dutch ship hold, she would die without a lie on her conscience. Even the rats stopped their scrabbling about to listen as she unburdened her deepest self.

Meriel told him all to his face, or rather she told it in front of the sound of his breathing in the dank darkness. She looked into the mirror of memory and recited everything from the moment she arrived in court and was mistaken by Chiffinch, kidnapped and borne away to the Tower, then taught the trade of a spy, albeit a spy for England. She said nothing of Felice. At last, she fell silent.

"You were a servant in Admiral Cheatham's household."

"Yes, personal maid to his lady."

"While you are in the way of truth, tell me . . . Felice is the traitor, and Chiffinch used you in her stead. Is that the right of it?"

She hesitated, but finally whispered, "Yes." She would not pile lie upon lie. She would tell him about her own web of deceit, but she would not tell the depth of Felice's wickedness, for which she had endured much to protect him from knowing.

"My countess a traitor against all I e'er fought for," Giles said in a wondering, agonized voice. "I am disgraced!"

Meriel rounded on Giles's faint outline. "How so, sir? No man can be disgraced by another. Your brave deeds are not diminished by what your wife has made of herself. She can not subtract from your glory. I think that is a male idea no woman would truly believe."

"And now you are a petticoat philosopher! Is there no end to your talent?" He was silent for long minutes, ashamed of that bitter sarcasm when it was obvious to him that she had pulled every painful word from her deepest self. "My pardon, mistress." He could not bring himself to call her Merry. He had buried that name to keep at least some of what it had meant to him.

Of a certainty, he was happy that Felice had been stopped in her betrayal, or at least exposed. But a question of equal importance haunted him: Had this woman who shared his captivity made love to him only as part of her masquerade, or had there been more to it? Surely, he could not be so completely wrong in what he remembered, the look on her face, the tenderness of her embrace, the tears. . . . Nay, he would swear the tears were real.

Finally, Giles lifted his head from his arms where it had rested during this entire tale. He was all amazed, and doubted he would ever be less so. He was not ready to share the first question on his mind, so he asked the next question. "Are you telling me that you learned to be a lady in less than a fortnight? That it is so easy for a commoner to transform to a coroneted peeress of the court!"

Meriel ruffled, thinking this *would* be the question an aristocrat would ask of a serving maid. "M'lord earl, you think it so difficult to imitate speech, manners, carriage! You imagine it unlikely that a servant could so quickly accommodate to silk, powder and jewels, not to mention seven meat dishes at the clap of her beringed and softened hands!"

Giles refused her an answer. But he heard her stand and begin to pace about, hearing her hands hit the mast that ran down the middle of the hold they were in, for balance, he supposed, against the ship's roll. He almost stood to support her before stopping himself from touching a body he couldn't trust.

"Nothing to ask now, my lord?" She was showing a temper, but she didn't care. "Allow me to tell you what *is* difficult to learn for a serving maid from a decent family. Expected to deceive a husband in the bed of others less worthy . . . many others . . . and glorying in it. Being kidnapped by a duke who does not keep his underlinen clean. Bowing low and pretending to respect those whose greatest career and delight is in scandal, whoring, cuckolding and cheating honest tradesmen of their due receipts."

In spite of his desire not to, he stood and came closer, facing her to stop her tormenting, too-truthful language. "Cock's life! You think to charm me with your truth now! You cozened my love from me and now I find it ripped away. I vow you have no pretty words for that, Meriel St. Thomas!"

Meriel's eyes, adjusting further to the dark, began to see shapes more clearly, especially Giles's broad shoulders as he faced her.

She would not shrink. Her guilt was now primed with anger because she had lost him. "I confess that I have done you wrong. Kill me if you will with that knife you hold in your hand. I do not ask your understanding. How could you . . . a man . . . a peer of the realm with the wealth and power of generations . . . understand what I am, what I need, what I can be made to do to live and to eat another day? Did you ever fight for a crust of bread? Endure a whipping? Sleep on filthy straw after the animals had finished with it? Were you turned a whore at twelve years by a brute of a stable boy, and left bleeding and in fear of being sent into the streets with a great belly?" Her breath gave out.

"You're asking something of me with this tale that I cannot give."

"You do not believe me?"

"Oh, but I do. Not even Cervantes—you remember Cervantes—could dream up a tale like that one."

Meriel shivered as the words, loaded with memory, reached her. Expecting the knife to follow, she braced herself. "Do it! Release me from this misery."

"No," he said. "I will not release you." He did not know exactly what he meant by those words, nor did he want to know. "Leave off this torment!"

He went to the farthest place to sit upon the hatchway stairs.

She spent the next hours watching the struggle that showed on his face in the faint light creeping around the hatch cover. . . . Much against her will, but without the strength to avert her eyes.

They were both sleeping, exhausted in body and spirit, when the hatch opened and de Witt, followed by Felice, descended into the hold.

Chapter Eighteen

~

The Salt Is Passed

Blinking against the sudden light flooding into every corner of the hold, Giles stood to his full height, his head thumping hard against the ceiling, but fearing a megrim less than appearing weak before the enemy . . . all his enemies, the Hollander, his wife and even Chiffinch's spy, whom he yet could not call by the name that had become completely dear to him.

"They are out of their bonds, Cornelis," Lady Felice said, looking around de Witt's shoulder, a bit of fright mixed with her cruel hauteur.

"I see that," de Witt answered, not obviously concerned. "There are more than eight hundred good Dutch seamen above, some of them with memories of fighting him last year, perhaps a match even for the Earl of Warborough." De Witt bowed without mockery.

Meriel stood, bracing her back as best she could against the moving bulkhead, refusing to grovel on the deck at their feet, or to imagine what Giles was thinking or not thinking. Or feeling. If he felt anything at all, and that was more than she allowed herself to hope for.

Felice stayed behind the protection of the Dutch plenipotentiary. "Cornelis, they must have a weapon."

Giles saw the uselessness of trying to keep the knife and bearing the indignity of having hands probe his person. He shrugged and handed it over to de Witt with an insultingly short bow. "It has served its purpose, sir. We had need to beat off your Hollander rats, fat on your cheese stores."

De Witt smiled, refusing to be goaded by the familiar English taunt.

Meriel thought de Witt a man much given to irony, and in a way he was rather enjoying the drama of a man with two identical wives unfolding before him. She stepped forward and grasped the mast. She would not allow this group of aristocrats to plague Giles or ignore her.

"You can be rid of us easily, my lord. Set us ashore." Her voice was one of command and it pleased her because she had not planned it thus. The tone had just been there when she needed it. Once again she wondered why command was more natural than submission, and she a servant her life long.

Felice laughed, and Meriel thought she had never heard so much of evil locked in merriment. "More like, we throw you to the fo'c'sle crew for their night's enjoyment. Surely, such a low person can jig and sing like the orange girls in the pit at the Theater Royal. Perhaps not so well as Mistress Nellie or—"

"Not so well as *your ladyship,*" Meriel responded, growing mightily irked at this lady libertine's superior manner. "Your reputation is no state secret. I found those universally high expectations of your bed's availability by every court spark the most difficult part of my disguise. It took all my strength to fend off your expectant lovers." She curtsied slowly to underline her disdain, and saw her words hit their mark, although the countess pretended to ignore them, turning her head away. Or perhaps she truly was not concerned with what was said or thought about her. There were such people. Meriel stared at Felice more closely than she had done afore, because to see evil in a face so much her own was just too distressing. A person with no evident conscience was surely in league with the devil or his minions on earth.

But Felice was yet concerned with the niceties of her noble position. "Giles! You would allow this lowborn counterfeit to—"

"Cock's life! This counterfeit, as you name her, asks no permission of me and needs none. I heard not one falsehood." Giles turned his back to his countess, and there was something of finality in that move, as if for him she was no longer in the world.

Meriel watched, her heart needing to understand more than it could. Yes, she thought she had detected something in his voice when he spoke of her. Not forgiveness, nor affection. No, never those. But some smallish speck of acceptance, even . . . and she dared much to think it . . . admiration.

De Witt descended into the hold completely, Felice staying behind on the stairs, holding her skirts in obvious fear that they would touch something foul.

Meriel had to smile at that. How could this countess be more befouled than she was already? Whore. Adulterer. Traitor. What was fouler beyond those?

Felice caught her eye, and Meriel saw from her thunderous expression that she must sense the thoughts behind such amusement.

"Giles, you were ever easily led by a pretty face." She laughed a court laugh, brittle and with no mirth. "Oh, la, as it seems now, the *same* pretty face. But you and your king will pay for denying me what was mine by right. You for withdrawing my funds—"

Lord Warborough did not turn to face her, but stiffened. "Monies that you were spending in depravity, even to having my heir torn from your womb."

De Witt looked back at Felice in some horror. "*Mijn God! What company have I hired?*"

Felice lifted one shoulder, uncaring of either man's opinion. "As for Charles Stuart! A king who chose Babs Castlemaine o'er me. Why would I serve such a husband as you, or such a monarch as he?"

"Because we are wed in the sight of God and you are English born."

"I serve the god and country of Felice, and ever have," she said, laughing at his scruples.

Giles bit his tongue to contain further responses, all seamen's curses. For some reason, the king's spy tempered his anger. He would not bring shame on himself in her eyes. That he thought of her regard first didn't surprise him, but he wondered at it. How could he be so willing to forgive deceit again?

De Witt raised his hands. "Enough! There is much important business I must conclude before my admirals meet tomorrow to make an end to our attack plans. My apologies, Lord Warborough, for believing some hours belowdecks without food would bring you to give up the defense plans for Sheerness Fort, and for the chain, especially the chain. I won't think so ill of your capacity for suffering again. You and your most lovely counterfeit"—he bowed, smiling to Meriel—"will be treated humanely and fed well."

"Bread will not make me traitor," Giles answered.

"Nor me," Meriel said, removing a steadying hand from

the mast centered in the hold, riding the ship with legs spread like a born sailor as it dipped to meet the next waves.

"Then hang *her,* Cornelius, if your dainty stomach will not allow you to hang an earl!"

His face thunderous, de Witt rounded on Felice. Even the countess could see that she had gone too far, and quickly climbed back up to the hatch and disappeared on deck.

De Witt sighed. "I cannot apologize to a man for his own wife."

Giles faced de Witt, mouth rigid with disgust. "I congratulate you, sir, for removing her from my sight and my country. God help you and yours."

"Indeed, my lord, I do think I agree with you. But for now, I will keep my bargain with her as quickly as possible. For you and . . . er, the other lady, I offer you better quarters in the small cabin adjoining mine. I'm afraid for some time. At least several turns of the glass until the battle is finished." He bowed with regret writ in his features. "I fear that the Lady Felice might attempt to carry out an execution on her own, thus I will lock you in near to me and keep the key on my person. I do assure you, my lord, she has no access to my person."

Meriel sat on her bunk in the small cabin, a plate of crumbs and a few bites of excellent eel pie in front of her. De Witt had been as good as his word, supplying them with blankets, food, thick Dutch beer and a pisspot. Giles had rigged a blanket that gave privacy to the pot.

After inquiring politely as to a stranger if she preferred privacy in her bunk and without waiting for an answer, he hung another blanket down the middle of the cabin so small that her foot could kick the blanket. She did not know if he behaved as a gentleman would in such circumstances, or as one wishing her well out of his sight. She suspected the latter.

"You have the salt box," she reminded him, keeping all inflection from her voice.

He pushed it under the blanket without a word.

"My thanks, sir," she said in a high tone.

Before she could ask, he sent the bread loaf and the butter crock and the ever-present cheese after the salt. She dipped in a finger and tasted the thick Dutch butter, which was easy to love.

She thought not to thank him twice for his reluctant service, but decided she would prove to have better manners than a peer of the realm and a Garter knight. "Again, sir, my extreme and absolute humble thanks."

Meriel was certain that he, as she, could hear everything in the small space, every sigh, every movement, every step of the four she could take from cabin wall to outer bulkhead. She wanted to plead with him for understanding, but she would not, though she knew he was a man who had understanding in him. Had she not seen it? Felt it? She spent some time and effort shutting her mind to the memories of what she had felt with Earl Giles.

Several times she thought he took a deep breath to speak only to fling himself into his bunk, roll over and soon sit up again. Finally, there was only the sound of Channel waves breaking against the ship, of winches squeaking as they turned on deck and sailors' shouts to break the silence. She sat, her arms folded, her mouth stubbornly clamped. 'Od's bods, he must speak first.

When he did speak, his voice was so suddenly all around her that she jumped and gave a little cry of surprise. He repeated the first words of his question.

"Did you not say that you swam in the Stour as a child?"

"Yes."

"Was that true, or part of a spy's story to make me believe you were Felice?"

"True."

"Then you were Canterbury born?"

"I don't know. I was named for Thomas Becket since I was found as a newborn babe on the cathedral steps one morning. I was taken thence to a foundling hospital, and when five years of age to a charity house for orphans . . . where my good Sir Edward Cheatham found me."

"Sir Edward? I know him and never heard him speak of you."

"Did you talk of your servants to him?" She didn't expect an answer to her counterquestion and didn't get one.

"And what is your age now?"

"Twenty and two . . . and not like to live to another nativity day by the way of things. What means these questions? Do you know aught of my parentage?" There was no answer, and she was not surprised. Yet she took a deep breath and spoke one word so sweet on her tongue it sounded of honey: "Giles?"

But Giles did not respond and her temper flared. "My lord, does talk only go one way in your noble world? In mine, that is considered poor etiquette. You know that French word for right manners, do you not, Lord Warborough?"

Silence. She could not goad him into breaking this crushing silence, forcing him to acknowledge her. She needed to hear his voice say her name, to have him hold her, place his lips on hers. . . . And elsewhere . . . especially elsewhere . . . a very sore need.

Meriel took a deep breath, and said one word. "Please." Then another from deep in her throat. "Giles—"

She heard a groan from behind the blanket, which was ripped away from its pegs at that instant to reveal Giles standing, his head bent to accommodate the low ceiling.

"I command you to stop this torment!"

His tightened muscles and half-growled words frightened her. And excited her. "What, my lord? What have I done? Is passing the salt box so onerous a duty. . . ."

He knelt before her, then pulled her roughly from the bunk to the deck and into his arms as she clutched the salt box against her breasts.

Meriel felt his arms tighten, while Giles devoured her buttery mouth as if he were starving for her kiss before another moment passed. *Yes!* She wanted to scream it. If they were to die in this place, she needed him to love her once more. She had to show him that she wanted him as a man and not as part of a spy mission. He had to learn . . . to know . . . to believe. She heard him gasp, then Giles released her so instantly that she fell back, the salt box spilling its contents everywhere on the deck.

"Oh!" She knelt, urgently tried to scrape the grains together in her hands and replace them in the open box. Where was the lid? Dizzied with confusion and heated surprise, not to mention a wildly pounding heart, she couldn't think or see clearly.

Giles bent to help. "Do not upset yourself so. This is my fault."

"No. My lord, I was too demanding. I should have waited until you were finished with your meal."

He forced a bitter laugh, since he had allowed himself to go against all best judgment, only to be completely misunderstood. Then the laugh changed to real mirth. "You delicious ninny! You think this is about salt?"

Giles's gaze smoldered with such a light that it was like

to set the wooden ship afire. Even in this small, windowless space, Meriel saw the desire she'd longed to see in his eyes. She smiled in her turn, licking the kiss still on her lips. "I would hope something much . . . much sweeter, my lord."

Chapter Nineteen

"The Better of You in All Ways"

This should not happen," Giles said, but he did not move away, could not move away from her. It was a puny power that told him to use his head and not his body to think with. And with a moment of clarity and honesty, he had to admit that his head did not rule him, either. It was his heart speaking and his memory of soft inner thighs like damp silk against his cheek.

"I know," Meriel agreed, with what he saw as a tentative smile, although she was beginning to untie her gown. "Do you want to stop me, or must I attempt to reject you? And how forcible would you have me be?"

Although he knew that she was making a pale jest to hide the truth of her own need, he didn't answer in kind. "You could favor us both and say no," he said, attempting seriousness, though he pulled his shirt over his head. When she didn't answer, didn't look as if she meant to ever speak again, her lips pursed a little stubbornly, but all the more kissable for that, he brought his hands curving up her sides and curled them about her breasts. He kissed one quivering handful and then the other, hearing her teeth chatter as if from cold, though he felt heat sweep through her body. She gasped, as if taking a first birthing breath.

All the hours of being close to her he had been in hot torment, hating her deception, trying to believe their loving had not been all playacting, longing for her, twisting this way, then that in his mind, until he thought he must be crazed. He had tried to ignore his insistent need, but he might as well ignore the air he breathed as his unexplainable desire for this spying woman who wore the face of betrayal. He had closed his eyes tight so that the sight of her body would not tempt him, but the memory of her behind his eyes was an even greater temptation.

Meriel, delirious to feel his hands on her when she had thought never to know them again, lost all caution and opened her gown to him.

"You are indeed a wanton." He breathed the words against her breasts.

"Hey, well, my lord earl, I can have a brain or a woman's part, but not both working together!"

His face fell forward between her breasts and he shook. She was amazed. This was laughter she felt, helpless laughter. With this man, she need not hide her secret thoughts, her second mind, as she had always done with every other soul on earth. She could be herself, all of herself, with Giles.

Giles lifted his face to hers, kissing her cheeks, her nose, her eyelids, a smile upon his face. "You are . . . you are—"

"Waiting, my lord," Meriel said, and began to stroke what parts of him she could reach.

Giles lost any will to fight his need for her, promising himself to examine it later, doubting that promise as he made it.

He kissed her throat from one side to the other as she arched her neck for him. They were hard, hot kisses because he had been a man who controlled men in battle and he could not control himself with one woman. He'd tried to convince her of his hatred. Did she believe he truly felt hate and was using her for his own needs? No, she was too strong for that or else she would not have dared so much. He must have known this from the first moment he saw her.

Yet how could he trust her again and not fear for his reason? How could he want this woman more than he had ever wanted Felice, even in the beginning? He forced himself to stop all thought, and it was as difficult as reining in a galloping stallion with the bit in his teeth.

"Answer one question, mistress," he said, not able to say the name Merry aloud. Not yet. He had no practice in dissembling, so he asked his question without making it pretty: "When we were together at Harringdon, were you loving me as yourself, or as Chiffinch's spy?"

"Sweeting," she said, enclosing him in her soft arms and using a dear name that she had never thought would be in her mouth. She felt his back muscles tense. "That was me, only me, and now that same woman is before you, undeserving but wild with want for you."

Because love had been denied for the many times Giles had wished it, whether confronting her in Whitehall, in his library at Harringdon, in the hold of an enemy ship bound hand and foot . . . he was fully ready. He had held tight to his need for as long as any man could.

He stood and reached down for her where she sat amidst the scattered salt grains, and they tumbled into her narrow bunk. "Please, Giles," she begged without ceasing against his lips.

"Please? What do you wish for? Say the words to me." His fingers were dancing from her breasts down to stroke her gently rounded stomach and further to the soft muff of dark hair, on into the cleft at the entry to her woman's cave, his fingers coming upon a slippery fire at the entrance.

She answered, "I want your body joined to mine, our parts grown together, never to separate."

Giles crouched over her in the dim light of the one lantern swinging from midcabin, his hot blood surging through him. He bent to kiss her where his fingers had first explored, tasting her sea-salty essence, his rough tongue moving her tender nether lips as it willed. Finally, at almost the last moment under his command, he slid his body up and she reached for him and guided him to the place that demanded filling and would no longer wait.

Meriel's eyes were full of searing tears, but she saw his face in the dim, wavering glow of ship's lantern light, his shadow moving up and down on the wall in concert with the ship's plunge to meet an oncoming wave. She could not see herself, but seeing him in flesh and in shadow was like being loved twice as hard.

Meriel reared up from the wooden bunk, feeling her heart pounding against Giles's chest, until with a cry she was drained of all the desperate desire she had held deep inside her, and he collapsed against her, gulping open mouthed for air against the hollow of her neck.

He closed his eyes, holding tight to this moment before he had to let her go, perhaps to never know another woman like Meriel. His senses vibrated with a strange unspoken prayer: *Oh, God, I don't know how I will ever live without you.*

Meriel spoke as she thought. "I love you, Giles. Whatever happens, I will always love you."

"Shhh. Don't speak," he said in a low voice, withdrawing from her reluctantly and readjusting his clothing.

"Giles, what have I done? Don't turn away—"

He put a finger to her lips and mouthed, "Quiet." Something in the way he said it and his movement toward the cabin door forced her compliance. As she quietly crawled forward, Giles had his ear to the door.

Many men's voices came from the cabin, and one woman's. Felice's high, brittle voice, speaking English and seemingly translated by de Witt for others.

"What are they saying?" Meriel whispered insistently.

"Council of war."

She moved closer to him. She had to look in his face, since his words had so little sound. His arm came around her and he held on.

"Michiel de Ruyter is there, and other admirals," Giles said, with Meriel following his barely audible words. "The damned French have joined them with twenty ships. That gives them near one hundred sail!" He bent even closer into the door, listening hard. "They are arguing, with de Witt against taking their fleet into the Thames."

"Why?" Meriel whispered, her heart gladdened at the thought the Dutch might fear to attack even with so mighty a fleet.

"An English squadron could come up behind them and they would be trapped between the warships at Chatham and the ones behind. A neat snare."

Meriel heard Felice say, "No, tell them the squadron is too far away, and I have two renegade English pilots ready to guide you to an attack on the fort at Sheerness."

Giles flexed his fists, and Meriel sensed the power of his hatred and dreaded to think it could ever have been turned on her. "They mean to attack Sheerness, and Felice has hired other traitors to pilot them in through the shoals in the estuary. After that, they can enter the Thames at will with only the chain to stop them."

She shook her head, biting the lips that had to tell him otherwise. "The chain is so heavy and so low in the water, a fairsized ship that draws less than nine feet could sail over it."

Anguished, Giles closed his eyes tightly. "Aye, the Dutch have many with shallow draft."

At last, after some time of talk and even shouts in Hollander that Meriel could not understand, all was quiet in de Witt's cabin. Giles was deathly white, his eyes haunted with worry about England's weak defenses. Unthinking, Meriel put out a hand to hover over his. She did not touch him, not yet knowing her rights, but he did not pull away. "Giles, Felice has finished her foul work. There's no help for that. Now it remains for us to find a way to stop the Dutch." Her voice was hard and uncompromising.

He nodded. His wife, who had been given every privilege of an English gentlewoman, was a traitor. This commoner . . . although a most uncommon commoner . . . had the courage and determination of a queen. He looked long at her . . . the last long look he would allow himself for how many hours or days he did not know. She had the heart and stomach of Elizabeth Tudor, though not the nose, thanks be. He wanted to laugh aloud at that absurdity, but he dared not. The king's spy, after days as a captive, was yet a soft beauty, and Felice, with all her paint pots, had turned ugly and hard as stone. This Meriel St. Thomas would never break, of that he was certain. Yet he must keep tight rein on such thoughts, in spite of the sweet time they had just spent. Indeed, he must forget everything, thinking only of the fight ahead. He shivered at that and wondered if he had caught an ague, or was he dreading a future without this woman? He was married for life, according to every law. Even if he could get an annulment from Felice, Meriel St. Thomas was a commoner he was forbidden to marry . . . and the Earl of Warborough must have a legitimate heir.

Giles could almost chart the leagues as they sailed swiftly south. "We'll reach the Thames estuary soon," he whispered.

"How do we warn the fort?"

"I don't know. Even if we overwhelm our guards when they bring our food and drink, there is always one that stands off with his musket primed, watching us."

"Could we call for de Witt in all pretense of cooperation?"

Giles shook his head. "Felice has given him as much as he needs to override his admirals' caution," he answered, each word dipped in bitter rue. "He would believe nothing we said. He knows we overheard the war plans, but he is so sure of himself now that he does not fear what we know."

"Then how do we warn Sheerness Fort?"

Giles had no answer, but stared at the stern bulkhead as if to see through it to some escape.

At last Meriel fell asleep in his arms, the deep sleep of an exhausted mind and well-loved body. When she awoke, hours had passed and Giles was now pacing with short steps in front of her.

"The ship is readying for action," he said. "I hear the starboard guns being run out and the gun captains shouting for powder and shot. We must be off the fort."

Meriel saw Giles's fists clench. It was painful to see a man of action unable to act, as shackled to inactivity as if clamped in irons. She watched as he moved to the small door leading to de Witt's large cabin, put his shoulder to it, then stepped back two paces and rammed into it again, harder. The oaken door did not move a hairsbreadth, though Meriel rushed to rub his shoulder back to feeling.

"Don't, Giles," she said, unable to bear his futile sparring with a door that would not give to any man's weight. "We will have a better occasion."

"I have not your surety or your great ease of sleep."

"Nor true knowledge of what I am thinking or suffering." She didn't bother to remove the sharpness from her words, though she regretted it almost at once.

He nodded in answer, and the pounding cannon soon ended any chance of talk between them. For an hour they stared overhead, as if they could see through the ceiling to the battle outside. At each broadside the ship heeled sharply to starboard. Several times the ship shuddered as an answering English cannonball found its target.

"Listen!" Meriel said, putting a finger to her lips.

A scrape of key sounded in the oak door lock, and it swung open.

Felice stood there, magnificent in lavender satin and strands of pearls, two pistolas in her jeweled hands, one pointed at Giles, another at Meriel, both weapons cocked.

For a startled moment, Meriel almost admired Felice. She was either fearless or without any idea of danger, because there was murder in Giles's face and absolute purpose in the way his hard body tensed to take her bullet. The hero of the Battle of the Four Days did not shrink from a small pistola.

But Meriel would not allow Giles to die for her fault. "I'm the one you want," Meriel said in Felice's high, clipped court voice, followed by hard laughter. "I took your place, easily made your lord husband love me as a truer wife than you ever were, and exposed you for a traitor. *Me!* A servant girl bested you, *your ladyship!*" As she had hoped, Felice's intense eyes and purpose changed their direction. Both pistolas swung to point at Meriel.

Giles leapt at his wife, knocking one weapon from her hand as they fell back through the door into de Witt's main cabin and scrambled on the floor. Enraged, Felice worked her mouth, but no curses came from it.

With a scream as they struggled, Felice brought the second pistola up.

Meriel kicked out at the weapon. Pray God, her aim was true. She yelled in triumph as the pistola skittered across the floor.

Giles lifted Felice to her feet as easily as if she were empty of substance and thrust her from him with a fury that Meriel knew had been kept tightly leashed for years. "Get away from me, Felice. Once and for all time, get away from me. If you come near me again, or near this woman, who has the better of you in all ways, I will kill you and save the Tower headsman the trouble." His words penetrated the tumult of a new broadside as if each word were an English cannonball.

Felice moved quickly toward the door leading to the deck. "We are not quit yet, husband," she said, regaining a bit of bravado as she reached safety.

Meriel looked on the scene as her heart near stopped. *The better of you in all ways,* Giles had said. Her mind raced to search out any other meaning, or could it be as he had simply said? She almost dared not allow herself to think he loved her, Meriel St. Thomas, and not this countess, though he had murmured words of love in her bunk.

She opened her mouth to ask him as Felice slammed shut the heavy door and locked it.

But hell exploded, knocking them both to the floor, Giles atop Meriel.

In the center of the cabin lay a shattered, smoking ruin of furniture smashed, stern windows blown out, the door to the cabin a smoking hole and the deck opened to expose the hold that had been their first prison.

Giles rose, his ears ringing, his bandage off and his head wound seeping blood. He kicked at the debris, then reached down for Meriel. He wouldn't leave her . . . couldn't leave her. "You must stay close. The eighteen-pounders at the fort can penetrate deep into any hull. If you stray . . . I might not be able to come back for you."

"My lord, you will need to match *my* speed!"

Giles pointed to his ears and shook his head, temporarily deafened. But he almost grinned because he did not need to hear her words to understand such a beautifully determined face. He stepped across beams and splintered oak to look out the stern windows, or rather where they had been. "My ketch! It's still tied below, praise be." He leaned out farther. "And not in any way damaged that I can see, and the railing repaired. The Dutch are too neat by half! Now I must free my crew, for I cannot leave them. I must change into Dutch clothes to gain the for'ard hold."

Meriel heard a sound like a kitten mewling. "Did you hear something, Giles?" she said, pointing to her ear.

Again, he shook his head. "Make haste! Felice could reach de Witt, or an officer come to report the damage at any moment!"

Meriel heard the mewling sound again. "There, I did hear something . . . something hurt. Perhaps . . ."

With strength that she did not know she had, Meriel joined Giles to move splintered wood and smashed beams where the main door had once been. A little more clearing, and Felice's ashy white face appeared on the floor, bloodied from oak splinters protruding everywhere . . . and—Meriel's stomach lurched—an arm sheered off by the cannonball.

Giles knelt close beside the wife he had thrust away forever just minutes earlier, using his black Dutch captain's coat to staunch the blood. Large pearls lay scattered across her breasts, shining like bright ivory against her pallor. "Felice, make peace with your God," he said, the words thick in the back of his throat, for though she deserved death, he could remember a time that she was yet uncorrupted.

Felice was not looking at Giles, or looking to heaven, but with eyes already draining of life, she fixed on Meriel and spoke.

"Mother—"

Meriel's heart near broke, remembering the woman in the painting. She bent close to hear Felice's last words.

"Your win, Mother, goddamn your immortal soul to hell!" Her last breath rattled away.

The lovely Countess of Warborough, toast of every noble cuckold in the merry court of Charles II, went to meet her maker with a strange curse on her lips.

Chapter Twenty

To the Chain and Beyond!

The Earl of Warborough closed the lifeless eyes of his dead countess and drew his coat soaked in her blood over her face. He acted with such a tender finality that Meriel was forced to look away and swallow to relieve the dry ache in her throat. As poisoned as had been Felice's life, her face in death held no hint of the malice she had intended, but had softened to the peace of early youth as she gave up everything.

Did Giles know or suspect what she meant by such a curse against her own mother? It was no time to ask that question, or any other.

Meriel searched for the two pistolas and saw one lying near the severed arm. Giles followed her gaze without speaking and moved to retrieve the weapon. She should not pity a man whose wife had been on a mission to make herself a widow, and yet she did. Her heart was breaking for him. Two women had betrayed his trust and love. Only a man with Giles's strength could come safely through such torment, standing tall and confident as he was this moment.

As if to confirm Meriel's esteem, Giles's mouth set in a

hard line. "Felice obtained the key from de Witt and meant to kill us."

"But de Witt said—"

"There is no man's person Felice could not gain access to . . . even an honorable man like de Witt."

"My lord, be that you above?"

Giles whirled to look for the familiar voice. "Is it Tom? Good Tom Barnes."

"In the hold below ye, my lord!"

Both Meriel and Giles saw the sea-weathered face of Tom Barnes appear in the shambles the cannonball had created.

Giles quickly grabbed the blanket that had separated him from Meriel for these last days and interred Felice's body under it, while Meriel, finding new strength, awkwardly shoved a beam down the shell hole to make a rude ladder. Tom soon emerged, followed by the rest of the *No Name*'s crew, pale and shaken, but grinning and tugging at their forelocks in salute.

"The Lord be praised," Tom said. "When the Hollanders moved us from the for'ard quarters away from their powder magazine, we be thinking never to see Norfolk again." He looked about him at the fractured cabin. "Lady Felice, it be good to see ye well in this place."

Giles did not correct him. He heard debris being shifted and Dutch voices calling from the upper gangway door. "Out the stern windows," Giles ordered. He looked at Meriel. "Can you climb down three decks?"

"Leave me to the Dutch if I cannot."

She caught a flash of admiration in his face.

It wasn't an easy descent, but she had gathered her skirts under her waist ties and was not hindered. There were toeholds that became handholds, and quickly she made her way down to the bow of the *No Name*, planting her feet firmly on the small deck. And she wasn't the last to arrive, to her great satisfaction.

It was dusk, but not full dark. Flashes of brilliant light came from the cannon of Sheerness Fort, answered by ten times their number from *De Zeven Provenciën* and the other ships of the Dutch squadron. The explosions sent waves of sound to beat upon their ears.

"Loose the cable," Giles ordered. "We must risk the Hollanders seeing us, yet hope they think we are merely adrift. Everyone below!"

"And what of you?" Meriel demanded.

"I will make myself small and keep her into the wind, or else she will run aground."

Meriel laughed. "You could never make yourself small, m'lord. I am of a smaller size and I will keep her heading. Sir Edward taught me well."

Tom Barnes looked from his lord to Meriel, and she smiled on him. She knew that he was thinking the marriages of lords were most amazing, and such a commoner's wife would be ducked in the village pond for a shrew. That is what she would have thought not so long ago.

Giles hesitated.

She lowered her voice, sending the half-angry words through her teeth. "You fear to be in the hands of an able woman, my lord of Warborough."

"I fear no man or no woman," he answered, and knew that what had always been truth might not be so now. This was a woman such as he had never met, with twists and turns of pride. . . . Aye, and of daring he had not seen in her sex. And strangely, for a spying counterfeit, she was without guile. "You may have the right of it. Yet I will stay at the hatch for your guidance. Now all below with no more speeches. Quickly!"

Meriel crawled along the deepening shadows of the deck, and reaching the wheel, drew a piece of canvas sail over her, sending the last of her tortoiseshell pins flying and her coif tumbling about her shoulders.

The *No Name* drifted away from the Dutch three-decker, and as the gap widened, Meriel turned the wheel slightly one way and then another. If any Hollanders were looking, the ketch would appear to be drifting aimlessly. But she gradually brought the bow into the estuary current and dropped behind the huge warship and away from the Hollander's fleet.

She heard shouts from the high stern taffrail over the smashed cabin.

"They see us," Giles said. "Tell me if any boats are put over the side."

Meriel watched from under her canvas cover. "Yes, they are putting troops ashore for an assault on the fort . . . barges full of soldiers. They are too busy to send after a ketch adrift." She also saw muzzle flashes followed by explosions and acrid smoke drifting down to choke her. "Giles, I fear there is little answering fire from the fort, and I think the walls are breached. The Hollanders will walk right in."

Giles, bending low, ran to her, ducking under the canvas. "We must get to the ships guarding the chain and warn them of the Dutch plans to come against them next."

"Surely, they will hear the firing."

"Aye, but they need to bring in more fire ships at once to disrupt the Hollanders' fleet. It is the only way to stop them, or they could reach London." He looked back to Sheerness. "The fort is lost. The chain is our next best hope now; after that, the warships anchored at Chatham. Beyond, all London and Whitehall lies exposed." He breathed deeply, his chest expanding in full, his voice intense with resolve. "The English will forever be disgraced if London falls. The king's majesty would never . . . never survive it. After plague and fire, there is already treason spoken openly in the streets. He does not lack for personal courage, this king. He showed it while fighting the great fire with his own hands and body . . . but he lacks a kind of diligence, loving his ease and mistresses too much."

Meriel, kneeling beside Giles, straightened her back and half rose. "Then his loyal subjects must have diligence for him."

Giles stared hard at her. "No woman needs be that right in such a political matter."

"My lord Giles, all women need be that right in *all* matters!" She tried not to smile when she said it, but her mouth seemed to want its own way, so she changed the subject as a woman must when she is utterly correct. "What can I do of real help to you? No nimblety-pimblety duty, but such a task as you would give Tom Barnes!"

He looked at her, a beautiful defiance radiating, his face very close to hers, and he tapped his hands on both her shoulders as if knighting her. "I will not say anything of how we two came to this, although we must speak of it in time. But I find you as you are, mistress, good to look at and be with and"—he paused and she held her breath—"er, well suited to help me in this adventure."

Praise? Awkward, yes, yet true praise. Her heart did not know whether or not to allow too much happiness at his words. Though he had spoken of love to her in the heat of lovemaking, flesh on flesh could make the words obey the body. Yet now they were two together in this fight against the Hollanders, but when it was over, she would go to whatever fate God or Chiffinch planned. Whate'er her future, Giles would not be in it. Of that she was almost sure.

Was it really true that you never missed what you had never known? If it were, and she feared its underlying truth, Meriel knew that she might someday soon wish she had never known Giles's love, for she would always know what she missed . . . know its touch and taste on her lips and . . . and elsewhere. Especially elsewhere.

Taking a deep breath, Meriel looked from Giles's face to the empty spars aloft. "Then, my lord, if we are together in this thing we should make all sail—" And since she did not mean to remind a ship's captain of his duty, especially one who was also an earl and could wear the blue sash of a Garter knight, she touched her forehead and added as humbly as she could, "As you command it, sir."

The command came immediately and the crew leapt to the halyards. A strong easterly wind caught the *No Name* and they sailed swiftly up the Thames.

Meriel looked back to see a small Dutch ship give chase, firing its bow gun as it came. She watched as Giles steered to take full advantage of every puff of wind, knowing his little ship and using the wheel as he'd used his hands on her body in de Witt's cabin: to the fullest advantage.

Several Hollander cannonballs plopped near their stern, spraying both Giles and Meriel with Thames water until, laughing and triumphant, they were thoroughly soaked but out of range.

They had not sailed far when the cannon fire from the Dutch fleet behind them ceased.

"The fort has fallen," Giles said, adjusting his heading to refill a sail as the wind shifted. "Mistress," he said, looking at Meriel in all pretend seriousness, thinking she would probably refuse, "you want a seaman's job and are not afraid of a little spray. Go below and outfit yourself as a sailor, then get ye to the bowsprit and lay out along it. Watch for any shoaling. Light a lantern in case some fool fisherman is on the river. Tom, men . . . and lady"—he made her a short bow, which showed some respect—"we go to save London from the Hollanders."

The men took time to yell, "Huzzah! Huzzah for our lord!"

Meriel joined the cheer, and Giles saw it with a swelling heart, though he quickly raised his gaze to his sails.

"And our brave lady," Tom shouted, and another "huzzah" rang out.

Within minutes, Meriel, changed into comfortable sailor's breeches, stretched herself along the bowsprit, balancing her lantern, aware that all could rightly see her form, but caring nothing for it. She had serious work and would not be distracted, though she wondered if Giles looked on her and was thinking: *What adorable curving hips!* Or with an excellent memory of his hands on her arse. *Hey, well, any woman would think thus! Wouldn't she?*

Villagers were crowding down to the shore, shouting to them, some putting out in small boats with their families and goods piled high, their gunnels low in the water.

"Get your muskets, good men," Meriel shouted. "Call out your militia trainbands. The Hollanders are in Sheerness Fort and will soon be at the chain. Arm yourselves for England and our king!"

She shouted until hoarse and heard Giles's voice behind her, his hands lifting her from the bowsprit as the river widened to a deeper channel. "Guard your throat. They think only of saving what they have."

"Aye. They have so little I do not censure them for it, my lord."

He hung the warning lantern, then held her against him, rather too tightly to be accidental, and the surprise of knowing his body again along all its length took away her speech, though saucy words kept bubbling near the surface.

But Giles had speech. "They fear the Dutch will kill and loot as we English did when we attacked the Hollander coastal towns."

"To our shame," Meriel said, her mouth close to his.

His voice was low and gruff. "In war there can be no shame."

"My lord, there, most of all, should men seek their conscience."

"You have philosophy on your side, mistress, but men know that in war there is only victory or defeat. I doubt we will ever see beyond that."

"What makes you think women are any less warriors? Don't I thirst to win?"

"If all women were your match, perhaps," he said, and she saw a grin escape his mouth. "But I fear you are singular amongst your sisters."

"Don't wager on it, Giles."

And there in the fading light of dusk on the deck of the ketch tossed by tidal surges, he kissed her because he could not help himself, or perhaps had stopped trying.

Meriel opened her mouth to the heat of his lips and held tight to him. Her legs seemed too heavy to move her away.

"This is most unwifely behavior," he said, a smile curling his lips.

"How should I behave, then?"

He laughed. "Dam'me, I can think of no better." And he kissed her again, spray soaking them.

In the next hour, shouts from boats poorly navigated and

several near collisions forced Giles to reluctantly haul sail, put in close to the shore and drop anchor for the night.

"But, Giles," Meriel questioned, eager to put more distance between the little ketch and the Dutch cannon behind them, "how can we stop for the night with the Hollanders so close by?"

"The Dutch will not risk bringing their many sail upriver at night. If they ran aground, our militia could pick off their men from shore, and they would need wait for another high tide."

He called to Tom Barnes. "Take two men and forage inland for some food and drink. Pay good coin for what you get. We will not pillage from our own."

"Aye, m'lord," Tom said, acting instantly on his orders.

With Tom gone, Meriel yawned, the tension of the last hours finally seeping through flesh to bone, forcing her eyes to close until she was almost asleep upon her feet.

"Get you below to my cabin, mistress," Giles whispered, taking a silent oath not to follow her. "When we have food, I will see you fed." He stared at her, his mouth slightly ironic to show a double meaning. "You have given of yourself most generously these last days." He handed her a lantern, lit from the candle of another.

She smiled more fully than he, licking her lips until they glistened. "I try always to be of a generous, giving nature, my lord." And then she stumbled away down the hatch to a hammock slung near the stern windows, trying to keep happiness at bay and failing, for what she saw in his face could only bring her joy. He wanted her despite all that was between them, or because of it. Didn't he?

Meriel settled into her swinging bed . . . after a third try.

Shouts and tramping feet on the deck above woke her. The lantern candle had burned down to half its length and the sharp scent of tallow was everywhere. She had slept for several hours and felt refreshed. Still, she had trouble climbing from the plaguey hammock.

The door to the deck opened, and Giles's feet, then legs, then torso appeared as he ducked his head into the cabin. "I've brought you a late supper, not exactly Longs or Lockets or even the Banqueting House, but enough to give you the strength you'll need," he said.

Meriel struggled to sit, but fell back. "Then I must eat it on my back, or I need your help, sir."

He grinned and looked nothing like the sober Earl of Warborough. "An interesting dilemma, mistress."

"For you?"

"Aye, and well you know it," he answered, gathering her in his arms and setting her on her feet, holding her a moment longer while she found her legs again in the gentle rolling shallows.

"I know nothing, Giles, but I hope for much."

He turned away at that and sat cross-legged on the bench under the stern windows, opening a hamper without issuing an invitation for her to sit.

She sat, anyway.

"A tavern keeper had not fled, hoping for business." He handed her a green glass bottle of ale, and broke off bread.

"No cheese, please you, m'lord," she said, with a little laugh.

He smiled and agreed. "A good English venison pasty will do you better." He held it out for her to bite, so that she had to bend double and open her mouth wide. Her breasts were loose and her sailor's shirt most revealing. She knew it and didn't adjust the ties for modesty. Modesty had long since fled her from lack of use.

"Mistress, will you have another bite?" Giles said, his gaze hot on her.

"My lord Giles of Warborough, I much prefer to be sweet dessert than a meat pie for a hungry seaman."

He took a deep breath and waited as it shivered out of his depths, but he could not resist so tempting a dish as Meriel St. Thomas.

"You torment me," he said, still refusing to use the name they had shared at Harringdon Hall in the big goose-feather bed and in the arms of the ancient oak. "I swear each time I lie with you that I will resist the next."

"Then, sir," she answered, sliding her lips across his un- shaven cheek, "if I were the Earl of Warborough, I would leave off swearing."

His hands were hot as he slid them into her sailor's shirt. "You make excellent sense for a . . ."

"Say it. A maid, a servant girl. Giles, I have no shame of where I come from. It was honorable, hard work. If you think on it, you have lived the same." She barely suppressed a giggle. "Only in somewhat better clothes." She said this while shrugging out of her own breeches, wondering only a moment at the wantonness that had been in her all the time.

He burrowed his mouth into the cleft of her shirt and kissed her soft, yielding breasts, licking their nipples hun- grily into erectness, supping on them as if he had not just had his fill, pulling her closer until she was on his lap, her legs wrapped about his back and braced against the stern bulkhead. He felt the heat of her open womanhood radiating against his cock as he slipped inside her. The pasty was for- gotten, as was the ale. He had a taste for sweets now and he saw nothing sweeter in the world than this woman before him.

The candle had burned down to a pool of tallow and a

floating wick when they finally lay close together on the wooden deck where they had tumbled, laughing. They quieted their breathing as the little ship gently rolled from side to side in the shallows.

Giles turned his head on his crooked arm to look at her in profile. A dimple showed in her cheek, and he knew that she was amused.

"What?"

"I was thinking how much I prefer your leafy perch in the woods of Harringdon Hall to this bed of oak boards."

He couldn't answer that. He wasn't ready to make that decision. But he could not take his eyes from Meriel. Her nose was most aristocratic, but shorter than Felice's by just enough to make a difference. Each time he looked at his dead wife's counterfeit, he saw the slight alteration in every feature that improved upon the original.

Until this moment, he had not had time to think of Felice or of her fitting end. He could not mourn her. She had died for him years ago, with the throwing away of his son and heir as if the half-formed babe were naught. That young and loving Felice that he had thought returned to him for so short a time at Harringdon was . . . what? Could be . . . what? He was a peer of the realm. She was a commoner. The divide was too deep. Wasn't it?

Meriel's lips were parted as if to speak, but he put a warning finger on them and she settled back into herself. He could not think what to do. His wife was dead, yet the best of what they might have had together lived on beside him. Better, oh, far better than what he'd ever hoped. He groaned under the weight of his tormenting thoughts, pressing his temples to get them out of his mind before they became speech.

"Sshhh, my lord," Meriel said. "Quiet yourself." She had

some idea what it was like to regret behavior that seemed beyond human control. "There is a greater matter to settle. We will know what is our future when England and our king are safe."

He stood and pulled her to her feet. "You remind me of my duty, mistress."

"Our duty," she whispered.

He nodded, and they climbed to the deck above, her hand in his. She did not need his help on the ladder, but she accepted it. She would take all Giles would give.

The first brightening of a new day lit the sky to the east of the ketch bobbing in the Thames, the morning breezes sweeping in from the Channel to tug at the furled mainsail.

"Hail, the deck!"

Meriel and Giles looked up to where Tom Barnes perched on the topmost spar of the mainmast. "A squadron of Hollanders, still out of cannon range, my lord!" he shouted.

"Cock's life! They lost no time. But we have twice their speed and half their draft. To the chain, men!"

The crew leapt to the halyards and they were moving at once. Meriel jumped to lend a hand as Giles ran to the wheel. Then she doused the lanterns, as the little ketch caught the current and swept upriver toward Gillingham, the wind singing in the shrouds.

"Will we be in time?" she asked, rushing back to him.

"We'll need all the luck that seems to follow you, mistress."

Chapter Twenty-one

From the Chain to London
and the King

Giles and Meriel, their hands sharing the wheel, steered the ketch toward the chain. High spring tides and an easterly gale combined to speed them there by the forenoon. Dropping anchor near the guard ship *Matthius,* Giles hailed the captain: "Sheerness is lost, and the Dutch are determined to come against you."

"Who speaks, sir?" the captain asked from his high stern deck.

"The Earl of Warborough."

"Captain Millett, m'lord, at your service. Every English seaman honors your name."

Giles nodded and rushed on. "I saw the walls at Sheerness Fort breached, and above eight hundred Dutch soldiers landing on English soil."

"What would you have me do, your lordship? I have few ships and have turned them broadside to the chain to gain maximum firepower. I have but two fireships loaded with pitch to send against them and some small pinnaces with oars. I have forwarded urgent messages to Commissioner Pett and the Admiralty for reinforcements, but money is scarce and seamen deserting for want of pay." The captain leaned lower over the port rail. "You sail into chaos, your lordship. Some capital ships lie near empty at Chatham. And in London . . . a run on the banks and men burying their gold guineas and silver plate in their gardens."

"But the Lord Chancellor Hyde—"

"Thinks the tortuous channels of the Thames will stop the Dutch."

"They have English pilots, sir, and a great fleet under de Ruyter's command."

"So many? But, m'lord earl, the chancellor busies himself fending off a London mob at his great new mansion in Piccadilly. They have torn down his gate, chopped down his trees and raised a gibbet. Think you he is concerned for us when he hopes to save his own neck?"

Giles waved away further shouted speeches. "Hold the chain, sir!"

"On my honor, I will do all I can with what I have. But I ask you to beg Commissioner Pett to send me more ships and men!"

Meriel spoke to Giles in low, urgent tones. "He cannot hold, Giles. We must get to London to report the Hollander's plans. Chiffinch and the Admiralty do not know the full threat to the city."

"Cock's life! We but waste precious time here."

"No, Giles, you do what is right, in proper order."

He commanded the drag anchor be raised, then laughed heartily, throwing back his head so that she saw the laugh travel up his throat to his mouth and into the fine dark eyes he turned on her. "You are a strategist, mistress, and will yet make a fine admiral."

Meriel curtsied at his extravagant praise and found her deep court curtsy just a trifle wobbly. She repeated it and this time accomplished it perfectly, though she had to pretend all the graceful sweeping moves of a gown and its train in cutoff sailor's breeches. She smiled up at him. "Sir, I would need a petticoat navy, because men would never consent to be ruled by a woman."

"Would we not, mistress? I think many a man would allow your rule, especially in such revealing breeches."

"I see only one man with the sense to both look and listen well." She was teasing, but so was he. Meriel knew that Giles was the last man who would be led by any man or woman. That he accepted her as full partner in this venture was almost past understanding. For an earl to join with a serving girl was more than any peer of the realm would think of, and she loved him all the more for it.

By this time, the port railing of the *Matthias* was lined with sailors, who stood silent as the *No Name* hauled anchor and headed toward London.

"How long?" Meriel asked.

"It could take two days without a pilot."

"We don't have so long. I will be your eyes. Can I not lie out along the bowsprit again?"

He clasped her about the waist, and his voice shook in his constricted throat. "Aye, my admiral," he said softly, with not a hint of sarcasm. "But we'll dock at Chatham and take a swift horse to Whitehall. The tide will not always run in our favor, and we have no time to wait for the turning."

Meriel watched his every move. To her, Giles seemed master of the wind, tacking expertly to keep his sails full, taking risks with his beloved little ship that spoke of his greater love of country. "I have found my true calling, m'lord," she said lightly, seeking to relieve his grim mood.

"Not as spy or servant or even countess, all of which I have mastered. A sailor, sir. That is what I would be, perhaps what I have always been. One day I hope . . ."

He looked away, his lips in a rigid line. He could not answer the question behind her words, though he knew she awaited his answer. How could she be part of his life? Would he see Felice every time he looked on this woman's face? The question nagged him, but the answer was missing. In this, he could not be ruled by his heart.

Giles swung the wheel to miss a large piece of driftwood and didn't see that Meriel understood his inability to define her future, or the pain of understanding pass across her face, although she banished it at once.

They sailed the rest of that day and into the evening hours, watching the banks as farmers and bands of villagers gathered in hastily formed militia units with powder, shot and muskets to repel the Hollanders from pillaging inland.

"We depended too much on the Thames to stop invasion," Giles told Meriel when Tom Barnes replaced her at the bowsprit. "We English did not count on de Ruyter's daring," he admitted.

"Well, my lord, I daresay he did not count on us!"

"Dam'me, mistress! I would more wish to have you by my side than a three-decker under my feet."

Meriel was too flushed with pride at the praise to point out that he could have his wish if he would but acknowledge her and trust her.

Giles drew his face a little closer to hers. "Although I'd take the warship, too. Think, Meriel, what we could do with a seventy-gun three-decker."

"Rule the Channel!" She thought again, and as usual the words came from her mouth before she could stop herself. "But I think me this little ketch is the best of all ships in the world." She bit down on her lip, knowing she had intruded too far into his heart with her own dreams, though every word was deeply felt.

Giles gripped the wheel until his knuckles whitened, and looked ahead. He dared not turn his gaze to her lest the mist in his eyes be taken for weakness. He could not think into the future, indeed had been holding it off with all his strength. This turmoil clouded his mind. Would Meriel be there beside him like this, or a memory less real with each new day and each new mistress? Would he forever search the faces of serving maids in the streets of London and around every corner, his heart quickening at the sight of every raven-haired miss in mop cap and smock, hoping to see her again?

Meriel saw his struggle and left him to it. She knew what she wanted. He had to decide on his own desire.

She went back to the bowsprit, and was again relieved by Tom Barnes when she thought herself unable to cling another minute.

He approached her gently. "My lady, ye be at yer post for better'n two turns of the glass. I be taking yer place now. There's small ale and a little bread aft. His lordship be sleeping."

"Thank you, Tom. It's shoaling now at low tide. Keep close watch." Stiff and thinking to never remove the imprint of the bowsprit from her body where it fit neatly between her legs and breasts, Meriel staggered aft. She was thirsty and hungry with an even greater need to see Giles, to discover if what she'd seen in his face earlier was still there, or had been a mere passing thought.

She found him sitting on the deck near the wheel, sleeping on his arms. She had scarce downed some ale and taken a bite of bread that had turned to near stone in her stomach when the helmsman shouted, "Chatham ahead. I be seeing the topsails of the great *Royal Charles* at anchor."

Thirty minutes later, Giles was hailing the ship, as it loomed above them under a clear, starry sky. "Your captain," he shouted up at the darkened decks.

A sleepy head appeared at the stern. "Cap'n be ashore, sir. Lord Arlington tells us we be ordered higher up river. Then First Commissioner Pett tells us we be ordered to stay at anchor. Eighty guns we have, sir, and no cannoneers. Pett even takes ships and men to carry away his own household goods to safety. All be in disorder at Chatham dockyard, sir. Too many lordships running things, begging yer pardon since I hear yer quality!"

Giles put the wheel hard alee past other capital ships, the *Royal James* and the *Royal Oake*, and made for the docks. "Can you ride, mistress?"

"Aye, sir." Had he forgotten her ride with Buckingham and Rochester through St. James Park? *Do we remember only as we wish?* The thought gave her hope that she could weather any future. "Should we talk with the master of the dockyard?"

"No, we need the highest authority. Not Pett, who seems easily swayed this way and that, or he would have removed the *Royal Charles* upriver to safety before now. Any fool can see the ship is a target. We will away to Whitehall by the swiftest horse." He gripped her arm and shouted to Tom. "Rest here, and I will return as soon as ever I can. There may be work for the *No Name* later."

They put a plank over to the dock, and Giles helped Meriel ashore on unsteady legs that near rolled out from under her. *Hey, well, I've been at sea for days!*

"I know a stable nearby," Giles said, and ready or not, her legs followed him. The hostler, spurred by the gold guinea glinting in Giles's palm, soon had a spirited horse saddled, and Meriel felt herself lifted up to sit within his arms against his broad, comforting chest, and they were away down the cobbled streets toward Whitehall.

Without a linkboy carrying a torch before them, the streets were dark and peopled by groups of men looting shops and shouting angrily after them. "We have been sold to the French Papists! Their armies gather at Dunkirk to invade us. All is lost!"

Only a sharp kick from Giles kept one man from grabbing their horse's reins. "Order has been broken," Giles said in her ear, and she nodded, lest her answering words be swept away behind them.

They made a detour around the worst burnt-over parts of old London until they clattered into the royal mews near Westminster. Leaving the horse, blowing and snorting in the care of boys dicing for coppers amongst the stalls, they hurried toward Whitehall Palace, past the red-coated guard who recognized and saluted Giles, thence up the private back stairs to Chiffinch's apartment, for only he could admit them to the king's privy closet.

Giles pounded on his door twice and put his shoulder to it before Chiffinch opened to them bursting through at the same moment, near to knocking him over. In his linen sleeping cap and gown, but minus a periwig, the spymaster looked like a rather large sleepy jester.

"My lord earl," Chiffinch began, unable to keep surprise from the grimly sardonic face he immediately assumed. He went no further when Meriel appeared from behind Giles, who towered above him. "Ah!"

"The king," Giles shouted. "We must reach the king!"

"Your pardon, mistress Meriel . . . it is Meriel, isn't it, and not Lady Felice? Yes, I see it is, for Felice would not appear at the palace in sailor's clothing, somewhat the worse for several soakings."

"My wife, sir, is dead by an English cannonball, as you probably know, so jests at her expense are unwelcome, if not dangerous to your health. You are but delaying us. Why? Is the king abed? Is the king not alone?"

"What news do you bring? As the king's spymaster, I will take it to His Majesty, as is my privilege and duty." He retreated into his office and began to pull on a pair of breeches.

Giles followed. "You waste time, spymaster, when there is no time to waste."

Chiffinch bowed. "Accept my deepest sympathy, Lord Warborough," he said in a faked mourning voice. "I had some slight communication from Sheerness Fort after it fell that a woman's body was brought ashore and buried by the Hollanders. . . . With all honors. I did not know until this minute whether t'was her ladyship or your present lovely companion." He smirked, obviously pleased with himself, and pleased to stop the earl's agitated advance. "I rather enjoyed the thought that they might still be confused between your wife and this young miss, perhaps believing neither."

Meriel could no longer contain the rage sweeping through her. "You *knew* that Felice had escaped to them, and you did not warn me."

"When we could no longer fool the Dutch with a counterfeit, we needed to confuse them as to who was the real countess," he said in a placid voice, as if he spoke such cruel, betraying words every day. "And I thought you might be persuaded with gold to give up your true identity to—"

"I gave up nothing to the Hollanders."

"Most admirable, mistress," he said in a mocking tone.

Giles stepped close to Chiffinch, and the spymaster drew

back, though Meriel doubted he knew the real danger he faced, for she felt the tension in Giles's body, like a lion readying its muscles to leap on prey.

"De Witt needed nothing from this woman," Giles growled. "He got everything from Felice, who gave him all willingly. But if you delay us longer from the king . . ."

Giles's support did not quell Meriel's rage. "Spymaster, you allowed me to walk into a trap. I say foul, sir!" And then she added words that no lady, whether counterfeit or real, should utter to her superior: "You take me for a dupe! Damn you for a whoreson bastard—" She could have gone on to apoplectic heights, but Giles looked her way in some dismay, and that was enough. "My pardon, Giles," she said, almost choking on the rage she had to swallow. "An English spy should not have to endure betrayal from her own."

Chiffinch looked bored. "We have grown mighty high in our ways, I see, from the servant you were a bare month ago. Do you not know her origins by now, my lord earl?"

"She told me, but I think even she does not know everything."

Chiffinch shrugged, though it was an answer he had not expected, honesty not being part of his repertoire. "Then you should also know that I would use the king's subjects as befits the need of the realm. Mistress, it seems you escaped any real harm"—he looked pointedly at her belly—"unless you now carry an earl's bastard. Yet, enough! You are a good spy, m'girl. I may use you again unless you are with—"

Meriel gasped. Chiffinch, in his uncanny way, had spoken aloud what she had thought possible since her first night at Harringdon Hall. And from the look on Giles's face, the thought was not new to him, either, but also not welcome from Chiffinch's mouth. Giles reached for his sword, and not finding it at his side, brought up his fist.

Meriel saw real fear in Chiffinch's eyes for the first time and caught at Giles's arm. "No, Giles. If I could be undone by words and names, it would have happened long ago."

Giles opened his fist slowly and wrapped his long fingers around the spymaster's throat. "Say that about her again in anyone's hearing and you die. Now delay us no longer."

The words that came from him were so hard and evenly spaced that each had the impact of a hammered nail. For once Chiffinch was silenced, finding no sarcasm to mine in this situation. "As you say, m'lord." The words gurgled in his constricted throat.

"The king? Where is he?" Giles asked the questions in a tone that brooked no more delaying wordplay from the spymaster.

"He is supping with my lady Castlemaine."

"Where?"

"You may not disturb—" But Giles's fingers crushed further advice.

"Where, you fool? The kingdom is about to come undone through your bungling!"

"The Duke of Monmouth's house."

"But is not the duke with the militia?"

"More like swiving all the country maids around."

"I know his grace's house," Giles said, having no time for court gossip about the king's bastard son. Giles released Chiffinch so swiftly that he stumbled backward into his writing table. Without another glance, Giles took Meriel by the hand, walking through the spymaster's apartments and out into the palace. "We must dress ourselves for the king's presence or risk not being admitted. I will come for you in minutes."

Meriel's voice was urgent. "Promise not to leave me behind, Giles. I would take this to the end, whatever is my fate."

He bent his head to her. His lips touched hers briefly, and repeated with emphasis: "I will change my clothes in minutes. Now make all haste."

Meriel hurried toward her rooms, taking a short way through the king's Presence Chamber, now empty but for sleeping porters. She had near forgotten the crystal chandeliers and rich crimson and gold damask hangings draping the walls. As her steps echoed on the marble floor past the dais holding the two thrones, she could yet hear the music of viols and oboes playing a sarabande, and smell the musk of a heavily perfumed noble crowd. For a few hours, this had been hers by right of birth. She smiled at that crazed bit of thinking. It had been hers only as being a queen on stage for a night was Nell Gwyn's true station.

She looked up at the gallery from which she had first glimpsed Giles in his living flesh. She fixed it in her mind and heart one last time. She would never again see it from this vantage.

No majordomo opened her door, and when she stepped into her apartments all was disorder. Her furniture removed. No sea coal in the fire with tinder close by. Chess pieces strewn upon a floor with no bright turkey carpet to warm her feet. Clothing was tossed about her bedchamber as if picked over by a hundred crows.

Agnes sat at the dressing table, looking at Meriel through the mirror, a crack running from top to side. "I ne'er expected to see you again."

"That is obvious."

"Nay, you mistake me. This is not my work. These lordlings and their ladies in Whitehall are like vultures. When Chiffinch reported Lady Felice was dead, they descended to apportion her furniture and fittings amongst them. To honor her memory, they said."

Meriel began to sift through what was left, thrown higglety-pigglety on the bedstead, shorn of its feather mattress.

Behind her, Agnes said, "I hoped you would return."

"How did you know it was Felice's body and not mine they buried?"

"I knew that you were too clever by far for the damned cheesemongers. Did they torture you?"

"Nay, but I cannot recount my adventures now. Giles will be here within minutes. Help me to be ready to gain admittance to the king's presence."

Though Agnes looked interested and obviously longed to know more, she rose and gave up her bench in front of the dressing table. "Let me dress your hair, m'lady."

"Hurry, I have but minutes. And don't call me m'lady."

"It is how I see you."

Although Meriel gave a swift squeeze to Agnes's arm, nothing more was said until Giles came through the door, shaved, dressed as an earl at court and armed with fine Spanish steel.

Meriel rose and curtsied to his formal bow as if they had not spent nights together at sea on the deck of a Dutch warship, not to mention on the ketch.

Giles surveyed the room and nodded to Agnes as she curtsied, nothing showing on his face. He was beyond surprise.

Agnes handed Meriel a hooded cape to match the bright blue velvet of her gown and to cover her lack of jewels.

"If I survive this, I will have you with me," Meriel said softly to Agnes.

"Did the knife—?"

Meriel smiled. "Most handily cut the ropes that bound us both."

And then Giles and Meriel were out the door and down to the Holbein Gate straddling King Street, where a carriage waited, flares held by footmen to light their way through the darkened thoroughfares full of Londoners crying doom.

Every window in Monmouth's house on Hedge Lane was ablaze when they drew up, and Giles lowered the steps and leapt out without waiting for help.

"Stop!" yelled an officer of the king's guards.

"I have urgent business with His Majesty."

"The king is occupied and no one is to be admitted."

"I am—"

"I know who you are, my lord earl," the officer said, "but my orders are to allow no one to disturb the king's pleasure."

"Who gave such orders?"

"His Majesty's keeper of the privy closet."

Meriel came up to Giles's side. "Chiffinch," she said as a one-word indictment. "He wants to take the credit, to be the hero."

The officer brushed her aside. "One more step, your lordship, and I will be forced to order you and your lady arrested and removed to the Tower."

Giles took two long steps, drawing his sword as he went, and Meriel thought she would never forget the hissing sound it made as the steel left the scabbard.

Chapter Twenty-two

Knowing a Strong Woman

Three guardsmen drew their heavier swords to meet Giles's lighter, faster Spanish steel dancing in front of them. He feinted to one side, testing the guards' defenses. With an easy smile and a thought to recommend a new fencing master to the king for his soldiers, Giles increased his pressure and broke through first one and then another's parry, not meaning to wound, just to teach a lesson.

Meriel could not stand to one side. She jumped into the melee, pummeling two and tripping one with her slippered foot.

"Stand back, Merry!" Giles shouted.

At that sweet name, the first time he'd uttered it since leaving Harringdon Hall, she redoubled her efforts. She staggered another guard with an elbow to the stomach, a move she'd learned long ago in the charity orphans' house. She dodged behind the swirling throng and shouted for the king, pounding on the door. She was at once grabbed from behind and held by other guards running to the sound of clashing swords.

She clawed and twisted her body like an eel caught in a

fisherman's net, but dared not call to Giles for help and distract him as he frantically parried a semicircle of thrusting blades attempting to disarm him.

Aye, this was her fight, as well as Giles's. *Hey, well, could any woman worth a copper stand aside when the man she adored was in danger?*

"Rally to your master!" she shouted at the footmen, who seemed content to goggle like ninnies and hold their flares aloft to light the scene.

Meriel could see that the guards were gradually pressing Giles back and back, and she redoubled her efforts to escape the tight arms about her. She hit her mark more than once.

At last, Giles ran around the carriage, swung through the door and out on the house side, catching two king's guards with his boot heels and laying them flat on the cobbles. "Bravo, Giles!" she sang, giving up her failed effort at silence. Who could not applaud the most brilliant fighting move ever seen?

But Giles was tiring; she could see that, too, and intensified her struggle, keeping two guards and finally a third too busy with her to join the fight.

At last one guard slipped his blade through Giles's defense and sliced through his coat, gashing his sword arm, which dropped to his side of its own will, although he did not lose his rapier.

Instantly, a half-dozen steel points were being held against his heart.

"Hold there!"

Meriel swallowed the scream in her throat as the king loomed over all.

With murmurs of "Your Majesty," the guards stepped back, saluting, freeing Meriel to rush to Giles.

"Your arm," she said, touching him and coming away with his blood on her fingertips.

"It's nothing. Sshh. Don't be such a woman." He was grinning down at her.

"I have it in my mind being more of one as soon as ever may be," she whispered quickly, before the king reached them.

Charles II moved regally down the steps toward them, tall and richly attired, but not as dandified with bows and ribbons as the nobles crowding at the door behind him. For the monarch of a lascivious court rivaled only by Louis of France and the spectacular palaces at Versailles, Charles was somewhat severe in his costume. Yet in Meriel's eyes, it only enhanced his regal authority.

"What mischief is this?" he asked, though he sounded more curious than vexed.

Meriel curtsied and Giles bowed, his arm dangling.

"You are wounded, m'lord earl. Our guards are overzealous in protecting our person. With London in disarray there is much fear of mobs. . . ." He sighed. "Indeed, we do know you intend us no harm, though we cannot vouch for this lady, sir, since she does seem to have crippled two of our guards, their shins in a tragic state of hurt." The king enjoyed spectacle and he had it in plenty before him, missing only trumpets and a fanfare.

Meriel curtsied most formally, wondering if this one would truly be the last one she would ever perform before being sent to the Tower or back to the scullery. She waited for Giles to speak, as was proper. Her time with Giles was now very short, perhaps hours, even minutes, and totally out of her control. Thus, it was right to show him this last courtesy.

Giles saw her open her mouth and hesitate, almost grinning at her unusual restraint; then he bowed to the king as best he could and spoke with no tremor in his voice, though his arm pained him damnably. "Your Majesty, the Dutch are coming against the chain and then on up to Chatham and—"

The king put up a warning hand. "Come inside, Giles, where we may speak privately with you and"—he smiled at Meriel, who was rising from her curtsy—"your lady, of course."

Giles and Meriel followed the king inside the candlelit Duke of Monmouth's house to face a furious Lady Castlemaine. "Charles, you have quite spoiled our hunt!"

"Aye, Your Majesty," said little Anna, Duchess of Monmouth, petulant in her extreme youth. "We were having such mighty amusement chasing the large moth from candle to candle."

The king smiled at her pout. "You will needs pursue it without us, m'dear, for the business of state intervenes. Now we must withdraw to speak of real hunts and serious matters."

The Countess Castlemaine stared at Meriel, a sneer marking her fading beauty, though she was now delivered of her babe and not so swollen. "Ah, the *other* little actress pretending to be what she is not."

Meriel realized the countess knew she was not Felice, and with her the entire court was in on her masquerade. Chiffinch must have seen some benefit to himself in exposing her. Who could imagine how many schemes he had in progress?

Her days as Lady Felice were truly ended, and she felt no regret at that. Yet she knew that Lady Castlemaine referred also to Nell Gwyn, her new rival for the king's affections, and also a woman who had risen from the gutter. Meriel laughed, gladdened as the sound brought a rush of color to

Babs Castlemaine's face. "Yes, m'lady, I am an actress of a kind, only such a one as acts on the stage of war against the king's enemies." She curtsied abruptly. "I leave the art of chasing moths at parties to you."

The king stifled a smile, but held his hand up for silence, since offended cries erupted from every corner. "Call for our good Dr. Wyndham to tend the earl's arm. Now, pray, excuse us."

Giles and Meriel followed the king through the doors of an adjoining room, its tables laid for cards. A guard was posted and the doors were quietly closed.

The king turned slowly and deliberately toward Meriel. "You object, we think, to a king's pleasures as his kingdom is under attack. . . . When distraction is perhaps most needed. We think that impertinent, m'lady." The voice was soft, even amused under the serious accusation.

Meriel knew this king heard less truth than any other Englishman, so she would not betray him with a further lie. "Aye, Your Majesty, I am quite impertinent. A necessary trait, I think, for a spy in these troubled times. Yet I pray you know that I was responding to m'lady Castlemaine's insult without you in mind."

"Come now, we think you would have us racing about the streets, sword in one hand, pike in the other. Don't you know it would only strike more fear in the populace to see their king in a terror?"

Meriel bowed her head, a bit ashamed not to have thought of this. But she had no chance to say so.

Giles stepped forward, holding his wounded arm in a tight grasp, blood seeping between his fingers, his voice urgent: "Your Majesty, there is so little time. We overheard the Hollander battle plans while held prisoner on *De Zeven Provenciën*."

"Indeed! This sounds a grand adventure that we must fully hear someday. But now, what news other than that which comes to our ears with the sound of cannon? The Isle of Grain is invaded, and we have the sad report that Sheerness is taken with much loss of life. The eighteen-pounders we ordered for the fort and watched installed last February were so poorly maintained that they jumped right off their carriages as the first shot was fired." The king clasped his hands behind his back, perhaps to hide the anger shaking them.

Giles brought the king back to the needs of the moment. "Sir, I fear there is now fighting at the chain and the Hollanders will be master of it soon, if not already. They were coming on behind us yesterday."

Charles paced up and down, and spoke seriously as if addressing his council. "'Od's fish! Think you they will come up as far as to Chatham and fire the fleet?"

"The men of the *Royal Charles* have deserted or been taken elsewhere by command. There is naught to stop the Dutch from working their will."

The king's face was thunderous. "First the plague, then the great fire. When no taxes can be collected, I cannot get monies from Parliament to pay my seamen and soldiers. They cannot eat the tickets we give them instead of coin, and they refuse to fight. It is no wonder the people think God has turned his face from England. . . . Or that their king has."

"The people, sir, hope that you will save London." Giles could not tell him that the people talked treason, though he did not doubt that Charles knew it. Although he appeared to be a man without much care, indeed Charles knew and cared for everything.

The king barely smiled at Giles's compliment. "You think the Hollanders would dare to come up so far as

London when we are in treaty negotiations? They want the port of Tangiers that came with my queen's dowry. And they would give us in trade the port of the former New Amsterdam, now called New York in the colonies." He blinked hard as if with a starting megrim. "Though we think a port in that far and empty country a poor trade." He paced forward, turning back immediately. "We ask you again, Giles, would they dare so much as our city of London?"

Meriel could keep quiet no longer, and certainly Giles would not have expected this much silence from her. "If we do not show them our teeth, your Majesty, de Ruyter will dare much, although de Witt will stop him if there is risk." She stepped close to the king. "I say we make it risky for them!"

Charles II looked down at her and she thought the look held admiration, but one could not tell with this man, who had learned in his cradle to guard his public face.

"And what risk would you have us take, Mistress Impertinent, when all Bedlam runs in the streets and in the very air?" he asked.

Giles bowed and then looked into his king's eyes, where they came to a man's understanding. Both knew strong women. "She would be an admiral, sir, but for now she is in need of my training."

The king's tone moved past such banter to urgency. "Give us your best advice, my lord earl."

"Fireships, sir, and many of them, indeed anything afloat. I will lead them to Chatham to confound the enemy. We must stop them there or they will come up to Whitehall to dictate their terms."

The king began his pacing again. "By law, we can commandeer ships in such times as these. If we sign a warrant of authority for the Admiralty—"

Giles interrupted in haste. "I will gather all that I can and move with barrels of pitch and tar from the naval stores downriver to Chatham and save our capital ships. But I must move before first light!"

"You promise much, m'lord."

"*We* promise much, Your Majesty," Meriel added, lest she be forgotten amidst these towering men.

"This is not woman's work," Giles said, unwilling to risk her life further and daring her to challenge him in front of the king.

"Was it not woman's work to board the Dutch flagship as a spy? Was it not woman's work to escape the—"

The king looked interested but weary of female discourse, since he had a palace full of it. "Do not o'er plead your argument, mistress, when you have won it at first salvo. We do not see in the Earl of Warborough the desire to deny you a triumph against the enemy that cost you so dear. We see only his loving protection."

Meriel blushed and curtsied again. Charles II bent his head and whispered for her ear alone as she rose, head bowed. "We give you our royal promise that our keeper of the privy closet will honor his bargain with the king's spy on pain of our displeasure. Our great displeasure."

"My thanks to you, sir," she said, and with her arm on Giles's bloodied sleeve she marched out of Monmouth's house past a glowering Castlemaine and gossiping lords, murmuring questions and surmises into each other's mountainous periwigs.

As the majordomo closed the front doors behind them, Meriel spoke quietly for Giles's ears. "You called me Merry when you were fighting."

"Did I?"

She dared not look at him, and he said no more.

The guard who had wounded Giles bowed and opened the carriage door. "I beg pardon, my lord."

"You did your duty and I commend you for it."

Dr. Wyndham sat inside, his physician's pack spread open on a lap grown a little more ample with success, his feet scarce touching the floorboard. "Come up, my lord earl, and let me see to that arm. My lady," he said, acknowledging Meriel as she was handed in. He beamed. "It is our great pleasure to see you alive and well. . . . And I hope happy." He shifted his gaze to Giles then back to Meriel, finding no confirmation in either face. "Ah, well . . ." And he began to cut away the earl's coat sleeve.

Giles called to his footmen. "One of you make quick passage to Whitehall and ask Sir Edward Cheatham to meet me at the Admiralty as soon as may be." When the carriage bounced, indicating the man had departed, Giles shouted out the window to his driver: "Now, to the Admiralty as fast as you can with safety."

As the doctor worked on his arm, Giles looked at Meriel, sitting across from him, her head resting on the upholstered seat back, with the look of a fresh court beauty, though her eyes were shadowed with fatigue. Tired or no, she had the finest steel for a spine. He tried to sort the thoughts in his troubled mind, but he could summon no resistance to her and little except desire. But how could he ever make a happy end? To interrupt his confusion, he spoke. "Sir Edward will know how we can commandeer every rowing boat, shallop and barge to be had."

"Yes, and he will help us," Meriel said, looking away from the gaping slash on his arm, now exposed to wavering light like a bloodied, toothless mouth.

"M'lord, you will need stitching, which I cannot do in this conveyance."

"Bind it, good doctor, with your infallible salve to provide its miracle to which this lady's complexion does endlessly provide a testament. You can do your surgery at the Admiralty while we await ships."

"As you wish, m'lord earl. In my younger days I healed many wounds from swordplay, although none of late since Jeremy Hughes, the great actor of the Theater Royal, was unfortunately stabbed by a jealous actress in a performance of *Macbeth,* Act Two, Scene Two, if you can believe such a thing in this modern day. That was before the fire of London. Since that sad time, my practice has changed somewhat, indeed more than once."

"I am eager to hear of it," Giles said, grinding his teeth as the bandage was twisted tight to halt the blood.

"My miracle salve has been much used by gentlemen of all rank, sir, to improve their . . . er, fading nature."

Giles nodded, his lips twitching. "I have heard it well spoken in that regard."

The doctor, though concentrating on his work, continued merrily. "And in the highest circles, m'lord, if you don't put me down as the worst braggart. But ah, more recently, I am much sought, sir, for the healing of marriages. Indeed, I give public lectures. 'Tis a skill not taught in any university of medicine that ever I attended."

Meriel laughed. "Well then, 'tis not taught anywhere upon this earth, I vow," she said. Upon seeing a fleeting upset on his sweet face, she quickly added, "But is a fine idea and sorely needed, I would imagine." She smiled at him, liking him exceedingly. "Yet is there enough bandage in the kingdom for such a wide practice?"

Dr. Wyndham looked up at her with a most confident grin. "You jest, m'lady, which is your way, but, in truth, it was you and his lordship here who gave me the idea at Harringdon Hall."

Sir Edward was at the Admiralty when they arrived, having worked through the night. At the sight of Meriel, he leapt up from a writing table covered with maps and drawings to embrace her. "Meriel, m'girl, I had such fears for you that were like to give me the apoplexy. Are you well? How—"

"I am as well as may be, sir, and I long to tell you all, but the tale must wait for—"

"Another time, with my apologies, Sir Edward," Giles said, handing over the king's warrant and proceeding to detail, with Meriel's interruptions, all that would be required to go against the Dutch fleet advancing up the Thames.

Sir Edward nodded and stood. "It is a hard thing to take a man's property, m'lord earl, but if we don't stop the Dutch, all London will belong to them. I will scour the river, sir, for everything that floats and every man jack who can pull an oar."

"And pitch and tar," Meriel added, "barrels of it."

Sir Edward smiled. "Aye, Meriel, you have not changed, thank the Lord of blessed name for that when all the world is full of ill change. I will use every man in the Admiralty as a press gang to round up men from—" He broke off his promise to execute it, calling for a servant to take the orders he was writing.

Impatiently, Dr. Wyndham tapped the back of a chair. "M'lord earl, I must be at my stitching. Delay will bring more pain, but be assured that I can take that away."

"No laudanum, my good doctor. I will need all my wits and Meriel's, too, these next hours."

Meriel stood by. The doctor first checked Giles's head wound and found it well along in healing. Thence, she made herself watch the slash being cleansed and closed, because she could bear to see the surgery, but not the pain on Giles's mouth that never became a single cry. "You are mighty skilled, Doctor. . . ." She bit down on her lip. "But I beg you do not prescribe your little red pills, for we have much hard work ahead this night."

"M'lady," the doctor said, not looking up but smiling, "you have a talent that is prime for happy marriages."

Giles straightened himself but said nothing, since he needed all his strength to concentrate the pain of knife and needle into a manageable place elsewhere in his mind. Besides, was all the world conspiring to tie him to this woman tighter than he was already? And could he resist?

"And what is that talent?" Meriel asked, especially since Giles made no comment. "I am no cook, being barely skilled enough to watch bread rise in its bowl."

"Why, m'lady, you have surely just shown it again. You see the truth of a thing through a jest, as in my little red emetic pills. And more important, you remember it so that it gets better with each telling."

"Oh, surely you do not prescribe your pills to heal marriages, good doctor!"

The doctor laughed heartily and wiped his eyes on his sleeve before taking the last stitch in Giles arm. "Ah, me, you have done it again. But a good humor is a true part of the healing of marriages, mistress. Yet I think you have the other necessary parts, as well."

Meriel laughed and because she could not stop herself from looking, she saw that Giles laughed, too, but silently.

Near dawn, when they boarded a pinnace loaded with barrels of pitch below Tower Gate, they were again smiling as Giles swung her to the deck.

But that was soon to end.

Chapter Twenty-three

To Win and To Lose

L ong before they reached the English capital ships anchored below Chatham, Giles and Meriel heard the continuous roar of cannon and musket fire, smelled the smoke of
burning ships and heard the squeal of buckling timbers. Yet
clasped together at the prow of a small single-masted fishing
wherry, they were most dismayed by the triumphant calls of
Dutch trumpets and drums issuing orders to the crews. The
pall of smoke and the cheers of the Dutch drove Giles from
Meriel's tight embrace to grab an oar, ignoring his bandaged
arm, and pull with all his strength with the outgoing tide.

Still feeling the remembered warmth of Giles's arms,
Meriel leaned hard against the rail, as if to urge the boat on
through burning wreckage with the force of her own body.
She smiled inwardly at the idea that she was admiral of the
motley fleet of commandeered small boats and barges
crowding behind them, even a Thames lighter used to carry
goods from the London side to Southwark. The tiny vessels
were loaded with pitch to set burning and send toward the
enemy. Wooden ships with tarred ropes and canvas sails
burned easily.

Then they rounded a turning in the river and sailed into a flame-lit hell.

"Steer toward the *Royal Charles*," Giles shouted to the man at the tiller, leaving his oar and returning to the rail alongside Meriel. "Cock's life! The Dutch are boarding her!"

Meriel counted the small Dutch boat's crew. "Giles, only nine men. Surely we can . . ." The rest of her protest was lost as they saw the Hollanders scramble aboard the flagship and strike the English flag to raise their own.

"Not one man to resist," Meriel said, putting words to the deep shame she knew that Giles was feeling, too.

He put an arm about her waist, since her legs seemed to want to give way. "Don't despair, Merry," he spoke into her ear past the noise. "We will send our fire ships against them. Better to burn the *Charles* than let the Dutch have her." He scrambled back amidships, shouting to the following boats to come alongside.

The first box of fuses was too wet to light, but the second box was dry as tinder and blazed readily. "Knock off the top of the casks," Giles ordered the crews as they came near. He took their men aboard and threw fuses at their open casks, and one by one he saw the fires start. With a mighty push, each of the boats took the outgoing current and drifted toward the Dutch.

"Stand by, men," he said, and steered for the *No Name* at the dockside.

With a heavy heart he watched the Hollanders take in tow the *Royal Charles,* the king's enormous gilt emblem carved on the stern transom, and retreat down the Thames, heading for the Channel.

"They'll never get her to the Medway," Giles said. "For her draft, she needs high tide."

"Look!" Meriel shouted, tears of frustration starting. The

huge English flagship slowly heeled over on its side and tow
lines pulled it safely over the shallow water.

Giles couldn't keep admiration from his words. "They've
shifted ballast and guns to lay her over so she could pass.
They're fine sailors, the Dutch."

The Hollander ship, *Agatha,* sailed alongside the *Royal
Charles.* Standing at the taffrail was Cornelis de Witt, and
even through smoke and distance both Meriel and Giles saw
his wide smile. Meriel raised a clenched fist, but if he saw it,
he was merely more amused.

Giles watched grim-faced as Dutch fireships rammed the
badly undermanned *Royal James* and *Royal Oake* anchored
near the shore, setting them both ablaze, the few seaman still
aboard leaping into the Thames. And with sinking heart,
Giles saw the Dutch sailors on the *Agatha* busy with long
hooked poles pushing away the fireships that he and Meriel
had sent against them.

"Nothing will stop them from coming on to London now,"
Meriel said, defeat written in the slump of her shoulders.

"Don't surrender quite yet," Giles said, ignoring his
wounded arm as he had all morning and hauling aboard men
clinging to debris from the river. Most sailors could not
swim, and these were no exception.

He mounted the small cabin amidships. "Men, we will
yet stop the Hollanders from coming up to London!"

Most of the tired men had been dragged from their busi-
nesses and off the narrow alleyways of Southwark by press
gangs and did not respond, their chins sunk in exhaustion on
their chests, though some looked at Giles as if he were crazed.

"With what weapons, m'lord?" one of the group asked,
appearing to have very little will.

"Our bare hands belike," said another, his face showing
anger.

"Aye, men, if needs be with our bare hands to save our city, your shops and homes," Giles said, walking between them, slapping each on the shoulder or back with his good arm.

"Aye," Meriel echoed him, holding her arms aloft. "And with these woman's hands. Are you Englishmen to let a woman fight where you would not go? Listen to Lord Giles. In truth, you know him by his past deeds."

"We know him, but what can 'e do, mistress? We be without guns, proper ships. We be no fighting men, but coopers and sedan chair carmen. How can such as we be keeping the Hollanders from London? All the men with rich goods be fleeing the city as fast as may be. We commons be left to do the fighting yet again."

Giles continued to walk amongst the men. "It is Englishmen such as you"—he pointed—"and you, who won the day at Crécy, again at Agincourt, and then kept the Spaniards' armada from these shores. If we have no weapons to hand, we have my good ship at the dock, waiting to take the fight to the enemy. And there are other ships here not worthy of the Hollanders' trouble and badly in want of brave Englishmen to man them. There is a way yet."

One man spoke up. "An how will ye be using what small merchant ships be left to keep the Hollanders from London, m'lord?"

All the men leaned forward.

"They have fired our capital ships, but the way to London is barred to them by the wreckage. I believe the Dutch will now try to sail their sloops and longboats crammed with marine troops up the small creeks and waterways to attack London by land."

Giles's strong voice could be heard above the Dutch cannon, each word an answering shot. "We will sink small ships at the mouth of each river and creek—" He paused. The men muttered in low tones amongst themselves for a few moments, then their spokesman rose. "Name's Robert, m'lord. Do ye propose we drown after we sink 'em?"

Giles raised his hand to stop that thought from advancing. "Not a bit of it, Robert. We scuttle and you walk safe home with my thanks, and more. Any man of you who applies to me henceforth at Whitehall for this day's good work will gain gold coin for his duty."

Meriel saw the men look up at Giles almost as one, a stirring of hope in their lined, worn faces, or if not hope, at least no longer abject defeat at the slender possibility that they would see their homes yet again. "What say you?" she yelled. "Shall we fight like men, or end in a Dutch galley on the Guinea Coast trade?"

"Don't overdo, Merry," Giles muttered. "The Dutch have few galleys."

"Aye, but they'd build one if they captured you and me."

Giles laughed heartily at the retort, and Meriel saw that his high spirit gave heart to the men in the midst of what seemed horrible defeat.

Robert pulled off his hat. "I be with ye, m'lord, since I'd rather have good English gold in me pocket than Dutch gulden."

The others nodded, some still reluctant, but the promise of gold enough to bring them together.

"One thing, m'lord," Robert said.

"Aye?" Giles ordered the man at the tiller to steer around floating debris and close on the dock where the *No Name* was moored. Tom Barnes stood in the rigging, waving his cap.

"How do 'e sail a ship, m'lord?"

Giles smiled. "There will be a good helmsman with each

ship, and you but do as he says with anchor and rigging. Hard work, men, but you all know hard work."

The men cheered, at first politely, then with good hearts.

As Meriel scrambled aboard the *No Name*, her gown no longer fit for a countess, even a counterfeit one, she looked about the ketch's familiar deck and felt at home, not for the first time. And then she remembered the similar feeling when she had first entered Harringdon Hall. Perhaps home was where Giles was. The sweet thought was not a happy one. It meant that in truth this might be the last time she would have the sense of belonging she had so rarely known in her life.

But she had little time for sadness, since she might not have a future of any kind unless they stopped the Dutch.

In seaman's breeches once more Meriel helmed the *No Name* that day, ferrying Giles, Tom Barnes and the other men from one ship to another and one creek to another, until the masts of sunken ships seemed to dot the shores of the Thames as if a forest had once grown underwater. She heard the guns firing below them at old Upnor Castle, and now batteries all along the shore cannonading the Dutch. But all the while, she looked downriver past her shoulder, expecting Hollanders to sail back for an attack on London to cap their victories at Sheerness and at the chain and the taking of the *Royal Charles*. After such success, even de Witt had probably lost his normal caution.

And each time Giles returned to her, more worn and wet, she thanked the God of blessed name for his safety.

As dusk fell, they were left alone on the *No Name,* sailing near St. Mary's Creek.

"No, Giles, you can't," Meriel said, reading his face.

"I must. My ship is no better than those of any other man's taken and sunk this day to save London."

The determination on his face silenced her, and she steered toward the mouth of the creek, while Giles was below, pounding caulking from the ship's seams.

Meriel felt the beautiful ketch settling sluggishly under her feet, taking a piece of her heart with it to the bottom.

They dove together from the bowsprit, slicing the water at the same moment, arriving on shore in near dark except for a perfect half-moon and stars. It was a clear night, though the smell of burning wreckage lingered. They walked onto the shore to stand there, shoulders touching, while the ketch disappeared beneath the water up to midmast, making scarce a ripple, as if in a pout for being treated so.

Meriel sat suddenly on the greensward, lying down in the cool grassy bed, dripping and exhausted.

Giles looked down on her and she could see the dark well of his eyes, but could not read their depths. Were they sad, or eager to draw a curtain over this strange part of his life? When he spoke, his voice told her what his eyes had not.

"Your work is done, Merry, all that any man, whether king or spymaster, could expect, and much more than I would ever ask." He had not meant the words to sound so final, but her black curls flowing across her creamy throat would tempt one of the old religion's saints and had put him on high guard. And if the curls had not entranced, her eyebrows had. They slanted slightly upward in that ironical way she had, as if she were always just about to laugh, as if life were the greatest jest of all. It was the thing about her face that he loved most . . . except for her lips, and the curve of her cheek, and the dimple in her chin, a chin pointed yet not severe . . . He closed his eyes tight before he had to decide on one favorite feature to remember over all the others. Because remembrance was all that there could be of this woman for him. There would be no acceptance in all the land of a marriage between low commoner and peer of the realm, with a title as ancient as any in England. All their children would be counted base-born bastards. Such a union would deny all that had ever been and ever would be for the house of Warborough. And yet . . . ?

"Aye, m'lord, all work accomplished," she said, taking his words as a dismissal. Another time she might not have heard it that way, but her emotions were rubbed raw. She would not plead. In her heart she had known that this day would come. It did not take an astrologer the likes of Dr. Ashmole to divine Giles's meaning.

Maybe she had simply imagined that he loved her for herself and not because they had been comrades in a great adventure. Any minute of the day, in every cottage and hamlet in England, a woman was fooling herself about a man, and apparently Meriel St. Thomas was no smarter. *Hey, well, I never claimed to be smarter about womanly things!*

Giles sat down beside her, then lay back, allowing his body to sink into the thick, tufty grass, sighing as if seeking a deep rest for his sore limbs. He did not touch her and he did not know what to say. So he said the wrong thing. "You can collect your reward now."

"Does that mean what you think it means?" she asked, half in jest, but with a need to know the truth. She would not prolong a good-bye if one was to be said. Even a servant girl was too proud to spread the broken shards of her heart at this lord's feet.

"I don't know what I mean, Merry."

Struggling up from what felt like the softest goose-down mattress, she started to rise. "I'll be off, then, m'lord. Good health and long life!" No woman could keep an edge from her words when she was being sent away with a "well done and true, little miss"!

With a throaty groan probably heard in Chatham Dockyard, Giles caught her arm and pulled her atop him. "I have scarce the strength left to stop you, but I don't want you to leave."

The sense of her body melting into his erased her anger in less than a beat of her heart. "You seem to have strength enough, Giles." *Hey, well, tired and wet have not made me less a woman who knows when a man's body is ready for sport!*

He smiled at her and she saw his teeth flash in the half moonlight. "You do seem to assist me in always gaining new strength, mistress."

"My pleasure, m'lord."

He laughed, one of those wonderful full laughs that he so rarely allowed, a laugh that shook him.

Giles rolled over, taking her with him. "Merry!"

It was obvious to her that he was struggling fiercely with himself and losing. "Giles, I know what it is you cannot say."

He kissed her, having no trouble finding her lips in the dark, and knowing that he would be forever finding them again in his dreams. His hand slipped inside her sodden sailor's shirt, finding a cold breast. "My love," he said, and parting the ties, began to kiss both quivering mounds until they turned warm. More than warm. He groaned again. "I should not . . . we should not. If I were to get a child on you, it would dishonor . . ."

She whispered fiercely against his ear, "Don't forever prate of honor"—she laughed to show the words were not angry—"especially when your breeches are down. They are down, aren't they, m'lord?"

He buried his face in her hair, not knowing whether to

laugh or mourn, her wet curls winding about him as if they would never let go.

She whispered, "If I am with child, you would leave me with that which is most precious to me, a part of you to hold by me when all this crazed time is gone and long forgotten."

Giles shivered, not with the night breezes against his rapidly drying shirt, but from the heat of their two bodies demanding to be joined. "Never forgotten, Merry. I pledge to you: never forgotten." He meant the words with all his heart and tried to imagine another woman not out of the scullery and of his rank at his side, her children in the fields of Harringdon Hall, another woman in his boyhood oak tree beside him sharing his longings. . . . Another woman who did not look like Felice, who every day would not remind him of a man's worst betrayal before the whole court.

Though her words were wanton, Meriel didn't care. "I have no pretense left to me, Giles. Please leave me with something to remember my love for you." She nestled against his check, kissing it, adoring his rough beard.

His arms tightened about her. " 'Tis said of love," Giles whispered in the familiar words of Cervantes, "there is no force able to resist it."

"Then cease your resistance," she said, and he did. She felt the hard strength of him moving against her leg, blindly thrusting against her, as she struggled with her sodden breeches until she finally kicked out of them.

"Now, Giles, now!"

Giles drove into her almost defiantly, taking her lips roughly with his at the same time, as if to finally conquer all his doubt by taking all of her.

Meriel rose to him eagerly, holding his cod inside as tightly as she could, as deeply as she could, and when it poured into the farthest reach of her womanhood, she cried out, gripping all the tighter to imprison him for as long as she could, making a final memory.

At last she let him go and, limbs shaking, he rolled to his back. "My God, Merry—" he said, almost choking on the name.

Meriel stood and quickly dressed herself, and without looking back began to walk away, swiping away tears as she went.

"Merry," Giles called softly, "you must understand how impossible . . . we are far apart in station . . . you look like Felice . . . you would never be accepted at court or in the shire. How would—"

"That is for you to decide, Giles, Earl of Warborough." Meriel continued walking, though there was still one thing she must know. "But it was Meriel St. Thomas, common serving woman, you loved, the Merry of the oak tree. Aye or nay. Not so difficult a decision for a brave peer of the realm."

"Aye," he said, his head in his hands, unable to watch her walk away. "Dam'me, aye! It was you. But you see, don't you, that you would be a constant reminder of Felice, all that was wrong and terrible before . . ."

When he looked, she was lost from his sight, but he heard her answer come sure and sweet on the night breeze, sweeping up the river. . . . My God, he would hear it forever. "I doubt Cervantes said it, but he should have. With love, Giles, good can always follow bad."

The brambles grabbed for her as if to force her to stay, but she walked on away from love into the beginning of nothing.

Chapter Twenty-four

What the Truth Drops Will Tell

Meriel stepped down the broad stairs leading to her back garden, which ran down to the Thames not far from Spring Gardens where Giles had kidnapped her and taken her aboard his ship. . . . Where, in truth, her life had begun. She shielded her eyes from the early August sunlight sending flashes of light from the polished cuirasses of the king's royal guard waiting in a barge at her dock to escort her to Whitehall.

"Careful of your court dress, m'lady," Agnes warned, holding it higher to escape the dew-drenched grass.

Meriel yanked the long train from Agnes's hands. "I would have you cease that m'lady nonsense or . . . or I shall have you whipped!"

"I tremble in my slippers, Mistress Meriel," Agnes said, a little faked fear in her voice to amuse herself.

"Well, you should," Meriel said, all but smiling. *Hey, well, now that I have been awarded my own establishment*

*and two hundred pounds a year, thanks to the king, I have a
right to be unreasonable. . . . Maybe more than one right!*

"Is your belly settled? Would you like some fresh bread
and butter new from the country?"

Meriel gagged.

"Some ale, then, to settle you."

"Leave be with eating! The oysters last night have quite
taken my appetite."

"Oysters did not put you off breaking your fast, and well
you know it."

Meriel snatched away her train, folded it over her arm
and gave Agnes a sharp look. Meriel knew well the warning
to forward servants, having received it often enough herself.
After which, since Agnes seemed unimpressed, Meriel
marched down the crushed gravel path to board the barge,
tossing a last order over her shoulder. "And tend the onion
beds. If I have a garden, I must have onion flowers."

Downriver at the palace water stairs, the officer in charge
bowed and handed her a loaf of bread wrapped in linen. "His
Majesty is in St. James Park, feeding his ducks and geese."

She walked toward the pond where she and Giles had
strolled just a little past two months gone, but she did not look
about for him. Gossip, that Agnes seemed to know almost before it was said, had Giles departing the palace and his duties
as gentleman of the bedchamber for some unknown place. He
had not been a party to the downfall of the king's chief minister, Lord Clarendon, who had taken the brunt of blame for
the dishonor of the Dutch attack up the Thames. Someone
must be the scapegoat. Who better than a minister Parliament
had long wanted to overthrow?

Though Meriel knew that Clarendon had been Charles
Stuart's teacher when the king was a boy, she also knew that
the elderly man had continued to treat the king at thirty-

seven years as if he were yet his student, with near daily lectures on governance and deportment. She stored that knowledge away. When her son was grown, she would treat him as a man with a mind and will of his own, and thus keep him close.

She stopped and clutched the loaf of bread tighter, her insides heaving, then hurried on down the path into the park, breaking a corner of the loaf and swallowing it to quiet her belly.

His Majesty was surrounded by petitioners as usual, and as usual was fending them off with tales of his ducks and a loud greeting to his favorite one-legged crane, for which the royal doctor Josiah Wyndham had fitted a cunning peg-leg. The crane loped awkwardly toward the king every morning, to his continual delight.

Charles II espied Meriel and motioned for her to come forward. "Ah, Mistress St. Thomas, will you not walk with us for some private discourse?"

She made a low curtsy, holding her gown a little high since the ducks, chased by the king's little dogs, were losing feathers and the contents of their bowels to an extreme degree.

They moved away from the courtiers, who looked and whispered behind their fans, since everyone thought they knew her strange story, which strange enough in truth had been embellished with every telling. As they whispered, they kicked the dogs and ducks away from their velvets and satins.

Meriel handed the loaf to the king, who examined it. "Do we not provide enough for your sustenance that you should rob our poor ducks? We would not be thought so ungrateful for your services to the crown of which, we must add, Babs is most jealous." He was jesting in his way, but curious, as well, and a king's curiosity must be satisfied.

"A slight indisposition, Your Majesty."

"Ah," he said, and inquired no more, since his multiple bastards gave him full knowledge of a woman's morning indisposition.

At that moment, the king lifted his head to the sound of bells from everywhere in the city, the nearest bells at the Abbey of Westminster sounding over all. "The Treaty of Breda has been signed."

"My congratulations on your successful diplomacy with the Hollanders, sir," Meriel said, though she knew little had been gained except for the New York port and some minor concessions of trade.

The king acknowledged the empty compliment with a lift of his mustache. "But, my dear, we did not call you to us to talk of policy, though we hear the Dutch now fear our women e'en more than our men."

He shook with laughter, and Meriel blushed at such praise.

"And do not the people take their hats off to you when you pass in the street?" He took his hat off to her.

"If Your Majesty pleases—"

"Your modesty is quite refreshing, m'dear." He replaced his hat after smoothing the long flamingo feather. "We have set our good spymaster the task of looking into the matter of your birth, mistress," he said, picking up a squirming little dog, kissing it and nesting it against his chest, its golden hairs clinging about his dark blue velvet coat.

"There is nothing to learn, sir. Sir Edward tried when he took me from the orphanage—"

"Sir Edward did not have Chiffinch."

Meriel couldn't argue with that.

"Let us continue our walk, for we would fully discharge our debt to you," the king said, and offered her his arm as courtiers began to crowd closer.

"It is discharged, Your Majesty, in service to England."

"Ha! You would have made a fine courtier, m'dear, yet we know you speak the truth of your heart, not particularly a courtly quality."

Meriel looked up at the king's dark face and lid-hooded eyes as he towered above her, the shadows of leaves and flashes of sun flickering across his skin as he moved down the curving path. She saw compassion occasionally slip through caution.

"It seems, m'dear, that Chiffinch has discovered your family in Kent near where you were a foundling."

Meriel stopped, her legs suddenly weak.

The king tugged her ahead since the petitioners were hard after them. "We think you must have guessed some of this story, but we will tell you all we know. Chiffinch is certain that your mother was the Countess Elizabeth, wife of the Earl of Basford and mother of Felice."

"But, Your Majesty—"

"Sssh, all will be made clear as ever can be, though we think the question might be already in your mind." They walked on for a moment and Meriel kept her silence, although it near choked her.

"The Lady Elizabeth was brought to bed of another girl child when Felice was but three years old."

"Me?"

The king didn't answer, but walked on at his usual pace, with Meriel half running to keep hold of his arm and at his side. "Earl William took the child from the birthing chamber and gave it to the midwife to dispose of."

"Kill? Why would he do such a thing to his own child?"

"It was not his, m'dear. He'd been at sea with the fleet for better than a year. Shortly, Lady Elizabeth committed suicide and the earl died of wounds, or an ill conscience."

"And my father, sir?"

"Unknown. The lady died with her secret."

Meriel was near out of breath and stopped, unable to move her legs. "Do I have any living family, sir?"

Gently, the king said, "The Countess Felice was the last known except for the earl's cousin, who has taken the title. Felice was probably your half sister, according to Chiffinch, who is never wrong unless he intends it." Charles II put his arm about Meriel's shoulders to give her strength. "There is no proof of any of this. The midwife was transported to Jamaica shortly after being questioned. Chiffinch keeps a close eye on my purse, if the woman should try future blackmail. He is thorough." He sighed. "You could be noble born or half-base born, if you are thinking of m'lord Giles."

Meriel stopped, unable to walk on.

His Majesty stopped, as well, and smiled down at her. "You should know that Giles was there enquiring shortly after Chiffinch, but found nothing. Of course, he would have a question. . . . The resemblance is too close."

"Your Majesty, I beg you, he is never to know what Chiffinch discovered. Please, sir."

"Why, m'dear? 'Od's fish! He loves you. We who know something of love, having felt it many times, can attest to another man's too obvious feelings."

"He is not to know, Your Majesty, and I will consider my service to the crown fully paid."

The king nodded. "As you wish, madame. Although we love your sex, we do not claim to understand your minds."

He escorted her back to the pond, where she made her curtsy and he gave her his hand to kiss, which she did, though mortified that a tear should drop upon his long royal fingers.

Later that day, Chiffinch arrived at her house with a signed patent of nobility from the king granting her the title of Lady Basford. "If I did not know you better, I would think the king is planning a *divertimento* with you, though I suspect Nellie Gwyn had a hand in this. You are the people's hero-ine, madame, and the king but plays to the pit, as Nellie says. She was most taken with your spirit at the Spring Garden—oh yes, I remember that escapade—and is an ac-complished intriguer herself, for one so young."

Meriel put the rolled parchment to one side after a single glance. "If it please you, master pimp, you may think what you like of the king's *divertimentos,* though I plan none with him."

"Tut. No need to take on airs with me even though you may be noble born and, as a fact, are noble since the king wills it. Perhaps, if you were more giving with me, I might do more searching and ferret the whole truth. Perhaps I al-ready know more."

Meriel laughed though she was tired and ached for her long chair in the garden. "You may search where you like, know what you like. You may prove me a queen, but you will never make me your *divertimento,* sir."

He frowned. "There is your pension at my—"

"You withhold my pension at your peril because I seem to have the ear of the king. And, sir, you will not take your usual ten percent."

She was delighted to see his ample backside disappear into his sedan chair. What with the living that percentages, preferments and the odd bribe had provided for him, the chair had grown a bit snug and his carmen less willing.

Later, Agnes brought the rolled patent to her garden chair. "M'lady," she said, suggesting she had read it.

Meriel shielded her eyes from the afternoon sun and scanned the parchment, the red waxen seals dangling. "His Majesty has named me—"

"Lady Basford, as is fitting for the younger daughter of an earl, with one-quarter the revenues from that estate—a good thousand a year, most like—and the right to the Basford arms, quartered." Agnes said it all in one breath.

Meriel glanced up and added, "With the bar sinister."

"Aye, m'lady, and well deserved." At Meriel's raised eyebrows, Agnes swiftly added, "No, not the bar sinister, but the honor for one who risked all. If the Earl of Basford knew, mayhap he would have been proud of you."

"Mayhap though I doubt he sounds much a forgiving man." The unspoken words hung in the air, so she spoke them. "Not many men forgive a woman's greatest deception."

"But now that you are the natural daughter of a countess, your station has changed. If Earl Giles knew—"

"No!"

Agnes shrugged. "M'lady, you defy scripture, for it is written in the Old Testament that a man must take his wife's younger sister to wed."

"This is the first I've heard of your interest in biblical commands. What about: 'Servant, obey thy master'?"

"I am not familiar with that one, m'lady," Agnes replied.

"Indeed, I do know it!"

By that time, they were both laughing.

Agnes placed a bowl of sweets near Meriel's hand and made an exaggerated curtsy before she left.

As Agnes turned away Meriel said softly, "I would have

him only if he wants Meriel St. Thomas, servant maid. Not because I am a noblewoman's bastard."

Agnes shrugged, rolled her eyes to heaven and did not argue. But she did mutter loud enough to be heard: "Pride is a cold bedfellow."

Meriel placed the patent of nobility carelessly over her face as a sun shield, happy to forgo further talk of Giles. She must forget. She *must*. The future would be a long, cruel time coming.

But it wasn't.

A few days later, during a hot, moist August morning while waiting for her coach to be brought round, Meriel stood on her water stairs looking downriver, seeking a cool breeze, but seeing memories in her head that were too real. Yet they pained her more because they were not. She focused on the pleasure boats crossing to Spring Gardens, laughing people disembarking. But that was little help.

A ketch rounded the bend in midchannel, flying all sails, even the jib on the bowsprit where Giles stood, holding to the rigging, shirt open and wide breeches rolled to his knees, brown as a common sailor.

Meriel passed a hand over her eyes, fearing a cruel vision. But when she looked again, he was gliding closer, growing larger and larger. And there was Tom Barnes hauling the helm over to spill wind from the sails and lose steerageway.

It was a dream at night, a wish in the day . . . a mind picture come to full life that felt like a blow to her breast.

"You knew I would come to you," Giles called across the water, as the distance between them closed.

"It would take a witch's magic to know a man's changeable mind."

"Then I have misnamed my ship."

She looked, and there on the bow in fresh gilt letters were the words *The Merry Mischief.* She swallowed, jolted by great emotions that became one question: What did this mean? Had the king told him of her birth? Had Agnes? Chiffinch, that dog!

Giles leapt upon her water stairs and rose up like the Greek god Poseidon from the river to stand very close to her, so close she could see the tiny lines beside his eyes that every sailor has. He was deeply tanned, and she saw his chest was even more finely muscled than when last she had occasion to see it. It took all the strength she had to stop her hands from touching him.

He was smiling at her and she forced her gaze away. She had learned as a young and helpless orphan child that showing any emotion only encouraged harm. And in truth, there was no need to look at him. She remembered all his faces. . . . Angry, sober, mirthful, pensive . . . his morning and evening faces, in full sun and by candlelight.

"M'lord, you are very welcome to *my* house." She held her body rigid and yet she felt it arching toward him, surely only in her mind.

"We have much to say," Giles said, looking down at her, and his hand touched her arm with an urgent pressure.

"I think not, m'lord."

"You think wrong, Merry," he said, and his was the solid male voice of a peer of the realm, a sash-wearing Garter knight, the hero of the Battle of the Four Days. A voice to be obeyed.

Her coach arrived, swinging around her house from the street with a clatter of hooves and wheels on cobbles.

Giles picked up Meriel, who despite all her expressed determination felt herself melt into his shoulder as he strode up the path, and placed her firmly in the coach. He sat close beside her.

Though he was touching her, she regained command of herself, if only a little. "Leave me," she demanded, knowing it was too late to run or to call for a constable. She felt his every touch as a repeated blow. She had steeled herself to his absence. Now she was without any armor for his presence, his adored face, the flood of memories like a coastal storm pounding against her body, the floating away of resolve, though she fought to hold it close to her.

"Where were you driving?"

"Hyde Park."

"Ah, the Ring Road drive. We have grown mighty high in the world to take the tour of a morning."

The coach jolted forward, and she said nothing. How dare he make a joke of the king's patent of which he obviously had heard? She stiffened. "You had something more to say, sir?"

"Since you are not happy to see me, are you at least happy to see the ketch, raised from the grave, newly caulked, painted and rigged. . . . And renamed to better suit her?"

Meriel's lips trembled and she turned away so that he would not misinterpret it as any more than it was: a pleasant surprise at a just end for a ship that had accomplished so much against the Dutch, and a greater compliment than that paid her by the king. She caught at her breath lest it sound the words she really wanted to say, and made a formal reply. "M'lord earl, I am happy to see her rescued."

He turned her toward him and faced her as they entered the gate to the park. It began to rain on the roof, splattering them with sound.

"I should never have let you walk away. I knew it was you I loved on that instant, Merry. It's you I see and not

Felice. You are different as—" He searched for a special way to say it, but Meriel interrupted.

"A countess and a serving maid?" She had to know if he were brought here by knowledge of her change in station.

He laughed. "As a countess *and* a serving maid, but a very special serving maid. Will you serve as my love for the rest of my days? And for heaven's sweet sake, if you no longer love me, tell me now before I die from waiting."

She surrendered to the lips that had been searching up and down her face all this while, and succumbed to the impulse to touch the muscles of his brown chest to see if indeed they were more sharply defined than she remembered. They were.

He kissed her as a drowning man comes up to kiss the air he must have or die, his hands moving and holding each part of her in turn as if to check that all was in its rightful place.

"You want me for your convenient mistress when you come to town. You want to be my keeper," Meriel whispered. She bit her lip, but still proud words issued. "I have no need of a keeper, having my own well-earned income and house."

He thrust her angrily away, but kept tight hold of her shoulders. "Why say you this? You will be mistress of Harringdon Hall and mate of *The Merry Mischief* after I make you my wife. I know now that I care naught for your station. Not even as I said it that night did I give a copper for it. I will petition the king this very day, take a bill to Parliament, anything . . . but you will be my wife, or no other will be." He caught her to him, tighter. "Is His Majesty in residence, or gone to Windsor for the summer?" He scratched at a shadow of beard. "I've been busy raising the ship as a wedding present to you, and have cared nothing for court news."

Her heart sang the words in her ears. *He doesn't know. He loves me . . . Meriel St. Thomas.*

The rain stopped and the sun came out hot and the Ring Road steamed under the horses' feet. They were clasped so tightly, very close to losing all caution, that they didn't notice a carriage slowing next to them.

Nell Gwyn stuck her red head out in greeting. "I recognize your coachman and give you good day, m'lady Basford . . . and, ah, m'lord of Warborough. This rain seems not to have dampened your full enjoyment of the park."

The king's head thrust out beside hers. "Is that Earl Giles?"

"A good day to you, Your Majesty, Mistress Nellie," Giles said, his face turned in question to Meriel. "I asked about Canterbury for your parentage, but could find nothing. Now Nellie calls you Lady Basford? Merry, is it true?"

Meriel nodded. "Chiffinch found the midwife. It's a long story."

He shook his head, believing the unbelievable. "That is what Felice meant at the end. She knew, and she wanted you dead for it. I think the first time when you looked at your mother's picture in the upper gallery at Harringdon you must have—" He grinned and his wide shoulders relaxed, a secret deciphered.

"'Od's fish!" the king called. "Our two heroes of the Thames together. We would warn you to beware the crowd of women ahead, likely to descend on you if you show yourselves."

"A crowd about of a morning, sir?" Meriel asked.

Nell laughed. "Aye, every wife, mistress and masked whore in London. Our good Dr. Wyndham presents lectures to women on a subject many seem eager to know more about."

Meriel smiled at the memory of the little doctor. "I do hear that he knows how to keep nature and age at a distance for both men and women."

Nell grinned. "Now we hear he advises women how to keep a man with his Infallible Truth Drops. Given a draught but once of the new moon at exactly midnight, a man will believe whatever a woman tells him and laugh at the knowing until the draught is renewed at the next new moon. I go to claim my bottle."

His Majesty laughed. "We will buy one to give to our ministers."

The royal carriage pulled away down the Ring Road, the sound of both Nell's and the king's laughter trailing behind it.

"You have no need of Truth Drops, Merry. I think I always knew everything about you that I needed to know . . . your wit, your beauty, your courage . . . the heart and stomach of a queen . . . remember?" Giles whispered the words in her ear and she shivered with longing as they swept through her, promising more later.

Hey, well, there is one little surprise growing in my belly that he does not know, which I will tell him. . . . Perhaps at the next new moon.

Author's Note

The English and Dutch fought three naval wars from 1652 to 1674, mostly for foreign trade dominance. Merry and Giles's adventure is set during the second of these wars, fought from 1665 to 1667, ending with the Dutch towing away the English flagship *Royal Charles*.

Once on a trip to Holland, I saw the elaborately carved gilt stern from the ship hanging on a wall of the Rijksmuseum in Amsterdam, never dreaming that one day it would play a part in a novel I'd written.

Although Meriel St. Thomas is a fictional character, there really were women spies during that time, the most noted being Aphra Behn, who went on to become a major Restoration playwright and a close friend of Nell Gwyn, the great comedic actress.

It seems strange to us today that Giles and Merry could not easily marry when they were so much in love, but social norms of the time were very rigid. A servant girl marrying a peer would have been illegal at worst, and at best, both would have been ostracized, their children with them.

The societal idea prevalent at the time was "the great chain of being," which stated that everyone was born to a place in the chain and could not move up; the greatest example being Charles II, who loved his mistress Nell Gwyn for seventeen years. Because she was a commoner, both Parliament and the court kept him from giving her a title or recognition. And Charles was the king of England! Giles would have had even less chance.

Those readers who have followed this Restoration romance series from *Lady Anne's Dangerous Man* to *Lady Katherne's Wild Ride* and now *Lady Merry's Dashing Champion* have seen another and rather mysterious love affair flourish: mine with King Charles. The more I learned of Charles Stuart, the more I adored him. Believe me, it's a strange sensation to imagine a long-dead ruler to the point when it seems you're channeling his personality.

Finally, I want to acknowledge Ellen Edwards for being the once-in-a-lifetime editor every author dreams of having.

And as always, I want to thank my husband, Gene, who, when I open the door and exit my writing room, always asks, "How many pages today?" And no matter what my answer, says, "Good work!"

LADY KATHERNE'S WILD RIDE

Jeane Westin

For years, Lady Katherne Lindsay's uncle has denied her noble heritage and treated her like a servant. But the night she foils his lecherous plan to steal her virtue, she becomes a suspected murderess with a bounty on her head. To avoid hanging from the king's gallows, she is forced to take shelter with a dashing actor and play along as his leading lady, despite the constant threat of capture....

Jeremy Hughes is notorious both for his performances upon the stage and in the bedchamber. But as Lady Katherne blooms into an accomplished actress and a confident woman, she can't help giving her whole heart to Jeremy and longing to win him for a lifetime of daring love and passionate adventure.

Also Available
Lady Anne's Dangerous Man

**Available wherever books are sold or at
penguin.com**